PRAISE FOR *EDEN*

?❧

"A stirring historical novel perfect for women's fiction fans."
— *BOOKLIST*

"*Eden* is not just another farewell-to-the-summer-house novel but instead a masterfully interwoven family saga with indelible characters, unforgettable stories, and true pathos. Most impressive, there's not an ounce of fat on this excellent book."
—ANITA SHREVE, *NYT* best-selling author of *The Pilot's Wife* and *The Stars are Fire*

"Reading this ambitious debut, which spans multi-generations and time periods, I was captivated by *Eden*'s sense of timelessness and deep yearning for something eternal. Jeanne Blasberg's gorgeous description of Eden—a family's magnificent seaside estate and the intimate stories it contains—reveals both the love that binds and the love that holds secrets and devastating losses. *Eden* is a beautiful, aching tale that will linger with you long after you've read the last page."
—JESSICA KEENER, author of the national best-selling novel *Night Swim*

"Jeanne Blasberg's touching debut novel, *Eden*, tells the story of Becca Meister Fitzpatrick, a family matriarch about to disclose a difficult secret over the Fourth of July weekend, 2000. As Blasberg's clear, affecting prose moves across time to tell Becca's story, the author also tells the story—heartbreaking, but ultimately hopeful—of a changing 20th-century America."
—LISA BORDERS, author of *The Fifty-First State* and *Cloud Cuckoo Land*

"With beautiful, big-hearted brush strokes, Blasberg seamlessly shifts between past and present, delivering a powerful and poignant family drama. As present-day challenges collide with long-buried secrets in the heat of a summer reunion, a family in crisis learns to accept truths, however uncomfortable, and how to navigate the closing doors and new gifts that change brings."

—SOPHIE POWELL, author of *The Mushroom Man*

"In this wonderful debut, Blasberg masterfully intertwines the stories of four generations of women, all forced to make difficult choices as mothers—first in the face of strict societal norms, and ultimately within the expectations of a family trying to live up to the promise of a place called Eden. I loved it from beginning to end."

—KATHERINE SHERBROOKE, author of *Finding Home* and *Fill the Sky*

EDEN

A NOVEL

JEANNE MCWILLIAMS BLASBERG

SHE WRITES PRESS

Published 2017
Printed in the United States of America
Print ISBN: 978-1-63152-188-1
E-ISBN: 978-1-63152-189-8
Library of Congress Control Number: 2016951922

For information, address:
She Writes Press
1563 Solano Ave #546
Berkeley, CA 94707

Cover design © Julie Metz, Ltd./metzdesign.com
Interior design by Tabitha Lahr

She Writes Press is a division of SparkPoint Studio, LLC.

This is a work of fiction. Names, characters, places, and
incidents either are the product of the author's imagination or
are used fictitiously. Any resemblance to actual persons, living
or dead, is entirely coincidental.

In loving memory of the mothers who came before me:
Anne, Mary, Betty, and Jeanne

The tide is not an independent force, but merely the submission of the water to the movement of the moon in its orbit. And this orbit in its turn is subject to other orbits which are mightier far than it. And so the whole universe is held fast in the clinging grip of strong hands, the forces of the earth and sun, planets, and comets, and galaxies, blindly erupting forces ceaselessly stirring in ripples of silence to the very depth of black space.

—AMOS OZ

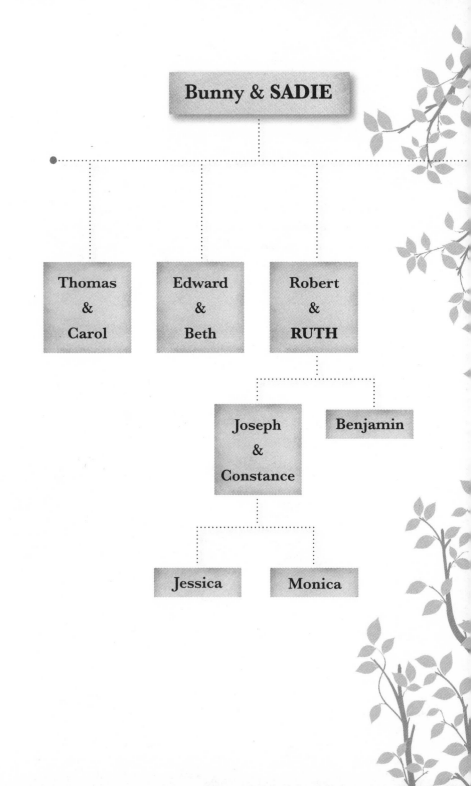

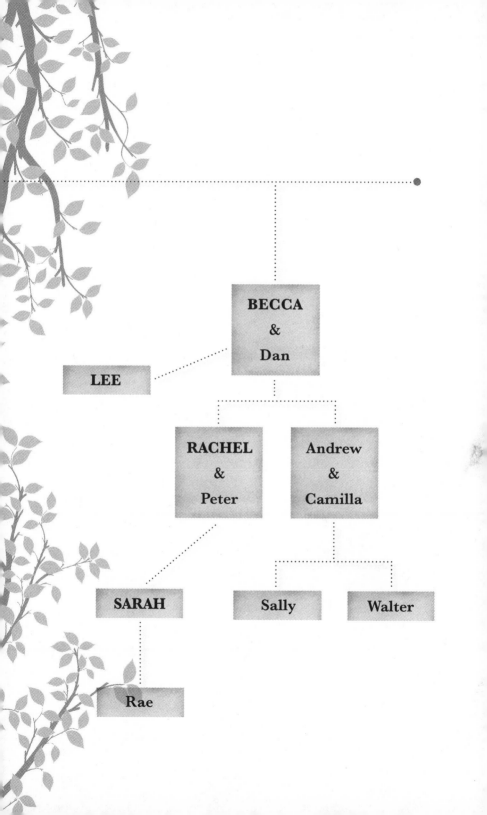

Chapter 1

LONG HARBOR, RHODE ISLAND
Tuesday, June 16, 2000

"I wanted to fill you in sooner," Becca said to her granddaughter, Sarah, who cradled a mug of hot tea in her lap, "but it's been hard to find the right time." She rubbed her weathered hands, adjusted the pillows at the base of her spine, and then straightened her skirt over her knees. The two of them were cozied up on Becca's favorite, down-filled love seat in front of the fireplace. She'd typically have lit a fire to take the damp out of the air but had opted not to restock the woodpile this year. Sarah waited with expectant eyes for her to continue. She twisted her tea bag around a silver spoon, squeezing out the last bits of flavor.

But Becca looked past Sarah, through the large, paned window with a view of the sea. The glass was streaked with salt and sand, and there were cobwebs between the screen and the storms. Outside a gentle rain was falling, a purifying springtime shower, and Becca paused to count her blessings. Number one, she was healthy. Two, she was ensconced in this beloved, ancestral home, Eden, for the summer season. And three, here was Sarah, all aglow by her side, pregnant, of all things, with Becca's first great-grandchild.

"So?" asked Sarah, peering over her dark-framed glasses.

"Well, this is quite difficult." Becca stopped again, looking up at the ornate molding and fidgeted with her wedding ring. She forced the words out of her mouth: "I discovered something quite alarming after your grandfather died."

Sarah squinted, and cocked her head, twisting her long red hair into a rope in front of one shoulder. Becca turned on a reading lamp, as the rainclouds were obscuring the natural light.

"Going over our estate with the lawyer, well, it seems he was not careful."

"Not careful?" Sarah gripped the love seat's worn upholstery with one hand and spread her other across her stomach, striking a melodramatic pose, as if safeguarding her unborn child from the unthinkable.

"With money."

"Oh?" Sarah's shoulders relaxed.

"Not that it was all his fault. Eden's antiquated plumbing and shingled roof cost a lot to maintain. We had to keep up appearances in New Haven, too, you know, given his position at the hospital." A warm flush spread over Becca's face. It was hard for her to confess Dan's failures, as she had always been the one to stand up for him. And sitting on this love seat, in what had once been her father's paneled study, conjured up his booming voice. "Doctors are notoriously bad with finances," he had said. "You'll need to keep an eye on things."

Sarah let out an audible "phew," and Becca looked up, surprised to see a smile on her face. "It's only money, Gran," she said. "It's not like Poppy committed a crime or kept a mistress."

"Of course your grandfather never kept a mistress!"

"So it's the money. Is that all?" asked Sarah.

"Yes. You act as if it's not a big deal."

"Well, actually, I thought you were going to tell me some awful scandal, something truly shocking."

"Sarah!"

"What I mean is that it's not unheard of, people making bad investments." The rain was falling harder now, and the sky had become almost black. Becca fingered her pearls as she considered the rolling thunder in the distance.

Sarah rose from her seat. "Gran, I'm just going to freshen my tea. Can I get you anything?"

"Please sit down. I'm not finished."

Sarah bit her lip and sat back down, folding one leg up under herself. Becca inhaled deeply, trying to shake the irritation that crept through her. She took in this vision of her granddaughter: single, a student at twenty-nine, trendily dressed in a ridiculous cotton sweater that barely clung to her shoulder. She was pregnant, with no source of income and no plan for paying her bills. How could she be so nonchalant about the fortune that had supported them?

"Sarah, it means I will have to sell my home in New Haven to pay off the debt, *and* my share of Eden. Thomas, of course, is salivating at the chance to buy me out. But this is likely our last summer. This house is a part of me. Just think of it."

Sarah shrank into the cushions. "I love it here, too," she murmured.

Becca couldn't help but raise her voice. "I won't be able to help out with your rent any longer. You and your mother can't expect anything from me. And I feel just awful about Lilly. She's been with us since your mother was born. I need to find a family that can take in a gray-haired, farsighted housekeeper." Becca swiped her index finger along the dusty windowsill to emphasize her point.

Sarah's face was downcast. "Does Mom know?" she asked.

"Not yet. I was about to get into it the afternoon you arrived. You walked in just as we were sitting down to talk."

"Oh."

"And ever since you made your announcement, she's been up in her room, getting all worked up. This is the last thing I can raise with her now."

"Gran—"

"And Lilly doesn't know either. She has no family left, and I don't want to worry her. God knows what type of place I'll end up in, but it certainly won't have maids' quarters!"

"Gran, I'm sorry."

"Don't you say a word to either of them. I'll be the one to tell them."

"You know I wouldn't do that." Sarah put a hand on her grandmother's shoulder. "I'm sure everything will sort itself out."

"Sarah, you don't seem to understand how this works. How all of this gets paid for." Becca made a sweeping gesture with her arm. "And it's never been more pertinent than now, what with you having another mouth to feed."

"I know how it works. I just thought . . ."

"Well, I suggest you do a whole lot more thinking. A baby is a lot of responsibility. And expensive, to boot. Maybe you should call that boyfriend of yours and see if you can't patch things up." Her shoulders were tense, and her hands were balled into tight fists in her lap.

"Gran, we've gone over this. Single moms can make it on their own these days," Sarah said.

"You don't think he'd be supportive?"

"No, he's quite angry."

Becca had never liked the sound of him—Sarah's professor, for goodness' sake. And how was a PhD in renaissance painting going to translate into a suitable income? "I know you're the new generation, Sarah, but . . ." Becca treaded cautiously. "I think you need to choose."

"Gran," Sarah interrupted, her tone defensive, almost condescending. "I am very close to finishing my dissertation, and then I'll be applying for lecturing positions. And if Alistair doesn't want to be a part of this baby's life, I won't beg him to change his mind. Women can have careers and babies these days, with or without a husband. You don't understand."

Becca bristled. She tucked a loose strand of gray hair behind her ear, squared her shoulders, and cleared her throat. "Sarah, I love you, but these have been a hard six months for me. Do you have any idea what it is like to lose a husband of fifty years and then to find out there's not a dime left?" She raised her voice a decibel higher. "And for you to sit there and tell me I don't understand? I have lived a full life, Sarah, and I understand plenty."

Becca felt tears welling. She inhaled deeply, then dabbed

the corners of her eyes with the tissue she kept tucked inside her sleeve. She retrieved a lipstick from her pocket, applied her signature peach, and rubbed her lips together to even out the color. "I thought I would fill you in on this financial crisis to inform your decisions with regard to your boyfriend and whether to go back to school or to get to work. Consider it a courtesy."

Now tears were rolling down Sarah's cheeks. "Gran, I've never seen you like this," she said, playing with the fringe of her sweater.

Becca inhaled, and her eyes softened. She did not like to be angry. "Sarah, this is a wake-up call for all of us."

"Gran, I want you to know that I've also considered not keeping the baby." Sarah blew her nose into a napkin.

"No," Becca said, shaking her head. "Write to him. He may respond to a letter. Invite him up here to talk it over. Consider every option first before you do something like that."

"Okay, I'll think about it," Sarah said, twisting her hair into an even tighter rope. "But in the end, it will be my choice."

Chapter 2

LONG HARBOR, RHODE ISLAND
Friday, June 26, 2000

B ecca's nostrils flared as she inhaled the briny air, elongating her stride and pumping her arms. She was already perspiring. Typical—last week she had considered lighting a fire in the study, and today was hazy, hot, and humid, the beginning of a heat wave. They were saying record temperatures, straight on through the holiday weekend.

Becca had walked the same crescent beach, one mile out and one mile back, most summer mornings for the past fifty years. She used to have the beach all to herself, had started back before it was in vogue to wear tight black pants and earphones.

Some mornings the tide was high, leaving only a sliver of sea-weed-coated sand for her to struggle through. Other mornings, like this one, it was delightfully low, exposing a broad and glassy, hard-packed surface that her aged legs glided over briskly. Although the beach's contours changed from day to day and winter storms often eroded the sand dramatically, the man-made landmarks beyond the dunes remained as familiar to her as the rooms of Eden.

Her springer spaniel, Hennessy, preferred nosing around the driftwood up by the dunes to her full-steam-ahead approach. He yanked on the leash, almost pulling her over. Becca relented and unclipped him, even though the week before he had bounded through the protective fencing around the piping plovers' nesting grounds. An irate park ranger had yelled at Becca for several humiliating minutes while she struggled to get the dog under control. Dan had never hidden his irritation at the expansive sanctuary claimed for the plovers, saying, "If those damn birds are ever going to survive in the wild, they shouldn't be coddled."

Becca tried to supplant that memory and her creeping melancholy with some enthusiasm for the upcoming season. Summer had always been her favorite; over her life, she had come to appreciate its unique cycle. During the cooler weeks just after Memorial Day, people were scarce. The weather was damp with spray to be washed off the windows. In July, houses filled, the sun heated up, and tides rose. By August, Long Harbor was in full swing, insects buzzed in the garden, and tomatoes ripened on the vine. As September approached, the tide slowly ebbed; hostesses grew weary of houseguests, parents happily delivered their children back to school, and one could pull the blankets back over the sheets.

Walking parallel to the lapping waves, Becca gazed somewhat sentimentally toward the Bancrofts' gray-shingled beach cabana, the Taylors' large stone "cottage," and the Whites' controversial renovation. She passed another five or six homes, each with a saga of its own. When she saw a porch light on, she made a mental note of who was in town, then allowed herself a few minutes of sorrow, anticipating her final summer among this exclusive band of neighbors.

But her nostalgia soon turned to dread as she imagined them, all upright people, aghast upon learning about Sarah's pregnancy, the gossip that would take place through the privet hedges. People would be whispering, although it didn't seem to faze Sarah a bit. She'd walked through the kitchen door just as Becca was about to discuss the family finances with Rachel. Sarah had dropped her overstuffed duffels with a thud, and her mother and grandmother had turned in their seats. "What a surprise! We weren't expecting you for weeks," Becca had said.

"I know, Gran. I had to leave. Alistair and I . . ." Sarah's voice trembled.

"Oh dear—did you have a fight?" Becca had predicted romance with a professor would end only in disaster, but she had been careful to keep her opinions to herself, knowing too well that Rachel was doling out a hefty portion of criticism.

Rachel stood up with the instincts of a mother smelling trouble. "Sarah, are you all right?"

"I'm all right," Sarah stammered. "I mean, I will be. I have some news." She looked nervously back and forth between them for several long moments.

Rachel scowled accusingly. "You're not pregnant, are you?"

Sarah nodded sheepishly.

"Oh, Sarah," Rachel said. "But your degree . . . Why? How many months?"

"Two . . . or three," Sarah said.

"After all the work you've put in? Now you're going to throw it down the drain?" Rachel shouted. She pounded her fist on the counter and marched out of the kitchen and had been holed up in her room ever since.

Becca cringed at the memory of her daughter's reaction to the news. She wished it could have been different, but it struck a raw nerve. Rachel had dropped out of college thirty years earlier, pregnant with Sarah.

Becca took her longest, most athletic strides now, inhaling the moist fog that enveloped her thin body and clung to her shoulder-length gray hair. Yes, people would be talking, or, then again, maybe they wouldn't. Maybe Sarah was right that these things were so common now: single motherhood, infidelity, financial ruin. Nobody would blink an eye. Regardless, Becca suspected there might be a touch of schadenfreude in Long Harbor when it came to her downfall.

She reached the one-mile mark and turned around. The early-morning sun was burning through the mist. Becca flipped her sunglasses down off the top of her head for the walk back. *Enough with the power walking*, she thought, and slowed to a comfortable pace. But she veered too close to the waves, soaking her tennis shoes and the hem of her tracksuit. She darted quickly for drier ground like a sandpiper flirting with the undertow.

Entering the narrow path through the dunes, she passed the pink beach roses ascending the sandy hill. It was from this higher vantage point that Eden always appeared most dramatic, a grande dame from another era. Her silver-gray shingles lent a touch of informality to her magnificence. She rose three stories in the middle and had a sprawling wing on either side, extending graciously across a lush green lawn.

When Becca's father, Bunny Meister, conceived of the home in the 1920s, he intended to take people's breath away, and from a distance, he succeeded. Even though its floral upholstery had faded into a state of classic "Yankee shabby," its paint was peeling, and bats made a home in the attic, the house welcomed her summer after summer, lulling her—indeed, the whole family—into a sense of immunity to the world's chaos. It was the one constant in her life.

Even though Becca could become accustomed to life without her husband, a life without Eden was an entirely different story. Even during the winter, the sheer notion of this place had buoyed her as much as the physical house did during the summer. Eden transcended time as the receptacle of the family's legends and most vivid memories. She associated Eden with love and tradition, a link between the generations, and it made her sad to think that Sarah's baby would miss the opportunity to run through its cool grass. The only thing sadder was the idea that Sarah might choose not to have her baby at all.

As Becca crossed the lawn and continued down the flagstone path, she noticed the dew still clinging to an intricate spider web on an eave over the back door. It reminded her of the summer she read *Charlotte's Web* to Sarah. Her heart ached. There wasn't an inch of this house that wouldn't remind her of something.

She wiped her eyes and reached for the knob on the screen door, pulling it open, the hinges creaking in the process. She should have replaced them long ago, but the familiar sound prevented surprise entrances through a door that was always left unlocked. Becca kicked off her wet, sandy shoes and socks and placed them on the mat before she filled Hennessy's water bowl.

It was now 7:00 A.M., long before anyone else would be down. The counters smelled lemony from the wipe-down Lilly had given them the night before, and yesterday's newspapers were stacked in a wicker basket on the floor. There was a sense of order in a room that would transform over the course of the day into the hub of Eden's activity.

The fog was lifting, the sun shining through the window and onto the kitchen table. Becca ran her fingers over the grain of its wood. If Sarah could be so bold, fearless in the face of single parenthood, maybe Becca could find the courage, too. It would feel so good to get everything off her chest. She had kept a secret of her own for so long, its tentacles had wrapped her from end to end. Her family would be convening for the Fourth of July weekend. It was the perfect opportunity.

Becca collected the centerpiece from the dining room and placed it in the pantry sink. She picked through the peony blossoms and refreshed the water, then buried her face in their browning petals, breathing in their calming aroma. Dan had tended the peonies with such love, just as her father had before him. The image of her father in the garden made Becca's eyes well with tears. She sniffed back her emotions and wiped her eyes. She would enjoy Eden's small pleasures while they were still hers.

Chapter 3

LONG HARBOR, RHODE ISLAND
1955

Bunny sat in his cushioned wheelchair on Eden's back porch. Lilly had deposited him there half an hour earlier with a scotch perched in his right hand, a blanket over his lap, and a mustard-yellow cardigan across his shoulders. He pulled the nub of a cigar from his chest pocket. He liked to sneak a few puffs before dinner where the women wouldn't complain. The pungent aroma of smoke wafting about his head, he meditated on the autumnal angle of the sun, its quick fade beyond the dunes, burning shades of yellow, orange, and red into the water below and the clouds above. When the sun set completely, he snubbed the cigar against a large clamshell he kept hidden behind a planter.

Bunny breathed slowly, the acrid taste of tobacco still fresh on his lips. There was a rattle in his throat, and he was conscious of a stiffening, a thickening, deep inside, gripping his chest. He could imagine it spreading slowly to his abdomen, his limbs, and eventually, probably in the not-so-distant future, to his mind. His life had been so beautiful—a blessing, really. But there was one thing that nagged at him. It had to do with Becca. She tried so hard to be the perfect doctor's wife, but Bunny caught her staring vacantly into space at odd moments. Sometimes he saw tears in her eyes. Certain topics were especially difficult for fathers and daughters to discuss, but if he was nearing the end, he had no time to waste.

He searched his memory for the point in time when she had changed. When she had stopped letting him call her Princess. He kept coming back to the year after the boys returned from the war, after she returned from that finishing school Sadie sent her off to. What was the name of that place? He hadn't even visited. Couldn't picture it. The one school he could recall was in the thick of Deutschtown, a densely populated wedge of Pittsburgh just north of where the Allegheny River merged with the Ohio. The American flag had hung at the front of his third-grade classroom. Bunny remembered standing erect, to the left of his desk every morning, his hand over his heart, his black hair pasted down, wholeheartedly reciting the Pledge of Allegiance. His father had been so proud that he was growing up a regular "American kid." "You see, Anna," he would say to his wife, "Bernhard speaks English without an accent. Nobody would ever know we are German."

Bunny took a last, long swig of scotch and put the crystal glass on the table by his side. He gripped the wheels of his chair in each hand and strained to turn himself toward the glow of the living room window. The room was fully illuminated, making him invisible to his twin grandsons, who labored over a jigsaw puzzle on the carpet inside. He saw Ruth, his daughter-in-law, walk through the living room and lovingly tousle young Joseph's blond curls. He radiated affection back in her direction. She remained poised, despite all she had been through. If only Becca had the same confidence.

He felt for those boys, grief-stricken in their own right, yet devoted to their mother's well-being. His own mother had depended on him, too. She had always been a foreigner in this country, learning passable English, but if she really had something to say, it was in Yiddish. She said, "Your father, he calls thees progress, but I can only theenk of vat ve haf left behind." She taught Bunny Hebrew prayers and urged him to recite them under his breath, in bed at night. Her facial expressions revealed the distaste she harbored toward his father's work in a meatpacking house, handling pork all day. She groaned about the Pittsburgh sky, always black with soot. Even though she scrubbed and scrubbed, the grime from the factories permeated everything and frequent floods from the Allegheny left their home cold and damp.

Bunny leaned forward in his wheelchair to tap on the window. Little Joseph turned suddenly from the puzzle, looking up toward the glass. Bunny leaned in close, tapped again, waved, and pointed toward the French doors. Joseph hurried to turn the knob with both of his little hands and stepped out on the porch.

"What are you doing out here, Grandpa?"

"I told Lilly I wanted to watch the sunset, but I think she's forgotten about me."

"Are you cold?" the boy asked, as he hugged himself against the breezy night.

"No, it's toasty under this blanket. Hop up on my lap, and I'll warm you up."

Bunny was arranging Joseph snug against his chest when Benjamin appeared in front of them.

"C'mon, there's room for you, too."

Bunny pulled the blanket over all three of them. Although they had once been rather rambunctious boys, nobody could predict when they might rebound from the shock of their father's death. Granted, Ruth had lost her husband and Bunny and Sadie had lost a son, but all Bunny's grief now centered on the fact that these boys would grow up without a father. He'd provide for them, sure, but that wasn't the point. A boy needs a man to get him started on the right foot.

His own father had been his greatest motivator, encouraging him at every point in his life. A rags-to-riches story himself, Samuel Meister had worked at H. J. Heinz for thirty years, being promoted from packing meat in the factory to floor supervisor and ultimately to headquarters, where he had worked his way up in the personnel department. Bunny had heard his mother complain that the factory was not clean, not kosher, but he admired the path his father had taken. His father waved his knife and fork in the air, commanding Bunny's attention at the dinner table. "Hard work, Bernhard, and taking risks at the right time—that's what it takes.

If your mother and I had never left Germany, we'd still be sleeping on a straw mattress in her father's attic!"

Bunny hugged his grandsons as the three of them stared up into the night sky. The trust funds were one thing, but who would guide them along the way? His uncles might, but nobody could replace a father.

Bunny's father had worked hard to move his family out of Deutschtown, making it possible for Bunny to attend private boys' school in Oakland and for his mother to have a postage-stamp garden. She may not have approved of the meat his father packed, but her demeanor certainly improved once she had her own bit of earth to plant. His father didn't mind when, wanting to sound more American, Bunny dropped the "h" from the middle of his name, becoming Bernard, later nicknamed Bernie by his team-mates. His father had been at all of his football games, watching proudly from the stands.

Bunny never told his father how the coach had yelled at the team during the halftime of their game against Deutschtown. They sat on a long wooden bench, down by a touchdown, several players injured at the half. "I want you boys to fight! I want you to remember who you are and where you come from. You're not going to let those filthy Huns and Jews come onto our field and hand us a loss. Let's send those meatpackers home with their tails between their legs."

Bunny felt a rush of heat under his helmet, fearful he'd be discovered as an imposter. He went back out onto the field, taking his position on the front line, looking at the ground, instead of into the eyes of his opposition, as he had been taught. What were the chances of somebody from the old neighborhood recognizing him or his father? Days later, after it had become clear that his class-mates assumed he was one of their own, his relief had turned to panic. It would take extreme vigilance to keep his family's origins a secret, especially considering his mother's accent.

Joseph interrupted Bunny's reverie. "Grandpa, do you think Daddy is in heaven?"

"Joseph"—Bunny stumbled over the mention of their father—"of course he is, of course." After a few minutes, he continued, "When you boys miss your father, think about him here, at Eden. He loved it and will always be with you here. He was a little boy here, just like you are now. His imprint is all over this place. He was by my side, rebuilding her, after the great hurricane. Hell, he saved his sister's life."

Bunny pointed a crooked finger toward the ocean. "See those dunes out there? When you climb over them, he'll be holding your hand. When you fish or go sailing, look for his reflection in the sea; listen for his voice in the waves. And when you look at the stars in the sky, think of the way his eyes sparkled."

Joseph nodded his understanding. "I will, Grandpa."

"Were you a little boy here, too, Grandpa?" Benjamin asked.

"No, not me. I never left Pittsburgh as a child."

"What made you come here?"

"Oh, well, I guess I just got it in my head. . . ."

He told his grandsons how the seed had been planted, one afternoon tossing the football on Michael Turner's front lawn. Michael was Bunny's best friend in high school and often went on about his summer plans. "We all go to Long Harbor, Rhode Island." His extended family had purchased a two-hundred-acre farm nestled into a peninsula, creating beachfront property on one side and a protected harbor and several coves on the other. "Bernie, it's perfect—we have the waves on one side and lots of boating on the other, and we escape the city's stench every summer."

Bunny tried to conceal his awe. He had never seen the ocean and was all too familiar with the stink of Pittsburgh during the summer. The only image he had of the Atlantic was based on the cold and stormy scenes in Rudyard Kipling's *Captains Courageous*. Not until he went off to Yale on a football scholarship would he have his first real-life encounter.

His friends at Yale opened him up to a whole new world. Bunny didn't tell his grandsons how Whitey and Stalworth used to barge into his dorm room, smacking a bottle of whiskey down right in the middle of a paper he was writing. "C'mon, Bernie, don't be such a grind," they'd complain. Eventually he learned how to play their game, donning his tie loosely, swinging his feet up on his desk, and hiding how much he studied by regularly mixing them drinks. He became a natural among prep-schooled Ivy Leaguers.

Instead, he continued the story by describing the time Whitey invited him to Southampton. The glare blinded him as he stepped off the jitney. Bunny held his hand against his brow to shield the expression of wonderment on his face as much to shade his eyes from the bright sun reflecting off the white sand. He had finally entered the sun-kissed world that Michael Turner had gone on about.

Whitey led him to a wide beach, where his friends, his sisters, and their friends were all spread out on blankets. "Man, Bernie, after that trip you must be hot! C'mon!" With that, Whitey bounded over the blankets toward the water, crashing through the foamy breakers, diving under the waves until he was far enough out to tread water easily. He floated higher and lower with every swell. Bunny marveled at his friend's skillful emergence into the calmer, deep water. He followed until the water reached his waist and splashed some onto his face and hair, then wrapped his arms around his chest, exaggerating shivers. It had never dawned on him to learn how to swim.

Whitey's youngest sister stuck close to Bunny while they hung around on the lawn, shaking out blankets and making plans for the evening. He helped to grill strips of steak and ears of corn, the taste of cold beer mixing with the salt on his lips, the skin on his forehead and cheeks tingling pink. The smell and sizzle of the steaks, the glow of the fire, the casual ease with which people munched on the corn, helped themselves to more beer, and kissed under the moonlight was bewitching. He was determined that this magic would be a part of his life, too.

His grandsons' small heads rested against Bunny's wheezing chest as he finished telling them his story.

Joseph asked, "Was that girl on the beach Grandma?"

Bunny laughed. "No, no. I met your grandmother years

later at a garden party in Pittsburgh. What a vision she was back then. . . ." The French door opened, and Ruth stood there with a look of relief on her face.

"There you are!" she said, making her way to the wheelchair.

"Grandpa can't swim," said Benjamin.

"What are you talking about? I've been looking for you," said Ruth, feigning exasperation. She never stayed cross for long.

"Ruthie, have you heard from Becca? Is she coming for the weekend?" asked Bunny.

"I don't think so. She and Dan are hosting a benefit for the hospital," said Ruth, deftly angling the chair toward the living room. "Boys, come down off your grandfather's lap. Lilly's been keeping your dinner warm in the kitchen."

Chapter 4

PITTSBURGH, PENNSYLVANIA
1915

Sadie accompanied her parents to the garden party at the Downings', but argued they needn't put her on display at every social event in Pittsburgh. She preferred riding her horses to looking for a husband. She held a parasol and wore a full white dress that was cinched around the waist, her mother having spun her dark red hair up onto the top of her head in the style of a Gibson Girl. She sipped iced tea and feigned interest in a game of croquet that two spirited boys, smothered by their formal dress and pageboy haircuts, played on the green lawn.

"Sadie Thompson, may I introduce Bernard Meister?" said Mrs. Downing, as she showed Sadie to her seat. "I believe you two are similar in age. You should find plenty to talk about."

Sadie let Bernard pull out her chair and smiled in his direction as he sat down next to her. He had a very strong jawline, olive skin, and jet-black eyebrows. She found his profile alluring and was awash with gratitude for her parents' insistence that she come.

While the men at the table discussed Andrew Carnegie's genius in translating his railroad empire into Carnegie Steel and his recent sale to US Steel, the women recounted the upcoming highlights of the social calendar. Sadie made polite conversation with Bernard. "Yale law school—my, my. You must have visited Manhattan often. Tell me all about it." He smiled as he spoke, his dark eyes enchanting. Sadie blushed and looked away, pretending to search for someone at the other end of the tent.

As their carriage drove away after the party, she thought only of Bernard, his silky black hair and cleft chin, and the way he looked at her. Her father broke her reverie as they bumped along the rutted road to their house.

"That Meister chap—I believe he works for Downing over at Heinz. Someone said he started in the factory, worked his way up."

Her mother added, "Can you believe that the son was seated next to Sadie? Did you hear the wife's accent? They're right out of Deutschtown."

"I'm sure Downing thinks they're quality people."

"You never know with Frannie Downing. She can be a troublemaker."

"Helene."

"If I had to guess from the looks of them, they're Jews."

"Stop, Helene."

Lying in bed that night, Sadie wondered if he would call on her. Given the demands of his law firm, she worried he might not find the time.

The next morning, Sadie's parents drove their carriage the mile to her family's church, which sat on the edge of their large estate, Lancaster Fells. They would pick up her grandmother on the way. Sadie and her siblings preferred to follow behind on foot. Sadie's mother leaned her head out the window of the carriage before they were beyond earshot. "Don't dawdle!"

Her brothers weaved through the tall trees that lined their drive while Sadie and her sister, Kitty, skipped arm in arm behind them. Sadie called out to her brothers to avoid the puddles, lest they cross their mother. All four of the Thompson children had red hair, carried down from their mother's side, and Sadie had heard their Thompson grandmother bemoan the fact that the only one it suited was Sadie. Her skin was fair, with a dusting of freckles over the bridge of her nose, and her eyes, crowned by high, arching, full brows, twinkled mischievously.

After the church service, the family gathered in her grandmother's cottage. She had moved there when Sadie was eight, after her younger sister, Kitty, was born. "I'm too old to live among the children," her grandmother had said. "Plus, Helene and I can't seem to share a kitchen." Sadie had liked when her grandmother had lived with them. She remembered the words her parents had exchanged when her grandmother insisted their traditional Sunday supper be moved from the grand dining room of the main house to her more modest one.

"Helene, my mother is an old woman; it's all she has left," her father had said, tired of the arguing.

As coffee was being poured, the minister's wife innocently commented on the number of weddings being held at the church that summer. "Every Saturday in June and July . . ."

Sadie's grandmother chimed in. "Well, our Sadie here, she's finished school, done the Grand Tour, made her debut . . . What was it, five seasons ago?" From the corner of her eye, Sadie saw the pained expression on her mother's face.

"Four," her mother corrected.

"Four. Right. Well, I was hoping for a wedding before I die!" The minister's wife sipped her coffee in silence.

"Well, please excuse me. While I'm still a free woman, I'm going to exercise Blue!" Sadie rose from the table and, with laughter in her voice, bade her farewells. She shook hands with the minister and kissed her grandmother on the cheek. Her mother could do all the worrying; Sadie was perfectly happy with her life the way it was.

She rushed back to the main house and changed into her riding clothes, then headed to the barn. She inhaled the familiar tanned-leather smells while brushing and saddling her prized quarterhorse. The sun shone on her face as she rode through the meadow and along the perimeter of the woods. She picked up speed as she came to the road. Blue was galloping alongside it when they came upon a hired carriage. She pulled back on the reins and slowed before overtaking it. She peered into its window to see dark hair and then Bernard's face, surprised and elated. He fumbled to open the window.

"Hello!" she said.

"What are the chances?"

"Out for a Sunday ride?"

"No, I came for a reason. You said I could call on you again, and that's what I am doing."

Sadie's heart skipped. "Oh" was all she could manage, as nervous surprise overtook her. She smiled, on the verge of gleeful laughter. "Make a left ahead and meet me at the barn!" She kicked Blue's sides, and he took off, her mind racing faster than her horse's strong legs.

That summer, Sadie avoided her mother's introductions to "eligible" men, spending evenings and weekends with Bernard instead. They walked after dinner, and she taught him to saddle and then ride a horse. He suggested they ride bicycles, and she teased him about his city upbringing. Sadie invited him to church and her family's Sunday supper, and he escorted her to two cotillions at the Hunt Club.

Bernard invited Sadie to his home in Oakland one night before the symphony. They sat in the small parlor with his parents, sipping sherry as Mrs. Meister served them cheese and bread on a porcelain plate. Bernard's parents were cheerful and animated. Mrs. Meister spoke with her hands to supplement her limited vocabulary, and Mr. Meister shook his fists for emphasis at the end of each sentence. Sadie had seldom encountered such self-made conviction. The men in her clan, while inheriting grand homes and positions, all left their offices midafternoon to play backgammon and drink whiskey at the Pittsburgh Club.

Sadie and Bernard walked to Symphony Hall, her arm wrapped through the crook of his elbow. "The way your father says your name—Bern-hard—it's almost two words; it sounds so harsh, like he might be about to punish you."

"Ha. I never thought about it."

"Really? Don't you have a pet name? Something they called you as a boy?"

"In school they called me Bernie, but I didn't think much of that."

"I'd say Bernard sounds too old, and Bernie sounds too sharp. I fashion you more of a . . . a Bunny than a Bernie."

"What?"

"Bunny. It's perfect. It's soft and kind and sweet."

"Soft?"

"Well, you know you *are* a lamb in wolf's clothing, a big, strong hulk with a huge heart."

"Of course, but I don't know about Bunny."

"Yes, yes, you *are*. From now on, that will be your name! Bunny Meister!"

"Well, all right. My college friends were always telling me I needed a better nickname."

* * *

"He asked your father for your hand, but we will refuse him," her mother said.

Sadie was silenced. Her mother's frostiness had always been humorous to watch, but now that it affected her, Sadie felt as if she had been kicked in the stomach. The thought of her parents spurning Bunny made her skin heat up. She felt for his humiliation, as well as for her own loss. She had been daydreaming about a life with him.

She left the house and headed directly to the barn, too mad even to speak to her mother. She brushed and mounted Blue, then galloped furiously through the meadow. She let him slow down along the long dirt road approaching her grandmother's house. When she spotted her grandmother sitting on the veranda, they came to a complete stop.

She waved, then dismounted Blue. She walked him toward the fence, tied the reins to a post, and joined her grandmother for a cup of tea.

"My dear, it is so nice to have you to myself for a change. I want to hear all about that handsome suitor of yours."

Sadie smiled sadly in reply.

"Well, what is the matter, child? I've never seen you at a loss for words."

"It's Mother," Sadie said.

Her grandmother sat silently and, without coaxing, waited for the whole story to come out. After Sadie was finished, her grandmother handed her a handkerchief. "Do you love him?"

"I didn't realize it until this happened, but I think I do."

"Well, that should be enough, then." Her grandmother's sage eyes twinkled as a smile of satisfaction spread across her face.

That night, Sadie heard muted, angry snippets coming from her parents' room: "she is practically beyond marrying age anyway" from her father, and "how dare she interfere?" from her mother. But in the morning, when her father joined her at the breakfast table, he announced from behind his newspaper, "We have changed our minds. I will call your Bernard today."

Sadie and Bunny married after New Year's in the family chapel at Lancaster Fells. Kitty was Sadie's maid of honor, and Bunny's father served as his best man. It was a small wedding party, and as they exited through the rear doors of the chapel, ahead of the invited guests, Bunny wrapped a white mink stole around Sadie's slight figure to protect her from the cold air outside. She looked up into his face and smiled as he helped her up into the horse-drawn carriage they would take back to the main house. As they sat side by side in the carriage, Bunny took her face in his large hands and leaned forward to kiss her lips. "I love you, Sadie Meister," he said.

"Oh, Bunny, I can't believe this is real," she said, a jolt of excitement rushing through her. "That I am actually your wife and we will be starting a life together." She would be moving out of her childhood room and into the small house on the other side of town that Bunny had recently purchased for them.

"It's a magical day," he said.

Guests rode and walked back to the main house at Lancaster Fells for a small reception. Sadie noticed Mr. Meister standing in the marble foyer, lending his handkerchief to his wife, when she arrived.

"Your parents are upset?" she whispered in Bunny's ear.

"My father is weeping because he is happy for me, and my mother is weeping because I married in a church."

Sadie searched Bunny's eyes for his own reaction. "Parents," he said, throwing his hands up in the air.

She caught sight of her own mother, standing stiffly in the dining room, making small talk with the preacher's wife. "Oh, yes, I know all about parents," she said.

"Never mind them, Sadie Meister. Let's go get some champagne."

* * *

Sadie and Bunny sat at their freshly polished dining room table, much as they had every evening for the past eight years. Their maid, Alice, who had started working for them after their oldest son, Thomas, was born, set plates down in front of them.

"Robert has his first loose tooth, and Thomas is riding his bike well now. He asked that you remove the training wheels this weekend."

"That's my boy." Bunny carved vigorously into his steak.

"And Edward is a little devil; he took his crayons to the wallpaper again."

They both ate in silence for a few minutes.

"And your day?" Sadie asked.

"US Steel continues to pay the bills. Just getting a small share of their legal work has the whole firm flat out."

"And how is it going with Stanley?"

"Better. He's still a thorn in my side, but I'm following your sage advice, my dear."

Bunny checked his pocket watch and turned the knob on the radio console they had set up near the table. It was time for the evening news, and they were both eager for some word on the war in Europe.

"Oh my," said Sadie, listening to the reporter describe the pending involvement of the United States.

"Kitty thinks Francis and Arthur might enlist right away."
Sadie looked for comfort in Bunny's face. "She said that Mother is
just beside herself."

When Sadie's brothers enlisted, the extended Thompson
clan was thrown into a confused mixture of anxiety and pride. Her
mother scratched her forearms continuously, to the extent that Sadie
insisted she wear long sleeves to protect her scabbing skin. Sadie and
Kitty took turns spending afternoons with her in the sitting room at
Lancaster Fells. On her days, Sadie would return home exhausted,
gathering her three boys after their baths and hugging them close in
one big bundle of arms and legs and tummies.

Over a candlelight dinner one cold February evening, Bunny
asked, "Any news from your brothers?"

"No. Kitty and I are just praying Mother receives a letter soon."

"Hmm. Well, I lunched again with some of the city council-
lors, and I got some important information. The P&E is going on
the block. It's just the opportunity we've been waiting for."

Sadie put down her knife and fork and stared at her husband
with serious eyes. Bunny took her hand as he laid out his plan.
The Pittsburgh and Lake Erie Railroad was a "heavy-duty" line
that occupied a prosperous niche in the industry, serving a relatively small yet extremely lucrative stretch between Youngstown
and Pittsburgh, catering to mills like US Steel's. Bunny, one of his
partners in his law firm, and two other local businessmen wanted
to form a syndicate to buy it, upgrade the track, and outfit the
cars, fashioning the line to specialize in transporting coal, iron, ore,
limestone, and steel.

"After that, we can sit back and watch the money roll in,"
said Bunny.

Although Sadie was proud of her husband's entrepreneurial
spirit, leaving the law firm and pouring everything they had into
his Little Giant made her nervous. But later, when his prediction
came true, she struggled to reconcile his business windfall with her
family's angst over the war.

Sitting in the parlor at Lancaster Fells, Sadie listened to her mother criticize their lifestyle. "You could be more sensitive, Sadie. Is it necessary to be so flamboyant?"

"But, Mother—"

"Don't try to make excuses. You should teach your husband discretion. People are talking about his nouveau-riche ways."

* * *

Six months after Bunny and his partners took another sizeable distribution from the P&E, Bunny returned from work wearing a new suit, carrying a bouquet of flowers, and bouncing with excitement. Sadie and Alice had just gotten the boys washed and seated around the dining room table. Sadie forced an exhausted smile in her husband's direction as he made his grand entrance. Bunny's appearance always resulted in a cacophony of cheers from the boys, who competed for a chance to speak and win their father's attention. He circled the table, exchanging kisses, distributing pats on the head, and laughing as Edward stood up on a chair and showed off his muscle.

"Bunny! Don't encourage them!" Sadie scolded.

Alice began to serve the meal, but Bunny couldn't sit still, clapping his hands and standing up suddenly. Sadie assumed he was going into the kitchen for the salt and pepper, but instead he came around behind her seat, pulled back her long, thick hair, and kissed the nape of her neck. She reddened as he touched her intimate spot, the place on her body that sent waves of desire through her.

"Bunny! Not now! What's gotten into you?"

Bunny put a small gift-wrapped box on the table in front of her, whispering, "I wanted to give this to you later, but I just can't wait." Sadie turned to search her husband's eyes. She lifted an elegant diamond necklace out of the black velvet box, and before she could chastise him on another extravagance, he got down on one knee in front of her. "Oh, Sadie, do you like it? And that's not all; that's not the main present!"

"What in heaven's name?" Sadie worried, raising an eyebrow as her sons jumped around.

"What, Daddy? What?"

Bunny removed a scroll of paper from his briefcase, moved some of the dishes aside, and spread it across the tablecloth. "This, my dears, is a map of Long Harbor, Rhode Island. And today your daddy bought a piece!"

Chapter 5

LONG HARBOR, RHODE ISLAND
Friday, June 26, 2000

Rachel retreated to her bedroom often. Inside its octagonal walls, she could ignore the unthinkable. Sarah, foolish Sarah, falling in love with an older man and showing up here pregnant, so naive about what it meant, what sacrifices she would have to make. Rachel closed the door and tried to forget, diving under her covers and swimming in the vastness of the queen-size mattress, so high off the ground. The tightly woven green carpet and antique dressing table in this room had been thoughtfully chosen years ago by her grandmother, who had decorated it for her mother, the only daughter in a family of rowdy boys. Even though Sadie might have overdone it with a frilled canopy over the bed, Rachel adored the room and its outspoken femininity.

Rachel liked to sleep with the windows open wide, welcoming in the cool nighttime air. The sea breeze wafted through the sheer curtains like a breath of life, CPR for her soul. She resisted ever closing them, even when, at the first hint of rain, Lilly bustled through the house, slamming every window shut. When Rachel was a teenager, her mother would burst into her bedroom at ten o'clock most mornings with an air of disgust, exclaiming that she was sleeping her summer away. She had been especially outraged those summers her cousins Joseph and Benjamin visited, as she had counted on Rachel to entertain them while her brother was off at the tennis courts.

"They're perfectly content going to the beach themselves, Mother."

"It's just that it's rude, Rachel. I promised Ruth we would show them a good time."

Her mother had always been a self-proclaimed morning person, righteously measuring people's worth by what time they got out of bed. Rachel, on the other hand, slept late, and the rituals she treasured most had to do with bedtime: fluffing up pillows, sipping a little wine, and reading a few lines of a book before giving in to heavy eyelids and full, consuming sleep.

Even better was the true summer luxury of waking up naturally, without an alarm. Rachel could lie still as her eyes adjusted to the light, reveling in the warmth of the down quilt, and listen for the sounds of the house. Water surging through the pipes meant her mother was showering; the kitchen door slamming was her daughter, Sarah; the crunch of the Lincoln's tires in the gravel driveway meant Lilly was off to the market. Rachel stretched her arms above her head and inhaled deeply, in search of breakfast in the air, but then remembered that since her father's death the previous winter, no one ate bacon anymore.

She sat up in bed, reached around several prescription pill bottles on the bedside table for her reading glasses, then picked up her battered copy of *Moby-Dick*. Another summertime ritual was revisiting the crazed and obsessed Ahab, so misunderstood and hell-bent on destruction. Lately she read it like her bible, opening up to a random page and just starting in, forcing her brain to materialize the correct context, and when she came upon her favorite parts, she put the book against her chest, its worn-out spine barely holding the pages together, and recited whole passages from memory. These literary calisthenics produced a self-satisfaction that gave her the strength to face each day.

Her growling stomach finally spurred her out of bed. In the bathroom, she caught sight of her reflection in the mirror. Dismayed by the dark, puffy circles under her eyes, she splashed cold water on her face, then twisted her long, gray-streaked hair into a clip on top of her head. She reached for the silk robe hanging on the back of the door and tied its belt around her belly. Her ex-husband, Peter, had brought it back from his first business trip to Thailand, almost thirty years earlier. Peter's anticipation of that trip had been a bright spot for them. Her uncle Edward had burst what small hope she had for Peter's future, however, when he explained he was sending Peter only because he was tired of watching him mope around the office.

Ah, how this robe brought back memories of her younger, sexier self, of Peter slowly untying the belt and reaching his hands around what then was her waist to pull her closer. A California boy at heart, Peter had never fit in in Long Harbor. This room and her fleshy body had been his refuge. The summer after they were married, before her pregnant belly swelled to the size of a beach ball, they spent long mornings in bed. He made love to her forcefully, as if it were the end of time, a violent storm brewing outside their door. And then, a few years later, when their marriage fell apart, it was these walls that absorbed the yelling. She'd pull the covers over her head to escape her mother's rebukes. "You certainly like giving people a reason to gossip," Becca seethed, upon first hearing of their plans. "There has *never* been a divorce in this family!"

Despite the struggles Rachel had with her mother, she had always been drawn to Eden. Their commitment to spend summer after summer together had become their own brand of love. They coexisted on different orbits of Long Harbor, Rachel moving to her own beat and her mother fussing over various committees. Despite her obligations, her mother managed to switch gears in Long Harbor. She expected Rachel and Andrew to keep their heads down during the school year, but after Memorial Day, she encouraged them to kick off their shoes. Summer was sacred, the grand prize for grinding away through a cold, dark winter. Her mother urged Rachel into the sun, the perfect antidote for her acne and the dark circles under her eyes.

But Rachel was certainly drawn to something more than the warm sun. She empathized with her father, who grumbled when obligations took him away for even a day or two. When Uncle Edward's children were married on Long Island in July, her father threatened not to attend.

And Lilly once complained that Rachel had never even made a run to the supermarket. It was true. Besides the house, the beach, and a visit down to the village ice cream parlor where she worked as a teen, Rachel hardly went anywhere.

"I'm sorry, Lilly, but the winter is so long," she had said. "I'm schlepping back and forth to work and to school with packages and book bags, and cooking meals. . . . When I get to Eden, I sort of collapse."

"Rachel, your grandmother hired me when I was sixteen years old to take care of you as a baby. I never dreamed I'd still be at it fifty years later!"

She opened her bedroom door and padded lightly down the hall, listening for voices. Grateful for the stillness, she proceeded toward the stairs as if it were midnight and she was about to raid the pantry. Although she treasured her solitude, Rachel sometimes resented the way she felt like an island, the flow of the house streaming around her, her opinions not mattering.

She was surprised to find the kitchen empty at eleven o'clock in the morning. Bright rays of sun shone through the window and against the wall. Hennessy's head perked up from his dog bed.

"Don't try to fool me, old dog. I'm not going to feed you," said Rachel.

Lilly had left the coffee on, along with a sectioned half of grapefruit and a buttered English muffin, ready to go in the toaster oven. Gestures like that proved that Lilly really did love her, even if she had been griping an awful lot lately about not being able to get into Rachel's bedroom to clean.

Rachel was poking around the liquor cabinet in the pantry, looking for the bottle of Baileys, when she heard her mother's voice. "What are you doing?"

Rachel jumped at the sound. "Mother!"

"I knew you'd come out of your room to eat eventually."

Rachel carried her dishes to the kitchen table and focused on her food. Her mother sat across from her, folding her thin arms across her pale-pink sweater set and pearls. As always, her gray bob was neatly coiffed. Rachel cinched the belt of her robe, then reached up to tighten her hair clip. "Just in case you're about to lecture me, Mother, I am planning on shampooing my hair after breakfast." She went back to the business of scooping out grapefruit sections, concentrating on squeezing the juice from the rind into her spoon and slurping up the ruby liquid.

"No, Rachel, it's not your hair. I want to talk to you about Sarah. I think you should talk to her. Think how she must be feeling."

"Mother, you're awfully sympathetic to Sarah's situation. Your tune has certainly changed."

Back in 1972, when she was a sophomore in college, Rachel had had to tell her mother that she was pregnant. It had been in the front seat of their station wagon. She had composed her speech during the long bus ride from Ithaca to New Haven.

It was pouring rain when the bus arrived at the station. The mad dash across the parking lot in her flip-flops soaked her frizzy hair and her Cornell sweatshirt. It was the one time Rachel remembered her mother holding her close and not rushing it, actually showing empathy. Her father had suggested that Rachel might give the baby up for adoption, but her mother wouldn't hear of it. She really put her foot down.

Rachel took a bite of her English muffin and chewed slowly. "One act of unprotected sex with Peter determined the rest of my life, Mother. You took over. You made the decisions, doors were forever closed, and the baby defined my existence," said Rachel.

"Rachel, that baby was Sarah. Please—you have a chance to do a better job at this. Just talk to her."

Rachel shook her head. Everything was for Sarah's sake. Her friends, fellow writers—gritty, bohemian, downtown types— ribbed her relentlessly about her highbrow summer home. But Rachel contended that she summered at Eden for her daughter's sake. "My parents are a pain in the ass, but I want to give Sarah the type of childhood where she can roam barefoot and collect shells on the beach."

Rachel never articulated what it also meant to her. Her blood pressure dropped as she passed all the old, familiar landmarks on the drive up from the city each June. The landscape's gradual transformation from urban to rural evoked in her a transition that she looked forward to all winter. She tooted the horn as they rolled up the driveway every spring, conveniently forgetting for those first, optimistic moments all the challenges she had with family harmony.

"Mother, Sarah just waltzed in here with that innocent smile on her face and announced she was pregnant. Since when has being unmarried and pregnant been no big deal in this family? Your hypocrisy just kills me. You never cared about anything besides appearances and your social agenda—oh, but when it comes to your precious granddaughter, all bets are off. I guess I was just born in the wrong generation."

"Rachel, you had Sarah and married Peter almost thirty years ago. It's ancient history. Things are different now, and besides, Sarah is a grown woman. She's capable. I think we should be supportive."

"Listen to you! What would Daddy have said to all this?"

"Rachel, your father is gone."

A lump formed in Rachel's throat. "I'm going back upstairs," she said, picking up her dishes.

"Please, Rachel. Talk to her. Talk to her before Andrew and Camilla arrive for the weekend, while it's just us in the house."

"Ugh, Andrew and Camilla."

"Rachel, Sarah needs a mother right now."

Rachel rolled her eyes and pushed an errant strand of hair away from her face. *Yeah, like you've always been there for me?*

"I'll think about it," she said.

Chapter 6

PITTSBURGH, PENNSYLVANIA
1923

B unny sat behind his large mahogany desk at the P&E, flipping through his copy of the *Long Harbor Prospectus*. He read it and reread it for entertainment, especially the paragraphs recounting Long Harbor's salubrious ocean breezes and all the healthful recreation. It spoke of the sea air's tonic effect upon the appetite and its ability to calm frayed nerves. Most important, the prospectus solicited those who would return summer after summer with their families in order to create a tightly knit community.

Bunny was mesmerized by the photograph of the light-house, perched at the tip of this small, rocky peninsula, dating back to the eighteenth century. It had been a lookout during the American Revolution, as well as a beacon for returning sea captains searching for the entrance to Long Island Sound. Even before that, it was the post from which mighty Chief Paupanaug had stood lookout for rogue Niantic or Narragansett warriors who might invade by sea.

As he turned the pages, he imagined the six men who, in 1885, seized the opportunity to buy up parcels of farmland. Coining themselves the Founders of the Long Harbor partnership, these men had known each other since boyhood, when they had summered in one of Long Harbor's grand hotels. Bunny traced the grainy photograph with his finger, picturing them puffing Cuban cigars and toasting with fine whiskey the night they closed the deal.

Their intention, they wrote, was not to rival the grand scale of Newport, with its Manhattan elite, but to offer a midwestern set of upper-class families a pristine enclave in which to gather and enjoy leisure activities such as boating and golf. This was to be a place representing the epitome of good taste, populated by the "right people."

Bunny had arranged for a business colleague to introduce him to one of the Founders a few years prior. The three men dined at the Pittsburgh Club, where Bunny casually dropped Michael Turner's name, back from his Philmore Academy days. The old-timer took the bait. "Is that the same Turner family with a connection to Long Harbor?" he asked.

"Actually, it is. The very one. I have heard so many wonderful stories and also admired the pictures."

"Well, Long Harbor is a magical place."

"Sir, I've done a bit of research, and I understand there are still some home sites available on the ocean side."

"That's correct," the old-timer answered, with a quizzical lilt to his voice.

"Sir, my wife and I are most interested."

The old man sized him up with a few questions. He was seemingly more impressed by Sadie's being a Thompson than by Bunny's Yale diploma or skyrocketing business success.

Back at his office, Bunny stuffed the frayed prospectus into his valise and gathered up his coat and hat. On the street he met his driver, who was arranging his luggage in the trunk. He looked up at the gray Pittsburgh sky before ducking his head into the backseat and heading off to the train station. He had been making trips east every couple of months to meet with his architect, Michael Henderson, justifying the journeys by lunching with his bankers in New York City before connecting with a train up the coast.

When he had kissed Sadie farewell that morning, her tiny body had been curled up under the blankets of their bed. She had looked up at him with puffy eyes and with a tired, scratchy voice said, "Have a safe trip." He wished she were more excited about the house construction but tried to sympathize with her mood.

There had been an awful tragedy in the Thompson clan. Sadie's brother, Francis, had been killed in battle early in the war, breaking the hearts of everyone at Lancaster Fells. Then, six months after they buried Francis, her other brother, Arthur, had been shipped back from the front with an injury to the brain and spine that left him paralyzed and mute. Helene and Walter had withdrawn to their upstairs quarters after delivering their son to an institution. When Bunny suggested they get out and walk in the fresh air, Helene stared at him accusingly, as if waiting out her days was all she could bear.

Since then, he had made an effort to contain his excitement, out of respect for the circumstances. He knew his exuberance over the photographs and the drawings Michael Henderson sent him risked crossing the line over what was appropriate during this time of mourning. At home, alone with Sadie, however, he couldn't help himself, thought it might help, in fact, to talk about something positive, "The building materials are being carted in from Kingston, twenty miles away, and hand-cut on-site."

Sadie looked up from her soup, forcing a smile, then went back to rhythmically stirring the contents of her bowl.

"The builders are true craftsmen, Sadie. They use saws, adzes, and broad axes. Sleeping shacks have been put up on the property for laborers so they needn't waste a day traveling back and forth."

"Oh, Bunny. This folly of yours, really. I don't know why you're wasting your time. How will we ever be able to leave Pittsburgh?"

As the train picked up speed, its swaying subsided and Bunny shut his eyes. He wanted so much to share his excitement with Sadie, for them to be doing this together. He wanted to show her the plans, the architectural drawings, but she was overwhelmed by her family's loss, her parents' needs. He had to be sensitive; she'd come around eventually.

* * *

Bunny's hands trembled with excitement on a sunny June morning in 1925. He folded the road maps and fidgeted with the luggage. His shiny black Nash 168 was packed and ready to pull out of the driveway once the goodbyes were over. He ushered Sadie, Thomas, Edward, and Robert through the drawn-out exchange of hugs and good wishes with Kitty and his parents. Sadie wept as she hugged her sister, but Bunny finally pried them apart and guided his wife into the passenger seat. Sadie's expression was still full of uncertainty. Nevertheless, Bunny drove away, his boys' arms waving out the back windows. He smiled in the rearview mirror, catching a glimpse of his mother dabbing her eyes with a handkerchief.

They made stops along the way at small roadside hotels. On the third day, dusty and weary, Bunny's heart began to race as they got closer to Long Harbor. He was panicked that Sadie would never be happy and that this house might not measure up to her refined tastes. He now wished he'd insisted she review the plans with him. He paused and took a deep breath before making the turn up the driveway.

When the structure finally came into view, he heard her gasp and saw her press her hands to her cheeks. The home's three stories anchored it in the middle, and its two double-storied wings stretched out like arms on either side. Void of landscaping, with nothing but ocean on the flat horizon beyond, the magnificent house appeared even more colossal.

Bunny tooted the horn ceremoniously as the family burst from the car. Sadie and the kids ran to the height of the dunes, eager to see the famous Atlantic Ocean, but Bunny emerged from the car slowly, wanting their first moments in this new, bright world to unfold in slow motion.

"It smells sort of salty and sweet at the same time," Sadie said.

Unable to find the right words, Bunny grabbed her around the middle and twirled her in the air.

"Oh Bunny, look what you've done," she said, giggling. Bunny kissed her delicate lips.

He continued to hold Sadie up in the air, then swung her legs over one arm and carried her through the front door. They stood quietly on the landing, admiring the sparsely furnished living room with a coffered ceiling and large stone fireplace. The ocean beyond the living room and back porch was framed by a wide expanse of windows that at first could be mistaken for a painting, rather than the actual sea.

They meandered through the house together, Sadie ahead of him, looking over her shoulder every so often, flashing large, approving smiles at the dining room and then again at the kitchen, connected through a butler's pantry.

At the other end of the first floor was a large study for Bunny and, facing the ocean, a solarium enclosed with windows. Two French doors opened onto a wide porch that stretched the entire length of the house on the ocean side.

"My man Henderson predicts the porch will be our favorite spot—perfect for reading, napping, cocktails, even dining," Bunny said.

Sadie headed for the grand, formal staircase, which flowed upward from the living room, "There's also a set of back stairs in the kitchen," Bunny said, as he jogged up ahead of her. The master bedroom was in front of them, at the top.

Sadie put her hand over her heart. "Oh, Bunny, is this our bedroom? With this view?"

He hugged her waist from behind and rested his chin on her shoulder. "Do you like it?" he asked, kissing her neck softly and rocking her from side to side.

Down the hall were six other bedrooms, varying in size and shape, sharing common but spacious bathrooms, and there were four small bedrooms over the kitchen for the help. A long, screened-in sleeping porch with six twin beds was accessed through five of the rectangular bedrooms, creating a playful, camp-like interconnected-ness. Bunny pointed out how they were all attached to one another with interior doorways, in addition to the common hallway.

"Why?" asked Sadie.

"Not sure, but Henderson says it's something they do around here."

The maids had arrived days before with the moving van and did their best to prepare for their first meal. Bunny had requested this celebratory event and had invited Henderson to join them. He trained it up from New York City for the occasion, appearing at the front door in a smart jacket and bow tie. He laughed easily when Sadie opened the door. "Well, the place is finally open for business!" Bunny slapped him on the back, almost knocking the slight man off his feet.

The dining table was set as properly as possible, amid the half-open crates and boxes. Michael chuckled and said, "Mr. Meister, it's okay to be informal, you know—this is just a beach cottage!" His laughter was contagious, but Bunny wasn't sure how to respond. Had he already broken an unwritten rule of the summering elite? Then again, Henderson himself had been the one to design a mahogany-paneled dining room—how did he expect it to be furnished? Bunny searched Henderson's expression again, but he was hungrily inspecting the dinner he had just been served.

Once the final plate was put down, Bunny stood, beaming, at the head of the table and held his glass high. The boys turned their heads toward him, becoming unusually quiet. Sadie put her finger to her lips, hushing the girls serving the meal.

Bunny waited for the sound of dishes in the kitchen to stop clanking. Once there was stillness, he spoke. "Now, *this* is a perfect moment," he said, looking around the table slowly and making eye contact with all present. "This is a day I have dreamed about for a long time, since before you children were born, and even before I met your mother. I really can't believe we're here."

His voice trembled, and he paused to gain control of his emotions. "I pray that your mother and I will grow old and prosper here and that this place will transcend future generations.

"Thank you, Sadie, for tolerating this outlandish vision of mine and allowing me to carry it forward." He blew Sadie a kiss across the length of the table. She gave him an embarrassed smile.

Bunny cleared his throat. "Now, as you know, all fine homes receive names. Because she represents my paradise and a new beginning for all of us, I would like to name her Eden."

The boys cheered and Sadie clapped, and Michael Henderson rose from his seat, stepped to the corner of the room and lifted a sheet revealing a block of granite engraved with EDEN—1925. "We will install this by the front door," Henderson said.

Later that night, with a full moon glowing through their unadorned window and the sounds of waves crashing beyond, Bunny undressed Sadie, taking her thick red hair out of its clips and letting it fall down her back and over her shoulders. He stood undressed in front of her, captivated by the moonlight, which turned her fair skin to ivory. He held her firmly around the ribs, supporting her backward onto fresh white sheets. They made love that night with an intense passion that had been dormant since Robert's birth. Their appetite for each other was reminiscent of the years before Sadie had fallen victim to the fatigue of motherhood and caring for her parents. Sadie wrapped her strong legs around Bunny's waist. He was invigorated, admiring the way the delicate lines of her collarbones and jaw interplayed with the light and shadow of the moon. As he held himself above her, his usually impeccable hair fell over his forehead like a schoolboy's. Sadie cried his name, and Bunny buried his face in the pools of her hair.

* * *

From his garden, Bunny looked up at the same bedroom window that had perfectly framed the moon the night before. He saw Sadie watching him and stopped raking, leaned on his hoe, and waved to her.

He had built a low, ornamental wall around three sides of the property from the pile of stones that had been overturned during the leveling of the building site. Then, using geometry to calculate exactly where shadows would be cast during the day and at different times of the year, he and Henderson staked the gardens and paced the yard, plotting the placement of trees and bushes.

In bed at night, after making love, he shared his vision: trees selected for their spring flowers, colorful fall foliage, and unimpeded views of the ocean, azalea and rhododendron shrubs flanking the cobblestone foundation with a colorful skirt. He would train wisteria vines that would someday climb onto the shingles above the porch, creating a lovely canopy of violet, conical blooms.

Bunny showed her where there would be future mounds of day lilies, snapdragons, and peonies, his hands animating the abundance he had in store for her. He planned the vegetable garden close to the kitchen door and the cutting garden alongside it, both able to thrive in uninterrupted sun. He set aside space for a large, level green lawn between the house and the dunes, perfect for croquet or as a playing field for the boys and their friends, promising grass as lush as the golf course fairways.

"Bunny," Sadie said, "I never knew this side of you."

"Ah, maybe I get it from my mother, but there is something about cultivating the earth." He closed his eyes and faced the sun and basked in its warmth, then took a sip from Sadie's lemonade before picking up his shovel.

Sadie stayed indoors, out of the sun, cheerfully greeting the tradesmen who were finishing up odds and ends, with hot coffee. She seemed fond of Paul O'Brien, who insisted on being called Mr. P. and asked if he might stay on to cook for the family. He had twinkling green eyes that almost matched hers, a reddish complexion, and a portly stomach that rose and fell with great belly laughs. Mr. P. arranged for regular deliveries of bountiful produce, seafood, ice, and milk. Local farms provided ample supplies of the beefsteak tomatoes, sweet corn, and berries that would become staples of their diet.

Bunny and Sadie ran into acquaintances from Pittsburgh often during their daily strolls to the village. They lingered along the sea wall to chat while the boys admired the sailboats.

"Welcome to Long Harbor! You two have really outdone yourselves."

Sadie always demurred, but Bunny accepted the compliments heartily. "Thank you. We'd love to have you stop by."

After one such encounter, Sadie gathered up the boys and continued silently back toward home. When the boys ran ahead up the driveway, Sadie turned to him and said, "I don't care who likes us here. If it's you and the boys and me living by the sea forever and ever, I'll be the happiest woman in the world."

"That would make me happy, too, but the community has so much to offer. We should try to be social."

"Bunny, these people are leery of outsiders. I just don't want us to—"

But Bunny cut her off. "I've followed all their rules, conformed to their architectural standards."

Sadie said, "The house may be built like the other houses on the shore, but her yellow, unweathered shingles brand her a newcomer."

"By next summer they'll have weathered to a silver gray," Bunny assured her. "Henderson promised their fanciful patterns would shimmer like fish scales when the sun hit them just right."

"I don't think the architectural style is the issue, Bunny. I think it's, it's . . . well, it's the grandeur." How could she explain that certain rules weren't written down.

Nelson Archibald, an old acquaintance of Sadie's father, came by one afternoon while Bunny was building his wall. He tipped his hat to Bunny, then ascended the steps to where Sadie was sitting on a rocker.

"Welcome to Long Harbor," he said.

"Thank you, Mr. Archibald," Sadie replied.

Bunny approached them while clapping dirt from his work gloves. He wiped his hands against his work shirt and extended one in the visitor's direction.

"I'm Bunny Meister."

"Well, young man," he said, "you've certainly set a new standard for Long Harbor. That little railroad of yours must be practically printing money!"

Sadie stepped down off the porch to stand firmly next to her husband.

"Yes, my little railroad. Quite a concept—shocking nobody thought of it sooner," Bunny replied.

The two men seemed to be at an impasse until Sadie spoke up. "Mr. Archibald, we'll have to have you over for supper as soon as we get settled."

He nodded silently in her direction.

The men shook hands and said their goodbyes.

"Give my best to Mrs. Archibald," Sadie called out, as their visitor walked in the direction of the driveway.

Once he was out of sight, Sadie went back to her reading on the porch. Bunny joined her, rocking for a few minutes in a chair by her side. She picked up a stack of envelopes and handed them to him. "Bunny, these invitations were in our post box today," she said.

He flipped through them.

"Accept them all," he said, handing them back to her, unopened.

"But, Bunny, we don't want to appear too eager," Sadie said.

"Accept them all," he said once more, before heading back to his garden.

Chapter 7

LONG HARBOR, RHODE ISLAND
Tuesday, June 30, 2000

B ecca stretched her leg over to what had been Dan's side of the
bed and felt the coolness of the sheets. It always took several
seconds to remember he was gone. Her spirit deflated even further
as she recalled the previous day's conversation with the accountant. She pulled a pillow over her face. Dan had been an adoring
husband, but how could he have been so irresponsible?

He had died last autumn, around the time the perennials
turned brown and coarse. It was only fitting that she had found
him in the vegetable garden, on the ground, among the withered
tomato vines. She had held him there for several seconds, putting
her cheek next to his, before heading into the kitchen to call 911.

Dan's summertime pleasures—bracing swims in the Atlantic
Ocean and sweet corn on the cob, dripping with butter—had kept
him invigorated. He had departed like a goose following the migra-
tion after Labor Day. It was a massive heart attack, there had not
been any warning, and the doctors assured her that he had not
suffered. Now Becca knocked around her life, wrestling with her
new title of widow.

She swung both feet onto the floor and dressed for her morning walk, zipping up her navy blue tracksuit with stripes down the
sides. She brushed her hair back into a clip and put on a baseball
cap. Her dark sunglasses and a dab of her peach lipstick were the
finishing touches. There was no time for self-pity, as the upcoming

Fourth of July weekend would be a busy one. More family arriving, they would be ten in all, and she wanted to take advantage of their assembling. It was time to tell them everything.

And she had to get an answer to the accountant soon.

Instead of taking the dog to the beach, she decided to walk on the road toward the village. She would pick up the newspaper at the general store. She clipped the leash on Hennessy and went to the study to get a dollar for the paper. The stack of envelopes sitting on the desk haunted her. The last letter from the bank sat on top of the pile. *Oh, Dan, if you weren't already dead, I would kill you myself.*

In a final act of desperation, she had telephoned her eldest brother, Thomas, in April. She had made the call from her car. She had been driving around the streets of Wallingford, Connecticut, the neighborhood where they had raised their children. The realtor had asked her to clear out of the house for a last-minute showing. As she waited for his secretary to connect the call, her heartbeat quickened. She pictured him, feet up on his massive mahogany desk, reclining in the leather chair that had been their father's. Thomas was in his element in that office. He took her call with a booming voice, "Good morning, little sister! To what do I owe the pleasure?"

"Oh, Thomas. Thank goodness I caught you." After a few pleasantries about the weather, she got to the point.

"It has to do with our estate," she said.

"And . . ."

Becca could hear her brother flipping through papers as she spoke to him.

"I've been going through Dan's affairs with our accountant, you see."

"Oh dear, Becca—so sorry. It must be terribly difficult for you. Do you need me to handle it for you?"

"No, Thomas, it's not that. Well, I'll just say it: Dan obviously wasn't planning to go so suddenly, and things are a mess." Becca felt the heat of embarrassed tears coming, certain Thomas also heard the tremor in her voice.

"How so?" he asked.

"Well, he took out loans, against the house in Wallingford."

"I see."

"It's on the market now, but I doubt it will fetch enough to cover the debt."

"Really?" She heard judgment in her brother's voice. He'd never thought highly of Dan, the way he had taken the reins at Eden, and it pained her to have to expose Dan's private business now, when he was no longer around to defend himself. But what choice did she have?

"And I was remembering," she continued, "that you mentioned, back when you bought Robert's share from Ruth, that you would be willing to buy all of our shares of Eden if we ever decided to sell."

"You want to sell, Becca?"

"Of course it's not what I *want* to do, Thomas. But I can't see what other options I have! The bank is sending letters every week."

"All right, let me know which bank. I'll give them a call, buy you a little time."

"Oh, Thomas, thank you. Really, thank you so much!"

"Eden would be three-quarters mine if I bought your share. Edward would likely sell the remainder to me as well at that point."

"I'm sure he would," Becca said, bridging a silence, "if that's what you want."

"Carol will want to walk around the place again, no doubt— kick the tires. Better call an appraiser, too. I'm not even sure what Long Harbor real estate fetches these days."

"Of course." Becca bit at the corner of her thumbnail. How could one put a price on Eden?

"We'll come out earlier this summer. We'll come for the Fourth and enjoy the festivities."

"That would be fine. Andrew and Camilla and their children will be here that weekend as well, and of course Rachel and Sarah. I'm sure they'll be happy to see you again."

She hung up feeling worse. She could always count on

Thomas, but kick the tires? It sounded like he was planning to haggle with her over what Eden was worth.

* * *

Becca was scanning the travel pages of the *New York Times* when Lilly descended the stairs to the kitchen. She sensed Lilly pause and glance over her shoulder on the way to the refrigerator.

"Anything good to report?" Lilly asked.

"I'm afraid not. And it's going to be another hot one today," Becca said, without looking up.

Lilly crossed the kitchen and got busy poaching their eggs, one hand on her hip. The large Garland stove was the centerpiece of the kitchen, outfitted with six burners, an iron griddle, and a broiler tray. Industrial-style pots and pans hung overhead. Becca recalled her mother's cook, Mr. P., getting pancakes, bacon, and eggs sizzling for a full house all at once.

Becca considered the frivolity of having a housekeeper poach eggs and start the coffee. Thinking about paying the next month's bills made her nervous. She needed to sit down and explain the situation to Lilly. But she was more than a housekeeper; she had been at Becca's side since Rachel was a baby. If Thomas didn't agree to keep her on, who would take care of her?

When the coffeemaker finished gurgling, Becca got up to retrieve their mugs from a shelf next to the sink. The kitchen had no cabinets, per her father's utilitarian design from an era when only women and servants entered the kitchen. Whenever Becca suggested remodeling, Lilly moaned, "Who wants all the houseguests banging cabinet doors, looking for the water glasses?" Lilly lined the exposed shelves with clean white paper every spring and eventually agreed to a new refrigerator and dishwasher, the only modern appliances in an otherwise timeless room.

Becca poured their coffee while gazing out the window. She caught a glimpse of Sarah in the garden. She was wearing Dan's floppy old sun hat. Her attempt to plant vegetables had been touching. She had gone out and bought young pepper, bean, and tomato plants soon after her arrival. Becca was grateful; seeing the garden barren would have caused even more heartache. Sarah didn't have the greenest thumb, but Becca was a firm believer that gardening was therapy. She found relaxation in all of it: fertilizing, dividing, weeding, and harvesting.

"You brewed too much again, Lilly." Becca wondered how much coffee cost.

"I know, I'm still not used to this, but Rachel will drink it later."

Dan used to say that rising to the aroma of coffee made him feel like a king. Back on those Sunday mornings, when the bedrooms overflowed, he had a statesmanlike manner of entering the kitchen smiling, inhaling deeply through his nose, and kissing all the ladies at the table good morning.

"At least I stopped buying bacon," Lilly said.

Dan had insisted on bacon with his eggs. He and their son, Andrew, had always gobbled down a plate before hustling out the door to the tennis courts. Rachel and Sarah, however, were nibblers, lingering at the table. They preferred rainy mornings that stretched out endlessly, with all outdoor activities canceled.

Becca carried their mugs across the kitchen as Lilly expertly slipped the eggs onto slices of toast with a spatula. They sat at their usual kitty-corner places at the table. Becca had a notepad and a pen at her side.

"I want to go over the menus for the holiday weekend with you. And I was thinking of inviting the Bells for a drink before the fireworks on Saturday, and maybe a few more of Andrew's old pals." If this was going to be their last Fourth of July at Eden, she would swallow her concerns about cost and splurge on the festivities.

And her son loved a party. He would be arriving from London with his wife, Camilla, and their children, Sally and Walter. It had been many summers since they had visited Long Harbor, as his wife preferred her family's estate in the English countryside. When Andrew was twenty-two, he had promised his mother the

London move would be only a "short stint," a bolster for his budding finance career, but he had met Camilla and never come home.

Becca looked up from her pad at the sound of the screen door opening.

It was Sarah. "I need a drink of water," she said, shedding her gardening gloves and hat on the counter. She took a glass off the shelf, filled it from the tap, and took a long sip. "What are you two up to?" she asked.

"Putting together a little guest list," said Lilly.

"Oh, Gran, what fun! A party! We haven't had one in such a long time!" She squeezed her grandmother's shoulders from behind.

"Just a few people for drinks. Not a party."

"Still," said Lilly, raising an encouraging eyebrow in Sarah's direction.

"Saturday will be casual, but on Sunday I want everyone here for brunch. I have some important news to share. Oh, and did I mention that Thomas, Carol, and Ruth will be arriving for the weekend as well?"

Sarah and Lilly exchanged confused expressions. "No, you didn't mention that, but how nice," said Lilly.

"Aunt Ruth?" asked Sarah.

"Yes, your great-aunt Ruth," said Becca.

"It's been so long since I've seen her."

"It's true, she was unable to attend your grandfather's funeral, but I spent some time with her after Joseph's wedding a while back, and every year since, I've tried to get her up here."

Sarah's eyebrows raised in interest as Becca continued. "Those twins have led interesting lives. Joseph has lived all over the world and married a woman named Constance. He met her somewhere in Asia. And then there's Benjamin, all involved in the high-technology boom near San Francisco."

"It's called Silicon Valley, Gran."

"Right—that's what Ruth calls it, too, but I never could find it on the map."

"And Uncle Thomas and Aunt Carol will be coming for the Fourth this year?" Sarah asked.

"I know, I know, it's a change for them."

"That's unexpected," said Lilly.

"Oh, come now, you two. Won't it be fun? We'll have a full house. Practically a big family reunion!"

"In that case, I'd better get busy making the beds," said Lilly.

"I can help," said Sarah.

"I'll try to get one of Jimmy's guys over here to finish washing the windows," said Lilly, ticking off the chores on her fingers.

"But, Gran, you've got me curious," Sarah interrupted. "You've got news you want to tell us all at brunch?"

"Yes, that's right," said Becca, taking a last sip of coffee.

"You aren't sick, are you?" asked Sarah.

"Oh, Sarah, I'm fine. But excuse me now—I want to change out of my walking clothes."

Becca climbed the back stairs leading from the kitchen to the second floor. Once she was out of sight, she wiped the corners of her eyes. She lingered among her mother's black-and-white photos adorning the stairwell. She straightened a picture of her parents standing proudly on the back porch, their first summer here.

Becca walked down the hall to her bedroom and shut the door. She shook her hair out from under the cap and inspected her face in the mirror. Then she crossed the room to the telephone on the bedside table. She picked up the receiver and paused before dialing the familiar number. It was time to invite the guest of honor.

Chapter 8

LONG HARBOR, RHODE ISLAND
1926

A waiter weaved through the crowd, carrying a silver tray of crystal flutes. Charles Butterfield, tall and tan, with glints of blond in his slicked-back hair, took two, offering one to Sadie as he stared into her eyes.

"Here's to new pals," he said, clinking her glass and smiling as if he knew a secret.

Sadie took a sip, a little flustered by Charles's attention. She looked around the grand terrace of this home belonging to one of their new neighbors. People were drinking cocktails, laughing, and kissing cheeks in the foreground of yet another breathtaking sunset. She took hold of Bunny's arm with her free hand and raised her champagne flute when she spotted Charles's wife, Maud, skirting through the crowd, trying to reach them.

Charles and Maud Butterfield were a golden couple, in their mid-thirties, thin and childless. Sadie admired Maud's long silk gown and wondered if she should order one of her own. Maud wore her hair cut short and close to her powdered face, which was adorned with a penciled-on beauty mark and glossy red lipstick. She was a sophisticated New York gal, the most glamorous thing Sadie had seen outside of a magazine, making Pittsburgh seemed like some sort of backwater.

"So," Maud teased, "you built the big place on the beach."

"Yes, we're still getting settled," said Sadie.

"Right, no doubt. You must have quite a brood," said Charles.

"Three boys," answered Bunny proudly. "How about you?"

"Oh, God no," Charles snorted. "Us, children?"

Maud laughed. "Oh, you are a funny Bunny! You must have not heard about us yet. No, we'd be completely unfit parents."

"That's right," added Charles. "Why, we can be downright naughty."

Sadie recoiled at their rebelliousness but checked herself, hating to think she'd inherited her mother's self-righteousness.

Charles was gallantly dressed in a white dinner jacket and black tie. The nephew of one of the Founders, and heir to a Pittsburgh coal fortune, he had met Maud at a party in Newport and married her three months later. Her chic style might have fit in better in Newport. She was antsy, tapping her toes and twisting her legs, rehearsing the latest dance moves along the balcony.

"Hey, this party's thinning out," Maud whispered. "Let's go have dinner."

She was like a magnet. Sadie and Bunny couldn't help but follow along.

Charles poured drinks for the road, and they climbed into the Butterfields' Rolls-Royce Phantom. Bunny's eyes widened at the sight of the car, and he squeezed Sadie's hand in the backseat. She eyed her watch and thought about her boys, hopefully in bed by now. She caught a glimpse of Bunny's smile—he was having such a grand time.

Charles and Maud whisked them off into the night. Charles sped around corners on Highway 1A to a spot up the coast with a great raw bar. He had a regular table and did all the ordering, making a display of how to slurp an oyster from its shell and wash it down with a martini. Bunny grinned like a child, ready to give it a try.

"Well, this evening certainly took an unexpected turn," he said.

"Look," Charles offered, leaning across the dinner table, "Long Harbor is something. Yes, it sure is. Now, Maud and I found out the hard way, but we figure we might as well make it easy for you two. You seem like nice folks; you don't want to have the rough time we did."

"Oh, Charles," Maud interrupted, "You make it sound so horrible. It wasn't *that* bad. I mean, the people are nice; they can be a bit dull—lots of small talk and all the parties to go to. You two won't have a hard time—just look how gorgeous you are!"

Charles continued, "All I'm saying is, get into the club—you'll have to kiss a few asses along the way, but it's important to get into the club. Do you golf?"

"Well, no. But I'd like to," answered Bunny.

"Good. I'll take you over tomorrow to meet the pro, set you up with a few lessons. An athletic fellow like you should catch on quickly. We can have some lunch in the men's locker room; there are a few guys you should meet."

Maud smiled at Sadie. "And you, my dear—you'll go to all the parties and be a perfect hostess in return, and you'll have no problem at all. Once they give you the once-over, you'll be in without a problem. Everyone is dying to see the inside of that house of yours. What did you name it? Eden? Isn't that prophetic?" She giggled. "I'll lend you the Social Register so you'll know who's who."

"And I hope you like to drink," Charles added. "In the end, Long Harbor is really just an island of shingled cottages surrounded by a sea of gin."

"One last thing, don't be prudish. People like to mix it up," said Maud, lifting an eyebrow and patting her shiny hair down along her forehead. "Actually, there's a lot of that."

"Oh?" said Sadie after a long pause, squeezing Bunny's hand under the table. She had never seen a married woman be so forward. "Mix it up?" she asked, feeling heat rise up her neck.

"You know what she means, dear Sadie?" Charles asked, with a wink. "Then again, we'd be happy to teach you that after dinner as well."

Sadie was stunned silent, beads of perspiration starting on her neck. She pressed her napkin to her lips, staring down at the shells on her plate.

Bunny cleared his throat, coming to her rescue. "So, what time should we meet at the club tomorrow?"

"Right, golf," said Charles, still fixing his gaze upon Sadie. "Well, I never plan anything before noon. I'll pick you up." Maud took a long drag on her cigarette, then turned her neck to blow the plume of smoke over her shoulder.

Sadie lifted her head to find Charles still grinning at her. He dipped a shrimp into the cocktail sauce and held it out to her. "Open up, love, and taste this."

Sadie wasn't sure, but she parted her lips slowly. Charles placed the shrimp's pink belly on her tongue, and she bit into it, tasting its sweet flesh mix with the horseradish's sting. She wiped the blood-red cocktail sauce from the corners of her mouth. Charles then lifted the toothpick from his martini glass and fed her a green olive. This time she met his gaze, rolling the olive against the inside of her cheek, sucking in its salty brine. Charles laughed, and Sadie smiled at his amusement, feeling the heat that had started in her face travel down her throat and fill her on the inside.

* * *

Long past midnight, while Sadie and Bunny undressed for bed, Bunny made a comment under his breath. "That's why all the bedrooms connect with interior doors."

"What?" Sadie gasped.

"Don't you remember Maud saying people like to 'mix it up'?"

"Yes," Sadie said hesitantly, falling back against her closet door.

"Henderson implied that people here move around in the night." She put a hand to her heart.

Bunny laughed. "Relax, love—I'm only kidding. You know you're the only one for me," he said, taking her chin in his hands, "and as far as the Butterfields are concerned, I'm sure it was just the alcohol talking."

But Sadie couldn't escape the memory of Charles's grin and the sound of his wicked amusement.

* * *

When Charles pulled up in the Phantom after lunch the next day, Sadie busied herself with the children. Returning from the club later that afternoon, Bunny relayed an invitation to join the Butterfields that evening for a night of dinner and dancing.

"Charles says the band playing at the Atlantic tonight came from Chicago."

"Oh, Bunny! I've been chasing three boys around all day; Maud gets to nap until cocktail hour. Let's just stay home tonight." His shoulders sagged in disappointment.

He let her have her way that night, but afterwards, Bunny insisted they do it all: swim, play tennis and golf, join the Butterfields' friends for all-day sails, then dance away Saturday nights at the Atlantic Hotel. The pace exhausted Sadie, so much so that she planned an excursion to New York City. Bunny had been after her to get the house furnished, and the idea of a shopping trip actually seemed like a respite.

He reserved a room for her at the Plaza. He had his sights set on Eden's interior being up to snuff by the following summer. He wanted to host a party of his own, and Maud had warned that they had about a year's leeway before the ruling class expected them to reciprocate.

He urged Sadie to spare no expense, arranging for a designer from Henderson's office to guide her through the process. But she soon discovered that choosing fabric samples and perusing furniture showrooms was both tedious and overwhelming. After a few hours of it, she handed over carte blanche authority to the designer and explored Manhattan instead. She marveled that it had been such a long time since she'd been free of the responsibility of taking care of somebody. She savored the opportunity to wander the streets, anonymous among masses of people, everything so different from Pittsburgh and Long Harbor. She surprised herself, skipping meals and strolling through museums, even happening upon a lecture by a woman named Margaret Sanger.

On the return trip to Rhode Island, Sadie sat on the train, reviewing the invoices and pictures of furnishings she had "selected" for Eden. She smiled as she recalled her conversation with the designer. "I promise, Mrs. Meister," she had said, "this will be our little secret. Enjoy the city."

She closed her eyes and daydreamed of the moon hanging over the ocean. She had been gone only three days but missed her family immensely. She would put her foot down when she returned and end the social whirlwind. There would be no more flirting with Charles and Maud on the dance floor. She wanted to spend time with her children, read bedtime stories, tuck them in, and kiss them good night before joining Bunny in their bed. Any stirrings would be directed toward him. She rocked back and forth in her seat and pictured her husband's strong, muscular back, until arousal sparked deep down inside her.

The train pulled into the Kingston station, and there he was, standing on the platform, tall and handsome. She felt a rush of romance as he scanned the windows for her face. Once the train stopped, she leaped onto the platform and hurried into his arms. He hugged her, then held her at a distance.

"Well, hello," he said.

"Oh, Bunny, I'm so glad to be back."

"So," he asked, "success? How long before the furniture arrives?"

"Where are the boys?" Sadie asked, peering behind him.

"At home with Alice."

"Oh, I wish you'd brought them. I missed you all so much. I can't wait to see them. But you, Bunny, I missed you the most." She tilted her chin, posed for a long, passionate kiss.

Bunny must not have noticed the desire in her stance. Instead of kissing her, he pulled a handful of invitations out of his jacket pocket. "Would you look at these?" he said, almost in victory.

When she saw the envelopes, fanned out like a deck of cards, her heart sank. "Oh, Bunny, really, I think I'm done for a while. Let's just go home and the five of us have dinner together."

His expression turned dumbfounded.

"But, Sadie, we must. It's important."

"We've met everybody. Who else could there be?"

"I've already accepted for dinner tonight at the Notmans'. Charles and Maud are picking us up at seven."

"All right, but that's it," Sadie said, breathing deeply.

At dinner she was grateful to be seated far from Charles, next to the host's daughter-in-law.

"So, you've been seduced by the Butterfields, I hear."

The woman's candor surprised her. "Oh," Sadie said, "they've been most kind to us."

"I'm Emily Notman," she said, clinking her wineglass with Sadie's. Then, leaning in closer, she added, "Maud Butterfield can be unscrupulous. I wouldn't leave that handsome husband of yours alone again!" Sadie blushed and for a moment felt her heart stop. *What on earth?*

She pushed her plate away with a trembling hand and adroitly changed the subject. Emily had two boys close in age to Edward and Robert, and Sadie warmed up to the fact that they had motherhood in common. Emily was the first one she'd heard admit to the challenges of balancing family time with Long Harbor's social expectations.

"I know what you mean. Bunny feels pressure being the new folks in town," said Sadie.

"I've been summering here since I married into this family ten years ago, and I'm still considered the new girl!" Emily laughed. "Have you heard about the big tug-of-war contest every summer at the beach club? On one end of the rope they have those who *are* Long Harbor, and they pit them against those who *married* Long Harbor. Even our own spouses need to make it clear where we stand!"

"Oh dear—we'll never fit in!" Sadie burst into laughter. Her eyes began to tear. It felt good to commiserate over the incongruity of what was going on here.

She wiped her eyes, then noticed Bunny staring disapprovingly from across the table.

Chapter 9

LONG HARBOR, RHODE ISLAND
Wednesday, July 1, 2000

S arah struggled to remove the ladder from its spot against the wall. She worked around old license plates, stakes for tomatoes, lobster pots, and minnow traps. There was a broken croquet mallet and an old badminton set, there were half-empty cans of dried paint, tomato cages, a wheelbarrow, fishing nets, and life jackets spotted with mold. Finally, outside the musty garage, she jiggled the ladder around on the soil next to the rhododendrons, checking to make sure it was secure. It was clear why the children in the family had always been assigned the unpopular chore of deadheading these massive plants, as they were nimble enough to weave around the interior of the branches and were impervious to the sap that ended up on their hands and stained their clothes.

Her grandmother had told stories about her older brothers turning this job into a contest. Whoever collected the biggest pile of dead blossoms earned a prize from Bunny. When she was a girl, her own grandfather had given her fifty cents for doing the job, once he had carefully trained her in his "pinch and twist" technique.

She stood on the ladder's top rungs, straining to reach the highest blossoms and leaning an arm against the house for support. From this peak, she could see through the kitchen window. She spotted her mother, wearing that ratty silk robe and pulling something out of the toaster oven. Sarah worked quietly around the window, not ready for a confrontation. Still, it was something that her mother had come down to the kitchen, was putting food in her stomach. Maybe she'd go back up and shower, change into something presentable, and sit down to dinner with Sarah and her grandmother. Around the table, they might be able to talk more naturally. Maybe Sarah could even coax a smile out of her.

It wasn't long before perspiration was dripping down Sarah's back, staining her T-shirt. She filled a paper grocery bag with withered, sticky blossoms, descended the ladder, and crossed the yard to the compost heap. As she dumped the contents of the bag onto the pile, she remembered her grandfather throwing the husks there each evening after they shucked the corn together. If he had still been alive, he probably would have found her pregnancy distressing: "Unmarried? Sarah, I know things are different these days, but I really think you have only one option."

Sometimes she thought it would be easier to have only one option. However, she had several choices, and that was complicated by the fact that, deep down, she hoped Alistair would reconsider.

But her last argument with him had been awful.

"Okay, that's good—just run away, Sarah," he'd said. "Don't deal with this. Just run up there to your mommy and your mansion on the beach."

"You don't know what you're talking about."

"I used to think you were worldly, but I was wrong. You're just a spoiled child!"

So spoiled that she was spending a beautiful day wrestling with bushes? She wiped her forehead, inadvertently spreading sap through her hair. Sweat dripped from her forehead and stung her eyes as she wondered how Alistair could be so cruel. She hadn't seen that side of him before.

The Alistair she had fallen in love with had adored her, had stared into her eyes across the table at their favorite café, taken both her hands in his, and tucked a wild strand of her red hair behind her ear, before leaning across the table to give her a kiss. Sarah wondered if this was his formula: he was an expert on young, idealistic grad students. He complimented her ideas, buoying her intellectual confidence. He treated her like an adult and helped her leave her girlhood behind. He cooked for her and took her to the theater. He surprised her with dress boxes containing sexy, flimsy outfits, suggesting she couple them with a pair of leather boots. He took her to the mountains for the weekend. He read her poetry in the bathtub and wrote her passionate letters. He knew every inch of her youthful body, kissing the freckles across her breasts and caressing her long legs, which shone like precious objects against his aging skin. He was wise, and he made her feel safe.

Her mother had accused Sarah of finding a father figure in a man almost twenty years older.

"Mom, that's not it," Sarah said.

It was that his salt-and-pepper hair was sexy. His ruddy, olive complexion, usually a few days unshaven, and his tortoise-shell-framed glasses turned her on. Tall, with broad shoulders, he wore jeans that flattered his muscular legs, and crisp button-down shirts. She liked how he hung his tweed sport coat on the back of his chair before starting class.

Alistair had been the one who had first noticed the symptoms of her pregnancy: her tender breasts and fatigue, her bouts of nausea. As she knelt on the bath mat, retching into his toilet, he poked his head through the door. "You should see a doctor," he said. "You're probably six or eight weeks along."

Peeing on a plastic stick and finding two blue lines confirmed his diagnosis. Even though a child didn't fit into her plans, it didn't seem impossible, either. She carried the proof into the living room, waving the pregnancy test in the air. Alistair was sitting in a club chair, reading the newspaper.

He was matter-of-fact. "Well, you'll just get an abortion."

She was crestfallen. "I just don't think I could do that."

"Why not?"

"I told you, my mother dropped out of school to have me."

"So?"

"Well, she and my dad didn't want a kid. My mom could

have had an illegal abortion, but that would have been the end of me. I wouldn't be here."

"Oh, Sarah, please."

"No, really, I think like that. This baby might be a very cool person."

Sarah smiled sweetly, flashing an expression that usually won him over.

"That's sentimental nonsense. You need to think rationally," he said.

"I think being a mother might suit me," she teased, sitting down on his lap and nuzzling his cheek.

Instead of nuzzling her back, he grabbed her arm and hissed, "I don't want any more children!"

"Let go of me!" she screamed, standing up. "This is not all about you!"

She left, rushing down the stairs to the sidewalk in tears. She walked the fifty blocks to her apartment, her mind vacillating between Alistair's reaction and visions of pushing a baby carriage.

A week later, a letter was hand-delivered from a lawyer's office. She stood in the hallway, reading it in the dim light.

"It's a document requesting your signature," the courier said.

The language boiled down to a formal request that if and when her baby was born, a paternity test be administered, and that if in fact Alistair Goldstein was the child's father, she would relieve him of all financial responsibility.

"They told me to wait while you signed."

"Well, that is not going to happen right now." She closed her door and stuffed the document into her purse.

Her roommate, Laura, had caught snippets of the exchange. "What was that all about?"

Telling her the whole story would just lead to a bunch of 'told you so's.' Laura had warned Sarah from the beginning that Alistair had a reputation for hitting on his advisees, but Sarah had refused to listen. She had refused to accept that she wasn't his one and only.

She now deadheaded with vigor, envisioning Alistair's neck each time she twisted and ripped off a wilted blossom. She tried to imagine him years from now, retired and alone, regretting having let that wonderful young woman and the child they had created together slip away.

Sarah squinted into the sun, pleased by the progress she'd made along the kitchen wing, moving toward the front steps. Just another half hour or so, and she would be done. She repositioned the ladder so that she could reach the last section. It was awkward fitting the feet of the ladder between the branches, and she was losing patience wrestling with the twisted, sticky blossoms. She climbed back up to the top rung. A branch sprang from below her. The ladder swerved, and Sarah lost her balance.

She yelled as she fell backward onto the ground. The ladder clanged into the side of the house. Sarah lay motionless on the grass. The wind knocked out of her, she sucked in a breath. Her shoulder had landed on a rock, sending a bruising jolt of pain through her arm. For the few seconds after impact, she stared up at the big white clouds blowing across the blue sky. Then she heard the kitchen screen door slam.

"Good heavens! Are you all right?" Lilly came running through the grass as fast as she could.

Sarah furrowed her eyebrows, looking up at Lilly's face. "I'm not sure. I haven't tried to move yet. My shoulder hurts the worst."

"Oh, Sarah, my God. Don't move. I think I'd better call an ambulance."

"No, Lilly. Calm down. Just wait a minute—let me see." Sarah rolled slowly onto her side.

"Did you hit your head? Oh dear—what about the baby?"

"I landed on my back, just got the wind knocked out of me. My head is fine." She rubbed her shoulder and then put a hand on her stomach. Sarah shut her eyes in concentration, still trying to catch her breath.

"I think I should call an ambulance. What were you doing up on that ladder anyway?"

"Lilly, no ambulances. I'll be fine. Let me go call my doctor in the city."

"Do you think it's safe to get up?"

"Well, if I can't get up, then I'm in real trouble. *Then* I'll let you call that ambulance."

"Just stay there, Sarah. You're all sweaty. Let me bring you some lemonade before you try."

By the time Lilly came back with a tall, icy glass, Sarah was feeling better, albeit rather bruised and worried. She sat quietly, listening for any sign inside her body that things were not right. She sipped the drink slowly, feeling the cold liquid slide down her throat, cooling her entire chest. She held the glass against her forehead for a moment. The condensation provided instant relief.

After several minutes, Sarah started to her knees, then to her feet. Lilly held her arm, and she limped into the kitchen. As they entered, Sarah felt a warm rush of liquid between her legs. She hurried to the bathroom and checked her underwear. Her throat tightened when she saw the blood.

She returned to the kitchen to find Lilly rinsing her mother's breakfast dishes.

"Lilly, we'd better go to the hospital."

Lilly gripped a dish towel, and her shoulders slumped in dismay. "Oh dear."

"Let me just get my purse," Sarah said.

"I'll get your grandmother."

"No. I don't want Gran to worry."

Chapter 10

PITTSBURGH, PENNSYLVANIA
1928

M rs. Meister, sometimes outside pressures can make a woman late," the old nurse in Dr. Hart's office said. Sadie winced as the woman's clammy hand gripped her bicep. She looked away from the needle drawing her blood and let out a deep breath.

Losing her parents and sorting through their belongings had been difficult, not to mention worrying about Kitty. And she and her sister were way behind schedule, as they had spent the better part of two days reminiscing. Instead of clearing out the cabinets, they had tucked their legs up onto the sofa in the breakfast room, clutching warm mugs, and faced each other in a way they hadn't since Sadie had married and moved away.

When the phone rang two days later, Sadie was halfheartedly folding her mother's sweaters into a box. She assumed it was another developer. They had been calling constantly, hovering like vultures, wanting to buy Lancaster Fells and subdivide the land. But when she answered, it was the old nurse's voice on the line.

"Mrs. Meister," the nurse sang into the phone, "the rabbit died! Looks like the stork will be visiting you again!"

Sadie sank onto a chair. "Could there be a mistake?"

"Oh, no, Mrs. Meister, never. Congratulations! You'll need to make an appointment to discuss your care with Dr. Hart."

When Sadie hung up the phone, she bit her lower lip and put her hand to her forehead. She sat motionless. *Damn. This can't be happening.* She had been using a cervical cap and chemicals to prevent pregnancy. She had to continue sorting through her parents' belongings, and Bunny expected to depart for Long Harbor in just three weeks. She still had to pack up her own household, on top of everything else.

Sadie returned to Lancaster Fells the next morning, determined to make more progress. But Kitty was waiting for her by the front door in riding clothes, a sad and vacant look on her face.

"Let's get the horses instead." Kitty said. Sadie agreed, even though she knew it was the last thing she should do.

They saddled and mounted the horses, crisscrossing the vast estate. They both had a lot on their minds. Sadie would never admit her despair over being pregnant to Kitty, since it was likely her sister would never have children of her own.

Sadie's breath was visible in the cold air, and her cheeks heated up with the exercise. She appreciated the expanse of their acreage as never before, now with the eyes of a steward. She caught up to Kitty as they neared the barn. "Thank you so much. You have no idea how much I needed that."

Cooling down the horses and putting the saddles away, Sadie had an idea. "Why don't you stay on at Lancaster Fells, Kitty? Operate the barn. You could take on tenant horses."

Kitty's eyes widened, and she smiled. "Really?" she said.

"Absolutely. I don't know why we didn't think of it sooner."

That night, when Sadie informed Bunny of their plan, he seemed surprised. "I thought you two were divvying up the china and silver. There's a killing to be made selling that place, you know."

"We don't need the money, and Kitty needs a home and a vocation."

"Well, living all alone at Lancaster Fells, she'll have to fend off the suitors with a stick," he joked.

"Bunny!" She swatted his chest. His ribbing was indelicate. Her sister, with freckles smattering her face and the family's red hair a bright orange on her, had never been a beauty and was now way beyond marriageable age. Sadie swallowed the irony that Kitty would remain free. She'd be the one who got to ride their horses across those beautiful fields every morning.

"I have something else I need to tell you, Bunny," Sadie said, looking up into his face, tears welling in her eyes. When she finally got the words out, he took her by the middle and swung her around.

"Oh, Bunny, stop it. Put me down."

He mixed two drinks and proposed a toast. "To my beautiful wife."

"Of course you're happy," she cried. "Another child doesn't change your life at all!"

"Oh, Sadie, come now. You're being hysterical," he protested.

"But it's true! Your days will be just as they always are. You don't know what it's like to be in charge of shaping a child, to draw him out, uncover his talents, to be there *all the time!*"

Even though Sadie directed the brunt of her frustrations at Bunny, she felt like a fool for having trusted Dr. Hart. A year earlier, Sadie had shown Dr. Hart the pamphlet she'd picked up at the Margaret Sanger lecture in New York City. "This is between the two of us," she'd said, pointing to the rudimentary rendering of a cervical cap. "Bunny is not to know."

Dr. Hart hadn't responded right away, sizing up her expression. An awkward silence lingered in the examining room.

"It's not like you'd be breaking the law," Sadie said.

"Mrs. Meister, I have never had such a request. I have used soluble pessaries and chemicals to treat infection before, but you are the first patient who wants to block entry to her uterus."

"Maybe just the first who's had the nerve to ask."

He looked at the pamphlet again and then put it in his pocket. "Is this what women are up to in New York City?"

"Will you give them to me or not?" Sadie's eyes narrowed.

"I'll do it. But I'd appreciate your keeping it *entre nous* as well."

Now, pregnant, agitated, and back in his office, Sadie crossed her arms and stared, steely-eyed, at Dr. Hart when he opened the door and greeted her. All he could offer was a shrug. "I didn't think it would work. These things are in God's hands, after all."

Sadie could barely listen as he stressed the risks for a woman of her advanced age. He told her to spend her final trimester in bed. Sadie flung open the door and walked right past the old nurse, who was calling her name.

On the sidewalk, she imagined the upright figure of her mother. "Walk tall and keep a stiff upper lip." Sadie knew she had no choice but to accept the situation, but she was almost forty. The boys weren't little anymore, and she had no desire, or, she feared, patience, to be up at all hours, caring for an infant.

* * *

Three weeks later, upon their arrival in Long Harbor, Sadie planned a cookout with the Notmans. Emily Notman had become her very best friend, and the whole gang of their combined families, barefoot, roasting frankfurters, and setting off sparklers on the beach, made her forget her troubles.

Over the past several summers, she and Emily had spent hours together, sipping gin and tonics and giggling on the back porch of Eden while all their boys played on the lawn below. They had sometimes shared stories about their husbands. When Emily had confided that she might enjoy intimacy with Ted more if she had a foolproof method of preventing pregnancy, Sadie had put down her glass and rushed upstairs to retrieve a folded issue of Margaret Sanger's *Birth Control Review*.

"My word, Sadie!" Emily had exclaimed. "Aren't you the modern woman!"

Sadie had indeed felt modern and triumphant back then for having demanded her right to birth control. "My family is complete," she had told Emily.

But now, as she sat with Emily in the living room at Eden, she felt like the joke was on her.

She wistfully polished the silver club championship tennis trophy that sat proudly on the mantel. "We won't be able to defend our title in August."

Emily offered Sadie a sympathetic smile and said, "You're an old hand at this. You'll have an easy delivery, and we'll be back on the tennis lawn next summer."

Their invitation to be full members of the Paupanaug Club had arrived the previous summer. Sadie had always been confident it was forthcoming, but Bunny hadn't been able to relax until it came. Only then did he become visibly at ease, branching out and making a variety of friends at the beach club and on the tennis courts. She was relieved by the diversity of his acquaintances and hoped this would put an end to his clinging to the Butterfields. They were dangerous. She couldn't pass Charles at a party without eliciting a naughty wink or a seductive kiss blown across the dance floor. Maud was more svelte than ever and had taken to wearing short fringed dresses and matching silk bands around her forehead.

Some evenings, Bunny talked Sadie into going to the Atlantic to dance the Charleston. She couldn't help complaining. "Look how gorgeous Maud is on the dance floor," she hissed in Bunny's ear. "My body doesn't even feel like my own anymore. I've never felt so run down, and the baby isn't even due until Christmastime."

"Now, now," he said, rubbing the small of her back.

"It must be a girl this time. I've heard they suck everything out of you."

Despite her chagrin about the pregnancy, it was a perfect excuse for declining social invitations. Dancing the night away was no longer an option once Sadie was visibly with child. Acceptable behavior meant staying home, although she continued to walk to the post office every morning. She passed the rest of the day framing family photographs and hanging them in the back stairwell. She organized the boys' clothing, sending castoffs to the Salvation Army. She embroidered several pillows and wrote long letters to Kitty.

* * *

Nine months pregnant, Sadie approached the holiday season in Pittsburgh as if it were one big chore. She knelt on the floor in Bunny's study, tying a bow on a red fire engine. She fretted over the piles of gifts, one for each of the boys, and placed the fire engine in Robert's pile in an attempt to make them equal. She hoped they would like the miniature train set she was having constructed to circle the living room, a perfect replica of Bunny's locomotives, down to the whistles. On her hands and knees, spreading the wrapping paper across the carpet, she felt a rush of warm liquid between her legs.

She hollered for Alice, who was baking cookies in the kitchen. Alice ran to her side, then fumbled with the phone, first dialing Dr. Hart's number, then Kitty's, and finally Bunny's.

The last thing that went through Sadie's mind before she inhaled ether in the delivery room was that if anything happened to her, at least there would be presents under the Christmas tree.

She came to just before the delivery.

"Mrs. Meister," the nurse was reassuring her by the side of her bed, "everything is proceeding uneventfully. The doctor is here now, and he needs you to give one final push."

Dr. Hart's figure came into focus as he positioned himself at the end of the tented white sheet covering her legs. The sight of him made her want to scream. She gripped the bedcover in her fists and pushed with a howl. The nurse helped propel her forward as tears streamed down her face. At the height of her pain, the insurmountable pressure that filled her pelvis released suddenly, with a squirm. She let go with a long groan.

Dr. Hart lifted the baby in the air, checked her physical characteristics, and handed her over to a nurse to be cleaned. In the seconds it took for him to do his inspection, Sadie felt the vacancy in her womb fill with something else, the seed of something dark, resentful, and ugly.

"Well, well, you've finally gotten your girl," Dr. Hart chirped, as he made his way to the swinging door. He was undoubtedly headed to congratulate Bunny, share their customary cigar, and collect a generous tip. The nurse stopped him in his tracks. "Doctor Hart, she's still bleeding, and it's turning bright red."

Dr. Hart made his way back to the delivery table and saw for himself. "She's hemorrhaging," he said. "Her uterus is not constricting." He snapped on a rubber glove and inserted one hand deep inside her while he massaged Sadie's outer abdomen with his other hand. The white sleeves of his coat were soaked with blood as his massaging took on a more violent urgency. Sadie's vision blurred as her head fell back against the pillow and Dr. Hart bore down even harder.

He hollered to one of the nurses, "Find Mr. Meister in the waiting room and tell him about his daughter, but prepare him—we're not out of the woods yet."

Chapter 11

LONG HARBOR, RHODE ISLAND
Wednesday, July 1, 2000

B ecca sat on the edge of the bed and stretched her arms in front of her, inspecting her hands, the age spots as much as the manicure. She took a deep breath. How could so much time have passed?

She and Dan had taken over this bedroom forty years ago, but even after all that time, Becca still felt like a trespassing daughter. Her mother's presence permeated every one of Eden's rooms, but it was right here, among her oil paintings, her dressing table, and her chaise lounge, that she sensed Sadie's disapproval the most. Becca got a pit in her stomach and goose bumps on her arms.

The pictures on the stairwell alone documented Sadie's transformation from athletic and healthy to gaunt and tired. It was no secret that Becca had been a late-in-life baby and her mother had suffered a great ordeal giving birth, but she would have taken that fate over what had happened to her. She would have preferred Rachel's lot as well, marrying a man she barely knew in order to keep her child. Only Becca was in the unique position to see what had happened and what was in fact still happening. She wouldn't be around forever, and she needed Sarah to understand what was at stake.

Becca reached for the phone on her bedside table, but she couldn't bring herself to dial the number. She curled up on the bed and pulled the wool afghan over her legs, remembering the evening fifteen years earlier when she'd first heard from Lee. She had just come out of the shower, still wet. She and Dan were expected at a cocktail party in thirty minutes, and she was annoyed that he hadn't yet returned from the golf course. With a towel wrapped around her wet hair and another wrapped around her dripping body, she rushed to the ringing phone, expecting a husband's typical excuses. She'd snapped a hello. There had been silence on the other end, as if the caller were reconsidering. Irritated, Becca repeated, even more sharply, "Hello?" and was about to hang up, when she heard a woman's voice say, "I am calling for a Rebecca Meister."

"I'm Rebecca Meister."

The voice continued slowly, "My name is Lee Hinkle, and I have reason to believe that you are my mother."

Becca felt her legs give out. She sank to her knees on the carpet beside the bed and clutched the towel around her chest.

"My Leah? Dear God in heaven, is it really you?"

"Did you give a baby up for adoption in Kansas City in 1945?"

Becca cried into her towel; the words would not come out. Then, between sobs, she finally managed, "Yes, I did. That was me. I'm your mother."

It was quiet on the other end. "Are you all right, dear?" Becca finally asked. "I mean, I never thought you would—"

"No, sorry, I'm fine." It sounded like Lee was fighting a few tears of her own now. "I really am fine, have been fine. I didn't imagine I would have such a reaction to just hearing your voice."

They spoke for several surreal minutes, but Becca began to fear Dan might walk in anytime, so she said, "Lee, can I call you tomorrow morning? There's so much more I'd like to say, but I'm afraid now is not a good time." Her hand was trembling so that she could hardly take down the number.

When Dan snuck, shamefaced, into the bedroom a few minutes later, Becca was still sitting on the bed, her wet hair dripping onto the crisp bedspread.

"Are you all right? Don't we have the Notmans' tonight?" he asked.

Becca wiped her eyes with the backs of her wrists. "Let's stay home. I'm feeling ill," she sniffed.

Her mother had assured her, and indeed she had believed, that keeping her secret would get easier as time went on. But the longer she kept it, the larger it grew. Pretending that Rachel was her first baby took more effort than motherhood itself. During her pregnancy with Rachel, she felt as if she had to fake amazement for Dan's benefit. Her guilt multiplied in the presence of his excitement.

Over the following weeks, Becca called Lee several more times.

"What are Rachel and Andrew like?" Lee asked.

"How tall are you? What color is your hair?" Becca asked.

Becca yearned for an intimacy that phone conversations couldn't deliver. So when Lee asked if they might meet in person, Becca jumped at the chance. Lee lived in Connecticut, where she had a midwifery practice, and offered to drive to Long Harbor one Sunday in September. As the day of their meeting drew closer, Becca felt queasy and had difficulty concentrating. She encouraged Dan to take their boat fishing that afternoon, and she put Brandy, their dog at the time, on a leash and walked to the village coffee shop.

Becca would never forget holding that precious baby to her breast in a Kansas City hospital and couldn't believe this middle-aged woman a few feet in front of her, ordering a coffee, was the same person. Time turned on its side. Lee was small in stature, wearing a denim skirt and a bulky beige sweater over her thick middle. She was sturdy like Rachel, with shoulder-length, wavy black hair and a ruddy complexion. Hands on her hips, she stood on the tiptoes of her leather clogs and pushed her glasses up on her nose, peering at the menu posted on the wall behind the cash register. With an unfamiliar tremble in her legs, Becca stepped forward to greet her.

"Lee?"

Her skirt twirled as she spun around in her clogs. "Becca?"

"Yes, it's me." The two women were grinning at each other when the teenage clerk behind the counter asked, "Can I get you something, Mrs. Fitzpatrick?"

"Oh, yes, small, black. Thank you." The teenager must have been one of her friends' grandchildren. She paid for both of the coffees and ushered Lee out the door. There wasn't a place in this town where she wouldn't bump into somebody, so she took Lee to the beach.

Once they were down by the water, with the wind in their faces, her trembling subsided. Becca resisted the urge to reach for Lee's hand as they walked side by side, and stole glimpses of her daughter's profile instead. She noticed how the skin around the corners of Lee's eyes wrinkled, the upturned crook of her smile, and her tortoiseshell eyeglasses. It wasn't until they actually sat down on a big piece of driftwood that Becca was able to take in Lee's full face and see the green sparkle of her eyes.

"I'm sorry for staring." Becca laughed. "I can't believe we're sitting here."

"I don't mind," Lee said, practically glowing. "It's the first time I have ever recognized myself in someone else's face."

"I thought about you all the time."

Becca didn't try to hold back her tears. Lee didn't cry right away but tried to comfort Becca, hugging her and rubbing her back. Becca rested her chin on Lee's shoulder, smelling the fruity scent of her shampoo, and whispered, "And I always wanted to tell you that I was sorry."

Lee dug a little packet of tissue out of her purse, the kind Becca used to have on hand for Rachel and Andrew. She unfolded one and handed it to Becca, who wiped her eyes and blew her nose. Their tears turned from those of sadness to those of laughter as the autumn sun cast an amber glow, bathing the beach and Becca in golden relief.

She was eager to know everything. The maternity home had assured her that her daughter would go to a wonderful family, and Lee confirmed that when she explained that she had been raised an only child in Cincinnati by wonderful parents who had recently passed away. Now that they were gone, she had felt free to follow up on an innate curiosity to find her birth parents. She said that her search hadn't been very hard, since Becca had registered Eden's address on all the paperwork. Lee commented, "Who would have guessed you'd be at the same house after all these years?"

"Your mother must have been a kind woman," Becca offered, "if she barely changed the name I gave you."

"She was a thoughtful, wonderful mother."

Becca felt a pang of envy but tried to continue seamlessly: "Nice girls from good families had few choices in 1945."

"Becca, I'm not here looking for an explanation. That's in the past. I guess I was just hoping we could have a friendship now."

Becca smiled and squeezed her hand. "Of course we can."

"And I was hoping you could lead me to my birth father."

Becca put her hands in her lap. Her face got hot and her chest felt tight. She cleared her throat. "Lee, you waited until your parents passed away before you searched for me, and, just like you, I also have people to think of."

"I don't understand. Is my birth father somebody you're still in touch with?"

Becca stuttered, "I-I can't take a risk. I have to protect Dan. You see, if he were to know I kept such a secret from him our entire marriage . . . I just can't."

And then, she thought, there was Rachel, who seemed to blame every problem she had on the way Becca had raised her. She could just see Rachel pointing to a long-lost sister as validation of her therapist's claim that Becca had been an emotionally absent mother.

A flash of disappointment spread across Lee's face, but she didn't push the matter any further. "Okay, I understand."

But when Dan died six years later, Becca had no more excuses. When Lee called to express her condolences and ask if she might like to meet for breakfast, Becca felt compelled to invite her back to Eden for a long-awaited tour of the family home. Rachel, Sarah, and Andrew had been around for the funeral, but had now returned to work and school-year obligations, and Becca was, with the exception of Lilly, alone for the first time in her life. She would invite Lee over.

On the agreed-upon day, Lee steered her Subaru up the long drive and stopped, wide-eyed and gaping, at the kitchen door. Becca went outside to greet her.

"Don't get too impressed by the house, dear."

"Becca, it's magnificent."

"Yes, but Dan left our finances a mess, and, well, I don't know how much longer I'll be here."

* * *

Becca snapped out of her daydream when she heard a booming crash from the yard. The kitchen door slammed, and Lilly shouted, "Good heavens!" She made a mental note to ask the window washers to be more careful. She checked her thin wristwatch; it was already 11:00 A.M. *Shame on me for letting the morning slip away.* She picked up the receiver and, with all the resolve she could muster, dialed Lee's number. Lee always picked up on the first ring, with a cheery "hello." She was a happy, upbeat person. It was refreshing.

"Lee." Becca spoke her name slowly, almost giving it two syllables. "The reason I'm calling, dear, is to see if you are available for brunch on Sunday. I think I mentioned that Andrew and Camilla are coming in from London with their children, and of course Rachel and Sarah are here, and then there's my brother and two sisters-in-law. I know it must sound intimidating, but I thought you would like to finally meet everyone."

There was silence on the line for a moment, before Lee answered, "Becca, you've finally told them about me?"

"No, not yet, but I will this weekend."

"Maybe you should wait to see how that goes before you invite me for brunch."

"Lee, this is long overdue. If we don't take this opportunity, Lord knows when Andrew will be back."

Again, a silence, then: "Okay, but only because I've been dying to meet my brother and sister. What time should I arrive?"

They settled the details, and Becca hung up the phone. *I am a seventy-two-year-old woman; I don't have to keep this a secret anymore.* Dan's portrait haunted her from its place on the bedside table. "I'm sorry," she said. Then she pictured her mother at her dressing table, elegantly putting on the finishing touches for an evening out with her father. Her mother glanced at Becca's reflection in the mirror while applying lipstick, making an exaggerated "O" with her lips. "Everything will be fine. You'll see. You'll be able to forget all about this. Nobody will ever have to know."

"But *I* know, Mother. And Lee knows. You never counted on her finding me, did you?"

"Oh, Becca, you're so dramatic. It's perfectly fine for a woman to have secrets. Not everything is suitable for public consumption."

"Mother, we're a family; we should be able to be honest with each other."

"Oh, Becca, why go and upset everything?"

Chapter 12

PITTSBURGH, PENNSYLVANIA

1928

It was difficult to open up her swollen eyes. She couldn't remember where she was as Bunny's hovering face came into focus. It was odd, the way he was smiling and crying at the same time.

"Sadie, you're awake! Oh, you gave me such a fright." He leaned down over the railing of the hospital bed and gave her a kiss.

"Bunny . . . why?"

"Shh, it's time to wake up and meet Rebecca," he whispered.

"Who?"

"Our little girl."

"But—"

"I named her Rebecca, for my mother's sister."

* * *

It took several days for the confusion and fog to lift from Sadie's mind. Nurses came and went, feeling her pulse, taking her temperature, bringing her trays of food she could barely touch.

"It's important that you eat; it's the only way you'll get your strength back," one of the older nurses said.

Sadie smiled weakly in response.

"And your little girl—Rebecca, is it? She's anxious to meet her mother."

Sadie smiled again and nodded, but she held her tongue, still perturbed that Bunny had gone ahead and named their baby without her. He'd explained that she'd been unconscious for four days, during which Dr. Hart had prepared him for the worst. The nurse maintained a serious expression below her neat white cap, replacing the untouched juice from the night before with a fresh one.

Kitty poked her head through the door, and Sadie sat up in bed a little straighter.

"Good morning, sister," Kitty said, beaming.

"Kitty, I . . ." Sadie almost broke down at the sight of her sister's fresh face. She wanted to cry and pound her pillow at the same time. Kitty rushed around to the head of the bed, and Sadie started to sob.

"Oh, Sadie, love, let me fix your hair."

"No, don't. I've decided to cut it." The words came out before she even realized what she was saying. It was a rash decision, but her long hair was matted and damp on the back of her neck.

"I can comb out the tangles," Kitty offered.

"Really, Kitty," Sadie continued, "if you want to be helpful, go out to the damn nurses' station and find a pair of scissors, then come back in here and cut off this gnarled mess."

"But, Sadie—"

"Kitty, just do it. I don't care how it comes out. I can go to the salon later to make it right."

An hour later when Bunny entered the room, his jaw dropped. Kitty was gone, but remnants of Sadie's long red tresses were still scattered on the linoleum at his feet. Sadie put down the newspaper she was reading. "I know what you're thinking," she said. "But don't you dare say a thing."

"That was an awfully drastic thing to do," he said.

"I can cut my hair if I wish."

He stopped short and considered her before speaking again, "Why don't I go down to the nursery and ask them to bring Rebecca in?"

"I don't like the name Rebecca."

"What?"

"I don't like the name. It doesn't . . . I don't know. It just doesn't roll off my tongue."

"Well, we can't change it now. It's been a week since I named her, and my mother is beside herself, telling all her friends."

Sadie glared at him.

"Rebecca was her sister, and she—"

"I know, I know. I know the whole story. I guess I'll call her Becca."

The nurse brought her daughter into the room and delivered her into Sadie's arms. She was bundled in a blanket and squirming to get her arms free, her face reddening quickly. Her little brow was wrinkled, and her eyes were squeezed shut into slits. Sadie heard small peeps coming from her mouth and sensed she was only seconds away from a full-blown cry. The nurse handed Sadie a bottle of formula, but she put it on the nightstand right next to her untouched juice from that morning.

"I'll try from my breast first," said Sadie.

"As you wish, but she's hungry," said the nurse.

Her daughter's frantic lips searched for a nipple but were unable to latch on to Sadie. Little Becca twisted her head one way and then the other, her skin mottling with fury. Sadie had been too weak for her milk to come in, but she longed for that immediate skin-on-skin bond breastfeeding created.

She was resigned to nudging the rubber nipple between her daughter's tiny lips. "I can't do this," Sadie muttered under her breath.

"Of course you can do it," Bunny encouraged, although the baby's persistent cries drowned out his voice.

A few seconds later, Becca's tiny lips found the latex and a peaceful quiet descended on the room.

Bunny stood, caressing her shoulder. Sadie burped the baby, then started feeding her again. "I've been waiting to tell you something else, darling. I'm so sorry, but Dr. Hart says no more children."

Sadie looked up at him quizzically. "That's fine with me,"

she said, mystified by the degree to which he just didn't understand. She returned Becca to her lap and nudged her lips with the bottle. She looked up in time to catch Bunny's forlorn expression. "Oh, come now—you couldn't have possibly wanted more than four?" she asked.

Bunny shrugged silently, caressing the crown of Becca's head.

* * *

Sadie's energy still hadn't returned the next week when Bunny took her and Becca back to their house, full of flowers and balloons. Alice, Kitty, and the new baby nurse were lined up in the front entry, holding the boys still in front of them. Thomas had crayoned a large WELCOME HOME sign that hung over the stairs. Sadie smiled weakly at all the fanfare for the sake of her sons. She handed the baby to Alice, then bent to kiss the children on the top of their heads. She spoke softly: "Thank you, my loves, for such a grand welcome. I will see you after your dinner. I've been craving a bath for weeks."

For the next several evenings, Sadie was roused from her sleep only when Bunny returned home from work. He would flick on the lamps and stoke the fire in the hearth, but all she wanted to do was rest. One evening, she felt his eyes upon her as she put on her robe and stuck clips in her uneven hair to keep it out of her face. "I don't know what I would do without Alice and the nurse," Sadie confessed. "They're managing everything."

"That's what they're here for, my love. And I hear Kitty came by today to stroll the baby in the pram."

"I don't think I'll ever feel like myself again."

"Yes, you will. Would you like me to ask Kitty to make a hair appointment for you?'

"No. I'm not up to leaving the house yet."

Alice brought the baby into the bedroom. "I thought you would like to hold her."

"Thank you, Alice," said Bunny.

Sadie pressed a wriggling Becca to her chest, trying to synchronize their breaths. She nuzzled the folds of Becca's neck, but her smell was foreign: formula mixed with the scents of the kitchen, warm cinnamon, lemon, and Alice's detergent. She handed Becca to Bunny. "Let's just get you to Eden," he said. "The ocean air and sunshine will have you back to normal in no time."

Sadie went to her dressing table and stared into the mirror at this new version of herself. She had stopped caring about the darkening circles under her eyes. Long gone was her healthy complexion, and even her short hair was feeling thin. Her mother would have admonished her to "make more of an effort, put a little rouge on," but Sadie couldn't fake it. The frustration that had eaten at her during her pregnancy had become something hardened, something deeper.

Bunny brought home flowers and made a grand display of shaking up their pre-dinner martinis, trying to fill the silence in the room with the day's gossip. But Sadie had no patience for his false enthusiasm or for Pittsburgh's small scandals.

Alice would bring the baby in for a good-night kiss, dressed prettily in her nightgown. The boys followed behind her, having been fed, bathed, and changed into their pajamas. One evening, Bunny sat in an armchair next to the bed while Thomas climbed up onto the mattress next to Sadie. "How is the littlest princess doing today?" asked Robert, standing on his tiptoes at the side of the bed. Becca's eyes bulged at his animated face, and her fist clung to his pinky finger. While Robert and Edward pretended to be secret agents charged with protecting the Egyptian princess, Thomas curled up close to his mother, a book in hand.

"Bunny, would you take the baby while I read to Thomas?"

After thirty minutes or so of family time, Alice herded them all off to bed.

"Well, I had quite a day," Bunny said, clearing his throat. "We closed on a big bank loan to finance a major upgrade of the tracks."

"But the P and E has never taken on any debt," she said, shocked that he would have done such a thing.

"The point is, we shouldn't sell our stock. The market is going gangbusters; we can borrow cheap money from the bank."

Sadie could hear her mother's criticism in her head: *that husband of yours, getting carried away again.*

Bunny went into his dressing room, unbuttoning his shirt. When he climbed into bed next to her, he began describing the mounds of tulips that were due to bloom in advance of their arrival at Eden. Her head fell sleepily against his shoulder, and her eyelids grew heavy, when there was a disruption out in the hallway. It was Alice. "Mr. Meister, come quick. It's Thomas."

Bunny was on his feet in an instant. Sadie was several steps behind him but hesitated when she heard the thrashing. Through the gap in the doorway, she saw her husband leaning over their son, who was shaking wildly on the floor. Alice stammered, "I was just checking on the baby down in the nursery when I heard him fall out of bed."

Bunny forced a calm voice: "Alice, make sure Edward and Robert stay in their rooms," Then he shouted, "Sadie, call Dr. Hart."

She hurried back to the landing and picked up the receiver with a jittery hand. She read the operator Dr. Hart's emergency number.

"Are you bleeding?" Dr. Hart asked immediately.

"I'm all right. It's Thomas—he's shaking out of control."

She returned to her son's bedroom. The tremors had ceased. Bunny knelt on the floor, cradling Thomas's head. Perspiration soaked through his pajamas, and foamy saliva streamed down his neck. Sadie leaned down to wipe the drool from his chin with the sleeve of her nightgown.

"Don't jostle him," Bunny whispered. Bile rose in her throat. She covered Thomas with a camel-hair blanket from the foot of his bed and rubbed his chilled feet in the palms of her hands. She and Bunny stayed like that in silence until they heard Alice open the front door for Dr. Hart.

When he got down on the floor next to them, he listened to Thomas's lungs and heart, felt inside his mouth, then shone a light in his eyes. "I don't know what to say." He directed his words toward Bunny. "Bring him to the hospital in the morning. We'll give him a complete examination."

Sadie paced the bedroom all night. Could he have fallen and hit his head? How would she know? The inadequacy she felt overwhelmed her. She scratched at her forearms. She gripped her hands at her chest and prayed silently, *Please, God, don't let anything be wrong, please. I promise to take better care of my children. Please don't take my sweet boy.*

* * *

Sadie was in bed two days later when Dr. Hart arrived. Alice knocked on her door and helped her downstairs.

"I'm sorry to have kept you," Sadie said. "I was tired, having a hard time sleeping at night." Bunny and Dr. Hart stood up as she entered the living room.

"I'm sorry to have interrupted your nap," Dr. Hart said, eyeing her bathrobe and disheveled hair. "I came to tell you about Thomas's test results."

Bunny leaned forward in his chair. Sadie looked back and forth between the two men, then picked at a loose thread in her sleeve.

The doctor continued, "I've consulted my colleagues. Many similar cases are documented, and I am quite optimistic about some young doctors at Harvard Medical School doing research on cerebral disruptions, calling it 'epilepsy.' We can arrange for them to see Thomas when you return to the East Coast."

"What if he has another fit before then?" Sadie asked.

"We don't know if he will or what might bring one on," Dr. Hart answered. Sadie hated Dr. Hart's lack of certainty. His steely eyes, his mustache—she just couldn't trust him.

"Why, it could happen anywhere; he could hit his head, or worse," she replied.

"He might also grow out of the condition. One just doesn't

know." Dr. Hart turned to Bunny now and spoke only to him. He instructed him to keep Thomas from sharp or dangerous surfaces, in the event of another seizure. He handed Bunny a small, barbaric-looking appliance to insert into Thomas's small mouth, to keep him from swallowing his tongue.

"We should inform his school," Sadie said.

"Nonsense. It's nobody's business but ours," Bunny said, eyeing Dr. Hart with a threatening stare.

From then on, the mere possibility of a seizure filled Sadie with fear. She found herself studying her son's face for a queer expression, a blank stare, a sign of what lurked beneath the surface.

Chapter 13

LONG HARBOR, RHODE ISLAND
Wednesday, July 1, 2000

B ecca's bridge partner, Sheila Murphy, shuffled the cards while
Becca ate a chocolate candy from the small dish to her left.
Sheila had a jerky, erratic way of doing it, with her fingers facing
in toward each other. Watching this had the same effect on Becca
as a child not being able to throw a ball properly had had on Dan.
He had shaken his head every time Rachel pulled her arm back,
her elbow bent awkwardly, ball in her fist. He had tried to correct
her, but Rachel had been stubborn, as usual.

There were tables of four everywhere, made up of Long
Harbor's older set, from a generation that had gotten hooked on
bridge in the corners of their Seven Sisters and Ivy League dor-
mitories. Becca was one of the few who had never gone to college,
even though she'd done a good job fudging. Dan had taught her to
play. He'd been crazy about the game.

After the hand was dealt, Becca concentrated on the bidding,
since Sheila fancied herself one of the better players at the club.
Becca was easily distracted by the voices at the other tables, where
lunch dishes were being cleared and the pretty little hydrangea centerpieces were being set aside. Theirs was always the first table to
start; Sheila had places to be.

Becca had strong diamonds, but she remembered Sheila's
past reproaches: "Diamonds are for fingers, Becca. Let's play in
a major."

"I'll pass," said Becca.

Sheila won the contract, four spades. That made Becca the dummy, and so she could relax—her favorite position at the table, quite honestly. She used to sit there, watching Dan play their hand expertly; he had the whole thing planned out from trick one. It was something they had enjoyed doing together, playing for an hour or two after dinner with another couple. That was how they had come to spend so much time with the Murphys. Dan had started playing golf on Saturday mornings with Dick, who had been the one to suggest the four of them play bridge.

"So, I hear your granddaughter's in town," Sheila said with a lilt in her voice, hoping for more. Becca just nodded, arranging her cards according to suit and counting up her points. Sheila was the one who usually disapproved of conversation across the table.

"Is she still in school?" she persisted.

"Yes." That was all Becca said, and her uncharacteristic brevity caused their opponents, Edith and Judy, to widen their eyes. Sheila dealt the next hand. She had a crisp way of snapping the cards down in front of each of them.

"Will she work? I mean, does she need work over the summer? Because I think my daughter is looking for some tutoring help with the kids," Sheila added.

"She's finishing up her PhD. She'll be applying for professorships next spring." Becca hated to play the PhD card, but it would shut them up. Things might be tight, but she wouldn't want Sarah taking odd jobs in Long Harbor.

"When do your grandchildren arrive?" Becca asked the table in general.

"Mine come Friday. Everyone loves the fireworks," Edith said, laying down trump with a satisfied smirk. She picked up the trick and led the next card.

"Ours arrive tomorrow," said Sheila. "I've got to get home right after this game in order to fit my nap in. I need to stockpile sleep."

"It's not feeling rested so much as *looking* rested that I care about," said Judy. They all giggled. Becca shuffled one deck, and

Sheila dealt. Judy gestured to the waitress; she was ready to move on to something stronger than iced tea.

"Wear sunglasses," said Sheila. "Takes off fifteen years."

"Vodka and cranberry, love," Judy said to the waitress. "Anyone care to join me?"

The others shook their heads, looking down at their cards.

"Howard naps every day, but I don't always need to," Edith said.

"Why don't you snuggle up with Howard in the afternoon?" Judy asked.

"Oh, he'd like that," Edith said, swatting the air demurely.

Becca noted that she and Dan had never gone to bed in the afternoon. Fifty years of marriage, and not once during the day, not once with the lights on. In the beginning, she'd been the one who was uptight, but Dan had also been as straight as they came, not one for change. On their wedding night she'd wanted them to be drunk, so worried he'd figure her out. And so had begun their habit of mixing drinks in the evening.

Becca wondered what more passion would have been like. Edith's husband, Howard, was a notorious flirt, and Edith frequently dropped hints about his "voracious appetite." How he exhausted her! Becca had heard rumors about other women, too. Ruth had even claimed once that Howard had made a pass at her.

Sheila won the contract again. She bid too aggressively. Becca looked up from the cards fanned out in her hands and surveyed the room. She was surprised to see her dear friend Mary Bell, who she thought had gone to New York for a doctor's appointment.

"Excuse me while Sheila plays the hand. Good luck, partner," said Becca, heading toward the ladies' room, purposely detouring around Mary's table. She bent over and kissed Mary's cheek while Mary deliberated which card to put down. "You're back from the city?"

"Never went. Appointment canceled."

"Everything all right?"

"Yes, female problems. An annoyance, that's all." Mary put down a card. "How's it going with you? Has Rachel come around?"

"Not yet."

"Oh dear. I'm sorry, love."

"Jason coming for the fireworks?"

"Absolutely." Mary put down another card.

"Please bring him by on Saturday night. I'm having a small gathering for Andrew beforehand."

"How lovely. How's it going over there with Sheila?"

"Hasn't made a contract yet."

Becca looked across the room to see Sheila shuffling the cards with her thumbs again. How had she ended up playing with those ladies? Because Dan had pushed her to partner with Sheila, to play with better people; plus, he had always wanted to get in with Dick, who was a bit of a man about town. If she'd remained Mary's partner, she would have been here trading recipes, instead of worrying about Sheila's complicated conventions. She nabbed a cashew turtle from the dish on Mary's table and headed back to her seat.

When she sat down, Sheila was frowning, as if Becca had held up the bidding. Becca just ignored her. "Time for Judy and Edith to get some cards and play a hand," she said.

"Becca, I wish you'd concentrate more on the game at this table," Sheila said.

Becca bit her tongue. Whenever Sheila went down, she inevitably blamed it on Becca.

Judy waved at the waitress to bring another vodka and cranberry while the cards were being dealt. After the waitress put the drink down in front of her, Judy turned to Becca. "So, is Mary Bell's son getting a divorce?"

"Not that I know of," said Becca. Why on earth would Judy care?

The sight of Judy's cranberry juice floating among the ice cubes above the vodka revolted her, and so did the gossip. She put up a wall against it, zeroing in on her cards as if her life depended on it. Dan would have been proud of the way she played. She even made a three no-trump contract. It was like he was up in heaven guiding her through the order in which she needed to lay down her cards.

She felt him whispering in her ear, watching over her shoulder. She clapped her hands in victory after picking up the last trick.

"That was good bridge," said Sheila, eyebrows raised.

Becca sat back in her chair, her heart pounding, satisfied and exhausted from all the thinking. Playing well was the greatest revenge. Sheila picked up the small "winners" envelope on the table and handed one of the bills to Becca.

"What got into you, partner?" asked Sheila.

"Oh Sheila, you underestimate me," said Becca with new conviction.

As Becca retrieved her lipstick from her purse in preparation for her exit, she saw the club manager approach Mary Bell's table out of the corner of her eye. He was bending down, speaking into her ear. Mary pivoted in her chair and pointed in Becca's direction. The manager spotted her and began making his way through the maze of chairs toward her table at the end of the dining room. My goodness, she had paid her annual dues, hadn't she? Or was this one of the balances her accountant suggested might wait? Dear Lord, not here, not now. He wouldn't mention such a thing in public, would he? Not in front of Sheila, dear Lord. It was too early in the season for him to be worried about past-due accounts.

She applied her lipstick with a trembling hand, pretending not to notice him.

"Good afternoon, Mrs. Fitzpatrick."

"Good afternoon, Michael," she said, stiffening.

"I'm so sorry to interrupt your game, but there is a phone message for you. It sounded urgent."

"Urgent? From whom?"

"A Miss Lilly. She said to tell you she is at the hospital with Sarah."

Becca's heart sank. Sheila circled the table and collected Becca's purse and sweater from the floor. Mary must have seen something was wrong from across the room and came over too. Edith and Judy whispered something, then discreetly helped Becca stand.

"Get her to the door," Mary whispered to Sheila. "I'll bring my car around."

"I'm sure it's nothing," Becca said. "Mary can take me." There was no need for the whole place to wonder what was going on.

Chapter 14

LONG HARBOR, RHODE ISLAND
June 1929

S adie's hands trembled as she unpacked her clothing at Eden. She knocked over some perfume bottles as she walked past her dressing table, her arms laden with scarves and blouses. "Damn it," she was exhausted, still unable to sleep. All she could think about was driving Thomas up to his appointment in Boston. As she put a pair of nylons in her lingerie drawer, they snagged on a jagged fingernail. Flustered, she zipped open a small pouch in search of nail scissors. She couldn't find them. She couldn't find anything. What was wrong with her? Forgetful, not sleeping, and now bruised from knocking into the furniture.

The house felt unnaturally quiet. The last she'd seen of Bunny, he was wearing swim trunks, off for a dip in the ocean with the boys. She put on one of her bright summer dresses. She would go down to the back porch and wait for him. He should call the hospital, make arrangements for Thomas. Outside, she settled into a chaise in the sun, began to breathe slowly, and was actually on the threshold of sleep, when Bunny appeared at her side wearing a smart linen jacket and slacks.

"Where are you going?" asked Sadie.

"Come with me," he said.

"Now?"

Bunny smiled sadly and escorted her, one hand on the middle of her back, around the back of the house toward the driveway.

She scanned the flowerbeds on their way, the seedlings that were already pushing their way through the topsoil. They would need watering this afternoon. But the car was waiting. He opened the passenger-side door for her and she got in. What was going on? She had no time for one of his silly surprises.

Bunny's hands quivered, and he fumbled with the ignition. Steering down the drive, he turned for a moment before planting his eyes back on the road. "Sadie, there's a hospital in Providence. It's called Banford. They're expecting us."

"Banford? What are you talking about? Thomas's appointment is at Mass General."

"God, Sadie, this is so hard." He wiped his eyes. Were those tears? She leaned closer to him. What was he getting at?

"You know you haven't been yourself since Becca was born. It's important you rest your nerves. I promise to take care of Thomas but you need to take care of yourself."

Sadie's throat tightened. It was hard to breathe. Bunny just kept driving, his eyes straight ahead. Tears streamed down her cheeks as he continued, "Alice and I pulled some of your things together, and it's only one hour from here," he said. "It's like a tranquil summer camp for adults. Dr. Hart says it's the Ivy League of sanitariums."

Heat rose up Sadie's spine at the mention of the name "Dr. Hart" and the word "sanitarium." She squeezed her eyes closed. The summer had barely begun; how could he betray her? And letting that Dr. Hart send her off to a madhouse? She put one hand on the door handle and pressed the other against the window. Each time the car slowed during the one-hour ride, she thought about jumping out. It wasn't until they were almost there that she found her voice.

"Bunny, please, this is so out of the blue. Can't we discuss it?"

"Sadie, love," he said, "I don't want to get you all worked up. It will only make matters worse."

She shook her head and wiped her tears with the back of her hand. "Bunny, you can't just make these decisions without me."

He looked at her with sorrow in his eyes and pointed to the discreet sign at the bottom of Banford's drive. "We're here," he said.

Banford looked more like a gracious mansion than like a hospital. Sadie stared into her lap, hiding her reddened cheeks, while Bunny completed registration forms. She lowered her gaze to the Oriental carpet and neatly painted baseboards. He must have been planning this for weeks. She wondered if Kitty was in on the idea, and a wave of nausea came over her.

She sobbed against Bunny's chest as they stood together in the lobby. She gasped for words like a child at the end of a tantrum. "Oh, please, Bunny," Sadie begged. "Please, take me back to Eden tonight."

She was sure he was wavering, sure she had reached the tender spot in his heart. But when he kissed her forehead and said, "Goodbye, my love," she broke inside. She stood stunned and alone until she noticed the orderly behind her. He took her arm, injected a syringe of clear liquid below her shoulder, then guided her down into a wheelchair.

* * *

Eighteen hours later, Sadie woke up conscious but numb. The sun shone bright through the window, the curtains pushed aside. She pried her swollen eyes lids apart, then rolled her face into the pillow to thwart the throbbing in her forehead. The bed linens' unfamiliar scent and scratchy texture made her remember where she was. *Good Lord, this is real.*

As she lifted her head from the pillow, the light reflecting off the bright white walls and muted gray floor was blinding. She touched her bare feet down on a cotton throw and rubbed the crusted sleep from her eyes. She took two paces toward the window, touching her fingers to the cool glass.

A voice came from behind her. "Mrs. Meister, you're awake." She turned to find a short nurse with tightly clipped brown curls. Sadie ran distracted fingers through her own short hair.

"Yes, I am."

"I'll give you some time to get sorted," the nurse said, "and then I'll take you to your physical."

Sadie sat lifeless on the edge of the examining table, suffering the weighing and measuring and a penlight shining into her eyes. The physical took up most of the morning. After lunch, she took a nap and then was led to her psychiatrist's office. Dr. Graham was perusing a file as she sat down. He began their meeting by referring to Dr. Hart's assessment of her domestic failings. Bile rose in her throat at the mere mention of Dr. Hart's name.

"Do not speak his name ever again," Sadie said, finding some resolve in her voice.

Dr. Graham raised an eyebrow, then turned a page in the file on his desk. "As you wish, Mrs. Meister. I won't mention him, but can you argue with his assessment of the situation?"

Sadie looked at her lap, and the hot tears came again. She shook her head. "No."

"I am going to prescribe an initial rest cure for your nervous exhaustion. This is quite common in women your age. I want you to remain inactive, which includes writing or reading. I don't want your brain taxed in any way."

"But, Doctor, how do you expect—"

Dr. Graham cut her off. "Your nurse will see to it that you are sedated enough to sleep comfortably."

* * *

The nurse clicked her heels on the polished linoleum floor every morning before pulling back the curtains in Sadie's room to let the sun in. She went so far as to unlatch the windows and pull them open, letting in cool air and the smell of grass from the lawn that lay beyond the evenly spaced iron bars screwed tightly to the sill.

Sadie usually slept through all of it, but one morning the sunlight caught her in the eye and she lifted her head off the pillow as if an urgent question had been planted in her mind. "What day is it? How long have I been here?" she asked her nurse, who was in and out with cups of pills.

"It's Tuesday the seventeenth. You have been here just shy of three weeks."

"It feels like I've slept through days and days. Has my husband called?"

"No, Banford won't allow visitors for the first two months."

"Two months? Oh no—I won't be here that long. You see, I have young children and they need me. I have a little baby. I must . . ." Sadie sat up in bed.

"You haven't had any visitors, but you have received some envelopes through the post." The nurse retrieved them from her station. One was particularly large and addressed in Bunny's distinctive hand. Sadie sat on the bed and carefully slit the envelopes with her index finger. Four of the photographs that she had framed the previous summer spilled onto her lap.

She envisioned Bunny taking them down from the walls and removing them from their frames. He had chosen one of her favorites, the three boys surrounding her at the beach. How she had failed them, failed them all so miserably. She choked on her tears. The nurse brought her a glass of cool water and dispensed pills from a small paper cup into her palm. After several minutes, the sharp edges of Sadie's sadness dulled. She stared blankly at the bars on her windows until they blurred and it was time to go to lunch.

She lost track of time at Banford, the meals of meats covered in gravy with sides of scalloped potatoes or canned corn marking her days. They were served on fine bone china with harmless cardboard utensils and, during the beautiful summer weather, outside on a stone patio surrounded by English gardens and long green lawns.

When the staff spoke, it was like she was underwater, their voices swimming somewhere near the surface. Other patients floated through Sadie's periphery. Their white robes caught the breeze and sailed past her like boats on the harbor. During moments of lucidity, she asked her nurse about them. Lying in bed at night, she heard sounds, random cries, and moans down the hall. But her nurse told Sadie not to worry about anybody but herself when she administered her bedtime injection. "I'm not like these people," Sadie insisted, as she fell into a sleep that felt impossible to climb out of. During the day, if she cried tears of self-loathing and shame, her nurse stood ready with pills that could put her back on a serene plane.

Eight weeks into her stay, with her dosage of sedatives reduced, Sadie could now spend her days taking walks, attending therapy sessions and arts-and-crafts programs. She surrendered to the pervasive slowness and whispered conversations of Banford. It was a place without loud noises or sudden changes.

She raised her voice only during her sessions with Dr. Graham, trying to convince him that she was ready to leave. "I want to return to my family," Sadie said. "I'm sure every mother has an adjustment period. Some just longer than others."

"Mrs. Meister, please. You are suffering very severe melancholia."

"I'm feeling so much better. Missing them is worse than anything else I felt at home." Sadie wrung her hands in her lap.

"You mustn't get so exercised, Mrs. Meister. See how you tremble when you discuss this with me? I might need to take the course of shock therapy."

She shook her head. "Please, no."

"In that case, I think it wise to give it a little extra time. There is a calmness here—one that does not exist outside our walls."

"But my husband surely—"

"Ultimately, your discharge will be up to him."

* * *

On an afternoon in August, easels with fresh white canvases and paints were set up on the terrace. Sadie fingered the horsehair of one of the brushes. "There is nothing as promising as a pure white canvas," said an older man, poking his head out from behind a neighboring easel. He was as diminutive in size as Sadie, with age spots on his balding scalp.

Sadie found joy in painting, in creating something where there had been nothing. When the lessons moved from landscapes to portraiture, her teacher suggested she paint her children. "You could paint them from photographs," he suggested. It had been too painful to view the pictures when they first arrived, but now they served a purpose, aiding her with initial shape and composition. Eventually she slipped them back into their envelope and painted from memory, obsessing over Edward's pouty lip or Thomas's dark eyes, the auburn curls that stuck to Robert's sweaty face or the rolls of baby flesh on Becca's neck. Sadie adored her, every last detail. How could she have overlooked the blessing of a daughter after three boys?

When she painted them, it was like being with them, but without Alice standing in between. There was no illness, no anxiety. Their innocence and perfection became clear. "I'm their mother," she repeated to herself. "Nobody will ever know them like I do."

With practice, she became skilled at contrasting light and dark, at skin tones, bringing out the glow of her children's cheeks.

Her bald neighbor pointed to the grin on Edward's face. "That one is full of mischief."

Sadie laughed. "Yes, yes, he is." She was determined to have her family back. She rubbed paint onto the canvas with the heel of her palm; she caressed their chins, their foreheads. When she admired the older man's moon on the water, she even felt a longing for Bunny.

He came around from behind his easel and placed a hand on her shoulder. "It's unfair—we artists, we feel too much. The secret is to be like an actor."

Sadie looked at him quizzically.

"Play to your audience," he said.

* * *

Sadie waited on Banford's front porch. She looked up from her book when she heard a car's tires crunch up the long drive. It was Bunny, finally. She watched him driving too fast, hitting the brakes when he came upon a parking spot. He removed his sunglasses and looked at himself in the rearview mirror. He stepped out of the car, slammed the door, and turned toward the building. It was the height of summer, but his skin was pale and his eyes were puffy. He patted down his hair, then placed his straw fedora in his hand.

When he looked up toward the building and spotted her, he smiled, bounding up the steps. "My darling," he said, taking her hands in his and kissing her cheek. She felt him searching her face, but she did not meet his eyes. He put his thumb to her cheek. "Darling, what's on your face?"

"It must be paint," she said, with no further explanation.

"My, you look stunning. How are you?" he said.

She knew she was no longer the beautiful, charismatic woman he had fallen in love with. She had seen her reflection plenty of times. Her face was thin, her hair brittle; even the sparkle was gone from her eyes.

"Are you taking me home?" she asked.

He looked down into his lap and squeezed her hands, his version of an apology. "Not today. I'm so sorry, love. I'm here to visit. . . . I'm just doing what they tell me is best for you."

Tears fell from Sadie's eyes onto their joined hands. They sat that way for a while in the warm sun. She wondered if things would ever return to the way they had been.

She asked about the children.

"Becca started walking; I noticed for the first time a few nights ago, after the boys and I came back from fishing." Sadie's shoulders sank.

"Robert and Edward like to dig a little hole in the sand for her to play in." Sadie looked away; it was too painful to hear.

"She's going to be a beautiful girl," Bunny continued. "Anyway, I'll be taking them back to Pittsburgh soon for the start of school."

Bunny stood up. She had forgotten how tall he could seem.

He coughed into his handkerchief and wiped his eyes. "It won't be much longer, darling. I'll return for you soon enough." He leaned over her and kissed the top of her head. She smelled his earthy perspiration through his shirt.

Chapter 15

LONG HARBOR, RHODE ISLAND
Wednesday, July 1, 2000

The tile floor, fluorescent lights, and antiseptic smell were the only clues that this was a hospital. The Westfield emergency room served only a few beach towns, handling a smattering of broken bones and household accidents. It must have been a particularly slow day, because the waiting room was empty. Only Lilly, Sarah, and a man with a very bad cough were waiting. Lilly watched him out of the corner of her eye, wishing he would cover his mouth, while Sarah completed a questionnaire on a clipboard. A few minutes later, a woman in a long white coat called her name. Lilly wasn't sure if she should stay in the waiting room or follow Sarah.

"Please, come with me, Lilly," Sarah urged, looking back over her shoulder.

Sarah hoisted herself onto a gurney behind a curtain, and a young doctor examined her for broken bones and a concussion. Then he ordered an ultrasound.

"They'll come to get you in a few minutes and take you to radiology," the doctor said, pulling the curtain closed behind him.

"Lilly, hand me my purse, will you?"

Sarah took out her cell phone and dialed her ob-gyn in the city. While Sarah spoke to the doctor, Lilly went back out to reception to make a phone call of her own. When she returned, Sarah whispered in her ear, "She said I did the right thing coming here." Lilly squeezed her hand.

"Sarah," Lilly said, "I have to tell you, I called your grandmother."

"Oh no—you didn't."

"I had to. I've worked for her for fifty years, and I've never kept anything from her."

Sarah put her phone back in her purse with a sigh.

"She was at the club, playing bridge. I left a message," Lilly said.

Sarah closed her eyes while they waited for radiology. Lilly brushed Sarah's mussed hair from her forehead and wiped the sap and the dirt from her neck. Lying there in that hospital robe, Sarah still looked like a little girl.

* * *

"Is this your first ultrasound?"

"Yes."

"If I can tell, do you want to know the sex?"

"No," Sarah said right away.

"Why not?" Lilly asked.

"Lilly, I just want to check things out, that's all."

The technician rubbed a cold gel over Sarah's stomach and then glided a wand around the area below her belly button. "See that pulsing?" She pointed to the screen. "The heartbeat is strong and steady."

Lilly leaned her face closer to the screen. "Well, would you look at that!"

Sarah attempted a faint smile.

The technician said, "Looks like you're at about ten or eleven weeks."

"Did I do any damage?"

"The doctor will take a look at the images and then come in to talk to you."

Lilly avoided Sarah's eye contact, not liking the sound of that. More waiting. About fifteen minutes later, the doctor came in. "Well, Sarah," she said, "the heart is beating normally, which is positive. The placenta, however, looks to be slightly detached. That's a problem. I am prescribing bed rest. Stay out of the heat, and drink plenty of water. This heat wave will dehydrate you, and that is the worst thing that can happen. Let's just hope there's no more bleeding."

"Bed rest? For how long?"

"Possibly a month, possibly the rest of your pregnancy. There will be no way to tell if your placenta is reattaching to the uterus until your next ultrasound. And come back if there's any more bleeding."

"Don't you worry, Doctor," said Lilly. "I'll make sure she follows your orders." She helped Sarah descend from the table and held her hand as they walked out to the car.

* * *

When they got back to the house, Lilly set Sarah up on the back porch, on a wicker chaise under the awning.

"I want you to drink this water and try to take a nap. If you don't stay quiet, I'm going to take you up to your bedroom."

"Not that, Lilly—it's so hot up there," Sarah said, sweat already forming on her brow.

"I'll get you some more ice cubes," Lilly said, although she wanted to tell Sarah that she'd do anything in the world for her. "Now, you need to follow the doctor's orders," she said, hearing her clipped Maine accent rise to the surface. Her wagging finger made Sarah smile. It was also the way she concealed her worry. "You'll be fine. You'll both be fine." Lilly sat, squeezing onto the side of the chaise and patted Sarah's thigh gently.

"I know absolutely nothing about this, but a detached placenta sounds serious," Sarah said, picking at her cuticle.

Lilly didn't like the sounds of a detached placenta either, but she didn't let on. "Think positively. I'm sure the ocean air and a little rest will cure all. I'll bring down some books for you to read," said Lilly, standing up. "And now I've got beds to make before it gets any later."

* * *

Upstairs, Lilly opened the doors to the linen closet. Becca had already given her instructions that morning about where everybody would be sleeping. One thing was for certain: Thomas and Carol should stay in the nicest and largest guest room, with its serene view, constant breezes, and private bath. Its white eyelet duvet and faded yellow wool carpet had been bleached by years of summer sun. While the rest of Eden had become threadbare, they had made an effort to keep the linens and upholstery in this room current for "special" visitors, even though nobody like that had visited in years.

Lilly dusted and put fresh towels in the bathroom. She sprayed a shot of lilac air freshener in the closet. As she bent over the vacuum cleaner, extending the power cord, Rachel opened her door.

"Perfect timing," said Lilly.

"Not now, Lilly," said Rachel.

Lilly gave her a pleading look, and Rachel did a huffy about-face on her threshold and started pulling the pillowcases off her pillows. She bundled all her sheets into a ball and carried them into the hallway.

"I'll put them down the laundry chute." Rachel had to raise her voice over the noise of the vacuum. "I'll make my bed later. You don't need to go in there. I was just on my way to find Sarah."

Lilly turned off the vacuum. "That's good! She's resting on the back porch. She had a bit of a scare," she said, handing Rachel a rag and a can of Endust.

"What happened?" Rachel asked.

"She fell from a ladder this morning. I took her to the hospital."

"Lilly! Why didn't you come get me?" Rachel threw the dust rag and Endust can down on the carpet. She headed toward the stairs, shaking her head.

Lilly carried fresh towels into the room where Andrew and Camilla would be staying. She opened up the windows, struggling to get the storm windows up and the screens down. She wiped the accumulated dust and dead bugs in her rag, confident that the fresh air alone was making the space more habitable.

They'd be staying in what used to be Thomas's room. Even though he hadn't been around much during her tenure, she had a strong impression of him. Working in their home, Lilly felt she knew things about the family that they didn't know themselves. She dusted and was in and out of all the closets, ones that Becca had stopped going into years earlier.

Thomas's bedroom was adjacent to the master because Sadie had wanted him close after he became ill. Then, just before Rachel's wedding almost thirty years prior, Becca had switched out the twin bed for a new queen size in order to accommodate her out-of-town guests.

Thomas referred to Becca's maneuvering as her "great land grab." He'd always assumed that, as eldest son, regardless of the time he spent in residence, he and his wife would inherit the master bedroom. But when they arrived for their two-week holiday, that was not the case. Lilly had overheard them arguing. "Very bold, little sister," Thomas said.

Becca shot back that his "patrilineal logic was ridiculous." Her family spent entire summers at Eden and supervised all its maintenance.

The domino effect was that Rachel took over what had been Becca's octagonal room, with its high ceiling, large windows, and flowing drapery. That really got to Thomas's wife, Carol. "Why should the two of us be all cramped up while your ten-year-old gets a spacious room with a view?"

Then Becca moved little Andrew into Edward's room. Edward confided in Lilly that his sister might have asked permission before she assumed his modest bit of turf. Each successive bedroom upgrade by Becca's clan left no doubt as to her intention that her line be in charge at Eden.

Lilly was impressed by the way Ruth watched calmly from the sidelines, even as her twins lived out on the sleeping porch, rain or shine. They made it fun. Many nights, Rachel and Andrew begged their mother to let them sleep on the porch with Joseph and Benjamin. In fact, Lilly often caught all four of the cousins with a flashlight, playing cards on the painted floor long after their mothers had said good night. Even as teenagers, when Joseph and Benjamin visited for a couple of weeks each summer, they insisted on sleeping out there. Lilly had gone out there one night in a rainstorm to bring them in, but Joseph had confessed that it made them feel close to their father. What a special boy.

Now, as Lilly surveyed the blue guest room, she thought about how best to tackle all the clutter. If she didn't give it a good once-over, Camilla would be sour.

Lilly had heard all her under-the-breath criticisms before. Originally, it was over their being "put" in the smaller bedrooms at the end of the hall. "We fly all the way over from the UK, and this is where she puts us." Camilla's pet peeve was the bathroom. "The plumbing is archaic." She hated the dimness of the pull-string light fixture as she applied her makeup in front of the small, mirrored medicine cabinet with its hexagonal glass knob. She scoffed at the claw-foot porcelain bathtub, with its rust stain around the faucet and the drain.

When Lilly raised the topic with Becca, she feigned ignorance.

"Oh, Lilly, Camilla reminds me of Carol. She takes things so personally. Why, they were the ones who insisted they squeeze in there when they were first married. When their kids were born, I just assumed they would prefer three rooms close together."

"It's like this," said Lilly. "Just after you greet your guests in the driveway, I watch the expressions on their faces when you tell them where they'll stay. It's not the men or the children who care so much—it's their wives. They think they're being snubbed when they aren't on the ocean side. I think whoever gets the room at the end of the hall, with the leaky faucet in the bathroom and the claw-foot tub, takes it as a downright insult."

So, for this visit, Lilly was determined to spruce things up for Camilla. She dusted bookshelves filled with tattered summer reading and carousel tokens awarded for snagging the brass ring. How the bedrooms always spilled over with the detritus of summer. It didn't help that Lilly was a sucker for nostalgia.

But not today. She would throw it all into her garbage bag. She hung a dozen new hangers in their closet. She removed the *National Geographics* from the bureau and the old sweaters from the shelves. She checked under the beds and in the drawers to make sure they were empty. The bedside table had a pen and pad on it, with some phone numbers written in what looked like Thomas's hand, left over from the previous Labor Day weekend. She checked the drawer and found a thick paperback: Tom Clancy, Thomas's favorite.

Before she returned the book to its shelf, she removed a folded piece of paper, a makeshift bookmark, sticking out from the yellowed and curling pages. Unfolding it, she saw it was a typewritten memo, FROM THE DESK OF EDWARD MEISTER. She scanned the top of the page; it was dated August. She read one more line: "RE: Offer to Purchase Eden." A prickle of shock. Were Becca's brothers conspiring behind her back? Should she show this to Becca?

She stuck it in the pocket of her apron and went to the closet to retrieve some fancy soaps. She unwrapped their expensive paper and placed them in the bathrooms. Her back was aching and her legs were tired. She hoped Camilla and Carol would be satisfied.

The last room Lilly entered was the red bedroom, Eden's nursery. A crib stood in the corner, although there hadn't been a baby in the house for over twenty years. Lilly sometimes went in there to hide, relax on the rocking chair. Her first summer, she had slept there on a cot next to Rachel's bassinet. When Andrew was an infant, the following summer, she had slept in there with both of them. She ran her fingers across the quilted bumpers on the crib and thought about Sarah's baby.

She had so much work to do in the kitchen, but the rocking chair always calmed her down. *Dear God*, she prayed, *let the placenta connect itself and let that poor child have some peace.*

Then she remembered the letter in her pocket. She held it in her lap and closed her eyes. If she read it and then just threw it into her garbage bag with the pile of old magazines, nobody would ever know. That might be better than handing it over to Becca—as if they all needed one more thing to worry about. Besides, she didn't want Becca to think she was snooping.

Chapter 16

PITTSBURGH, PENNSYLVANIA
1929

Bunny asked his secretary to dial Dr. Hart. When she buzzed that he was on the line, Bunny lifted his receiver and barked into it, demanding Thomas be prescribed Dilantin, despite the specialists' warning that he was too young. His household was coming apart, and he couldn't be thrown into chaos every night with those horrible convulsions.

And then there were Edward and Robert. The school principal had sent a note home. Apparently, the teachers were concerned by their uncharacteristically subdued behavior. He'd had to give them a stern lecture: "You two need to buck up, get on with it, and bring home some good marks. I have enough to deal with."

He remained strict with his boys, certain a tough demeanor would produce strength in them, an ability to stand on their own two feet, a determination to succeed. Inside, however, he was guilt ridden. He couldn't get the picture of their disappointed faces out of his memory. He'd pulled the car around the circle by the kitchen at Eden after his trip to Banford in August. Even though he hadn't tooted the horn, the three boys had sprung from the kitchen door to meet him. They surrounded the car, confused, searching for their mother in the passenger seat.

Dr. Hart put up a small fight but, in the end, agreed to write the prescription. Putting the telephone receiver back in its cradle, Bunny ticked off item one on his list. It made him feel in charge and hopeful. He would ask his secretary to pick up the medicine during her lunch hour. He would put things right again.

He looked at the next item on his list and pulled the number for Banford Hospital out of his private desk drawer. He picked up the receiver again and heard a distant, crackling tone after he dialed the number.

"Banford Hospital. How may I help you?" an operator answered.

"I need to speak to Dr. Graham," Bunny said.

"May I ask who's calling?"

"Bunny Meister."

"Please hold."

Bunny tapped a pencil against the edge of his desk, waiting. It was time to get his wife home. He missed her, and, by God, those kids needed their mother. He leaned back, put his shoes up on the desk, and examined their shine. He tapped the pencil against his thigh, waiting. Sometimes he wondered whether committing Sadie to Banford had been the right thing to do. There was no denying how desperate he had felt last spring, and Dr. Hart had been so convincing. Kitty had been the first one to raise concerns. "She's in bed most of the day, sobbing, and doesn't dress," she had told Dr. Hart.

Bunny had defended his wife. "It's because she's awake most of the night, listening for Thomas."

"And the baby—how is she balancing Thomas's illness with the demands of the baby?" asked Dr. Hart.

"She doesn't," Kitty interjected. "Alice has minded the baby from day one."

"Mr. Meister, is this true?" asked Dr. Hart.

Bunny conceded, "Well, she had nurses when the boys were babies, too, but, yes, I must admit she is less involved this time."

"It is not uncommon for new mothers to experience a distraught mental state," said Dr. Hart.

Bunny slammed his hand against Hart's desk, as if his wife's melancholy were his own personal failing. "There is nothing wrong with my wife's mental state." But in the end, Hart had convinced him, after Kitty had left and they had poured some scotch. Hart explained how common it was for women to spend a little time in a sanitarium when their nerves were frayed.

The crackle on the line got louder, and Bunny sat up in his chair and put his feet on the ground. The operator's voice eventually came back on the line. "I'm sorry, Mr. Meister," she said. "Dr. Graham is currently in session. May I ask him to return your call?"

Bunny spelled out a clear message for the operator, along with his phone number. "I'd like to hear from him by the end of the day. After lunch, if possible," he said.

He stuck his head into the office of one of his junior partners and asked him to lunch at the Pittsburgh Club. The younger man briefed Bunny on the status of the track's capital improvements over sliced roast beef. The P&E's expansion plan was the one topic that directed Bunny's mind away from his troubles. US Steel wanted more and more capacity. Steel and aluminum were in great demand, as the Department of Defense had recently commissioned several warships. The young man was full of optimistic projections. Bunny smiled. He would make it all right again; the future was looking bright.

As Bunny looked over the dessert menu, his thoughts turned to Sadie and the fact that Dr. Graham would be returning his call that afternoon. Could he get her home by the weekend? It was only Tuesday, after all. If she got a train tomorrow, she might make it. How the children would be delighted. He could practically hear their shrieks of joy pealing through the house.

"A slice of apple pie with whipped cream on top," he said when the waiter came back to take their order. Sadie might even be baking her own apple pies in their kitchen by the end of the month. His young partner continued to describe the timetable for their expansion, but Bunny was no longer paying attention. His wife's face filled his mind, her green eyes, the way her long red tresses fell about her body when they were first married. Maybe her hair had filled out over the past months at Banford. Wouldn't that be a wonderful surprise?

As Bunny scooped the last bits of whipped cream off his plate, a solemn-faced man hurried into the dining room with tousled hair and his suit coat askew. Bunny noticed him with a touch of distaste; how awkward it was when a wayward soul had to be ushered out of the private club by the maître d'. But the man didn't leave. Instead, he positioned himself in the center of the dining room and looked around at every table, as if he were searching for somebody. He threw his arms up in the air and shouted, "The stock market is crashing! The stock market is crashing!"

Bunny didn't know whether the man was crazy or not. But diners rose from their tables and rushed out the front door. Bunny stood up, disbelieving, and put his hat back on his head. He refused to panic, but, out on the sidewalk, he and his partner jogged back to the office. The phones were ringing like mad. It was true. In one day, the value of all of the P&E's non-railroad assets had plummeted to a small fraction of what they had been just the day before.

Bunny's partners roiled over the devaluation of their investments in light of the bank debt they had taken. The phone wouldn't stop ringing. His secretary hurried in and put the bag from the pharmacy on his desk. Bunny looked blankly at it, not remembering about Thomas's medication. He took off his necktie and unbuttoned the top buttons of his shirt, which was soaked through with sweat. Pouring a tall glass of scotch from the decanter in his office, he chastised himself for having let the junior guys take care of so much. "I really took my eye off the ball." Bunny's personal portfolio had disappeared in one fell swoop as well.

Dr. Graham returned Bunny's phone call in the midst of the chaos, but he couldn't take it.

His parents stopped by the house unannounced that afternoon. They arrived when the boys came home from school, and stayed for dinner. They said they wanted to be there for the children, in the face of Sadie's absence, but Bunny felt their eyes on him, his untucked shirt and disheveled hair. His father must have known what a crash meant, how far Bunny had extended himself.

His mother rocked Becca, singing her an old German lullaby,

while his father read a book to Robert, glancing every so often over the pages in Bunny's direction. He had to escape to his study to get away from all of them. If he could just go over the state of his affairs in private, some sort of a solution might become clear. Lit by a sole desk lamp and a bottle of scotch within arm's reach, he added and subtracted the length of a tablet, trying to figure out how he'd keep absolutely everything from crashing down around them.

His parents were at the house again when Bunny returned from the office late the next evening. The children were already in bed, and his mother and father sat alone in the living room, eyeglasses perched on their noses, reading the newspaper. His father stood up when Bunny entered. "Bernhard, I'll sell the Oakland house. And I liquidated my Heinz stock after I retired. I kept the cash in a savings account. You can have it all."

Bunny put his briefcase down, took two steps forward, and embraced his shrunken father, bending over to rest his head on his shoulder. Tears flowed. He had never imagined a slide backward. Once he started crying, he couldn't stop. Sadie's absence had left a hole in his life. He wept, thinking of her sitting alone at Banford, and he wept some more, thinking of Thomas choking down those awful pills before bedtime.

Close to midnight, Bunny sat in the master bedroom, Sadie's empty chaise next to him, staring at the red embers in the fireplace. Wind whistled through the shutters outdoors, and a dank winter draft seeped through the window. His parents' generosity wouldn't solve his financial problems, but it would bridge a short-term gap. He made a list, reviewing what was expendable. He could part with everything, except Eden. He would sell both his and his parents' houses and talk to Kitty about accommodating all of them on the grounds of Lancaster Fells. Maybe it was better that Sadie be spared this stress.

Bunny called Dr. Graham the next morning from his bedroom. "Things are complicated for us here," he said. "I have to put the house on the market, and our son . . . well, his seizures just aren't under control yet."

"Ah, Mr. Meister, enough said," the doctor replied. "We certainly wouldn't want Mrs. Meister returning to a strained atmosphere."

Bunny walked over to her closet and opened it. The perfume Sadie wore still clung to her dresses. He took a step forward and caressed his cheek with the silk fabrics. They were cool and feminine. He inhaled the sweet air a few more times, before backing out of the closet. He turned toward their bed and collapsed, fully dressed, onto its unmade sheets. He pounded the mattress with his fists as the pillows muffled his sobs.

Chapter 17

ESSEX, CONNECTICUT

Thursday, July 2, 2000

“Why do babies always want to be born in the middle of the night?” Lee yawned, bringing a mug of hot coffee to her lips.

The expectant mother reclined in a birthing tub while her husband massaged her shoulders. Lee's eyes made contact with theirs, and they smiled at each other, the acknowledgment that the moment had come. For Lee, there had been hundreds of these moments, but they never failed to bring a rush of excitement. She turned down the lights in the hallway and the bathroom and lit scented candles. She turned up the volume on the boom box—James Taylor's "Fire and Rain."

Lee got down on her knees and put her elbows up on the edge of the tub. She lifted the mother's hand from the warm water and looked at her wristwatch. "Okay, remember to breathe, you're getting close. It won't be much longer now."

"You're doing great, hon," her husband said.

"An old pro."

The three of them had been through this before. It was their third child, and mother, father, and midwife were working in unison. They all knew what to expect, the atmosphere was relaxing, and the mother was healthy, having never had any complications. Lee measured her dilation. "Good," she said, with a confident voice that she knew would make everyone relax.

How this contrasted with her experiences twenty-five years

prior, just after her graduation from nursing school at the University of Cincinnati. She had gone right to work in the maternity ward, and from day one, everything about birthing and babies had seemed magical to her. But the veterans on the ward had complained a lot about the mothers and seemed unimpressed by it all, and the male doctors had often arrived to deliveries wearing golfing attire under their scrubs with an air of being inconvenienced. She thought they might do a better job of coaxing things along naturally, instead of reaching for the forceps or pressuring mothers into C-sections prematurely. The fluorescent lights and stainless steel flew in the face of the miracles she witnessed. She asked one of the older nurses if they had ever thought about making the rooms more homey for the mothers.

"Impossible to clean. Every once in a while, things go wrong, Lee. Blood goes everywhere."

The mother groaned as the jolt of her final contractions overtook her body. She rocked in the tub, causing the water to slosh over the side.

"Breathe," the father said, rubbing her back.

"Almost time to start pushing," said Lee. She got back down on her knees, creating a cushion of towels between her and the hard tile floor. She submerged her arms up to her armpits. Water splashed onto her chest, and she laughed, "Here we go." The mother couldn't speak through the effort, instead locking her eyes on Lee's face.

As Lee knelt with her arms in the tub, waiting for the next contraction, she whispered a silent prayer. It was the same one every time: *Dear God, grant this precious soul a peaceful life.* For Lee, it was just that simple. When new friends in Connecticut asked about her occupation, she described her life's work as welcoming babies into the world.

It made sense, given her own origins. She had been obsessed with trying to piece together the details of her own birth ever since her parents had told her, when she was twelve, that she had been adopted. They assured her that they couldn't love her any more if they tried, but they wanted her to know the truth.

"Then who are my real parents?" Lee had asked nervously.

"We don't know the answer, darling. All we know is that your mother was a young girl, no husband, and she hated to leave you. When you are twenty-one, you'll be able to request the file, if you'd like."

Lee felt a deep allegiance to the only mother she had ever known, but after that day, she had never stopped wondering about her young mother with no husband. What did she look like? Was she sad or angry or relieved about the adoption? Did she ever think about the baby she had left behind?

Her obsession with her birth mother subsided as she got older and attended college. But when Lee first started in the maternity ward, it resurfaced. There were newborns everywhere; there were flowers and balloons and congratulations. Some women didn't have visitors or ask to hold their babies, and that's when Lee caught her breath and checked her emotions.

The brave mother's face reddened, and her eyes bulged.

"Keep pushing. There you go. The baby's crowning." The mother let out a loud groan with her final push. Lee's expert hands lifted the slippery infant above the surface of the water. It was a boy. She encouraged him to take his first breath. The father followed Lee's directions, draining water from the tub and retrieving a warm towel and terry-cloth robe for his wife. Lee placed the boy on his mother's breast and cut the umbilical cord. Lee looked up and saw a ray of light reflecting off the beveled edge of the bathroom mirror. The sun was rising. Their two older daughters tiptoed into the room, holding their father's hands. "Meet your little brother," he whispered.

The girls squeaked like baby birds, kneeling by their mother in awe. The mother cried softly. Lee prepared an area to clean the baby and wrap him up, but before she took him away, she watched this most beautiful scene unfold on the ordinary bathroom floor.

For Lee, these ordinary, intimate settings symbolized the magic of midwifery. For most American women, having a baby in a hospital was a foregone conclusion. The medical community scoffed at the idea of giving birth outside the sterile atmosphere of a hospital, without anesthesia or various other medical instruments.

By the time Lee had washed and wrapped the baby, waited for the pediatrician to arrive, taken care of the mother, and helped clean everything up, it was late morning.

As she was pulling out of the driveway, her cell phone rang. She glanced at the caller ID, which read BECCA MEISTER. She stopped the car and deftly flipped open the phone.

"Hi!" Lee answered.

After a hesitation, Becca began speaking. She sounded run down. Her voice had been much brighter back in May when she had left that message: "Lee, dear, it's Becca. . . . Can I pop down to Mystic on Sunday and catch a movie with you? Maybe a bite? Your birthday is coming up, and, well, you've been on my mind." Lee had listened to that recording multiple times and hadn't deleted it. *This is the voice of my mother*, she thought. *Mother. My mother.* With its singsong lilt and energy, it was the voice of a friend, somebody who wanted to hop in the car, drive an hour just to see her, watch her blow out birthday candles—the voice of a person who had actually experienced her birth. Lee didn't have any photographs of the two of them yet, but she had that recording, and that meant much more than a picture could.

But this morning Becca was calling with an invitation to Sunday brunch at Eden with the entire family. This would be it. Lee had set this chain of events in motion, after all, and she couldn't back down now. Just like the siblings of the baby she had just delivered, she would be meeting her brother and sister for the first time.

She had first telephoned Becca after her own mother passed away. She was sorting through her old files, and her mother had left the envelope clearly labeled "Lee's Adoption" right on top, as if she were encouraging Lee to search for her biological parents. Lee figured if her mother had been a teenager when Lee was born, she would be in her seventies now, most likely still alive and well. But Lee was hesitant, constructing a list of pros and cons that boiled down to two basic scenarios: *Pro: my mother will be happy that I found her and will love me. Con: my mother will be unhappy I found her and will turn me away . . . again.*

After she completed some paperwork, got her signature notarized, and sent the request off to Kansas City, the file from the Willows Maternity Hospital was mailed to her. She had no idea it would be so simple. Rebecca Meister, Westfield, Rhode Island. Why, that was less than an hour's drive from where Lee now lived. Lee was convinced it was providence that had charted her course east and that contacting her birth mother was her fate.

She finally dialed the number on a Saturday evening in September. Lee hadn't expected the phone number she had been given, the one that had been in the Willows' files for the past fifty years, to be the only one she needed. The officials at the adoption bureau in Kansas City had warned that she would probably meet dozens of obstacles during her search. But Rebecca Meister actually answered the phone. It took Lee a minute to speak as her heart thumped in her chest.

"My Lord, is it you? Is it really you?" Becca had wept and carried on, getting more emotional and then putting down the phone at one point to get a handkerchief. As Lee had listened to Becca on the phone, she'd felt a tugging in her heart. The curiosity Lee had initially felt turned into a visceral desire. Becca's voice was what lured Lee, pushing her to take the next step.

When Lee sat face-to-face with Becca on the beach, perched on that long piece of driftwood, she did not feel disloyal to her own mother, as she had been afraid she might. She couldn't stop searching Becca's face for what was recognizable, and when Becca showed her a photo of Rachel, that was when Lee's heart really raced. "Oh my goodness. I have a sister? Oh! And we look so much alike."

She would meet Rachel this Sunday. Lee pictured the two of them having a glass of wine, going to a museum, maybe even traveling together. She decided that when she got home, she would pull all the shades and get some sleep. She wanted to be rested for Sunday. Lee shifted the gear into drive and started moving forward, humming to the music on the radio.

Chapter 18

LONG HARBOR, RHODE ISLAND
1930

On a cloudy afternoon in May, Sadie waited in the lobby, wearing a hat and a long coat, her bags packed, staring impatiently at the door. When Bunny finally walked through it, Sadie stared into the glare. Only her husband's voice and height were recognizable. Where was his strong jaw, his cleft chin? He looked bloated. His jet-black hair had turned salt and pepper and was fully gray at the temples.

"Sadie, love," he said, coming toward her.

She stood and faced him, her knees starting to tremble. "Bunny."

He took her by the waist and leaned down to kiss her, but out of the corner of her eye she spotted her nurse and painting teacher, who had come to say goodbye. She put her hands up against his large chest, pushing back. "Bunny, not here, not now. I'd like to say goodbye to some people." She pointed to her bags in the corner. "Why don't you take those to the car?"

Bunny's shoulders slumped as he gathered her luggage. An orderly followed Bunny to the car with Sadie's portfolio and her many canvases. Sadie reached the parking lot as Bunny was struggling to fit them all in the backseat.

"Please be careful," she said.

"I'm trying," he said, as perspiration gathered on his forehead.

Once he turned the key in the ignition, he turned to face her.

"I can't tell you how much I've missed you," he said, his eyes softening. She sensed his face moving closer and his desire to kiss her.

"Have you really?" Sadie pulled back and crossed her gloved hands across her lap.

"Of course I have, and the children are beside themselves with excitement." Bunny said, heading down the long drive.

Sadie eyed his profile skeptically, then shifted her gaze through the passenger-side window. She spoke as she watched the scenery speeding past. "You may have missed me, but it will never equal what I have missed. One year of my life, Bunny. One year."

"Sadie, I—"

But she cut him off. "And what did you tell the children? Where did they think I was all this time?"

"I told them you weren't well."

She sighed and shook her head. What if they didn't remember her?

As the car approached Eden's driveway, Sadie's heart raced and tears crept from the corners of her eyes. There had been days when she had doubted she would ever go home again. Bunny tooted the horn ceremoniously, a signal to all that they were home. And then there they were, like a vision, standing shoulder to shoulder, waiting for her alongside Alice and Mr. P. They were so much taller and thinner than they had been when she'd left them, fidgeting with their pockets, their shirts buttoned up, their wet hair parted and combed. They had likely been instructed to be calm, but all she wanted was for them to run into her arms, to bowl her over with affection.

She had been training herself to convey calmness and control. Indeed, Sadie had learned to thicken her skin and play the part of a healthy woman for Dr. Graham. She rose early, lest he label her depressed. She no longer spoke of Thomas's malady, lest he label her obsessive. She feigned an aching for Becca, lest he label her unfit. She did all these things to convince Dr. Graham she was well enough to return to her family, a concept that had become increasingly amorphous with each passing week. Now that she was on the precipice of reentering her life, the moment she had been dreaming of for an entire year, she didn't know how to act. She felt the corners of her mouth rise. She hadn't smiled, hadn't felt joy, for such a long time. But here it was, the sight of her children—pure joy. It stunned her into a strange silence, as if she couldn't know what might come out of her mouth.

Bunny herded everyone into the house, where they gradually migrated to the living room. Sadie cried silently, tears of disbelief and happiness. Hesitant hugs were exchanged, then kisses, followed by shy giggles, then, eventually, heartier ones. Oh, how good it felt to laugh again. By late afternoon, the boys were hanging off her. Little Becca disappeared for a moment, then came dashing through the living room without her clothes on. She was a cherubic toddler with a mound of red ringlets springing off her head. She had a freckled face and pouty pink lips that glistened with drool. She screeched in delight, circling the sofas and coffee table.

"Becca, stop that!" said Robert, as Edward cut her off and picked her up under the armpits.

"Alice!" Edward shouted. "Becca's naked again!"

"She doesn't like to wear clothes," Robert said shyly to his mother.

Sadie found herself just staring as Alice picked up Becca and took her up the stairs.

Robert dug out a deck of cards and suggested they play a big game of hearts. "I've missed playing with you, Mommy. I think I'm much more clever now," he said, swaying from side to side. Bunny smiled from his lounge chair while Sadie played cards with the boys and caressed Becca's cheek. "Oh, how you've grown up!" Sadie lifted her daughter onto her lap while Edward dealt the cards, but Becca scrambled down, running back and forth between the kitchen and the living room. Sadie leaned across the card table and kissed the boys' smooth faces and whispered, "I missed you all so much."

Later, during cocktail hour, Alice returned Becca to the living room, freshly bathed, powdered, and dressed in a white nightgown. "Time to say good night, Becca," said Alice.

Edward lured her to the sofa and bounced Becca on his knee, singing, "Little Becca-roo went boo-hoo. Her daddy took a ride in his big choo-choo." This act roused laughs from everyone, and Becca begged for more attention, alternating between Edward's knee and Sadie's lap. Sadie sensed Becca's curiosity about this new woman trying to hold on to her. Becca resisted her cuddles. Sadie knew her thin body was no match for Alice's plump softness.

"It's time for bed, sweetheart," Alice said, standing at the bottom of the stairs.

Becca scampered off the couch. Sadie watched her leave, occupying herself with the bowl of mixed nuts and crackers while Bunny stood to mix their second drink in his silver cocktail shaker.

If Becca had changed the most physically, Sadie saw a drastic difference in Thomas's personality. He wasn't silly or affectionate but glanced at her accusingly, as if he took her disappearance personally. Sadie pointed to her paintings and came up with a story about art school and influenza, a long recovery and an awful train strike, praying a combination of all these vague tales might satisfy him.

After dinner on Eden's back porch, with mosquitoes and june bugs buzzing around the lantern, Bunny gathered Sadie in his arms.

She stiffened. "Bunny, please," she said, pushing him away.

"Darling, I've missed you."

"If it weren't for your bruised ego, I wouldn't be a stranger in my own home."

"You're not a stranger, and I was only doing what I was told was best."

"Bunny, who should decide what's best? You should have come for me."

"Sadie, I was struggling, too. The P and E lost everything. We almost lost everything. If Kitty hadn't taken us in at Lancaster Fells—"

"But, Bunny, I missed so much."

"And, luckily, in May, the government placed large orders with US Steel to build warships, so the P and E should have a steady stream of revenue for a while. I restructured the bank debt. I sold off . . ."

She stopped listening. All he could do was calculate assets and liabilities.

Later, in their bed, once Bunny had fallen asleep, Sadie slipped out from under the coverlet and crept down the long second-floor corridor. She opened Thomas's bedroom door and stood on the threshold for several minutes, then made her way to Robert and Edward, finishing by Becca's crib. When would this little girl allow herself to be held? She adored her sleeping stillness and innocence, the moonlight glowing on her skin. She lost track of how long she'd stood alone like that, but the result was her rising late the next morning and arriving at the breakfast table about an hour after Alice had shooed Robert and Edward out the door in their starched tennis whites.

Thomas had given up on sports. Bunny had explained that his medication interfered with his moods. "I want to stay at home," he said to Sadie over breakfast, "and read with you." Sadie hugged him around the shoulder and sat down next to him at the table. Alice brought her a cup of tea while Becca crawled after a ball on the floor. Sadie had to pinch herself. She was finally home. "Where are Robert and Edward?" she asked.

"You might not remember," said Alice. "Tennis clinic at eight."

"Right," said Sadie, stirring her tea. There was so much she had forgotten about their days, their lessons, their playdates. She watched Alice at the stove, deftly stirring a pot of soup while preparing a chicken for roasting, Becca playing at her feet. Alice fed her children and was the one to dress them in clean clothing. She knew them inside and out and had been dependable, even if her discipline was a little lax.

"Thank you, Alice," Sadie said.

Alice turned from her place at the sink. "Ma'am?"

"I want to thank you for taking care of my children."

"Of course," Alice said, nodding.

"It means an awful lot to me," Sadie said, taking a sip of tea.

"But, you see, I'm back now, and I'd like to establish more order."

"Order?"

"Becca needs to be on a more regular schedule."

"All right," Alice said, turning back to the stove.

"She needs to nap after lunch and go to bed by seven P.M. She was up awfully late last night."

"Well, it was a special occasion," said Alice, stirring the soup.

"And," Sadie said, with an extra measure of authority in her tone, "please take care to keep her out of the sun. She's got the Thompson complexion and can get quite a burn."

"Yes, ma'am," Alice said, her voice tightening.

After their tennis lessons, Edward and Robert remained outdoors. They rigged jumps for their bicycles, built a tree house, and found ways to make their small skiff run faster. They even had leftover energy for concocting practical jokes and setting off fireworks. Sadie shook her head at the sight of them rigging a rope swing off the tree house. She complained to Bunny that they were running wild.

"They're going to kill themselves! Somebody needs to discipline them!" Sadie said, finding Bunny in his study. He was always there, huddled over a stack of papers.

"I probably should have stayed in Pittsburgh for the summer; there is so much to do."

Sadie looked at him, crestfallen. "But I guess there was the small matter of bringing me home. And making sure I'm suitably maternal." She cringed at the sound of insecurity in her voice.

"Oh, Sadie, please. Don't be so sensitive." She saw the dark circles under his eyes and softened.

Sadie also wondered about Bunny's withdrawal from the Long Harbor social frenzy. Invitations still arrived at the house, but now Bunny ignored them. There had been no sign of the Butterfields, either. It wasn't until she spoke to Emily Notman that she realized what they were up against.

"We can have lunch at the club, but that might be too public," Emily said on the phone. "Why don't you come over to the house instead?"

As they sat at her kitchen table, eating sliced tomatoes, Emily confirmed that Sadie and Bunny had been the center of the town's gossip.

"I asked him where you'd gone off to, and I wasn't going to give up until he gave me an answer. Well, he went on about you recuperating. He said you nearly died delivering Becca. That you had 'female problems.' Then he got all flustered like men do when it comes to talking about female parts. He would never even tell me *where* I could write to you."

Sadie was silent; then she asked, "Was there anything else people were talking about?"

"Well, that Bunny had to sell most of his assets and crowd your entire family into Lancaster Fells."

"Yes, he did that." Sadie nodded. "Was there any talk about him and Maud Butterfield?"

"Oh, sweetheart, I don't think you have anything to worry about there. No, she's been spending her time in Newport. Absolutely not."

"You'd tell me the truth?"

"Of course I would! No, Bunny behaved himself. I was just so concerned about you," Emily said with a loving smile.

Sadie squeezed her friend's hand. She would never tell her where she'd been, although she knew Emily was smart enough to imagine. "Let's not speak of it again," she said. "I'm back now, and that's all that matters."

Chapter 19

LONG HARBOR, RHODE ISLAND
Thursday, July 2, 2000

S arah flipped her sunglasses down over her eyes and slipped a hand under her T-shirt. "Hang in there, little one," she whispered, rubbing her stomach, inhaling the perfume of the Oriental lilies, and admiring the violet wisteria hanging on the pergola overhead.

She sank into the wicker chaise, watching the sun shimmer on the water. Her eyelids grew heavier as the sun's warmth tempted her to sleep. Her breathing deepened, and her arm twitched at her side. The fright of her fall had faded; she wished only that the doctor could give her a definitive answer that everything would be all right. Instead, he uttered a phrase she always dreaded: "We'll have to wait and see."

She allowed herself to enter new territory, mulling over potential names in her head. For boys, she liked Chase and Dylan, then figured they could be girls' names as well. She tried different combinations of first names and middle names. She would definitely give her child a middle name. She didn't have one herself and had always wished for one. Her mother had said that by the time she came up with a first name that made everyone happy, she was exhausted.

Just before Sarah surrendered to full-fledged sleep, the distant sound of her mother coughing and the scuffle of her slippers on the hardwood floor reined her back in. She opened her eyes, supposing the moment for them to talk had finally come. She took a long sip of water in an effort to wash the sleepiness from her head. The footsteps grew closer, eventually stopping at the screen door.

"*There* you are," her mother said, in an exasperated tone that was all too familiar to Sarah.

"Hi, Mom," she answered, stiffening her back and craning her neck around.

The wicker lounge next to Sarah's squeaked as her mother flopped down into it. The sight of her still wearing that awful robe, with her greasy hair piled high on her head, was disheartening. Rachel had also been a single mother, and Sarah couldn't help comparing their situations. She would do it deliberately, whereas her mother had been divorced at thirty-two and had never let go of the scars of her hasty marriage.

"What's this about you falling?" her mother asked. "Lilly mentioned it in the midst of her cleaning rampage."

"Oh, I was up on a ladder, deadheading. I fell backwards, and you know Lilly—she wanted to take me to the hospital, just to be safe." Sarah knew she should tell her mother about the baby's heartbeat and the placenta, but the thought of it exhausted her.

Her mother seemed satisfied with that brief explanation, wiping perspiration from her brow with the sleeve of her robe. "Ugh, it's hot for June. I guess this global-warming thing might be real after all. Hey, do you know why Lilly's going gangbusters with the vacuum?"

Sarah was familiar with her mother's tendency to engage in a good bit of small talk before broaching the more important topic. She would go along with it, hopeful the sharing of bits of intelligence would help to smooth things over.

"It's because she just learned that, in addition to Andrew's family, Aunt Ruth, Uncle Thomas, and Aunt Carol are all coming this weekend."

"They are? Why am I always the last to know?"

"Gran just told us at breakfast this morning."

"So, when do the Brits arrive?" Rachel asked.

"I think Gran said that Jimmy would drive up to Boston to meet their flight tomorrow afternoon."

"Well, one more day of peace, at least."

"And Gran wants to have a cocktail party on Saturday before the fireworks. Kind of a welcome-back for Uncle Andrew."

"Really?" her mother asked in a curious, albeit sarcastic, tone. The resentment her mother harbored for her uncle was never far from the surface. Sarah had listened to countless complaints about Uncle Andrew's being the favorite, even though she found it hard to imagine Gran playing favorites.

"She wants to invite some of Uncle Andrew's old crowd."

Her mother rolled her eyes.

Sarah was not surprised by her mother's reaction. She knew what her mother thought of her uncle's "crowd." They had been the popular and athletic ones, the boys who drank beer on the beach, who stuck with tennis and golf lessons until they mastered both. Her mother said Andrew had been handed more trophies in his sweaty tennis whites than she could stomach. He still carried the mantle of club champion, even though his victories had occurred back in the days of white tennis balls and wooden rackets. And the worst thing, according to her mother, was that Gran and Poppy took so much pride in all those trophies. Having an athletically accomplished child seemed to raise their stock in Long Harbor. Her mother said she used to stay home, smoking cigarettes out her bedroom window, while the others attended the awards banquets at the club.

Despite her mother's disdain, Sarah had a soft spot for Uncle Andrew and Aunt Camilla. During Camilla's first-ever visit to Eden, she and Andrew had been the ones to whisk Sarah away from the drama of her parents' final knockdown fight. They had taken her for ice cream and then for a sail, anchoring Uncle Edward's old sailboat near one of the sand bars created by the 1938 hurricane, where they swam off the bow.

"Come with us, Sarah," Camilla had offered at breakfast. Sarah had been clutching her spoon, pushing the remaining Cheerios around a surface of milk, hopeful that the fighting the night before hadn't been as bad as she'd thought. Her parents' shouts had woken her up. She strained to hear what was happening, then stuck her thumbs into her ears to block out the anger.

Sarah had always blamed herself for her parents' fighting. In fifth-grade science class, they had studied the gestation periods of different mammals. An elephant carried its baby in its womb for twenty-two months (the longest period for any mammal), compared with the human gestation period of nine months. These scientific facts had never been presented to Sarah in such a way. Sarah raised her hand, "But, Miss Clark, is it always nine months with humans? Can't it sometimes be six?" Tara Brandon, the only fifth grader to wear a bra, laughed at her. Miss Clark shot Tara a disciplinary stare and responded rather matter-of-factly, oblivious to Sarah's earth-shattering epiphany. "No, Sarah, it's always nine months' gestation in the case of a normal, healthy human."

Miss Clark continued the lesson, but Sarah didn't hear a thing. She double- and triple-checked the math on her fingers, but there were just six months between her parents' May wedding date and her November birth.

Sarah had asked her mother about it after school that afternoon, expecting an explanation that would erase all her doubts. Instead, her mother had become defensive. "Sarah, I never spoke to you about it because it shouldn't matter. If that pregnancy was devastating for anyone, it was me." She slammed her empty wineglass down on the counter. That was the moment when Sarah realized she was the "problem," not the blessing her grandmother always told her she was.

As she lay on her chaise lounge now, with an embryo growing inside her, Sarah attempted to relate to how her mother must have felt, unwed and pregnant all those years ago. Yes, there was trepidation, but to create life, it felt miraculous. And she hadn't turned out so bad—why couldn't her mother be grateful?

Her mother cleared her throat and shifted the conversation. "When you pulled into the drive, your grandmother and I were just drinking coffee in the kitchen. I was totally taken by surprise.

'Guess what? I'm pregnant!' No hint of remorse, not apologetic at all."

"Apologetic? It's not like I committed a crime. It's unfortunate timing, yes, but I can deal with it."

Her mother's arms trembled. "I just thought you might show me some respect, or at least sensitivity to your grandmother's generation. Maybe in your world this sort of thing is commonplace, but in places like Long Harbor, it is still considered verboten!"

Sarah shriveled from her mother's anger and fought back tears. She couldn't believe the direction of this conversation. Not "Sarah, you'll have some tough times ahead, but I'll be there for you." Not "How are you feeling?" Not even "I was there myself, and hey, it didn't turn out so badly."

Her mother wasn't through, either: "I think you were scared to call me—always running into the arms of your grandmother."

"Mom, I don't see why you're taking this personally. I had no idea you would get so upset. I'm not a kid. I'm almost thirty, and it's my life."

Sarah knew her mother wanted an apology—that was how their fights usually went—but she wouldn't budge this time. "Mom, can't you please just accept this situation?"

No reply. A standoff. As she studied the dark circles under her mother's eyes, a wave of pity tugged at her heart. She might have folded, offered some conciliatory words, but the clamor of the French doors opening interrupted them.

"There you are!" her grandmother shrieked. "My goodness! You had me so worried. Mary drove me to the hospital as fast as she could. By the time I found a nurse, she told me you had already come home! What happened? Where's Lilly?" Sarah pictured little old Mary Bell driving a speedy thirty miles per hour through town. Despite it all, her grandmother never perspired. She still had a crisp crease in her slacks. The purse she carried matched her shoes.

"I fell off a ladder while I was gardening. Lilly took me to the emergency room. The doctor ordered me on bed rest for a while.

Something about the placenta." Sarah blurted out the last parts, staring at her mother.

"Oh dear," her grandmother said, frowning.

Her mother shook her head in disbelief, squinting at the horizon. Sarah tried to see if there was some compassion there but was blinded by the sunlight reflecting off the ocean. The shimmering light had the effect of blurring the line between the dark blue of the water and the light blue of the sky.

"Well, don't you have all the luck?" Her mother finally spoke. "A doctor actually told you to stay in bed?"

"For a few weeks," Sarah said. It was the story of her life, her mother finding sarcasm in everything. She turned toward her grandmother, who had a look of sad bewilderment on her face. Sarah offered up a small nugget of positive news. "But the ultrasound showed the baby has a strong heartbeat."

"Well, we have that to be grateful for," her grandmother said, clutching her purse in her lap. "Does your health insurance cover emergency-room visits?" she added. It hadn't even occurred to Sarah, and the question, combined with all her other insecurities, made her feel even less prepared. She slouched in the chaise between her mother and grandmother, aware that neither of them would be able to help.

Chapter 20

LONG HARBOR, RHODE ISLAND
1931

B ecause Becca was so much younger than her brothers, she often rambled through the house alone, playing under tables, in deep closets, or behind sofas. But the summer Nana and Opa came to Eden, she had an ally in the guest bedroom.

The excitement began when the whole family traveled to Long Harbor from Pittsburgh on the train. Becca was thrilled upon boarding their fancy compartment, but as day turned to evening on the first day of the journey, the rhythm of the train lulled her into drowsiness. She sat next to her mother in the dining car, picking at the food on the fine china in front of them. She wasn't hungry anymore and turned her attention instead to rubbing the red velvet of the seat one way and then the next, making small swirls in the plush fabric.

The grown-up conversation bored her, although she took in the tones of the exchange. What she absorbed was the togetherness of three generations traveling and the jumbled emotions between her father and his parents. She eyed her brothers in the booth across the aisle, playing cards. Edward eventually got bored and sprayed the deck all over the place. Thomas shouted he would never play with Edward again. Alice rushed down the aisle and scolded them. She said it was time for bed and shuttled them down the aisle to where porters converted their seats into horizontal sleeping berths with starched white linens and warm woolen blankets.

From her makeshift bed, Becca still heard the comforting droning of the grown-ups' voices. "Some way to travel?" her father said. Nana replied, in her unmistakable accent, "Vell, Bernhard, it is like nothing I could have imagined. When your papa and I came from Germany, we traveled like animals packed in a crate. This is all so much, I can't imagine how expensive it must be."

"Mama, don't worry. We all share track, do each other favors."

"What on earth do people do all day in this place? There is no work? Just beach and sand?" Nana asked.

Her mother's high giggle. "Not to mention tennis and cocktails."

"Mother, there are many delightful things to do," her father said. Nana sighed heavily.

"Anna," Opa said gruffly, "everyone is making sacrifices, so we live with Bernhard and his family now. If traveling to the shore for the summer is your biggest problem, count your blessings."

Opa spoke again. "Yes, this is wonderful, Bernhard. Who could imagine—we will wake up tomorrow in New York City. The last time your mother and I were there was when we passed through Ellis Island."

Her mother's voice was directly above Becca now as her hand reached down to stroke her tangle of curls. "Good night, everyone, and, Anna, don't worry. There will be much for you to do. You can help me decorate Becca's bedroom, something frilly for a little girl, and I'm sure Bunny will need your help in the garden."

* * *

In Long Harbor, Becca woke up much earlier than the rest of the family. But she always knew Alice would be standing at the stove down in the kitchen. She ate her oatmeal early, then liked to play "store" in the butler's pantry while Alice cleaned up after her brothers. The pantry was a long, narrow passageway that separated the kitchen from the dining room, with floor-to-ceiling cabinets of china and crystal. She jumped at the sound of the bell ringing near the ceiling. It could be an alarm in the fire station—

time to suit up and board the fire engines! Becca tried to swing the large door separating the two rooms. "Alice, it's the bell!" she called urgently, then backing up into the pantry to avoid the large door swinging back and knocking her over.

"Ooh, Becca, sweet, you are just going to pinch those wee fingers of yours again," Alice beckoned, catching the door. "Come out here with me while I finish the silver." The bell sounded again, and this time Alice noticed.

"My goodness," Alice said, peering up at the small red light on the signal box. "And I bet I know who's calling us again. Guest room one. Your grandmother."

Becca accompanied Alice upstairs. Alice knocked lightly, before pushing the bedroom door fully open. "Good morning, Mrs. Meister. How are you feeling?"

"I am the same. I ring the bell for you, Alice, because Shmuel did not bring up any breakfast today." Becca held on to Alice's apron tightly, stretching on her tiptoes to see over the high bed. Her nana looked kindly back at her. "Becca, go find a book for us to read."

Her nana wasn't feeling well and hadn't left her bedroom since she had arrived at Eden. Her mother told Becca that when her nana was resting, she wasn't allowed to knock on the door.

Alice pleaded with Becca to stay put in her room during her naptime. "Please, Becca. I'll come get you when it's over. I don't want your mother to be cross with me."

But Becca got bored, thought maybe she'd been forgotten. It had happened before. She opened her door a crack and watched. After a few minutes, she walked down the hallway and decided to look for Alice. She headed down the back stairs to the kitchen and was concentrating on taking quiet steps when her mother almost ran into her, coming the other way. "Becca! What are you doing?"

"I'm up from my nap, Ma."

"Well, you *are* up, now, aren't you?" her mother said, checking her wristwatch.

"Why doesn't Nana leave her bedroom? She doesn't seem sick to me."

"No, she doesn't, does she?" her mother said in an irritated voice. "Nana is just happier in her bedroom, that's all. It's nothing for you to worry about."

Her mother took her by the hand and led her back up the stairs and down the long corridor toward the boys' rooms. Robert was counting coins on his floor, but he stood up straight at the sight of his mother.

"Ah, Robert. Be a love and take your sister outside to play. Alice must be at the market, and I've got to lie down. Try to keep her clean."

Stuffing the coins in his pocket, he took Becca's hand and led her down the porch steps to the yard. "Tell me about the bunny family, Robert." He smiled at her, repeating their favorite story, that bunnies lived in their gardens and that if they were very quiet, they might find the hole leading to the animals' big underground house. Eventually, he took her around to the kitchen door and sat her on the grass. He emerged with a hand full of ginger snaps as Edward rode up on his bike.

"Robert! I've been looking for you! The fish are biting like mad. Grab the rods."

Robert hurried Becca into the kitchen door and told her to go find Nana. "She'll tell you a story—now go on." But she lingered in the quiet of the hallway, listening to the gulls squawk outside and feeling the warm pile of the rug under her bare feet. She wandered farther down the hallway to her nana's room and cracked open the door. She moved a wooden chair over to the bed and climbed up. Her nana was awake, propped up on pillows, writing a letter.

"Will you look who's here! My love!" Her nana's face brightened.

Becca handed a ginger snap to her nana, who smoothed the crumbs off the duvet. "Are you all alone? Is your mother home?"

"She's resting."

Her nana let out a *humph*, then brushed the hair from Becca's face, before entertaining her with stories of when she was a little girl in Germany. "My sister—your namesake, Rebecca— and I would sneak to the neighbor's yard and pick apples. . . ."

Later, her nana taught her to count to ten in German. *"Ein, zwei, drei, vier . . ."*

* * *

In the hallway outside her parents' bedroom was an antique secretary chest in which Becca hid pictures. She liked to open and close the small drawers, putting messages in the various letter slots. She pretended she was stationed at the front desk of a busy hotel and accepted letters and messages for important guests. She used a pad of paper and a pen and a make-believe telephone receiver that she spoke through. Sorting messages in the various compartments one afternoon, she heard her father raise his voice in the master bedroom and then her mother's icy response. "Well, given the way your mother and Alice indulge her, not to mention *your* doting, consider me a counterbalance."

There were some things she couldn't make out before her mother said, "I'm tired of you making all the big decisions in this family without me."

Her father's deep voice bellowed, "Sadie, you know how the boys put you on edge."

Becca put together the pieces. Her father had made arrangements for Edward and Robert to attend boarding school in New Hampshire the following fall, the same time Thomas would be heading off for his freshman year at Yale. Even though her parents' arguing worried her, Becca felt a rush of excitement when Edward and Robert confirmed it. Mother and Father all to herself!

That August, Becca watched from the periphery as her mother folded clothes into steamer trunks. She offered to help, but her mother, with tears rolling down her cheeks, said that she and Alice could manage. All month, her mother made lists of what each boy might need for nine months. She stocked up on medication for Thomas, as well as shirts, ties, blazers, dress pants, warm overcoats, scarves, hats, and gloves. She collected Edward and Robert's sporting equipment. She folded their socks and packed several pairs of shoes.

"I'm not leaving you, Mommy," Becca said softly from the hallway.

"I can't believe it's over. It was just yesterday they needed me."

"I need you, Mommy," Becca said, with a tremor in her voice. Her mother turned her head and smiled weakly from her seat on the floor.

"I know you do, sweetheart," her mother whispered. But Becca wandered, crestfallen, into the kitchen. Alice seemed to read her mind. "Now, Becca, dear, you mustn't be upset by your mother; she's very tired and worried about your brothers."

"I know," said Becca.

Becca overheard her father insist that there was no need to inform the dean of the college about Thomas's condition. "Don't worry, Sadie—Thomas will make it through just fine." Becca heard her mother slam the door to her sitting room.

There was a picture in the back hallway of her mother swimming in the waves with Thomas. She had long red hair, down to the middle of her back. Becca barely recognized the woman in the picture. Over the years, Becca pieced together the timeline of her mother's transformation. Robert told her that when he and Edward and Robert were little, their mother had put on puppet shows. Edward recalled baking cakes and cookies together and Mother letting them take long, bubble-filled baths. She couldn't imagine their mother so carefree. She asked Robert what had happened.

"She went away after you were born and came back different," he said.

Becca stood by her mother's side in the driveway at Eden when her father left with Thomas, and again a week later, when he took Edward and Robert to New Hampshire. Her mother stood up straight, reached out to squeeze each of her brothers' shoulders tightly, gave them light kisses on the cheek. She walked stoically back into the house each time the car drove away, but Becca knew her mother cried in private.

Chapter 21

LONG HARBOR, RHODE ISLAND

Thursday, July 2, 2000

Becca heard the Lincoln's horn toot a rough rendition of "Take Me Out to the Ball Game" as it climbed the driveway. She smiled at the tradition that had begun with her father and brothers, seeing who could be more clever with the syncopation of their horns when arriving with special guests. It was charming that Jimmy, her longtime handyman, had picked up on the custom, or maybe it was Andrew, reaching over to the steering wheel and pounding out the tune on the horn himself.

She felt a pang of excitement, placing her knife and cutting board in the sink. Wiping her hands on her apron, Becca looked with satisfaction at the big clock on the kitchen wall.

The dog perked up his head from below. "All right, Hen," Becca said. "We're right on schedule." Her purse sat on the telephone table, a few short steps away. She ran a comb through her hair. She opened her compact mirror, applied a quick dab of lipstick, and was out the kitchen door, calling over her shoulder, "Lilly, will you run up and tell Rachel they're here?"

It was unlikely that Rachel, the one who always kept her windows open, hadn't already heard the car's horn, but she always needed extra prodding. Back in the day, her father had insisted his entire brood line up to welcome houseguests, and Becca clung to the tradition even as their numbers dwindled. It certainly didn't help that Sarah was on bed rest.

Becca pushed the screen door open and squinted into the brightness. There was her boy, sitting in the passenger seat of the Lincoln, the window rolled down, smiling. He climbed out of the car and jogged a couple steps toward her. "Oh, Andrew, dear, marvelous to have you—just marvelous, really," she said, her arms stretched out wide.

Becca embraced her son, then held him at arm's length, looking up and taking in his face. The number of wrinkles around the corners of his eyes had increased, and she had to catch her breath at his likeness to Dan. His fair complexion, piercing green eyes, and thinning red hair evoked not only her deceased husband but something of her brothers as well. It was eerie but also a lovely reminder of the men in her life.

Andrew didn't pull back from her prolonged stare. Did he see her as grayer and smaller, too? Eden rarely changed, after all; maybe he expected its timelessness to extend to her. The last time he had pulled into Eden's driveway, Dan would have been bent over in the vegetable garden, wearing his wide-brimmed hat, happily plucking tomatoes. Now it was just Becca, an old woman, and the gardens, left to Sarah's feeble efforts.

Becca kissed Andrew's wife, Camilla, and her grandchildren, Walter and Sally. Sally was tall and leggy like her mother, with long, dirty-blond hair. Walter hadn't sprouted yet, was still pudgy in the face and stomach, just as Andrew had been at that age. Lilly emerged from the kitchen. "Oh, Andrew, let me take a look at you!" She planted a kiss on his cheek.

"Lilly, are you keeping my mother out of trouble?" he teased. "You know, the only reason I've come back is to make sure you ladies haven't gone wild with no men to keep an eye on things." Everybody laughed. Andrew's joviality had served him well. He knew just when a punch line was needed.

* * *

Becca ushered them all into the house, where they settled in around the kitchen table. "It's quite warm here," said Camilla, "compared with what we left in London."

"Yes, they're forecasting the heat wave to continue through the weekend," Becca said.

Lilly poured iced tea, then put some sliced apples and cheddar cheese on the table. Camilla nodded approvingly at the healthy snacks, and Walter and Sally helped themselves.

"Aren't Rachel and Sarah here?" asked Camilla.

"Poor Sarah isn't feeling well. And Rachel . . . I think she must be upstairs," said Becca, searching Lilly's face for an indication. Lilly shrugged apologetically.

Camilla nodded and pursed her lips, making her long nose and angular features even more severe. She was not aging well, the skin around her neck and chin already slackening.

Andrew asked about Becca's weekly bridge game and her charity work, tiptoeing around the fact that the house seemed empty. His cheerful voice signaled he didn't want to venture to the sad topic of his father's passing.

"So, what's new around here?" Andrew asked.

"Not much new in Long Harbor. Things stay the same."

"Oh, there's always some scuttlebutt, Mother." Andrew winked.

"Nothing really, Andrew." Becca wondered why the persistence.

"Nothing we should discuss?"

"No . . . ," Becca said, with a questioning lilt in her voice. What was he getting at? What did he know? The triviality of their small talk was ridiculous, but they had just arrived and it was too early to broach all there really was to discuss.

"Mother, Uncle Thomas called and said he and Carol were coming for the weekend."

Aha, so this was it. "He called you?" Becca tried not to react.

"Yes, he did." Andrew nodded, deftly conveying that he was in the know. "He wanted to tell me there was some business that needs looking after. Said we needed to see how we might salvage things around here. Mom, why didn't you tell me how tight things have gotten?"

Becca sat upright. "There was no need, Andrew. I can manage my own affairs."

"Well, it affects me. And Rachel."

"Andrew, please."

Was her financier son really sitting across the kitchen table, flashing a gold Rolex and questioning the size of his inheritance? And to speak to Thomas behind her back? Becca made an effort to remain calm. They had barely arrived, after all, and the children were at the table. She turned away from Andrew to face the others.

"Your aunt Ruth will be coming for the weekend as well," she said, taking back control of the conversation.

Walter asked, "Who's Aunt Ruth?"

Andrew answered, "Ruth was my uncle Robert's wife, Walter. Lord, I haven't seen Ruth in years. She wasn't at Dad's funeral, was she?"

"No she wasn't able to come."

Sally swept her hair away from her face and asked, "Gran, do you have an Internet connection here?"

Camilla rolled her eyes. "Sally, you'll survive a long weekend without it."

The screen door slammed, and Jimmy lumbered through the kitchen with luggage in both arms. Andrew stood up to help.

Sally snapped at her mother, "This was your plan all along, to make sure I couldn't be in touch with my friends!" She picked a shred of apple skin from her metal braces.

"Oh, Sally, your friends will still be there when we return from holiday."

"Ugh, what do you know?"

Lilly put her arm around Sally's shoulder. "Let's go upstairs. I'll show you where you'll be sleeping." They walked slowly past Sadie's famous picture gallery hanging along the back stairs. Most children loved the old photos, but Sally breezed right past them. Becca followed closely behind with Camilla and Walter. She stopped on the top step and pointed. "There's your father as a baby. Have you ever seen this picture before?"

"I saw it last time I was here, Gran." Walter showed no interest, either. Becca inhaled deeply. It had been a while since there had been adolescents in the house.

When the four of them came upon the door to Sarah's room, Becca poked her head in and said, "Look who's here!"

"Hi, Sally!" said Sarah, sitting up in her bed. "Oh, and Aunt Camilla and Walter! Welcome!" The three of them crammed into the doorway.

"Can we come kiss you, love? You aren't contagious, are you?" Camilla asked.

"Of course I'm not contagious!" Sarah said, with a wide smile on her face. "I'm just pregnant!" Camilla stopped in her tracks.

"Had a bad fall, and now I'm on bed rest for a while." Sarah put her hands up in the air and shrugged.

There was an awkward silence, before Camilla and Sally said "Wow" at the same time.

Walter added, "Congratulations!" Camilla forced a smile, walking to the bed to kiss Sarah, with an air more of condolence than of congratulations. Becca noticed Camilla's raised eyebrow and a smirk in her daughter's direction, but Sally didn't return her mother's glance, seeming rather nonplussed by the announcement.

"So," Sally asked, pointing to Sarah's belly, "like, who's the dad? Are you getting married?"

"Sally!" said Camilla.

"No, it's okay. I don't mind talking about it," Sarah said. "He's this guy I was dating for a long time, but now, well, we've sort of broken up."

"Really? Wow, *that* sucks."

Becca watched her granddaughters' exchange. Even though they were fifteen years apart in age, they would always be comrades of the same generation.

"Well, pretty cool that you're having it," Sally went on. "I mean, most of the girls I know who get pregnant have abortions."

Camilla put her hand to her forehead. Sally seemed to relish her mother's discomfort. "I think you'd be a cool mom," she said.

"Thanks," said Sarah. "So, Lilly told me you'll be sleeping on the porch. Maybe I'll join you one night. This heat is suffocating; plus, I love hearing the waves crash as I'm falling asleep."

"My biology teacher told us it's similar to what a fetus hears in utero. You know, there's this whir of the mother's blood circulating and the rhythm of the mother's heartbeat, which sounds like being at the beach. Wow, I can't believe I just remembered that—how random."

Becca was dumbstruck by Sally's fluency on the topic, and by her feistiness. She was certainly no longer the timid girl Becca remembered.

"Why don't we get our things sorted and get cleaned up?" said Camilla, herding her children toward the door. Becca was walking down the hallway ahead of them when she heard Jimmy yell, "There!"

And then Andrew's voice chimed in, "Now! You almost got him!"

Becca began to walk more quickly.

Rachel opened her bedroom door. "What's going on?" she asked.

Andrew was in the blue guest room, swinging a tennis racket, while Jimmy clutched the handle of a broom like a baseball bat. "Shut the door!" Andrew shouted.

"Well, hello, brother," said Rachel.

"Hello, Rachel. Sorry, now's not a good time. Could you please shut the door? Goddamn it. I will not hear the end of it if Camilla sees a bat in our room!"

"For heaven's sake," said Rachel, "hand me that towel. I'll catch him. You haven't been here five minutes, Andrew, and already the drama's begun."

Andrew stopped swinging the racket and Jimmy stood still with the broom in the middle of the room while Rachel held a towel in one hand and stealthily followed the bat with her eyes. It flew in frantic circles, avoiding the walls and the light fixtures. It swooped, and they all ducked before it ascended, again, toward the ceiling. It made a dozen dizzying laps around the room and finally landed on a curtain to rest. Becca could see the little creature's body inflate and deflate rapidly, could practically hear it hissing, as they all held their breath. Then Rachel snuck up behind it, snapped the towel quickly, and swatted the bat to the floor. She pounced over its stunned body like a cat and threw the towel down on top of it.

"Now, Jimmy, just scoop up the whole bundle and set it free outside," Rachel said.

"Impressive," said Jimmy, following her orders and scurrying out the door with the towel bundled tightly in his hands. Becca didn't quite know what to say next, standing in a room that her adult children had upended. She considered her offspring for a moment: a perturbed son, reaching in his pocket for a neatly pressed handkerchief while sweat beaded on his forehead, and a wild daughter, her hands balled into angry fists.

Camilla poked her head around the doorsill. "Is this where we were meant to stay?"

Becca sighed. "Not to worry. We'll switch things around." Andrew and Camilla would have to move to the big guest room now and Thomas and Carol would stay here. She could just picture their irritated faces.

Chapter 22

LONG HARBOR, RHODE ISLAND
1938

Bunny slipped a silver letter opener through the day's mail. A creamy envelope had arrived from Kitty. He bit his lip while he read it. There was a smallpox scare in Pittsburgh, and the start of school was delayed three weeks. Kitty was concerned that she might have been exposed, but her symptoms were mild so far. They should not worry but should postpone their return to Pittsburgh until further notice.

He didn't know whether to share the letter with Sadie. It was addressed to both of them, but bad news could agitate her. Then again, if anything happened to Kitty, she would never forgive him.

"I'll catch a train tomorrow. Can you book it?" Sadie said, the letter still in her hand.

"Tomorrow? Sadie, are you sure it's wise?" Bunny asked.

She didn't blink. "I'm all she has."

Bunny wasn't sure sudden changes were good for Sadie, but he wouldn't mind staying behind in Long Harbor with Becca. Mr. P. and Alice always took very good care of them, and why not experience one of those famous New England autumns he had always heard so much about? He would schedule some fishing excursions and plenty of golf, and delighted in the idea of puttering around his garden.

* * *

Not long after classes began at Yale, Robert decided to return to Eden for the weekend. He had never been an enthusiastic student, and the mention of eking out one last round of golf with his father was too tempting. But when Bunny awoke to dark clouds on Saturday morning, he was afraid their plans to tee off were dashed. Becca's face brightened at the breakfast table, and she asked if that meant they could stay home together and play. Mr. P. said he would make a warm, hearty stew for their dinner, and Alice announced she'd use the day to can the bounty of tomatoes from the garden.

"Daddy, can you, Robert, and I play cards? Alice can be the fourth!" Becca was persistent.

"Becca, your mother left instructions for you to read." Bunny wagged his finger at her and then, in his best schoolmarm impression, continued, "Don't think you can play around here all day just because fourth grade has been delayed."

"But Bobby's home!" She giggled.

"He'll be sleeping for a while. Go on up and grab your books and bring them down to my study," Bunny said. "You can read on the sofa while I catch up on some work. Afterward, we'll have a gin rummy marathon."

A big grin spread across Becca's face, exposing the gap where she was missing a front tooth. She darted from the kitchen to gather her books.

Bunny was absorbed in his newspapers, passing occasional glances at Becca on the sofa, and didn't hear the wind pick up. When he walked into the living room to investigate just before lunchtime, he saw waves cresting above the height of the dunes. Sand and dune grass were blowing everywhere. He ran up to the second floor and went directly to the sleeping porch, from which he could get a better view.

"Jesus Christ," he muttered, watching the black sky closing in. He hollered for Robert, Alice and Mr. P.

Robert was wiping sleep from his eyes as he opened the door to his room, confused by all the tumult.

"Robert, put some clothes on. Looks like we're in for a big storm."

Bunny rushed back downstairs to his study and gathered up Becca, book in hand, with an afghan over her legs. He went to his desk and picked up the telephone. Looking for information on the weather, he dialed the golf club, but there was no answer. He turned on the radio. Despite the crackly reception, he deciphered bits about a massive storm coming up the coast. The power was knocked out in Manhattan above Fifty-Ninth Street, the subway was flooded, and trees had been uprooted in Central Park. The sound of the wind whistling through Eden's shutters made it impossible to hear the broadcast, so he turned the dial off. The lamp on his desk flickered, and outside the window two of his favorite trees bent almost ninety degrees in submission to the wind.

"Daddy, I'm scared," Becca whimpered.

"Don't worry, sweetheart—we'll be fine," Bunny said, feigning calm.

He wanted to put his new Cadillac in the garage at the bottom of the driveway to protect it from the falling branches. He settled his daughter at the kitchen table and wrapped the afghan around her shoulders. Just as he walked out the door, the rain deluged. He sprinted to the car and started it up, then rounded the circle in the driveway and headed the car into the garage. Just opening the large barn doors against the wind proved difficult. He propped the doors open with two boulders and pulled the car in. He was drenched, his shoes soaked through.

He struggled back to the house and gathered Becca in his arms again. "Okay, Princess. Good thing we're here to protect Eden from the storm." Becca blinked her eyes wide. Bunny headed upstairs to retrieve dry clothes from his room, and as he crossed through the living room, the waves broke over the dunes, just fifty feet from the house.

"Daddy, look!" cried Becca. He held her, captivated, then squeezed Becca hard as a gale-force wind gust blew out a windowpane in the dining room. Becca's shrieks mixed with the sound of glass breaking.

Bunny's mind raced, caught between a fear for their lives and the desire to protect his property. He hurried back to the kitchen, still carrying Becca, trying to think of comforting things to say along the way.

"Dad!" It was Robert, crouching by the large Garland range, trying to turn off the gas.

Bunny took Becca to the same interior wall and huddled next to Robert. He wasn't sure where they should go or what they should do. He called out, "Alice! Mr. P.!" once again.

"To the market," Becca whispered.

"What?" Bunny asked.

"Alice and Mr. P. went to the market to buy the meat for the stew."

"Ha," said Bunny, thinking how that morning at the breakfast table he had been tempted to break it to Mr. P. that he had never liked stew.

While he was considering their options, the large window by the kitchen table burst. The floor on which they huddled was now covered with glass, water, and sand. A rush of water forced them all up against the wall. He was momentarily blinded, his eyeglasses swept from his face, salt water filling his mouth and nose. Two feet of seawater sloshed above the linoleum floor. When he pulled his spectacles down from his forehead, he realized Becca was no longer next to him.

"Becca!" he screamed.

Her body was underwater, and another surge was headed their way. As Bunny struggled to his feet, he saw Robert hurdle across the kitchen floor and snatch up Becca by the slack in her collar. He hoisted his sister into his arms and against his chest. He thumped her on the back until she coughed up the seawater she had swallowed. Becca dug her face into the nape of Robert's neck. She clung to him with one arm, her soaking-wet book still pressed against her chest.

Bunny stood against his children, protecting their faces from blowing debris with the breadth of his back. Whipping wind, sand,

and shattered glass made it too dangerous to stay. Forcing his feet into a pair of gardening boots behind the kitchen door, Bunny grabbed jackets, although they were all soaked, and ushered his children out the door. They got to the road, Robert carrying Becca over one shoulder, and started jogging toward town. It was slow going against the wind and the sting of sand hitting their faces. Maybe they could seek shelter at the Atlantic. When they got to the crest of the hill overlooking the harbor and the hotels, it was apparent that those grand buildings had also fallen victim to the powerful storm.

"We should stay on high ground, Dad," Robert said.

"The golf club?" Bunny suggested.

"Too many flying branches."

Just then, a set of headlights approached them on the road. The driver stopped and reached over to unlatch the passenger door. "Get in!" he shouted.

It was Mary Thaw's son-in-law, heading on a last run to pick up some of Mary's elderly friends. She had spread the word that people could ride out the storm at her house, a large stone mansion on Long Harbor's highest ground.

Once they arrived at the Thaws', Bunny and Robert got Becca situated and then helped carry the older women into the house. Sitting on one of the kitchen chairs, dripping on their floor, Bunny felt like a coward for deserting Eden. He was fearful for Mr. P. and Alice, and then for Edward, who must have felt the storm's impact in New Haven.

One of the Thaw daughters handed Becca a dry set of clothes. "I don't know if these will fit you, sweetheart, but at least you'll be warm and dry." She handed a few things to Bunny and Robert as well. "Feel free to go upstairs and change," she said. "Oh dear, you're bleeding. Are you hurt?"

"Oh," said Bunny, unaware of his hands. "Just some scrapes. I'll be all right." He examined Becca's arms and legs. Miraculously, she was unscathed. Robert had a bruise on one cheek and a few cuts on his legs from the shards of glass.

The ballroom-size living room had cavernous fireplaces roaring with flames. Haggard people milled about. Damp clothing and blankets were strewn here and there, and Bunny recognized that even the most proper Long Harbor matrons were completely disheveled, huddling together. Old Mrs. Notman held court in one of the wing chairs while her eldest son poured her tea. One of her friends suggested they find some cards and start a bridge game.

The Thaws were fellow Pittsburgh natives, and their home was a replica of an Italianate villa nestled on a hill, overlooking the harbor. Ironically, the Long Harbor Founders had given Mrs. Thaw a hard time for veering so far off the accepted architectural path, but, in the end, if hadn't been for her foot-thick granite walls, they wouldn't have had a bunker during the storm.

From their perch on the hill, Bunny, Robert, Becca, and the others were able to see the destruction unfold. "Daddy, Daddy, look!" Becca cried.

It was Fort Point, a crescent-shaped isthmus of land framing the harbor, featuring a two-lane road and some of the community's most prominent homes. The rooflines were disappearing into the sea. The old women cried in horror. Becca hid her face in her father's chest as boats smashed up against docks and water flowed over the harbor's sea wall, which now seemed laughably low.

After the last house sank below the water, silent disbelief filled the room. The combination of a hurricane, the autumnal equinox, and a full moon had created actual tidal waves. In the middle of the quiet, Mr. Woodward began speaking in a soft, small voice. "It's worse than the destruction I witnessed during the Great War." He swallowed. "The knowledge that Long Harbor was here was always what kept me going." Tears streamed from his eyes. Bunny choked.

Following the devastation, panic set in. Mrs. Notman was desperate to be in touch with her family, but phones were no use and there was no way to send a wire. Power lines were down, trees were upturned, and roads were impassable. The Thaw sisters lit candles after dark, illuminating ashen faces. That night, Robert and Bunny curled next to Becca and tried to sleep on a corner of rug. He shuddered, remembering the state in which he had left Eden. He lay awake all night, listening to his neighbors' sobs and hushed conversations.

Toward dawn, a loud voice raised above the din. "You folks gonna run out of food real soon. Someone oughtta head on up to the golf club and raid that freezer before everything goes bad." Bunny jumped, praying he wasn't dreaming Mr. P.'s voice. He had never been so happy to see a man standing.

Becca ran into Mr. P.'s arms. "Where's Alice?" she asked. He had insisted Alice stay put at the grocer's in Westfield until he returned for her. He'd had to abandon the truck a quarter of a mile before he'd reached the village and walk through the wreckage.

Later that afternoon, once the wind had calmed, Bunny told Mr. P. he couldn't stand it any longer—he needed to see Eden for himself. After all the financial maneuvering he'd done in order to keep her, having her wash out to sea would be a cruel twist of fate.

"Robert, stay here with your sister."

"I think I should go with you, Dad."

They left Becca at the Thaws', and the three men walked the mile to Eden.

They made it to the base of the driveway. Even from there, the sound of the turbulent surf created a consistent din. They managed over downed branches, stopping at the battered garage. Bunny peered in what was left of the structure, hopeful they might have the use of the car. As he approached the front lawn and looked up at Eden, he was relieved to see her facade intact, but when he pushed open the kitchen door, he recoiled.

Eden's magnificent exposure to the sea was her downfall. The waves had crashed over the dunes and beat on her relentlessly. Even though her strong stone foundation had acted as a buttress against most of the tidal surge, the basement had filled with water. The majority of the windows had broken, letting in more sea- and rainwater. The back porch had come apart, and the sleeping porch on the second floor had collapsed. Seaweed was strewn across the living room furniture, sand covered the floors, and outside, Bunny's gardens were barely recognizable. He looked up and down the beach toward his neighbors' homes. The few houses that survived also had massive stone foundations, as well as sizable dunes around them, to buffer the ocean. But there was no sense to it; the spots of wreckage in Long Harbor appeared almost haphazard.

Bunny leaned back against a wall, his body shaking. He put his head in his hands and sank to the floor, sitting among shards of glass, sand, and kelp. It was not only his own loss that evoked such emotion, but the widespread destruction of Long Harbor. What would happen to this place?

After a few minutes, he felt Mr. P. patting his back.

"It's not pretty, Mr. Meister, but she's still standing."

"Yes, she is, P., yes, she is," said Bunny, standing straight, attempting to regain his composure.

"You'll have a chance to make her right again."

Mr. P. retrieved several portions of fish and meat from the big freezer in the kitchen. The men scoured the larder for anything else that was salvageable. Bunny went into his study to see what was left of his papers. There were a few inches of water on the floor surrounding his desk.

"C'mon, P., let's bring that food over to the Thaws'. It's not safe to stay here."

"Okay, boss."

"But, you're right, P. I'll rebuild her. I won't give up on Eden."

"We'll do it together," said Robert.

Later that night, one of the Long Harbor Founders appeared at the Thaws'. Everyone circled him, instantly recognizing somebody who'd emerged from "civilization."

"How widespread is the destruction?" they clamored.

"Has the news of the damage spread?"

"Is help on its way?"

He assured them that the roads were getting cleared and that aid would be coming quickly. People lowered their voices when they spoke of the death toll, fears about those out on boats or docks, and those unable to evacuate from their homes down on Fort Point. The full moon meant that it had been a very promising day for fishing, and some men, both commercial and sporting, had left before sunrise, never to return.

At dawn the next morning, sitting by the Thaws' large window, the one from which he had witnessed the storm's devastation, Bunny watched the sun rise orange into a clear violet sky. Not a cloud was visible, and the whistling wind had dulled. A flock of swallows dipped and soared above while a fox scurried across the Thaws' lawn. As the sun heated up, raindrops began to evaporate from the panes of glass and rays of light refracted against the water droplets into the colors of the rainbow.

* * *

New Haven also looked like a war zone after the storm. Robert got word from Edward that classes at Yale were canceled for two weeks. Bunny wanted Robert to return to his studies as soon as possible, but Robert refused to leave Long Harbor. He petitioned the dean for a leave of absence in order to assist in the aftermath of the tragedy. Bunny did send Becca and Alice back to Pittsburgh, however, after three weeks' time. Every able-bodied man remained behind. Bunny and Mr. P. were two of the leaders of the effort, surveying the group to determine what kind of muscle was left to help with the cleanup. Robert was the youngest and strongest of the men remaining in Long Harbor. It was obvious they would have scant outside assistance, and many of the remaining men were elderly.

The crew that remained continued to sleep on the Thaws' living room floor while working for the better part of two months. They stabilized the damage before the weather got cold, boarding up windows with scrap lumber to last the winter.

When he finally returned to Pittsburgh, Becca presented him with a scrapbook of newspaper articles chronicling the storm. The Great Hurricane of 1938 was the worst disaster ever suffered in

North America, made worse because it had caught everybody by surprise. Residents along the North Atlantic coast had little or no warning, and in a matter of hours, 688 people were killed, 4,500 were injured, and more than 75,000 buildings were damaged. Bunny choked when he read the inside cover: "My daddy, my brother, and I survived this storm. Bobby kept me from washing out to sea. He is my hero."

Chapter 23

LONG HARBOR, RHODE ISLAND
Friday, July 3, 2000

R achel forced herself out of bed at a decent hour on Friday morning, despite her significant role in having polished off two bottles of white wine the night before. Her window wide open, the sunlight and singing birds woke her up. She squinted her eyes against the bright rays and hoped she hadn't missed everyone at breakfast. The day's plans were always hashed out at the kitchen table, and showing up late put her three steps behind or left out altogether. She wanted a voice for once. Not that she minded being a follower, but this weekend seemed to hold some significance for her mother. Since Thomas and Ruth were arriving, and given that Sarah was on bed rest, she should be more outgoing.

She padded down the stairs to find Andrew's clan sitting with her mother, dirty breakfast dishes in front of them, negotiating the logistics of the day. She poured a cup of coffee and listened to Andrew's relentless attempt to squeeze tennis into an already jam-packed schedule.

"I hate tennis," said Sally.

"How could anybody hate tennis?" asked Andrew. "Walter will play with me, won't you, Walt?"

Walter rolled his eyes at his sister, crossed his arms at his chest, and said, "Sure."

"Great, so Walt and I will head to the courts while you girls go to the beach."

"The beach?" said Rachel from across the room. "Now, that's just my speed. I'll join you for that."

"Just be cleaned up by six," her mother added. "We'll have cocktails, then sit down for dinner at seven."

"Rachel, could you be ready in fifteen minutes?" Camilla asked, pushing back from the breakfast table.

Rachel nodded. She hadn't remembered Camilla as a beach person, not with that milky complexion. She was so British, so pale, so fragile, couldn't even walk the path through the dunes barefoot without complaining the sand was too hot.

* * *

That first time Camilla visited Eden, Rachel had already been married to Peter for seven years. Sarah was seven and quite cute, running circles around her uncle Andrew, asking to be put up on his shoulders or for him to ride the waves with her. Andrew hammed it up playing the "fun uncle," relishing Sarah's adoration. His ease with her made a favorable impression on Camilla, similar to the way big guys might borrow puppies to impress girls in the park.

That was the summer the entire house had been kept awake by a loud argument, her mother reprimanding her afterwards as if she were still a girl. "So distasteful, Rachel—think of poor Sarah. And your brother here, all the way from London, with a new girlfriend."

"Goddamn it, Mother," she retaliated. "Thinking of the rest of you is what got me in this mess. You were the one who insisted we get married; you wouldn't hear of any other option. It was you who pushed this from the very beginning. And now, if everything isn't all peaches and cream, don't look at me like I'm to blame. I have tried. I have tried everything. Peter does not love me. What am I supposed to do?"

In most instances, Rachel's parents cut her a great deal of slack. After all, she had given birth to their first grandchild, and she hadn't run off to live in England. These facts usually granted her immunity to her mother's criticism and put her on a stratum above her brother, but divorce was crossing the line. What's more, Camilla and Andrew were so damn attractive, Ms. Leggy and Mr. Broad Shoulders. With sparkling eyes, easy smiles, and sun-bleached curls, they stood on the back porch, he in a natty blazer with cream chinos, she in a tight-fitting, high-cut cocktail dress, shaking hands with their well-wishers the night of their engagement party. Camilla was always pulled together. Even after Andrew married her and she became one of the family, she still entered the kitchen fully dressed in the morning, as a houseguest might. It was odd.

* * *

It took Rachel twenty minutes to return to the kitchen in her cover-up, and Camilla was slathering sunscreen all over Sally's body.

"My God, that's enough, Mother," Sally snapped.

"You'll burn, Sally."

"So will you."

"I've already put mine on." When Camilla was finished with the tube of sunscreen, she offered it to Rachel.

"Ah, no thanks," said Rachel. "Never use the stuff."

Camilla looked at her scornfully.

"If Aunt Rachel doesn't use it, then why—"

"You will wear sunscreen. End of discussion," said Camilla.

The three of them left through the kitchen door and grabbed beach chairs in the garage. They trudged down the path and over the dunes. When they reached the beach, they took a few steps to the left and unfolded their chairs. Rachel retrieved the novel she was reading from her bag, along with a bottle of Coke and half a bag of potato chips.

She extended the bag in Camilla's direction. "Want a chip?"

"No, thank you," said Camilla, disapprovingly, as Sally reached in for a handful.

After sitting and looking at the waves for a few minutes, Camilla stood up.

"Sally," she said, "let's you and I have a walk along the shore."

"No," Sally said.

Looking at Rachel, she added, "A little mother-daughter time."

Rachel looked up from her pages, smiled, and nodded.

"Get out of that chair now, Sally."

"Mother."

"Now."

Rachel watched them depart. They walked at two different speeds. Camilla wanted to get some exercise, while Sally looked pained. Finally, Camilla slowed down and tried to take her daughter's hand. Rachel wondered why some people couldn't just relax at the beach, sip on a soda, snack on chips, or even just take a nap. Rachel was hardwired a napper, born into a family of walkers.

She had never walked the beach with Sarah—that was her mother's thing. Instead, she took her down to Katy's, the ice cream parlor in the village. Besides Eden, that had been her other refuge in Long Harbor. Just thinking of those cones brought back the memories of the summer after she'd turned sixteen, about the same age Sally was now. Her father had found her napping on the back porch and announced, "Rachel, your mother and I have decided you should get a job."

Rachel sat up, not sure she'd heard him correctly. "Is Andrew—"

Her father cut her off. "This is not about Andrew; it's about you becoming a responsible member of society."

Rachel studied her father's expression to see if he was really serious or just delivering an edict from her mother.

"All right, Dad," she said.

Whatever retort he'd prepared was stuck in his mouth. "Okay, then," he said, satisfied, and headed back to his vegetable garden.

She'd headed to the village, where there were HELP WANTED signs in the windows of both the pizza parlor and the ice cream shop. She liked pizza, but the idea of the ice cream shop made her smile instantly, as she knew her mother would never set foot in the place. It had always been her father who took her and Andrew after dinner. She could hear her mother's protests: "Dan, don't go stand in line with all those tourists. We have ice cream in the freezer."

Maybe it was the school insignia on her sweatshirt or the confidence with which she reached over the counter to shake the owner's hand, but Rachel carried herself more impressively than the typical hippie teenager looking for work in 1968. When she told the owner her name, something seemed to light up in his face.

"Wow," he said, "you're Becca Meister's girl?"

"You know my mom?"

"From a very long time ago." He said his name was Mr. Fabbrizzio but that she could call him Sal, and when Rachel mentioned her flexibility and that she would be in Long Harbor until Labor Day, he hired her on the spot. "Here, wear these to work with khaki pants or shorts," he said handing her three red collared shirts with the shop's logo embroidered on the left breast pocket. "Keep your hair pulled back, and wear tennis shoes." His eyes twinkled as he described the frenzy that would descend in a few short weeks. "It just about kills me every year," he laughed, "but it pays the bills and then some."

That night at dinner Rachel had beamed, describing her new job. She'd already memorized all twenty-four flavors. Her father slapped her on the knee. "That's great!" he said, but her mother seemed to stiffen in her seat, the corners of her mouth turning down.

"Mr. Fabbrizzio said he knew you, Mom. You never mentioned that."

"My family's lived here eighty years. A lot of people know who I am; that doesn't mean I know them, too," she said.

Andrew asked whether he and his friends could get free ice cream. "Absolutely not!" Rachel fumed.

* * *

Camilla was one of those intense mothers who signed Sally and Walter up for all sorts of lessons—tennis, violin, French—as soon as they were six or seven years old. Rachel had never signed Sarah up for a damn thing. She liked that Sarah stumbled upon her own fun, finding things entirely new to both of them. One rainy afternoon, Sarah had been up in the attic, going through old relics, and had come across a dress box containing a blue taffeta cocktail dress. She had tried it on in Rachel's room. Oh, how they had laughed at the startled expression on Becca's face when she had happened upon Sarah dancing in front of the full-length mirror.

The mother-daughter walk must have ended prematurely. Sally reappeared first, collapsing into her beach chair and putting her headphones back in. That she had turned into a rebellious teenager gave Rachel great pleasure. When she and Walter were lovely little toddlers, Camilla had dressed them in smocks and pinafores, a big white ribbon in Sally's hair, to have their portraits taken. Expensive black-and-white prints, presented to their parents as gifts, exquisitely framed, adorned the shelves at Eden. Sally and Walter certainly couldn't be dressed up and pranced around anymore.

"Why aren't there more kids my age on the beach?" asked Sally.

"Long Harbor teenagers hang out at the wall."

"Where's that?" asked Sally, looking around.

Rachel pointed. "Way down there, by the jetty. Better surf."

Rachel remembered how her friends straggled in over the course of the afternoon, the girls flipping through magazines and the boys bodysurfing, until a quorum of sorts had arrived. Some brought towels or low-slung chairs, but most just sat up on the wall and plotted the evening's activities, where the party would be. Rachel relished the grittiness of sand in her sheets even today; it sent her mind back to beach parties full of flirtation and innocent kissing.

Rachel worked at the ice cream parlor with a couple of kids who frequented the wall. She remembered the thrill of learning her parents were going away for a wedding and realizing she might be the one to host a party at Eden. She cozied up to Andrew early in the week, trying to get a read on whether he would snitch or not. He resisted at first, calling Rachel's friends "freaks," and wondered aloud how she planned to get past Lilly's watchful eye. She remembered buying him off with $20 and agreeing to do his chores for the rest of the summer. Rachel figured Lilly would be engrossed in her television programs up in her room around nine o'clock, so she would tell the kids that the party would start at nine thirty.

That Saturday, she rode her bike down to the wall after work. She waited for the right moment to casually speak up. "We could probably party at my house tonight."

Late that afternoon and through dinnertime, word spread that Rachel Fitzpatrick's parents were away and the party was at Eden. At about eleven, Lilly padded down the thickly carpeted main staircase through the living room and into the butler's pantry just in time to find Rachel on her knees, pulling bottles out of the liquor cabinet. A boy was on the floor beside her, reading the labels. Just as Rachel was about to pour the contents of the scotch bottle into a mayonnaise jar, Lilly raised her voice. "Rachel!"

When Dan and Becca returned to Eden on Sunday evening, Lilly described the situation, the band of kids on the lawn, the siphoning-off of alcohol. But, to Rachel's surprise, her parents were light on the punishment, maybe impressed that she had attempted some social overtures.

Camilla returned, her skin glistening with water droplets. "The water's lovely—a little cold but refreshing."

"Hmm," Rachel said, without looking up from her book.

Camilla checked that Sally was plugged into her music and then moved her chair closer to Rachel's. "So, do you think Sarah will marry the chap?"

"What's that?" Rachel turned the page.

"You know, the father."

Rachel bristled. Heat rose to her face. "Unlikely. I think the affair is over."

"Pity," said Camilla.

Rachel flipped the page of her magazine. She had no interest in discussing Sarah's pregnancy.

"So, how is your mother doing?"

Rachel finally looked at Camilla. "Doing?"

"Yes. How is she doing after your father's passing?"

"Well, I guess as well as can be expected." Rachel had no intention of discussing her mother's welfare, either, with Camilla, of all people.

"Andrew says the finances were left in a mess and she'll have to sell Eden."

What on earth was Camilla talking about? Rachel was grateful for her oversized sunglasses.

"Sell Eden? No, no, no. Mother would never sell Eden. Mother owns Eden with her siblings, Camilla. Her father left it in her care. A person can't just sell Eden."

"Isn't that why Thomas and Ruth are coming this weekend? To start sorting through it all?

"I . . . I . . ." Rachel hated feeling uninformed, and to be less informed than her sister-in-law was the ultimate humiliation. She couldn't speak.

"Who knows, Rachel?" Camilla said, as she waved her arm at the ocean in front of them. "This could be your last summer here."

Chapter 24

LONG HARBOR, RHODE ISLAND
1939

Walking through the front door was difficult. Becca was still haunted by the broken glass, losing hold of her father as the wind and waves swirled about them, and choking on seawater on their kitchen floor. She reached an arm toward her mother for support but felt only air. Her mother had backpedaled and was leaning against the unpainted door frame for support. It sounded as if she was also holding back tears. "Your father tried to prepare me, but I never imagined," she said, her voice trailing off.

Becca turned toward her mother, forgetting her own trepidation. She looked for something that might buoy her mother's spirit. "Daddy said your photographs are still in the back stairwell and are unharmed." The comment elicited the faintest hint of a smile. How her mother loved those photographs. After a few moments, Becca's shoulders relaxed as she watched her mother stand straight and smooth her skirt, albeit with trembling hands.

"Don't worry—Daddy said he would have Eden back to herself in no time." She continued to study her mother's face.

"Well, I guess we'll have to do this sooner or later," her mother said, running a hand through her unkempt hair, flattened by the day's travels. "Come, let's have a look around." She took Becca's hand and walked slowly toward the large picture window in the living room. It was a mild spring day, and the sky was clear, with pillow-like clouds on the horizon. The ocean was calm, waves just lapping on the beach. Even though her father's trees, the ones that should have been in full bloom at this time of year, were no longer, having been pulled from the earth by the great hurricane, Becca was grateful for the day's peaceful landscape.

Her mother tugged on her hand gently, slowly heading into the dining room. Everything that was ruined had already been cleaned out: furniture, drapery, carpets. Shaking her head, her mother said, "What a waste." Becca didn't want to tell her that if she had heard the roar of the wind on that awful afternoon, she would understand it was a miracle the house was standing at all.

"Well, I guess we'll just have to start over," her mother said, tracing a finger along the water-stained wallpaper.

"We don't need much, Mother. We can use sleeping bags; it will be like camping."

Her mother looked down at her with a skeptical smile. "I don't think we'll have to go to those extremes, darling. Your father's assured me the mattresses upstairs are fine."

"Oh, I'd rather not go upstairs."

"Well, maybe you can talk one of your brothers into camping down here with you. You can come upstairs when you're ready," said her mother, swinging the door to the butler's pantry open. The door open wide, her mother stopped in her tracks and gasped. "Oh dear," she cried. "My grandmother's china." She began picking through a box of chipped and broken shards. "I wish your father had just thrown this away, too, instead of leaving it like this for me to see."

"Some people have nothing, Mother," Becca said, trying to coax her mother's attention away from the loss of their china. "Not even walls to keep the wind out. Anyway, Daddy said the insurance will cover it." Becca's stomach flipped as they got closer and closer to the kitchen door.

"I know, darling." Her mother squeezed her shoulders. "We have a lot to be grateful for; it's just there's something about what gets passed down in a family. No insurance in the world will make a difference."

Becca nodded silently. Her mother was opening the door to the kitchen. "I think I'll go out to the beach," Becca said, hurrying past the sink and the stove, her eyes on the back door. She didn't want to risk any more bad memories in the kitchen.

"Okay, but don't stay long! Alice and I are going to need your help unpacking and pulling supper together!" her mother hollered, as Becca picked up speed, heading toward the dunes.

Later that afternoon, her father and brothers came in from the work they were doing on the exterior of the house. They walked slowly and stiffly and made little conversation. "And tomorrow offers more of the same," said Edward, descending into a kitchen chair.

"Oh, come now, boys—it's just a little manual labor," her father said, pouring a scotch at the kitchen counter. Robert took beers from the icebox and tossed one to each of his brothers.

"You boys are going to have to scoot out of the way," her mother said, reaching for the oven door. "We're roasting some chickens, and I need to check on them." Becca smiled in the midst of her parents and brothers all gathered in the warm kitchen, the smell of roasted chicken and rosemary filling the air.

"Robert?" said Becca, as supper came to an end and her brother pushed back from the table, looking like he was about to turn in for the night.

"Yes?" He looked across the table at her, rising, his scraped-clean plate in his hands.

"Will you camp in the living room with me?"

"Camp?"

"I'm afraid of going upstairs, and I'm afraid of being down-stairs alone," Becca said as tears welled up in her eyes. He looked back at her sympathetically. She did not need to explain herself, as they had weathered the storm together.

"Of course, Princess," he said. Her father patted them each on the shoulder as he passed by, taking his dishes to the sink.

They zipped up their sleeping bags after the family finished a game of cards on a makeshift table by the hearth in their father's study. A low-burning fire and its hot embers erased the spring's damp chill; Becca could feel it spreading a glow across her face.

"This is fun," she said.

"I guess," said Robert. "But my back sure is sore."

Becca fidgeted around until she got comfortable. After a while, her eyes became accustomed to the dark. "Bobby, do you remember when you used to take me out to the dunes to look for where the bunnies lived?"

"Ha. You remember everything, don't you?"

"How do you think they fared in the storm?"

He didn't answer right away. Becca spoke up again: "I mean, all that time people were missing and the fishing boats never came back, I kept thinking about our bunnies and their holes getting filled up with seawater and drowning the little bunny families."

"Becca, I think the mommy bunnies could sense a storm coming and took their babies far away before the waves got them."

"They would have had had to get pretty far away."

"Not really—just to higher ground. All animals have a sixth sense about that. It's a fact of nature."

"Are you sure?"

"I'm pretty sure."

"Will our rabbits come back to live at Eden?"

"Sure they will, but maybe you should leave some carrots out in the yard to make sure. Father's garden won't be much of an enticement this summer."

* * *

During the following night's supper, her father explained the order in which repairs needed to happen. Her brothers didn't seem to pay attention, as if they'd heard it a hundred times before. No, her father was making it as clear as possible for her benefit. "It's safe and sound now, Princess. Don't you worry."

He said the water had structurally compromised parts of Eden, which had been replaced, including the entire sleeping porch. Where the floors had buckled and water had dripped through the ceilings, they had already excavated to the root of the damage to ensure the house's structure was intact.

Instead of hiring laborers to buzz around Eden like a colony of ants, as they had when the house was originally built, Becca's father and brothers had done most of the work this time. Mr. P. had also traded in his apron for a hammer that summer and helped her father cobble together a small crew. They sent for supplies from Pittsburgh because there was such a high demand locally.

Even Thomas shed his businessman's persona, although Mother yelled if he went up on a ladder. "Let Edward and Robert do it! You shouldn't be up there!" She got angry with Becca's father for allowing it. "My Lord, Bunny, you should know better, with Thomas's medication and all! What are you thinking?"

Alice sewed slipcovers. Becca was in charge of cleaning walls and baseboards with a solution of vinegar and bleach to battle the mildew that had spread throughout the course of the winter. With the warm sun helping, they opened the doors and windows wide to dry out the damp plaster walls, then painted the new windowsills. When Becca's jobs were done indoors, she went out to try to restake her father's gardens.

They bleached pillows in the sun and put anything that appeared to be beyond salvation in a heap by the road, where families with much greater needs could take their pick. Instead of spending the afternoons lunching with friends, Becca's mother worked in the kitchen, preparing trays of food for all the men. She wore Mr. P.'s big white apron as she expertly held the handle of the frying pan in her left hand and a spatula in her right. Oil spattered about the burners of the big Garland stove. Becca marveled at this sight, as her mother's involvement at mealtime had previously consisted of writing the menu and arranging the centerpiece. Becca had always assumed that Alice and Mr. P. were the only ones in the household to possess such skills.

"I didn't know you knew how," she said to her mother.

"Don't be silly. Of course I know how," her mother said suppressing a laugh. "Why, these things are second nature."

Becca dipped chicken parts in batter before passing them to her mother, who darted about, flipping the pieces and peeking at their undersides to make sure they were nice and brown. Becca licked her fingers, delighting in the savory warmth and buzz of her mother's energy.

Once the meal was prepared, Becca rang a large school bell and her hungry father and brothers came down off the neighbor's roofs to long tables set up on a flat stretch of lawn. The sound of saws and banging nails ceased for an hour while they all sank their teeth into a good meal.

When the sun set, the men wiped their foreheads and put their tools away for the night. They were getting dark tans on their necks and backs. Her mother massaged her father's shoulders at the end of the day. "I'm not as young as I used to be," he groaned.

Thirty-eight locals, among the 433 total in Rhode Island, had lost their lives in the hurricane. Becca attended all the memorial services at the Long Harbor chapel with her family, even though her mother said it might be better for her to stay home. But Becca felt a need to be there. She was one of the few who had experienced the storm firsthand, and it took all those sermons and hymns, and shedding of tears, to move through the emotions she felt. Each time she approached the chapel from the crest of their hill, she had to face that barren spit of sand wrapping the harbor and remembered the afternoon the houses on Fort Point washed into the sea.

She started a diary.

The services are so sad, one after another. They are the same in many ways, but with each one it is a different family's turn to sit in the front pew and wear black. We cry for all of them, all the same. But I feel bad, because when we are home, I am so happy. Everyone is home, and really home—helping to rebuild Eden, instead of going out at night with their friends. Mother and Father have no cocktail parties. With all the funerals, it wouldn't seem right. We stay up to play a few hands of hearts before collapsing into bed. Bobby and I are camping in Daddy's study. The others just don't understand how scary it was. But Mother is laughing. And Mother and Father are hugging again.

* * *

And then it all came to an end the afternoon Becca came bounding into the kitchen with a basket of wild blueberries. "Can we make a pie?" she hollered.

"Shh," her mother said, pointing to the radio. Her father and brothers were sitting around listening, too. There was a war in Europe. From that afternoon forward, radio broadcasts played night and day. Becca set up a game of solitaire. She pretended to ignore the man's voice on the radio but spied her mother's worried glances and then her father gently rubbing her mother's shoulder in response. Her mother left the room while the man on the radio was still talking. Becca could hear her pacing in the pantry, and the banging of plates as she put away the dried dishes.

She heard her mother on the telephone with Mrs. Notman. "All our boys are the right age," then a silence as Mrs. Notman spoke, then, "They'll be expected to fight." Becca's stomach lurched. Her mother dabbed her eyes with a handkerchief and said, "During the Great War, well, that's exactly what happened to my brothers."

Chapter 25

LONG HARBOR, RHODE ISLAND

Friday, July 3, 2000

L illy felt that old jolt of energy that came with hosting a crowd at Eden. She poured water in the coffeemaker upon entering the kitchen, while the route for her errands percolated in her mind. She rinsed the breakfast dishes more quickly than usual, then tucked her pocketbook in the crook of her elbow and clung to it tightly. She scurried out the kitchen door before Becca could come down from her shower. Not telling Becca about the letter was weighing heavily on her, and Lilly fretted that the tic in the corner of her eye might give her away.

Besides, she didn't feel like another debate over where to market. Lilly preferred Dade's, the old family-run market in the center of downtown Westfield where they'd always had a charge account, but Becca's bridge friends were raving about the selections at the superstore that had recently opened on Route 1. "I hear the prices are lower, too," Becca had said, clearing her throat, adding a few last items to the shopping list.

Lilly's fists wrapped tightly around the plastic handle of the shopping cart as she entered Dade's produce section. She dug her reading glasses out from under Edward's letter. Squeezing the limes, she remembered Becca and her brothers when she'd first started at Eden. She'd known them as young adults, still the children of the family, celebrated and grieved with them, and helped them raise their own children. She wouldn't have imagined back then that it would be her and Becca growing old together. She selected the grapefruit, chose the bananas, and put her pocketbook down on the seat of the grocery cart.

"Morning, Ron," she said to the graying man at the meat counter. The butcher at Dade's dated back as far as she did. She'd blushed at his flirting, until she caught him winking at other customers. But he did hold on to her wrapped sirloins for an extra second, making her tug and then meet his eye. "Have a nice weekend," she said to him, steering her cart toward the cheese display.

The woman in line behind her was Mrs. Bancroft, a friend of Becca's, perfectly coiffed and wearing a peach V-neck sweater with the Paupanaug Club insignia on the breast. She demanded Ron's attention, urging him to import her favorite prosciutto from Manhattan, at least for the summer season. Lilly chuckled at her pompous tone as she hunted through the fancy cheeses for the brie Becca liked. Lilly had served Evie Bancroft at Eden countless times, but concentrating on the cheese spared them both the need to say hello. She hated when those hoity-toity friends of Becca's acted like they didn't recognize her.

Mrs. Bancroft reminded her of Sadie, so caught up in her own world, sometimes she forgot basic kindness. Sadie used to make such a production, all aflutter, in those early years, getting ready for Ruth and Becca and her grandchildren. She expected Lilly to live in the nursery with the babies—no privacy at all, due to the fact that Alice wanted the maids' quarters to herself. Sadie could ignore poor Mr. Meister, too. All she came to care about was being a grandmother, sneaking Ruth's twins candy from the village.

Lilly picked out a good carton of eggs, gallons of milk, orange juice, butter—the list went on and on. She had almost forgotten how much food they needed for a full house. Alice had done most of the marketing in the beginning, and the cooking as well. Lilly had been in charge of the children. The boys were straightforward, but Rachel had been sullen even as a toddler. Lilly had to coax her out from under their umbrella: "Come play in the water with the boys." Little girls at the beach formed cliques early on, giggling along the sand with their pails and shovels. It made Lilly sad that Rachel had few friends.

Rachel had always been her worry, and this summer's mess with Sarah was sort of the crowning blow. Pregnant with no husband, Sarah needed understanding from her mother. But Rachel could be so stubborn. Luckily, Sarah had Becca. She'd turned out to be a patient grandmother. Sarah and Becca were cut from the same cloth, early risers, walking the beach together. Sarah even helped in the garden. "Usefulness seems to have skipped a generation," Becca liked to chastise.

Rachel's aggravation only mounted as she sat up in her bedroom window, watching her daughter and mother pick tomatoes and clip flowers. Lilly tried to comfort her. "It's not uncommon to have friction with your mother," she said, setting a pot of tea down on the writing desk. "It's why I left home at sixteen, traveled down from Maine with some older girls looking for work. I happened upon Long Harbor just as Sadie was advertising for somebody to help Alice."

"Lilly, I just can't relate," Rachel said, scribbling poem after poem in those journals of hers.

Lilly understood what that felt like. She had never fit in with the other help, what with all their gossiping. They'd offer up nuggets of scandal from their own households, hoping to lure Lilly into a conversation about the goings-on at Eden. A friendship with them would have meant betraying the family.

Happily, Rachel eventually found a set of friends. It was the summer she started working at Sal Fabbrizzio's ice cream shop. He'd hired five teenagers in total, two of whom would become the closest friends Rachel would have in Long Harbor. Even when she wasn't on the schedule, she was drawn to the carnival-like feel of the village. The tourists standing in line for the carousel, enjoying cotton candy and popcorn, seemed miles away from the Paupanaug Club's private beach and tennis courts.

Lilly lingered in the bakery section, enticed by the various round peasant loaves, with their poppy-seed toppings and yeasty smells. Abigail Waters, the Notmans' cook, came up beside her and pulled two French loaves in their white paper sheaths from a basket.

"Oh, Lilly. Is that you?" Her eyes were rimmed red, and she wiped her nose with a tissue.

"Abigail! Hello. Stocking up for the weekend?"

"I tell you, I've just about had it. Do you ever want to spend a holiday with your own family?"

Lilly hesitated. The Notmans were close friends with the Meister clan, but they were known to be difficult. "No," she answered, although it wasn't entirely true. She had been on the verge of leaving once. After all, Rachel and Andrew had both gone to college. She had gotten as far as writing her recently widowed sister in New Hampshire, asking if she would like some company. She had been just about to break the news to Becca and Dan when they returned from a visit to Cornell and announced there was going to be a wedding.

"A wedding? Who?" Lilly asked, startled.

"Why, Rachel! Who else? She's taking a leave from Cornell and marrying her beau."

Lilly searched both of their faces. She hadn't heard of a beau. It took a few minutes to figure out, and then she felt their shame. Lilly never put words to it, just went on cheerily with the wedding plans, choosing the flowers, the menu, a tent for the lawn.

"Make it a big tent, something special for our Rachel," Lilly said.

"Don't be silly. You know Rachel," Becca said. "She is so anti-everything."

In the end, they planned the ceremony to be on the back porch, just family, with a small reception in the living room. No live music, just a tasteful luncheon, lobsters and Cobb salad.

"So, what's this lad Peter like?" Lilly asked, as she ironed napkins in the pantry.

"His family's in the ranching business, from California," Becca said, as if it were outer space.

When Lilly finally met Peter, she liked him right away. He

was tall, with shaggy hair and the face of a boy. He came into the kitchen and shook her hand, oohing and aahing over the view. He didn't pass through quickly, like most folks did. He put down his bags and stood by the sink, accepting her offer of iced tea and admiring a robin's nest with her, the birds flying in, one twig at a time, right outside the kitchen window.

During the ceremony, he stood, dazed, next to the minister, waiting for Rachel to appear. When she finally did, his face went white as a sheet. Peter's mother had to lean forward in her seat and remind him to smile. It was a tough day's work for the photographer. Dan's face was stern, and Peter's father didn't look too pleased, either. The only ones smiling and laughing were the guests, their classmates from Cornell who had been smoking marijuana and drinking wine on the beach. They brought their own records and played them on Dan's turntable in the living room. They frolicked, held hands in a circle, some of them barefoot, with wreaths of flowers in their hair, and danced around, Rachel and Peter in the middle. Becca complained they all needed haircuts, but if it hadn't been for them, the day would have been so depressing.

Lilly wrote her sister back that she couldn't leave now; Rachel didn't know the first thing about caring for a baby.

* * *

Lilly signed for the groceries, then asked the bag boy to take them to the car. He loaded one bag after another into the trunk of the Lincoln while she scrounged in her change purse for a tip. Then she checked the shopping list. It read: "Vodka, scotch, and white wine" in Andrew's scratchy hand. Lilly grumbled, hating to select wine for the family.

"What are you serving it with?" asked the salesman at the liquor store.

"It's for a cocktail party." Lilly explained.

As he guided her through the choices, Lilly recalled the way Bunny Meister used to line up the wine bottles on the sideboard before a big dinner. Back when she was maybe eighteen or nineteen, after Alice passed away, Lilly began serving in the dining room. Bunny explained in a kind voice how to open a wine bottle, and how to pour so as not to drip on Sadie's linens. She remembered him giving her a proud grin as she leaned in over the guests' shoulders, finishing each pour with a small twist, just so.

* * *

The salesman loaded the cases of wine into the backseat. The dry cleaner would be Lilly's last stop. Even in this heat, Becca prided herself on looking fresh in sweater sets and pearls. She'd dressed beautifully when she and Dan entertained, back when an invitation to Eden was the pinnacle of social achievement. Becca always told her she couldn't have done it without her.

Becca was thoughtful that way, even helped Lilly overcome her Maine accent as they polished the silver and organized the pantry. She taught her the snooty way to pronounce "tomahto" and "bahthroom," and she showed her how to make little cucumber sandwiches with dill to serve at her bridge parties. There was a Long Harbor social register published each summer, and Becca ticked off the names of their dinner guests with a felt-tipped pen, just like Sadie used to.

It was as if Becca set out to do her mother proud, as if she owed it to Bunny and Sadie to devote her life to Eden—to the whole town, for that matter. Her brothers never felt the same pull as she did. After Bunny and Sadie had passed, Edward's wife had tried to stir things up. Lilly had been passing through the living room, collecting empty glasses after Sadie's memorial, and Edward's wife had fallen silent at the sight of her. But Lilly had gotten the gist: something about selling Eden and splitting the money. Becca had gone on a tirade. As far as Lilly knew, the subject had never come up again—until she found that darn letter from Edward, of course.

* * *

Lilly checked her watch as she pulled into Eden's driveway. The errands had taken all morning and then some. Becca was standing at the screen door. "You've been gone such a long time; we've got to get busy!" she said. "Here, let me help you with those." Noticing the logo on Lilly's shopping bags, Becca scolded, "Oh, Lilly, Dade's? You must have spent a fortune!"

Lilly heard the stress in her voice. Edward's letter would have to wait.

Chapter 26

PITTSBURGH, PENNSYLVANIA
1941

Sadie's new radio console was housed in a polished wood case with a silver mesh face and stood centrally in the living room at Lancaster Fells. She turned the gleaming brass dials to tune in to the news after supper every evening during the winter of 1941 and sat down in the living room with Bunny, Thomas, and Kitty.

"Becca, it's time you went to bed," Sadie said.

Her daughter kissed them good night and headed upstairs. Sadie didn't want her listening; she was too young to comprehend the enormity of war on the horizon. She feared a declaration by President Roosevelt would see her sons off to fight. The thought paralyzed her with worry that her mother's nightmare was destined to repeat itself. She suspected Robert and Edward, however, with their youthful sense of power and immortality, were facing the news with the same courage and duty they had shown in the aftermath of the hurricane.

"We should stay out of Europe's affairs," Bunny steamed. "This country still hasn't recovered from the Depression. How can he even think of mobilizing?"

"Shh," said Sadie, hating it when Bunny spoke during the news broadcast. The reporter described Germany marching through Europe, having gained huge victories in France and Poland. US involvement was inevitable.

Thomas said, "President Roosevelt signed legislation committing US weapons to the Allied powers. It's practically a declaration of war already."

Sadie couldn't stop worrying about her boys. Edward was a banker at J.P. Morgan. He enjoyed an independent life in Manhattan, sharing an apartment with two classmates and prowling after-work haunts with his Wall Street friends.

Robert was still at Yale and had fallen madly in love with a Smithie named Ruth Meyer, whom he met at his college's mixer the first weekend of the fall semester. Once football season ended, he spent nearly every weekend driving to Northampton, staying at Rahar's, a rooming house on the fringe of the Smith College campus. He wrote his parents: "Ruth is bright and studious, very funny, and somewhat of a night owl, and she loves motion pictures. She has dark brown hair, brown eyes, and a beautiful smile. She has introduced me to new authors, new foods, and, last night, Carole Lombard in *My Man Godfrey*."

Bunny didn't hide his dismay over Robert's spending so much time with a girlfriend, instead of dedicating himself to his studies. Sadie assumed Robert's latest letter was what had him agitated on that Monday afternoon in December. He called Sadie into the living room and asked her to sit down next to Kitty and Thomas, before turning up the volume on the radio. President Roosevelt was speaking with urgency.

"Dear Lord," said Sadie, ignoring the fact that Becca was standing behind the couch. The President was saying that Japan had attacked Pearl Harbor. She wrung her hands, staring into the radio grille. The President coined it "a date that would live in infamy." This was the final straw. She huddled against Bunny's chest as Roosevelt's crackling voice declared war. There would be fighting in the Pacific, as well as in Europe.

"I'm enlisting first thing in the morning," Thomas said.

"Oh, Thomas, don't be ridiculous. You can't do that," Sadie said, dabbing her eyes with a handkerchief.

"Why not?" he replied, glaring.

"Your mother is right—you'll never pass a military physical.

Thomas, there will be plenty we all can do to help from home," said Bunny.

"We'll see about that," he said, stomping up the stairs.

Thomas returned from the army recruitment office in Pittsburgh the next afternoon, dejected. Sadie guessed the military doctors had echoed what Bunny had said and hadn't delivered the news as diplomatically. She watched as her son's condition evolved from something Bunny had managed secretively into a documented disability. She saw Thomas's devastation mount as he watched his younger brothers and friends enlist. His presence in Pittsburgh at age twenty-six, with an outwardly healthy appearance, was sure to launch gossip.

Sadie set her sights on the one spring weekend they could all manage together at Eden between Robert and Edward's completion of basic training and shipping out. It wasn't exactly as she had imagined, as Thomas chose to stay behind in Pittsburgh and Robert wanted to bring his new girlfriend along.

She planned one of Mr. P.'s clambakes out on the back porch for Saturday night. It was a chilly evening, and everyone was wrapped in sweaters. Sadie watched the group's laughing profiles and twinkling eyes. She watched them gorge on lobster, lick butter off their fingers, suck on beer bottles, and help themselves to more corn and more chips. They were carrying on as if they hadn't a care in the world.

Sadie fixated on Becca's smile across the table as she guffawed at her brother's jokes and looked at Ruth in awe. Then her throat suddenly began to tighten. Poor Becca, giggling away as any thirteen-year-old might, had no comprehension of the dark cloud looming.

"Becca, help me clear the dishes, please." Sadie felt a need to rein her in. Her daughter dutifully rose and took two plates to the kitchen. "Even though we're together at Eden," Sadie said, as they rinsed the plates in the sink, "I think a somber mood is more appropriate under the circumstances. All this lightheartedness in the presence of war is disrespectful, unpatriotic."

"Why not get mad at the boys? They're the ones cracking the jokes in the first place."

"Becca, can you even imagine what your brothers must be facing? You, on the other hand, need to show more restraint."

* * *

For the rest of the war, Sadie modeled restraint. Like her neighbors, she kept the house dark at night, drove less in order to conserve gas, and cut back on meat, sugar, butter, and coffee. She bragged that Bunny grew his own vegetables long before victory gardens were the rage.

Even though they were bumping around, trying to find their way to bed by flashlight, Sadie was content at Eden. Many of the midwesterners dared not even come to the East Coast, for fear of the Germans attacking across the Atlantic. Sadie didn't care; it made her feel closer to her sons in their overseas posts.

Throughout the war, Long Harbor social activity came to a halt. Bunny and Sadie kept to themselves, dining with Becca or with the Notmans, whose sons were also off fighting. Sometimes she would stroll down to the harbor with Bunny to watch the few sailing regattas that the yacht club continued to host. The older members claimed keeping their class of Herreshoff designs in the boatyards all summer amounted to "no less than a travesty." But the races were never too far out of the harbor and starting guns were not used. All tennis tournaments were canceled, along with any golf events or fireworks. Becca reported watching various army trainees practice amphibious landings on the beach and occasionally spotted submarines just beyond the lighthouse.

Whenever she bumped into their fishing rods or golf clubs, Sadie was reminded of Robert and Edward. It was almost easier returning in the fall to Pittsburgh and Lancaster Fells, where she hadn't hung photos of her sons up and down the stairwell.

In Pittsburgh, Sadie and Becca volunteered to roll bandages and staffed blood drives for the Red Cross. They took simple dinners in the kitchen while Bunny and Thomas worked late at the P&E. The commandeering of steel and defense materials put increased demand on their line. The P&E would eventually profit handsomely, but ramping up capacity required more investment. Bunny stayed up late, a sole desk lamp lighting his work, reviewing loan documents, as well as the security of their contracts with the steel mills and with the US government.

In the midst of their simplified lifestyle, Alice moved back to her family's home to take care of her aging parents. Sadie didn't even try to find a replacement. For the first time in her life, she had no staff and let her standards drop, ignoring the dusting and polishing. Bunny spent the free time he could manage in his gardens, but both Lancaster Fells and Eden sagged from wartime neglect.

One summer afternoon, Sadie found Becca lingering wistfully on the back stairs at Eden with a basket of laundry in her arms. She stood in front of the black-and-white photo gallery and pointed to the one of Sadie hoisting the Paupanaug ladies' tennis championship trophy above her head.

"Mother, when I look at this picture now, it seems just impossible."

"That was taken ages ago, before you were even born."

"I never knew that side of you."

That was what she looked like before Thomas's seizures began, before her time at Banford, before the crash, the hurricane, and a war that took two of her children a continent away. It was another life.

"I guess you never did," she answered.

* * *

One morning, Sadie heard the thud of the mail being pushed through the slot. She put down her sewing and rushed to the foyer. The highlight of her existence became the receipt of v-mail from either Edward or Robert, with news of their progression. She slit the edges open with extreme care and unfolded the thin paper carefully. She would read the letters so many times, they were practically committed to memory. She only wished they weren't so short. The military allowed for only one folded side of paper so all the soldiers' mail wouldn't take up too much cargo space.

That evening, a new letter in hand, Sadie turned off the radio, stood in the living room, and read aloud to Bunny, Becca, Thomas, and Kitty. Edward's correspondence never divulged much. He wrote about facts and dates and coordinates on the map. He complained of the food and the weather but mostly encouraged his parents not to worry and said he was looking forward to coming home to a "whopper" of a shindig at Eden whenever the day came. "I'll write again when it's time to put the beer on ice!"

But three weeks had passed without any news from Robert. Sadie began to drop dishes in the kitchen and pace more than usual. She went to the chapel every day and lit a candle. "Dear God," she prayed, "keep them safe. You can take me, but please don't take either of them."

One night, after a particularly frightening radio broadcast, she was undressing for bed. Bunny came up behind her and surprised her. He said, "Darling, I phoned Dr. Hart. He's prescribed something to calm your nerves. If you can be soothed, it might help us all relax, especially Becca." Bunny handed her a small paper sack.

Anger rose from the pit of Sadie's belly. The mere mention of Dr. Hart's name caused her to clench her jaw. How she hated when Bunny went behind her back. Her hands formed into fists, her fingernails piercing the heels of her palms.

She wanted to shout at her husband, but she humored him, all the while resenting that he followed her into the bathroom to observe her swallowing the pills. When she woke up the next morning, she felt sluggish and confused; it reminded her of those first days at Banford. She tossed the contents of the vial down the toilet, deciding it better to be alert to her heartbreak than to sleep through it.

* * *

One cool Long Harbor afternoon, four years after her sons' departure, Sadie received two telegrams. She had been feeling hopeful ever since victory had been declared. She dissolved into tears as she read the words saying both boys would be shipping home in the coming months. She ran to the chapel with tears running down her reddened cheeks to offer a prayer of gratitude. Back at Eden, she found Bunny in the garden. She showed him the wrinkled telegrams, held tight in her fists.

They embraced, then went into the kitchen. Sadie didn't bother to wipe her face or fix her hair. She was crying and smiling up into Bunny's face at the same time. When Becca came into the kitchen and heard the news, the three of them became dizzy with relief and elation, twirling and jumping, then almost collapsing into Bunny, who held them all up.

Chapter 27

LONG HARBOR, RHODE ISLAND

Friday, July 3, 2000

S arah had never thought it possible to tire of her bedroom at
Eden, but the doctor-ordered bed rest was doing the trick. She
had always loved the room's cozy proportions, the floor only as
long as the twin bed nestled against the wall. But that had been
before she'd had an adult body burning up in a heat wave, and
before she had been told to stay in bed for the unforeseeable future.

She had migrated to this tiny room when she was twelve, squir-
reling herself away in here during afternoons to read. She'd discovered the maids' quarters on a rainy day and returned to its narrow
pinewood hallway and one empty bedroom when she wanted solitude. She giggled, listening to her grandparents call her name as they
searched everywhere. But her mother always know where to find her.
"I used to do the same thing when I was your age. If you want to
disappear in this family, it's as simple as going to the maids' quarters."

Eventually Sarah extended afternoons of reading into bedtime and started sleeping in her new favorite spot until the room
officially became hers. "She just sort of squatted there," her
grandfather joked at breakfast when Lilly asked if it was a permanent thing.

There were bookshelves built in above the bed's headboard
that she filled with her childhood favorites, including *Charlotte's
Web*. The soft cotton coverlet spread on the bed matched the white
curtains, both embroidered with fine pink thread that matched

the light pink of the walls. Across the hall, Lilly's room was mint green, as if maids in general were drawn to the pastel hues of ice cream flavors. Lilly slept with her door open to catch the breeze, and Sarah liked seeing the silhouette of her prone figure when she made her way to the bathroom in the middle of the night. She also liked to wake to the sounds of her grandmother puttering around in the kitchen below before her daily walk.

But now Sarah hobbled out of bed, needing to empty her bladder. She felt stiff, her internal clock out of sync. She napped most of the day and lay awake, restless, at night, anticipating the holiday weekend. Upon returning to her doorway, she caught sight of the full "strawberry" moon in the window. It hung over the water like a face, almost yellow and so large, it consumed the entire pane of glass. The paper had said that this moon, on the heels of the summer equinox, would appear the largest to the eye and create extreme tides. The waters would swell, building pressure, an undercurrent of tension that had the potential of permeating everything. *Great, just what we need,* Sarah mused.

She also thought back to the astrologer's report in the previous day's paper, something about the summer moon being responsible for feelings of vulnerability and high-strung emotions. Was that why she was on the verge of tears all day? Why her mother was so unreasonable? Why her grandmother was making them all wait for some earth-shattering announcement?

Sarah reached for the notebook and pencil by her bed and the calculator, too. Rent, food, clothing, babysitting—she calculated what she would need to earn. It was a lot more than they'd offer a lecturer. It was going to be nearly impossible without her grandmother's financial help, and how would she ever complete her dissertation? The applications had all been forwarded from the university, and she was late returning them. Research might be possible, but there was no way she could fulfill the teaching assistant responsibilities that went along with her doctorate program. Did they offer extensions? Maybe she could call her advisor to discuss? Ha! Not when her advisor was Alistair.

Oh, Alistair. She had written him a letter, just as her grandmother had suggested, asking if he'd come up from the city so they could talk things over. She'd given it to Lilly to post yesterday. Thinking about him didn't make her angry anymore. She actually missed him. She wouldn't be surprised if he didn't reply, but her grandmother was right: it was worth one more shot. She put her hand to her breast and let the calculator and notebook drop to the floor.

She threw off the gnarled top sheet to look at the clock. In a few hours, Lilly would be clanging away in the kitchen. Gran would take Hennessy for his walk, and Andrew's family would be having breakfast. Maybe they'd be going to the beach. It might be all right to join them; she could just sit quietly in a beach chair. She wouldn't dare wear a bathing suit, though. All she had were bikinis, and even though her stomach was still basically flat, her boobs were swollen beyond the size of any top she owned. She'd just wear a cover-up. *Dear Lord, I'm turning into my mother.*

Everyone in her family loved the beach, but at this moment Sarah craved a swimming pool, something crystal-clear and calm, with turquoise water, that she could wade through serenely, instead of being on the lookout for waves that might knock her down. She imagined steam rising about her body as she submerged into the aqua liquid. Her grandfather would turn in his grave, hating swimming pools the way he did. He'd made such a scene the time one of the girls in her tennis clinic had invited her to a pool party.

"Why would anybody build a swimming pool when the Atlantic Ocean is just a few steps away?" he'd asked.

"Because, it feels cleaner, it's warmer, and there's no seaweed or jellyfish."

"Oh, poppycock, Sarah! Don't be silly, and don't turn into one of these precious creatures who can't enjoy nature. You come from hardy stock. You should be swimming in the ocean."

* * *

Sarah closed her eyes and focused on her breathing, inhaling through her nose and extending her exhalations. One, two, three—she counted her inhalations and put everything else out of her mind. Long exhale. Exhale her worries away. It might be fun to finally spend a day on the beach. She'd basically be on bed rest once she got down there. She'd need only to cross the backyard and then take the path through the dunes. She could take a book, eat the picnic lunch, and come back to the house if she started to feel too warm. She would be fine, if she could just get a few more hours of sleep.

She stared at the moon. Lazily running her fingertips across her belly, she eventually drifted off to sleep.

Chapter 28

LONG HARBOR, RHODE ISLAND
July 1945

Just before six in the evening, Becca's father's car roared up the driveway, followed by horn tooting and all sorts of hooting and hollering. She ran down the stairs and bounded through the door. Two men who looked much older than her brothers ducked their heads as they emerged from the vehicle. Were they Robert and Edward? Her mother cried, "Who are these handsome men?" They hugged and kissed their mother in turn, then picked Becca up in the air and twirled her around.

"Wow, you've gotten big!" said Robert.

"Becca, you're not a little girl anymore. You turned into a woman while we were gone!" said Edward.

Becca blushed. She was seventeen now. She knew she had the face and the body of a woman, and the wavy red hair she had inherited from their mother was no longer in pigtails.

Her mother's gloom seemed to evaporate in Becca's brothers' presence. Whatever special ingredient they brought to her life, it was something Becca just didn't possess. That first afternoon they were home, her mother kept reaching for their arms, as if she had to convince herself they were real. "Thank God," she said over and over. Her gratitude and patriotic excitement hit a high pitch when she decided they would host a victory celebration that August. "It will be a celebration not just for our boys," she said, "but for the entire community, for the whole country!"

Her mother shifted into a gear Becca had never seen before. She outdid herself, and the party was shaping up to be the talk of the town. Her mother described how she would illuminate Eden in its entirety. "The grounds, as well as the porches and interior, will shine brilliantly. It will be a complete contrast to the air raid–enforced blackness we've had to endure." She ordered a large tent to be erected on the great lawn, with colorful rows of paper lanterns hanging from its scaffolding. Her father ordered a fountain of flowing champagne, a parquet floor for dancing, and an elevated stage for the Billy Dugin Orchestra, which he hired to come all the way from New York City.

Down in the village, Becca overheard both good things and bad. The Meister boys had returned home unscathed, and Bunny Meister's business, linked as it was to the steel industry, had actually profited from the war, rubbing many a patriotic inclination the wrong way. Even though their friends were giddy about the party, Becca knew there were others who whispered about the garishness of it all.

Those first days of the boys' being back were uncharted emotional territory. Her mother could get laughing with Edward and Robert, then suddenly start crying over the state of the moth-ridden clothes they had left behind. Becca couldn't quell her curiosity: "What did France look like?" she asked at the dinner table. Edward only stared back in silence, shaking his head and taking a swig of beer.

"Don't keep peppering them with questions!" her mother hissed. "Nobody wants to know what horrors they witnessed."

Robert's sweetheart, Ruth, arrived amid the preparations, and Robert couldn't stop beaming. Becca liked how easily Ruth pitched in. Together, they made dozens of trips from the kitchen down to the lawn, setting the tables under the tent. Her father said, "Hell, any girl who can walk barefoot across the gravel driveway is a keeper."

The morning of the party, the kitchen was chaotic, Mr. P. having returned with a crew of men to cook alongside him. The company that supplied the tent unloaded linens, silverware, and crystal.

Alice, who had returned once the war ended, ticked off items on her clipboard, directing deliveries to their appropriate places. She and Mr. P. smiled proudly, watching Eden regain her former pizzazz.

"How did we ever get along without you?" Becca's mother wondered aloud, as she scurried from the tent to the kitchen.

"We barely did!" Becca whispered to the two of them. "We'd sit in the kitchen, a small candle lighting the room, choking down mother's cooking."

In the midst of all the activity that morning, a dress box arrived via parcel post from Bonwit Teller in New York. Her mother called out, "Becca! Your dress is here. Let's go upstairs and have you try it on."

"A dress?" Her mother had never surprised her with a gift before.

"I had given up on its arriving in time!"

Enormous quantities of food and champagne were arriving at the house, and now this? Becca had never seen anything but her parents' spartan side. When had her mother had the time to think about a dress for her?

When she opened the box and folded back the tissue paper in her mother's dressing room, she found a beautiful, light blue taffeta dress with a cocktail-length full skirt. "Oh, Mother, I had no idea. . . ."

Her mother helped her put it on, and they stood together, admiring its fit in the mirror. The thin shoulder straps and tight bodice flattered Becca's figure and showed off her neck and shoulders.

"Just beautiful."

"Mother, I don't know what to say."

"Sweetheart, with everything that's been going on, I know I've ignored you. I was hanging up your blouses when it dawned on me you had nothing suitable for the party."

Becca had been resigned to wearing her Sunday best; now she felt like Cinderella. She would finally be experiencing Eden the way it was depicted in the pictures hanging along the back stairs.

Cars streamed up the driveway all afternoon while Edward made multiple trips to the train station. Horns honked as cars approached the house, followed by spontaneous, gleeful shouts of welcome, and feet and suitcases thumping up and down the staircase. Aunt Kitty even came in on the train from Pittsburgh, exclaiming, "I've been looking for a good excuse to visit, and you know how I love a party!"

With each arrival, Becca's mother got teary. She'd put down the task at hand, embrace the guests, and say, "Thank you so much for joining us!" When she showed people where they were sleeping and handed them a fresh set of towels, she apologized for the cramped quarters, but they were expecting a full house. Becca watched her brothers' reactions. With Edward there was lots of backslapping, but after Robert proudly introduced Ruth to his friends, he seemed to shrink into a hushed sadness, probably thinking about the ones who hadn't returned from France.

Thomas, on the other hand, puffed out his chest. Becca sensed his resentment of all the hoopla. Her father stroked his ego: "Robert and Edward may be returning to heroes' welcomes, but *we* transported the ore that made the steel that built the tanks that fought the fight. We had a hand in victory as well!"

Thomas stuck by his father's side all night. They both wore immaculate white dinner jackets and bow ties and stood on the back porch, overlooking the tent with crossed arms, rocking back and forth on their heels. The contrast between Thomas's portly figure and those of the returning soldiers, excruciatingly lean and modestly dressed in college-era sport coats, was stark. Edward and Robert both waved up to their big brother—"Come down! Have a beer with us!"—but Thomas remained on the porch above, sipping scotch with their father and Charles Butterfield.

Once Dugin's orchestra struck up the swing tunes, even more people seemed to arrive, and the shiny brass section wailed as if it had been holding back for years. The calm ocean carried the music down the coast, casting an open invitation to the night, and Eden's doors were thrown open for anyone who wanted to celebrate.

Becca was standing, wide-eyed, on the perimeter of the dance floor when a handsome man in uniform grabbed her by the wrist and began twirling her around the parquet. The live music filled her head and throbbed through her body. It took her only a few minutes to catch on to the right moves. When there was a break in the music, he introduced himself. "I'm Sal," he said.

"I'm Becca," she said, smiling.

"You certainly are a sight in that dress," he said.

"Thank you," she said, feeling the redness rise in her cheeks. There she was, among Long Harbor's finest, back in their glittering dresses and black tie. She bumped shoulders with Mr. and Mrs. Notman, who seemed surprised upon recognizing her. She was smiling so hard, her cheeks hurt. She giggled at some of the girls from her tennis lessons, who lined the dance floor with astonished expressions, watching her balancing in her high heels and swishing her taffeta skirt.

Careful not to stare, she stole glimpses of Sal. With his black hair, dark eyes, and suntan, he was what she imagined a younger version of her father might have looked like.

"Did you just come home from serving?" she asked. Sal explained he had been fighting in North Africa, that he had grown up in Westfield and his parents owned some of the buildings in Long Harbor village. "You know where the ice cream shop is?"

"Of course!"

"That's one of ours."

"Will it reopen?" Becca asked, as Sal handed her a glass of champagne.

"Now that I'm home, it will!" he said.

Edward passed by them, noticing the glass in her hand. "Be good! That's my little sister you're dancing with."

Becca smiled, embarrassed, but Sal saluted Edward, then put his hand over his heart. When he turned back to face her, he seemed doubly pleased, as if dancing with the guest of honor's little sister made him special. They danced for a while and then took a break for some food. Becca went through the buffet, hungrily gathering fancy bites of shrimp and crab cakes. Sal returned to her there, carrying more champagne.

A little surprised and light-headed from her first two glasses, she placed the flute daintily on her lips, the way she had seen it done in the movies, determined to conceal the fact that she was only seventeen. It tasted sweet and fizzy, but Becca wished mostly that it did a better job of quenching her thirst.

The band came back from their break, and Sal took her by the arm again, insisting they dance, pulling her away from what should have been her dinner. "Oh, Becca, you have no idea how much I've missed dancing!" he shouted over the music. They stopped just long enough to have another glass of champagne.

Sal told her he missed Long Harbor, although the place he spoke of was not the one with the golf club and the beach club. He was a local. His family made their living off summer people like the Meisters. What he missed was getting up at the crack of dawn and fishing in the waters off Block Island. He missed the sun turning his back a deep bronze, jumping in the ocean after work, and enjoying a cold beer with his buddies at one of the bars by the state beach.

With each sip of champagne, Becca felt as if she had been transported from a world of dark clouds and sadness to a carefree dream. At one point, Sal looked into her eyes and she thought he would cry, telling her all he was grateful for: being home, being alive, being young, and, for the first time, being treated with respect and admiration everywhere he went. Tonight he was on top of the world. "And to be dancing with the prettiest girl at the party—what else could a guy ask for?"

The dancing continued long past midnight, and Becca needed to cling to Sal's shoulders in order to stay steady. Out of the corner of her eye, she saw her mother disappear into the house with Aunt Kitty, and her father and Thomas eventually went into the living room with the older people. Becca sensed a shiny sheen of perspiration coating her skin and her hair, causing it to fall out of the twist Ruth had done on the top of her head. Sal leaned over and whispered in her ear, "Can we go someplace quiet where we can talk?"

She took another sip of champagne in order to avoid answering Sal right away. She did not know what to say, but the last thing she wanted was for this evening to end. The dance floor was still packed, and Robert and Edward were in the middle of the throng. She knew nobody would notice them leave, so they slipped out the side of the tent and followed the flagstone path toward the dunes. Becca kicked off her high heels at the end of the path. Then Sal put his arm over her shoulder as they walked toward the waves, onto the hard sand, and then turned left to proceed farther away from Eden.

"This sand," Sal said.

"What about it?" she giggled.

"This sand is from eroded rock on the ocean floor. It's as old as time. Have you ever thought of that?"

Becca's girlishness rose to the surface, and she dashed toward the water, dodging the breaking waves. Sal chased her, caught her from behind, and circled his arms around her waist. He lifted her off the ground and carried her to the softer sand at the edge of the sea grass. She tried to suppress her hiccups, and that made her giggle even more. When he laid her down on her back, her head began to spin.

She remembered Sal craning his neck upward and telling her to "look at that moon, will ya?" before leaning over and kissing her. She remembered that kiss and maybe the one after that, but no matter how many times she tried to recall what happened next, she drew a blank.

Chapter 29

LONG HARBOR, RHODE ISLAND
Friday, July 3, 2000

Ruth disembarked the train in Kingston after the six-hour ride north from Washington, DC, and took a big gulp of fresh air. It wasn't like the old days, when one could crack the windows and smell the marshy sea breeze as the train snaked up the coast. She remembered the time Robert held her proudly and protectively around the waist, her stomach a mixture of nerves and excitement, the first time she would meet his parents. It felt like yesterday, although it had been over fifty years ago. Even though she was arriving alone and Becca would be picking her up, this place still conjured up the same nervous excitement.

She took another deep inhalation of the air she associated with summertime. It tasted of salt, was less humid than Washington's, and lifted the wispy hairs off her perspiring forehead. The sun radiated off the concrete, warming the soles of her shoes as she searched the heads for Becca. She stood on her tiptoes, peering over the stream of people, when she came face-to-face with none other than her brother-in-law. "Thomas?"

He turned with a surprised expression on his face.

"It's Ruth!" she said.

"My God, Ruth! I had no idea." He grabbed his wife by the elbow before she could wander any farther down the platform. "Carol, stop. Look, it's Ruth!"

"We must all be going to the same place," Ruth said, smiling, "I'm sure Becca is here somewhere."

"Were you on our train?" asked Carol.

"Yes, all the way from DC."

"Oh, we boarded in Manhattan," said Carol. "Funny I didn't see you in the first-class cabin."

Ruth laughed demurely. She had prepared herself for every variety of awkward exchange with her in-laws over the holiday weekend, but she hadn't expected one this soon. She loved them, and missed them so much that it pained her sometimes, but they could be a challenging group, as the sight of Thomas and his wife, as large and imposing as ever, reminded her now.

"Yoo-hoo, yoo-hoo!" Ruth was grateful to see Becca scurrying across the parking lot, waving her arm in the air.

"There she is," said Ruth, pointing. Thomas and Carol turned their necks stiffly, following the direction of her finger. Becca must have seen Ruth first, running straight into her arms. They were the same height and the same build. It reminded Ruth how much like sisters they had been, swapping clothing all the time.

"Oh, Ruth, thank you. Thank you so much for coming," Becca said, standing back and clasping both of Ruth's hands in her own. It was obvious Becca wasn't yet aware of Thomas's presence, and Ruth sensed his impatience behind them.

"Sister," Thomas bellowed, "you're here to meet us yourself. What an honor."

Becca pulled back from Ruth's embrace. "Oh, I didn't see you! Thomas, Carol, look at you!" They exchanged air kisses before Becca led them all to the car. Thomas struggled across the parking lot with Carol's luggage while Ruth slung an overnight duffel over her shoulder. When they got to the old Lincoln, Becca fumbled with the keys to the trunk.

"You doing okay?" Ruth asked, the others still out of earshot.

Becca just inhaled deeply and gave Ruth a wide, exaggerated grin. Ruth remembered Sadie's telling them how important it was to "put on a happy face."

The car ride back to Eden was packed with chatter about the heat wave, until Ruth and Thomas, who sat next to each other in the backseat, politely started catching up on the last thirty years. Ruth let Becca focus on the road; she would get Becca alone once they arrived at the house. She also figured diverting Thomas's attention was a favor she could do now for her sister-in-law. Some things never changed.

"And Joseph and Benjamin?" Thomas asked.

"The twins are wonderful. Joseph and his family live in New York. He was married eight years ago. I thought he'd be the consummate bachelor, but he met a marvelous girl in Singapore. Her name is Constance. Becca came to the wedding."

"Ah, that's right. I heard he married an Asian girl."

Ruth was taken aback. "Yes, Constance is Korean. Uh, and then there's Benjamin. He's been living in San Francisco for many years."

"Both successful," Thomas said. Ruth wasn't sure whether he meant it as a question or as a statement.

"They have been, thank you." Even though she knew Thomas measured success in wealth alone, she was proud of how gentle and kind her boys had grown up to be.

"Then again, they had a nice head start."

Ruth looked at him quizzically. She wasn't sure what he was referring to.

"Their inheritance—my father set them up nicely. But it sounds like they were smart investors, too."

"Oh," Ruth said, surprised by his audacity. "Yes, they were."

Then Thomas leaned toward her and hushed his voice, pointing his finger discreetly toward the driver's seat. "Not like some people in the family."

Ruth bulged her eyes at his callousness and turned her attention toward the scenery passing by. She hadn't bargained for this.

As they drove up the driveway, Ruth spotted Lilly, already waiting for them outside the kitchen door. *She always did have eagle ears*, Ruth thought, as her heart warmed at the mere sight of the maid. Her hair was thinning and white, but she still had her freckles and that ever-present smile. Lilly waved, then ducked down to peer into the Lincoln.

Ruth couldn't wait and rolled down her window. "Lilly! It's me! Can you believe it?"

"Why, Ruth! You don't look a day over twenty-five!" Lilly said, jogging alongside the car for the last few feet before it stopped.

"Look who's talking, you spring chicken!"

After they unloaded the luggage, Thomas and Carol begged off to the second floor for a nap. "Where do you want us?" he asked Becca, turning toward his sister in the kitchen.

"Oh, Thomas. Don't be cross, but I've got you in the blue guest room. There was a misunderstanding when Andrew and Camilla arrived." Becca waited for his reaction and seemed especially relieved when there was none. "But leave your suitcases down here. I'll ask Andrew to bring them upstairs for you."

Ruth listened as he began lumbering up the back stairs, accentuating his age with each step, Carol behind him, carrying the glasses of water Lilly had fetched for them from the sink. Lilly put on the teakettle and joined Ruth and Becca at the kitchen table. "It's just like old times. I can't believe Ruthie is back!"

Ruth noticed a tilt in Lilly's head, one that hinted she was intrigued about how Ruth's visit had come about. "It's a shame you've stayed away for so long," she said, fishing for an explanation. *Why this weekend? Why now?* But it wasn't Ruth's place to spill the beans, not even to Lilly.

"Becca's invited me so many times, and I finally told myself, *Ruth! Enough sitting alone in sticky DC on the Fourth of July. Pack your bags and go to Eden!*"

Sitting in the kitchen, she did regret having stayed away, and letting that special bond with Becca deteriorate into an exchange of polite phone calls and holiday cards. But their relationship had strained after Sadie died and Becca and Dan took control of Eden. Ruth had resented the way she was marginalized in the household. But, in retrospect, Becca had probably bristled at the intimacy

Ruth shared with her mother. She had first seen it in Becca's face when Sadie hung the photograph of them, arm in arm, on the beach. It had always been one of Sadie's favorites and thus was framed larger than the others.

When Joseph and Constance announced their wedding and Ruth mailed her allotted invitations, she looked forward to a reunion with her extended family. Becca wrote she'd be attending alone but asked if she might stay on for a night after the wedding. "It's high time we have some one-on-one time," Becca said.

Ruth was exhausted after the wedding, but Becca treated her to lunch, suggesting they bundle up afterward for a long walk down the Mall. And that was when she divulged the whole story, what had happened the night of Robert and Edward's party, leading all the way up to the phone call from Lee. Ruth could tell that simply voicing the words was liberating for Becca. Ruth held on to her, and for the first time tears flowed, from both of them, fifty years' worth.

"Sadie set it all up?" Ruth asked, handing Becca a tissue.

"You remember how good she was at making plans."

"Oh, Becca, I really loved your mother, but this explains so much."

Ruth promised she would be there when Becca told the rest of the family, "whenever that might be." She was the one who convinced Becca it had to be done, and the one who called every couple of months to keep the idea alive. "I wouldn't dream of letting you go through that alone."

"Would you like some more tea?" Lilly asked her now.

Ruth got up from the table and walked to the sink where she could take in the view from the picture window. She craned her neck in both directions, yearning for the full panorama. "No, thank you," she said. "What I'd really like to do is go out and take a look at the waves."

Chapter 30

LONG HARBOR, RHODE ISLAND
1945

Although the summer of 1945 had been spectacular, it was ending like any other, with the annual pantry-cleaning ritual, covering the upholstered furniture with sheets, and draining the pipes for the winter. Becca worked alongside her mother, delivering items to the third floor or fetching boxes from the basement.

Her mother's elation at having her family assembled together at Eden that summer had subsided now that Becca's brothers were gone again, either searching for work or drawn away by romance. In the aftermath of the homecoming celebration, August seemed to vanish into the steamy air. Now, with the mix of dread and sadness that always marked the end of the season, they prepared to return to Pittsburgh.

Becca was awakened in her father's study by her mother's jostling and an irritated tone in her voice. "Wake up, Becca. There's still a lot to do."

"Sorry, I must have fallen asleep while I was pulling together the newspapers and magazines."

"What's wrong? Are you feeling all right?"

Becca stretched her arms in the air. "I'm just so tired. Do you mind if I take a little nap?"

She slept right through dinner. In the morning, Becca began retching into her washbasin. Her mother came up behind her and held her forehead.

"Darling, have you been ill all night?" she asked.

"Oh, Mother, it's been like this for a few days now."

Her mother squinted her eyes and tilted her head but didn't confront Becca until later that day. She came in to Becca's room carrying her car keys in one hand and her pocketbook in the crook of her elbow. "Okay, let's go," her mother said. "Time to get you to the doctor."

Becca voiced her surprise. "To the doctor? For the flu?"

Once in the car, her mother followed the route to the interstate, instead of taking the turn toward their local physician's office. "Becca, I made an appointment for you with a Dr. North in New Haven."

"We're going all the way to New Haven, Mother? Why?"

"We can't risk talk in Long Harbor." Her mother looked into the rearview mirror and pulled the car over to the side of the road abruptly. She turned toward Becca in the passenger seat. Her mother stared at her for a long time, then closed her eyes and let out a deep sigh.

"Mother, what is going on? You're scaring me."

"Becca, do you have any idea why you've been vomiting every day? Why your breasts are swollen? Why you're tired and falling asleep in the middle of the afternoon? You have all the signs of being in the family way."

Becca's eyes widened as she sucked in an audible gasp.

"Becca, please do not sit there with that dumbfounded look. A girl does not magically become pregnant. What indiscretions have you been involved in, and with whom?"

Becca began to sob. Ever since the night of the party, images of Sal had played in her mind. For several days afterward, she hoped to hear from him, but he seemed to be avoiding her entirely. She finally got up the nerve to ask Edward if he had seen him around town. He'd seen them dancing together, and would know what her question meant. "I heard his old man's got him working at the dock on weekends, and during the week he's a mechanic at the Long Harbor Garage. Probably working 'round the clock."

The following Saturday she walked past the Fabbrizzios' docks, seagulls squealing over the remnants of fish carcass. She saw Sal tossing a line to a tourist fishing boat. She stood there for a while, shading her eyes from the glare. He looked her way, then quickly turned back to his task of unloading the passengers. Even from a distance, she sensed his discomfort. Since then, Becca had avoided the village altogether, venturing only to the beach with her friends. When Robert and Ruth couldn't even persuade her to join them for the ice cream parlor's reopening, Robert figured it out. "What's the matter, Becca—afraid to run into your local boy?"

Sitting next to her mother in the front seat of their family car, she struggled to put the pieces together. She traveled back to the dance floor, to all the champagne and to giggling as she ran down the beach with him, but this was where her memory grew hazy. They were lying down and kissing; then he unzipped her dress. She remembered fretting that her taffeta skirt would be ruined in the sand, but when Sal touched her breasts, she forgot everything else. The sensation thrilled her. She remembered the rush through her stomach and legs. Her head was spinning, and bile inched up her throat.

The next thing she knew, she was opening her eyes to see Sal with the predawn violet sky behind him, her head throbbing with an unbelievable pain.

"Becca," he said, "I've got to get you home. It's late. Well, it's actually early. It's almost dawn." He jostled her arm further to wake her up. He helped her to stand, then zipped up her dress and shook its shape back into place around her hips. He took her hand, and together they walked back toward the house. That was when Becca felt moisture between her legs and realized her panties were gone, but she was too embarrassed to ask Sal about it. In fact, they walked in silence.

As soon as they reached the pathway to the house, she picked up her shoes and let go of his hand. When Sal leaned in to kiss her, Becca pulled back, whispering, "Shh . . . my mother gets up early."

She trotted to the kitchen door, slowly opening the screen

door and easing it shut behind her. She tiptoed up the back stairs and past the maids' rooms, where many of her brothers' friends were sleeping. Thankfully, the doors were all shut tight, the sounds of drunken snoring echoing through the hallway.

Once she slipped into her room, she shed the sandy dress onto the floor and kicked it into her closet. She pulled her nightgown over her head, drew the shades on her windows, and slipped between the sheets. The sand in her hair sprinkled across the pillow.

"I'll ask you one more time," her mother asked from the front seat of the car now, "What indiscretions have you been involved in, and with whom?"

Becca finally found her voice. "The night of the party, I was dancing with a boy from town. I drank champagne, too much. I was really dizzy. I went out onto the beach with him, but I can't remember everything."

* * *

Dr. North wore a disapproving scowl as he examined Becca on a cold, stainless-steel surface. She shivered, dressed in only a hospital gown with the opening in front. A nurse entered and took Becca's arm in one hand, a syringe perched in the other, to draw blood.

The following day, the nurse telephoned with expedited test results that turned out positive. Sadie said, "Well, Becca, I guess this leaves no question as to what happened on the beach." Her mother's disappointed eyes pierced her.

Becca clung to her mother's shoulders and cried. She sensed her mother's own mounting anxiety but remained there, against her shoulder, increasingly afraid of what lay before her. Her mother rhythmically rubbed her back and spoke in a low voice. "Oh, Becca, I'm to blame as well. The way that dress cinched at your waist. You developed quite a figure while your father and I weren't paying attention. I let you wear makeup and let Ruth put your hair up. It made me happy to see you laughing at my dressing table. Why, your father even commented on how glamorous you looked. I should have insisted on something more modest."

Her mother held her for several minutes in the kitchen. She opened a window to let some air in. The sun was dropping, and the glare in Becca's eyes brought on a headache. They sat at the kitchen table quietly, until her mother began to ramble on, thinking aloud about what needed to be done. "Robert and Edward made it home safely. This must be my payback. If Bunny finds out, it will destroy him, destroy the family entirely. Bunny would find the young man and kill him. Ha—then Long Harbor would really have something to talk about.

"Becca, there are places where girls in trouble go. I've heard about some well-established homes in the Midwest. I'll find the best one, Becca, and you will go—right away, as if you are spending your senior year at finishing school. I'll tell Daddy that you have been asking to go ever since you heard about Eleanor's experience, and that I think it a splendid idea. I'll tell him that I've gotten good reviews from Eleanor's parents and all the materials from the school. He's so preoccupied with getting Edward and Robert set up in New York, he'll be more than happy to let me handle all the details."

"But, Mother, right away?" Becca asked.

"I know it's scary, but the academic calendar provides a perfect cover. Right now, protecting your reputation is my highest priority. Listen to me, Becca—this may seem like a great injustice, but it's just the way things are. Young men who engage in sex, well, it actually enhances their masculinity. But young women, girls, in the same situation, who become pregnant, for heaven's sake, they're shunned by family and friends. You wouldn't be allowed to return to school. Your father and brothers would never look at you the same way. This indiscretion would be a permanent stain on your reputation and on our name. Given your father's position, this would be very damaging in Pittsburgh, not to mention the scandal it would cause in Long Harbor."

"But Daddy wouldn't—"

Sadie cut her off. "Becca, don't kid yourself. Your father isn't the perfect man you make him out to be. Going away and giving up this child is the only option. You'll forget it ever happened in no time at all."

Becca's face flushed while her mother rapped her fingernails on the table. "You will stay there to convalesce after the baby is born in April. I will come in May to your 'graduation' and bring you back to Pittsburgh. You'll be back at Eden for Memorial Day weekend." Becca turned toward the window, one hand pressed to her forehead. Her mother's tone became more assured as her plan gained momentum, but all Becca wanted was for time to rewind, for the film reel of her summer to go back to the beginning, so she could stay in the kitchen and help Alice the night of the party.

Chapter 31

LONG HARBOR, RHODE ISLAND
Friday, July 3, 2000

S arah entered the dining room. It felt good to be showered, out of her bedroom, and a part of the activity. Her grandmother pulled out the armchair at the head of the table. "Thomas, would you like to sit here?" she asked, unusually attentive to her brother and his wife.

"Why, thank you, sister," he said, gesturing to the chair on his right for Aunt Carol. "Sarah, why don't you sit on Thomas's left, across from Carol?" her grandmother asked.

"I'd love to," she said, making her way there.

Gran took her seat at the opposite end, Uncle Andrew pulling out her chair with gentlemanly grace. Everyone else filled in between. They were an even ten, finally a crowd large enough to warrant the dining room table. Sarah loved hearing the cacophony of voices; this was what Eden was supposed to feel like. When the conversation had run through what was new in their lives, the reminiscing began. Gran, Uncle Thomas, and Aunt Ruth told one story after the next.

"You mean, the entire sleeping porch was knocked off?" Walter asked.

"Yes, and the windows all smashed in on the ground floor and the entire house filled with rain and seawater," Gran said.

"Was anyone home?" Sally asked.

"Yes! I was here with my father and Robert. If it hadn't been for his fast hands, I might have drowned."

"Afterward, Father and I spent months on ladders, getting things straight," Thomas said.

"And my mother and I were in the kitchen 'round the clock, cooking for all the men," Gran added.

Everyone was entranced by stories of the hurricane—everyone except, from the looks of it, Aunt Carol, who stared at a water stain on the ceiling. Sarah asked her about her charity work in Pittsburgh, attempting to distract her.

Then her grandmother clinked her crystal glass with a teaspoon in order to get everyone's attention. "I'm so happy we could all be here together tonight," she said. "I'm very lucky. We haven't all been together since Dan passed away. To have you all back at Eden now, during the summertime, is really wonderful. You know, my mother and father built this house for family, and the place really comes alive when it's full. I've even asked Ruth to invite Joseph and Benjamin and their families to visit next week."

"That was very generous," Aunt Ruth said, "and I think Joseph, Constance, and the girls would love to come." Sarah noticed her mother raise her eyebrows in surprise. After a general acknowledgment that it would be wonderful to see Joseph and meet his wife, the table fell back into silence and all eyes turned back to Gran. She looked as if she were considering something important but then stood up rather abruptly, announcing that dessert and coffee would be served in the living room. Aunt Ruth had helped Lilly make the blueberry pie and went to the kitchen to serve the pieces. Gran asked Sally and Walter to clear the dishes.

Sarah pushed back from the table and straggled into the living room with everyone else. Her mother, Uncle Thomas, Aunt Carol, Uncle Andrew, Aunt Camilla, all stretched their arms overhead and yawned from full stomachs. "Good Lord, it's hot. Andrew, can you open a window?" her mother said.

While Uncle Andrew struggled with a window that seemed painted shut, Thomas wandered slowly throughout the grand space, casting a critical eye on the beams and the floor joists. He knocked his fist against the mantel. Sarah's mother relaxed into the plush furnishings, oblivious to the due diligence that was taking place. "It's probably the first time we've sat in here since Dad died," she said to nobody in particular, wiping beads of perspiration from her forehead with a cocktail napkin.

Sarah bit her fingernails, anticipating her grandmother's announcement. The night before, tossing and turning in bed, she had concluded it was terminal cancer. What would she do without Gran? Just thinking about it caused her eyes to tear up.

Aunt Camilla sat down on the sofa next to her. "I take it the negotiations are about to begin," she said in an all-knowing tone.

"What do you mean?" Sarah asked.

"Ah, dear Sarah," Aunt Camilla said, patting her knee. "You know—divvying up this place. It's obvious from the state of the bathrooms alone that Becca stopped maintaining it long ago."

"That's what you think Gran's announcement is about?"

"What else could it be?"

Sarah thought her grandmother wanted to keep her money problems private, but what a relief if it wasn't cancer after all.

* * *

Rachel sat on the other side of the room, eying her brother. He oozed irritation, scowling at his children's bored faces. "Did you enjoy the tennis today with your dad?" she asked Walter and Sally, egging them on, having heard the quarreling when they got out of the car. Walter shrugged, and Sally rolled her eyes.

"They didn't care for the tennis or our walk to the harbor to look at the boats," Andrew said.

"What a shame," said Rachel.

Andrew smirked at her.

She returned his expression with a rascally grin of her own. No matter how old they got, put them together for a few days, and they were kids again, antagonizing each other in the way only siblings knew how. It had always been easy to get under Andrew's skin, read his disappointment that they no longer dressed for dinner. Her brother had clung to the portraits that glorified their uprightness: silver-haired, austere Bunny Meister with his buttoned-up Ivy League boys; his modest daughter, a product of the finest finishing school; and a serene, well-composed wife by his side. Andrew had to face the fact that their legacy had deteriorated into a middle-class morass replete with unwed pregnancy and overweight divorcees.

Sarah interrupted her mother's jousting with Andrew by suggesting a game of Scrabble. Sally rolled her eyes again. "That game takes forever!"

Andrew jumped right in, as if to demonstrate for his children how one might enthusiastically engage with others. "I'll play!" he said.

"Me too," said Rachel, upping the ante. She was, after all, the reader, the wordsmith, and a contest with letters would always be hers. The rest of the day had been filled with athletic pursuits and physical exertion, leaving her on the sidelines.

"Great. Aunt Camilla, will you round out the table?" Sarah asked.

Rachel watched her pregnant daughter, down on her hands and knees, searching through the board games in the cabinet. Backgammon and Monopoly were in there, alongside some random checkers and chess pieces and three incomplete decks of cards held together by dried-out rubber bands. When Sarah found the old Scrabble board, Rachel helped her set it up on the card table.

"Everyone take seven tiles," Sarah instructed. This was for Camilla's benefit, as the rules ran deep in Rachel and Andrew's veins. They took turns picking tiles, placing them deliberately into their racks. Then they each picked up an additional tile, Rachel delighting in the "K" that earned her the right to go first. Rachel deliberated her opening move, only peripherally aware that her mother had joined them all in the living room, along with Aunt Ruth, who carried a stack of dishes, and Lilly, who carried a tray laden with pie and ice cream.

Lilly put the heavy tray down on the large coffee table in front of the sofa and began to pass out plates. She handed Thomas and Carol napkins and forks and the last of the pie as they settled into the love seat by the fireplace. She wiped her hands on her apron and was about to take the tray back into the kitchen, when Becca said, "Lilly, please stay. You're family. I want you to hear this, too."

That declaration got her attention and caused all the others to look back and forth at each other. Lilly sat down slowly on the couch next to Camilla, creating the effect of everyone sitting in more or less a circle within the oversized room.

Becca and Ruth sat side by side in the swiveling armchairs by the window. Lilly would always think of them as Bunny and Sadie's favorites, especially toward the end—the way they swayed slowly from side to side, balancing a book on one knee, the page illuminated by sun rays beaming through the large plate window.

Lilly turned her head toward the sound of Thomas clearing his throat. "Let's not get ahead of ourselves here, sister. You and I should speak privately first."

"Oh, Thomas, no," Becca said. "That's not what I want to discuss now."

He nodded. "Okay, then."

Lilly was surprised to see tears forming in Becca's eyes. Ruth passed a handkerchief to her. Walter looked up at the ceiling and stretched his beefy limbs, hot and sticky in the living room. Sally sat in a chair beside her mother, both of their right legs crossed over their left knees. Everyone was quietly waiting for Becca, all but Rachel, who was arranging her Scrabble tiles. She looked up suddenly. "We're not going to play? I was about to lay down a bingo, with a 'Z' to boot!" Andrew shook his head.

"If you don't mind, Rachel, I think it's important we have a discussion," Becca said. "I don't know that we've ever talked about something this serious as a family before. I know when I was growing up, many things were never spoken about." Lilly couldn't imagine what on earth was going to come out of her mouth next, but Ruth seemed to be in the know. She nodded at Becca with encouragement, mouthing, "You can do it."

"I don't quite know how to start. I hope you all can be open-minded. You see, when I was seventeen and my brothers came home from the war, not Thomas, just Edward and Bobby," Becca stammered, "well, Mother and Daddy threw a big party here at Eden. I had never seen such a celebration; it felt like the festivities lasted for days. It was a very happy, exciting time for everyone. Well, Thomas was there, and Ruth was there—you can ask her."

Ruth nodded. "Yes, I was there!"

Becca had everyone's attention now. Even Walter and Sally seemed entranced, probably at the idea of their grandmother, once young, attending a multiday party. Lilly had pointed out the pictures of their celebrated great-uncles Edward and Robert on the back stairs. They had been so handsome in their khaki uniforms, posing with their arms around each other.

"I had always been a reserved girl. You see, my mother was worried during the war, and even before that she was anxious because Thomas was sick."

Thomas shook his head again and asked, "What does that have to do with—"

"I'm sorry, Thomas; let me finish."

Thomas nodded skeptically. Carol looked at him, worried.

"Thomas had epilepsy, you know. Well, nobody understood it or called it by that name back then."

"Becca! How dare you!" Carol said.

"I'm just trying to explain what it was like back then."

Carol folded her arms across her chest.

"And during the war, well, Mother was an absolute wreck and Daddy was working all the time. It was difficult. When the war ended and my brothers came back . . . Well, Ruth remembers, too—you see, Robert and Ruth were so in love, and so all of a sudden my mother was happy; she had all her children home, and there was a wedding on the horizon. Really, in my whole life I had never seen her so gleeful. She even surprised me with a beautiful new dress, such an extravagance. I still remember the way the skirt twirled when I spun around.

"The party was magical. There was a big tent and a live band playing swing tunes. There were lanterns strung around the tent and in the yard. People were everywhere. Daddy even ordered a big fountain for the center of the tent that bubbled champagne all night long.

"I guess that's where the trouble began for me. It was my first drink of alcohol—you know champagne can be sweet, and I was thirsty from the dancing and the warm weather and all, and I drank much more than I should have."

Becca avoided everyone's stares and fixed her eyes on Ruth's encouraging face. Lilly now suspected where this story was leading. She recalled the afternoon the previous winter, a few weeks after Dan died, meeting a woman in the kitchen. Becca had introduced her as Lee, but she was a dead ringer for Rachel. Lilly had had a feeling then, a what if, but had stored it away as impossible. Poor Rachel, still fiddling with her Scrabble tiles, had no idea what was about to hit her.

Becca looked into her lap and took a deep breath. "The young man I was dancing with was drinking as well, and it got very late, and we felt—I felt—so free. For the first time, really, there were no worries hanging over us. And nobody had ever paid so much attention to me. I was inexperienced, and I didn't know how to act. Well, we went out over the dunes and we sat in the sand together, and things got carried away." Becca stopped speaking, as if collecting her thoughts.

* * *

Sarah watched as Sally leaned forward in her seat, mouth agape. She wished her cousin could hide her daytime talk show–like surprise for Gran's sake. Sarah twisted a long strand of her hair and put a hand on her stomach. She felt something against her ribs, a little flutter, a sensation she had never experienced before. "I just felt the baby move!" She put her hand over her mouth, realizing the disruption she had created. "Sorry, Gran."

Her grandmother smiled in her direction, and Sarah noticed the trails of tears on her cheeks. "This is where our stories collide, Sarah. Toward the end of that summer, it became clear—at least to my mother—that *I* was pregnant."

Sarah's mother let out an audible gasp.

Her grandmother looked back at Ruth and continued, more rapidly, "You know, this sort of thing could cause quite a scandal in those days. My mother insisted nobody know, not even my father or my brothers. She arranged for me to go to a maternity hospital in Kansas City. Everyone thought I was attending finishing school. I even came back with a counterfeit diploma." Aunt Ruth handed her a handkerchief.

"I stayed there until spring, I had a beautiful little baby girl. Mother came to collect me and brought me back to Eden. I think Robert and Ruth got married about three weeks later, so all the fuss over the wedding took the attention away from me. I've kept that secret for fifty-seven years."

Sarah's mother spoke up. "You mean, you never told Daddy?"

Her grandmother looked directly at her mother. "No, Rachel, I did not." She paused. "There were many times I wanted to tell him, but I felt a great deal of shame, and of course my mother insisted I forget the whole thing. Then, when you and Andrew were born, I thought I could bury it, pretend you were my only children. The more time passed, the harder it seemed to tell your father."

"But when I got pregnant with Sarah," Rachel said, "you insisted—"

"I insisted you keep your daughter. I didn't want you to have the same—"

"You wouldn't hear of any other options—"

"Rachel, please stop acting the victim. Look at Sarah, your beautiful daughter, sitting here with you. How do you think your words make her feel?"

Sarah's skin got hot; she could tell she was reddening, as Sally and Camilla were now staring at her. "Uncle Andrew, could you try opening that window again?" she asked.

"My God," said Thomas. Carol sat fixed by his side, gripping her husband's leg, her eyes wide open, exaggerating the wrinkles on her forehead.

Her grandmother continued, "And so, since we are all together this weekend, I have invited Lee to Eden to join us for brunch on Sunday. She wants very much to meet you."

Sarah stood up and went to give her grandmother a hug. "Oh, Gran, I'm sorry. I'm so sorry for you."

"Can you understand why I want you to keep your child?"

Sarah swallowed hard and nodded, her eyes moist. She collected a stack of plates with untouched pie and melting ice cream and carried them into the kitchen, then went directly to the driveway to inhale the fresh air.

* * *

Lilly went to Becca's side and hugged her. Camilla stood by as well, but Lilly could sense her smugness over the fact that the family was not woven from the strong moral fiber her husband always trumpeted.

"Wow, Gran, that's an intense story. Knocked up—that was like . . . like . . . date rape!" Sally said.

"Sally, heavens no," Becca said. "I had never thought of it like that, like I was the victim of a crime."

"Well, today you would be."

"That's enough, Sally," Camilla said.

"I can't wait to meet her!" Walter said, as if anticipating the next episode in a mini-series.

Camilla ushered her children upstairs, and Thomas and Carol slipped out onto the back porch. Lilly gathered the remaining dishes onto her tray and headed into the kitchen to give Becca some time alone with Andrew and Rachel.

* * *

Rachel stared at her brother's hand, turning letter tiles over one by one. Once everyone else left, she looked fiercely at her mother, demanding further explanation.

When none came, Rachel shouted, "Hypocrite! You did one thing but expected the opposite from me!"

"Hold on a second, Rachel," Andrew said. "Mother, do you have any idea about the whereabouts of the baby's—Lee's—father?" he asked.

"Yes," she said. "He's . . . he's actually in town."

"In Long Harbor?" cried Rachel. "Oh my God!"

"He never knew about the baby," Becca continued. "We never spoke after that night. He came to the party because he had just returned from overseas, just like my brothers. He looked just like all of Robert and Edward's other friends, so handsome in his uniform. Mom invited the whole town."

"Who is he, Mother?" Rachel demanded.

"Sal Fabbrizzio."

"*My* Sal Fabbrizzio?"

"Yes."

Rachel swept all the Scrabble tiles onto the rug. "Shit," she said, before marching up to her room.

Chapter 32

KANSAS CITY, MISSOURI
1945

Day turned into night and then into dawn again. The sun rose as a porter poked his head into Becca's compartment. "Fifteen minutes until we pull into Union Station," he said, setting down a basin of fresh water and a tray of tea and toast. Kansas City was the end of the line, and Becca heard the other passengers shuffling about in the aisle, collecting their hand luggage.

It had been over a twenty-hour journey, and although the train had a dining car, all she could stomach were the saltines and ginger ale her mother had packed. Her mother had also tucked a Charlotte Brontë novel into her purse, but Becca had given up on that and gazed out the window, glimpsing the reflection of her own sad eyes and downturned mouth. She was tired of her mother's stowed-away surprises.

She stretched her arms overhead, fighting the tightness that had settled in her neck and shoulders. Dr. North was right: even though her outward appearance was no different, her body was working overtime. She yawned as she stood, pins and needles numbing her legs. After gathering her few belongings, she peered out the window. All she had seen in daylight so far were miles and miles of cornfields, but now all the signs of an urban center were coming into view. It might have been Pittsburgh, but these were all strange buildings and there was something different about the light, the color of the sky. Separated from her family, and amid everything unfamiliar, Becca continued to stand and stare out the window as her fellow passengers began to crowd the aisle.

The brakes squealed on the tracks before the train lunged forward to a complete stop. Becca waited while the other passengers rushed down the aisle ahead of her—theirs were most likely happy homecomings or reunions with loved ones. She was in no hurry at all.

When she finally stood at the door and looked up and down the length of the steamy platform, the station's grand scale surprised her. She took the Pullman porter's outstretched hand for balance as she made the last, oversized step off of the train. A tall Negro man in a navy suit and driver's cap approached and said, "You must be Miss Meister." When Becca nodded, he continued, "I'm Ronald. Since you was the last one off, I knew it must be you. You girls is never in a rush to get off that train."

"Oh, thank you," Becca said, trying to smile, passing over her hand luggage. He showed her to a bench inside the main lobby, where she waited for him to retrieve her steamer trunk. The station's ceiling was extraordinarily high and painted with a towering mural of clouds and cherubs, and an enormous gleaming brass clock hung from a buttress in front of her. A blond woman in a pretty pink suit and matching hat stood waiting, tapping her foot and checking her wristwatch. Suddenly emerging from the crowd, a handsome young man rushed to her side. She smiled and they kissed, before heading for the doors arm in arm.

Ronald returned with her trunk on a dolly. "Okay, miss, if you're ready now, it's this way to the car." Becca was silent, still following the pretty blonde and her beau with her eyes.

"Miss?"

"I'm sorry, I just wasn't expecting such a big station," Becca said, her eyes turning toward the magnificent ceiling.

"We got a dozen lines here. This here Union Station is the biggest in the country. Makes sense, don't it? We're smack-dab in the middle. All the lines crisscrossing the nation run through here."

In the car, Ronald explained that Kansas City's central location, along with Missouri's progressive adoption laws, had resulted in its becoming home to pioneering maternity hospitals. For approximately thirty-five years, unwed girls in trouble had made their way to Kansas City, and by the time Becca arrived, there were a dozen such hospitals, both large and small, caring for girls like her, in an unfortunate condition.

"Of all the maternity hospitals in the city, none is as confidential as the Willows," said Ronald. "Some folks call it the Waldorf because it's the fanciest, too."

As Ronald made a careful turn into the Willows' short drive, Becca remembered her mother's reassurance that this would be more like a home than like an institution. It looked as if it had originally been a grand Victorian residence, painted light green with dark green trim, but expanded several times in order to accommodate all the girls and their babies awaiting adoption. It had a massive wraparound porch, where several clusters of girls were sitting in the fresh air, and across the street was a beautiful park. Her mother had been right, it did look homey, but Becca didn't feel like making friends or rocking on the porch and suddenly craved a sterile cell block where she could just be anonymous.

She followed Ronald onto the porch and read the bronze plaque by the front door: THE WILLOWS HOME, FOUNDED 1910, DR. AND MRS. EDWIN LAWTON. Ronald held open a large mahogany door and led Becca into the parlor, which served as a welcome area, furnished with a hotel-like registration desk. Two girls sat in red leather chairs by the window, looking up from their knitting when Becca entered.

An older woman, resembling a kindly Mrs. Claus, with reading glasses perched on her nose and her gray hair pulled back in a bun, approached. She wore a blouse, a suit jacket, and a full skirt. She smiled, looking into Becca's eyes, and cupped Becca's chilly hands in hers. "Well, hello! I'm Mrs. Lawton, and you must be Becca. Your hands are cold. I guess winter is around the bend!" Then she picked up a large envelope with "Becca M." written on the front, saying, "There's quite a bit of material for us to go over, dear, but that can wait. You've had a long trip. Ronald will show you to your room. I suggest you rest a bit before supper."

Maybe it was her plain, midwestern friendliness or a well-tuned, empathetic nature, but Mrs. Lawton made Becca forget her immediate worries. She had feared the Willows would reinforce her sense of shame, but, instead of passing judgment, Mrs. Lawton couldn't have been kinder.

Ronald hauled her trunk up the back stairs and set it down at the foot of Becca's twin bed. Holding his driver's cap over his heart with his left hand, he waved goodbye with his right. "Miss Meister, I sure hope it goes okay for you."

"Thank you, Ronald."

He turned and left, gently pulling the door closed behind him.

Left alone, she spun on her heels to survey her home for the next seven months. The gray-painted floor was covered with a pale pink hooked rug. A large, sun-filled window illuminated a white desk below it. A silver tea service and a side of sugar cookies sat on the desk, and against the wall was a single bed with white sheets and a cotton quilt. The room was filled with light and cheerful touches, but Becca closed the blinds, switched off the desk lamp, and turned her back on the tea service.

She opened the drawer of the bedside table and found a Holy Bible. She took it out of the drawer and sat on the bed, turning it over in her hands. Maybe she would read this while she was here. It would probably take seven months as well. Becca's head was throbbing, and she suddenly became aware of her fatigue. She lay down.

The sound of a clanging bell startled her awake. Wiping her eyes, she stood and opened her door. A stream of young women clamored in the hallway. Becca's stomach growled as she followed them to dinner.

The Willows' oak-paneled dining room was filled with a dozen or so large, round tables covered with white cloths and each adorned with a centerpiece of chrysanthemums. She watched as girls congregated in groups around the tables, continuing conversations that had been on hold since the bell had rung.

Becca slipped into a chair at one of the empty tables along the wall. In the center were glass pitchers of ice water and milk, droplets of condensation running down their sides. Three girls with enormous bellies approached her with curious expressions on their faces, and she realized that she was interloping on their table. They concentrated on lowering themselves into their seats, then looked up at her.

"A new arrival!" one of the girls said, though she was scowling.

"I'm sorry. I didn't know where else to sit," said Becca.

"That's okay," said one with a softer face. "There's room. Our numbers are dwindling."

"My name is Becca."

"I'm Mabel," said the one with the scowling face. They were interrupted by a waiter delivering roast turkey, green beans, and mashed potatoes. Mabel surveyed the trays. "A little early for Thanksgiving, isn't it? I don't think I can stomach this. I've been craving tomato sauce all day."

Becca was careful not to take too much at first. Even though her appetite had returned for the first time in days, she was conscientious about deferring to what she assumed were the larger appetites around the table. But they took tiny portions, picking over the turkey and the beans. Mabel spooned only a lump of potatoes onto her plate.

"Becca, was it?" Mabel asked.

Becca nodded silently.

"Well, Becca, you're welcome to sit with us, but you might want to stick with the new girls. You'll be as far along as they are. We used to be eight and filled this whole table. You don't want to wake up one morning and have all your friends gone. And you don't want to be hearing about all our aches and pains before you need to."

Becca looked down at her food. She hated that she couldn't control the tremble of her lip or the hot flush in her cheeks. Lately, she felt as if anything could hurt her feelings or make her weepy.

"Now, Mabel," said one of the other girls at the table, "you've upset her. You could be a little more welcoming. It's her first night."

"Clara, it's never too soon to figure out the way things work around here. I would have been appreciative on my first night if someone had informed me that my roommate would go off in the middle of the night a month into my stay and never come back. After everything I had shared with her, that was just one more heartache I had to suffer."

Becca dabbed the corners of her eyes with a napkin, then looked up to see waiters coming around again. She listened to snippets of gossip at dinner, centering on one girl or another's sad tale. Although she'd been taught that gossip was impolite, she found it reassuring in a morbid way; knowing which cases were more heartbreaking than her own brought her comfort. After listening to Mabel go on and on, Becca was grateful that she hadn't suffered any brutality, and that Sal wasn't her cousin or her stepfather.

The next day, she went over all the rules, her schedule, and medical forms with Mrs. Lawton. On all her paperwork, her name was printed as "Becca M." Mrs. Lawton explained that under no circumstances were last names used at the Willows; it was part of the establishment's confidentiality policy. When Mrs. Lawton excused herself for a moment to answer the telephone, Becca noticed a passage from the Bible, Exodus 2:1, framed and hanging behind her desk.

A certain man of the house of Levi went and married a Levite woman. The woman conceived and bore a son, and when she saw that he was good, she hid him for three months. When she could hide him no longer, she got a wicker basket for him and caulked it with bitumen and pitch. She put the child into it and placed it among the reeds by the banks of the Nile.

Becca noticed that Mrs. Lawton had returned to the office and was watching her.

"You see, Becca, since the beginning of time, mothers have had to give their children away. Sometimes it's meant to be," she said.

Chapter 33

LONG HARBOR, RHODE ISLAND
Saturday, July 4, 2000

L illy handed the silver ice bucket to Andrew as he passed through the kitchen. He'd been back and forth so many times for the gin, vodka, scotch, tonic water, and club soda. Lilly knew exactly how he'd line up the glass bottles; it was in his genes. He'd learned it from Dan, and Dan had learned it from Bunny. All three of them had a way of tending bar on the porch, rocking on their feet, their shoulders back, as they surveyed the lawn, the dunes, and the ocean beyond. Andrew made yet another trip into the kitchen for white wine and cranberry juice for the women. Lilly asked, "Do you have soft drinks for the kids?"

"They can fend for themselves."

"I don't want them running through the kitchen," said Lilly.

Andrew turned to face her with a look of surprise, probably because he wasn't used to her speaking her mind. She followed him out to the porch with a stack of paper cocktail napkins. They stood together at the bar, arranging the last few things, and she looked over one shoulder and then the other. She leaned in particularly close to his side. "I need to talk to you, Andrew," she whispered, removing the folded paper from her apron pocket and handing it to him as if they were conducting an illicit transaction.

He looked at her skeptically, spreading the letter out on the bar. He pulled his reading glasses out from the inside pocket of his blazer and put them on, before pouring himself a vodka and cranberry. Lilly watched him take a sip of his drink and sensed her bad timing; he hadn't had time to recover from the bombshell his mother had dropped the night before.

"What is this?" he asked.

"A letter I found when I was making up the bedrooms." Andrew seemed to have perused only the heading before he folded up the letter and handed it back to her.

"Your uncles want to sell Eden."

"So?" He didn't appear surprised.

"I thought you should know."

"Thanks, Lilly, but this is none of your business," he said, swirling the ice cubes around in his glass.

"Somebody needs to stand up to your uncle. For your mother's sake. Selling this house, after all she's been through?"

"It's under control."

Lilly was suddenly struck by the fact that putting Eden up for sale was not a big deal to Andrew. "Then you've spoken to Thomas?" she asked.

"Lilly, this is family business. But thanks for bringing me the letter."

"I just worry about your mother," she said.

"Be assured, I worry about my mother, too," he said with a nod, suggesting the conversation was over. "I'll get through this blasted brunch with my new 'sister,' and then I'll sit down with Mother. She's been in denial about her future at Eden for a while."

Lilly frowned. Andrew had been playing the good son all day, manning the grill, flipping the compulsory Fourth of July hamburgers and hot dogs, but underneath he was selfish and spiteful. Why would he care if Becca and Rachel and Sarah lost Eden? He hardly came to visit anymore, and Camilla clearly couldn't stand the place.

His children weren't any better. "I thought the Fourth of July was supposed to be fun," Walter had whined as they stood around the grill, Andrew scorching the hot dogs and forking them onto the platter Lilly held for him.

"Tonight will be fun," Andrew had said. "Entertaining is what this family does best."

Lilly looked at her watch and realized guests would be arriving soon. She decided it best to leave Andrew at the bar with his cocktail. As she took a few steps toward the living room door, she spotted Walter and Sally clamoring over the dunes with towels wrapped around their bathing suits. Andrew must have spotted them as well. "The two of you better get showered and changed quickly!" he screamed over the porch railing. "Our company will be here soon."

They ran around the side of the house toward the outdoor shower, Walter snapping his sister with his beach towel.

Lilly was back in the kitchen, cutting celery sticks and florets of cauliflower, when she heard Andrew come back into the butler's pantry. "Mr. Bell drinks bourbon. Isn't that right, Lilly?" he called to her.

She raised her voice so he'd hear her through the swinging door. "I remember that to be the case, Andrew." She saw his figure through the gap, hunched down on his knees, the clink of glass bottles barely masking his grumbles.

Lilly turned her head to see Thomas enter the pantry. "Pour me a scotch, would you, Andrew?"

"Neat, okay? My ice bucket is out on the porch."

"Of course."

Lilly was not surprised that Thomas wanted a quick drink before guests arrived. He was not a fan of the intergenerational gatherings that were de rigueur in Long Harbor. He'd always been a man's man, and the prospect of having to mingle with women and children made his eyes narrow.

"Ah, well, my boy, that was some story your mother told last night." Thomas put his empty glass down on the countertop with a clink.

"Unfortunately, it was more than that. Not just a story, I mean. It's all true," said Andrew. Lilly turned off the faucet to hear better.

"I can't believe it. I mean, I was in Pittsburgh the winter she attended that bogus finishing school, and I never suspected a thing. At first I didn't know where she was going with it all. At my age, surprises aren't a welcome thing," said Thomas.

"At any age, really."

"The woman's been through a lot." Lilly opened the door of the refrigerator in order to be a little closer to the swinging door. *Damn right she's been through a lot.*

"Yes, only seven months since Dad died. She isn't back to being herself."

"No, she isn't."

"Say, we need to discuss how to get her out of debt," Andrew said.

Lilly frowned with distress. She hadn't realized Becca was also in debt. She felt an awful pang of guilt about having shopped at Dade's all summer, paying no attention to the prices.

"I've been giving it some thought," said Thomas. But then the doorbell rang and the men stopped talking and Lilly took some sour cream out of the refrigerator and shut the door.

"Would you like me to answer that?" she called.

"No, I've got it," said Andrew. "Old-timers are always early." Lilly followed a few steps behind him anyway with a tray of crudités.

It was Becca's old friend Mary Bell and her husband, Whit, with their grown son, Jason, in tow. Lilly remembered his fancy wedding a while back, but here he was, hands in his pockets, standing alone, behind his parents.

Andrew led them all onto the back porch. He popped the top off a beer for Whit, then turned on the charm with Mr. and Mrs. Bell. "I'll mix your first drink; then it's summer rules," he said.

"Oh, heavens, Mary, you've arrived," Becca said, pushing open the screen door. She'd been upstairs, putting the finishing touches on her ensemble: a simple red cocktail-length dress and, draped over her shoulders, the same American-flag silk shawl that she always wore for the holiday. "I lost track of time and didn't hear you all out here." She kissed Whit on both cheeks while Andrew poured her a glass of white wine.

"Great view you have here, Mrs. Fitzpatrick," Whit said, as he relaxed into one of the cushioned armchairs. Lilly put the tray down on a low table and wiped her hands on her apron. The doorbell rang again. She passed Ruth and Sarah in the living room on her way to answer it. They were flipping through an old photo album that lived on a bookshelf.

It was all of Andrew's friends at the door, arriving en masse with their wives and children, everyone glowing from a day in the sun, well scrubbed and ready for a festive evening of iconic Long Harbor. Lilly showed them out to the porch, before returning to the kitchen.

Rachel came down the back stairs and poured herself a glass of wine out of the refrigerator. "Don't you look pretty," Lilly said. Rachel wore standard Fourth of July garb: white slacks that flared at the bottom, wedge sandals, a loose navy-blue crewneck sweater, and a red scarf tied around her neck. Her hair was pulled back from her face, and her oversize sunglasses covered the circles under her tired eyes. She even wore makeup and red lipstick.

"Ugh," Rachel said. "Trying." She took a big gulp from her glass, then refilled it to the top.

"Now go on out there and join the party," Lilly prodded.

Lilly followed behind with a tray of deviled eggs. As they crossed the living room, Camilla was just coming down the stairs. She wore a lime-green cocktail dress, dense to the fact that the Fourth of July meant red, white, and blue. Lilly paused so that Rachel and Camilla could go through the door in front of her.

Andrew and Camilla gravitated toward one corner of the deck, where they hoisted glasses with his old pals and reminisced about their well-spent youth. Lilly passed the hors d'oeuvres, hoping all the expensive food from Dade's would get eaten up. She lingered among the wives and the smaller children, helping them with napkins and deviled eggs.

Lawrence Henningsen was the only one of Andrew's group with a second wife and their toddler, Lawrence Jr. Little Larry, as he was referred to jokingly, was a three-year-old towhead wearing red, white, and blue seersucker overalls. Lilly asked his mother if it was all right for him to have some cheese and crackers. Kneeling down with the child, Lilly heard the wives' attempts to include Camilla in their conversation: Where did they live in the winter, where did their children go to school, did they have any pending travel plans? But Camilla was a pill, didn't even try to disguise her boredom.

The Bells were the first to leave. Lilly collected empty glasses from around the porch. It was seven o'clock, and the wives began to nag the men with reminders of how far away they'd have to park at the fireworks. The kids undoubtedly wanted to leave. After the obligatory squirt of mosquito repellent on their bare ankles and calves, they planned to get lost from their parents, in the direction of the popcorn and cotton candy, balloon artists and face painting, and, for the teenagers, maybe behind the caddy shack to sneak a beer.

The fireworks party at the club was infamous for drawing over a thousand people, requiring tables to be set up on the turf, extending from the porch all the way to the eighteenth green. Although Lilly had never attended, Becca always went to great lengths to paint a picture for her. She described the long stretches of buffet with roasted chicken, salads, cole slaw, corn on the cob, dinner rolls, and even a carving filet, followed by ice cream for dessert. A brass ensemble played patriotic favorites and Dixieland during cocktails. Helium balloons in red, white, and blue arrangements were tied to simple floral arrangements on the several hundred tables.

Lilly stood at the kitchen door as the family packed into several cars for the short ride over. "Have a good time," she said, then returned to the kitchen to do the dishes. As she loaded the dishwasher with glasses, she wondered what sort of plan Andrew and Thomas would concoct. Was this to be Becca's last summer at Eden? And hers as well?

Chapter 34

KANSAS CITY, MISSOURI
1945

B ecca took small steps down the long corridor leading to the medical wing. A tall nurse with straight brown hair stood waiting for her at the threshold of the examining room, clipboard resting against her sizable chest.

"Becca M.?" she asked in a deep voice. She must have stood six feet tall, reading glasses perched on her nose as she looked down at her papers.

"Yes," said Becca, noticing a large mole on the nurse's chin.

"Okay, come in. Up on the scale. Every week, expect the same routine: weigh-in, blood pressure. Be sure to tell me if you see any blood or feel any pains." The nurse said all this rapidly. "Then, in the last trimester, the visits will be more involved," she added, pointing to a table with stirrups against the wall. The nurse smelled of cigarette smoke and coffee as she leaned closer to listen to Becca's heartbeat through a cold silver stethoscope. Becca crossed her ankles tightly as the nurse sat back on her stool, filling out a form on her clipboard, her big hand swallowing up the pen.

"Do you have any questions?" the nurse asked in a gravelly voice.

"Will it hurt?" Becca managed to ask after a few seconds.

The nurse was quiet and took off her reading glasses. She looked Becca in the eye and coughed into her hand. "Sweetheart, it's different for everyone. And I wouldn't dwell on it, but yes, in the end, for a little thing like you, it's going to hurt." She looked up to check the clock on the wall, removed Becca's form from the clipboard, and placed it in a basket labeled WEEKLIES.

Becca's heart raced. She stared at her feet. They were small, just like her mother's.

"Make sure you eat all the vegetables they serve and take plenty of naps," the nurse said, rising to indicate the exam was over. Becca buttoned her blouse quickly, anxious to leave this part of the Willows. Besides the oversized nurse, it was the noise that made her anxious, the combination of hungry newborns crying in the nursery and intermittent moans coming from farther down the hall.

Returning to her room, she found a note under her door from Mrs. Lawton saying that she had received several large boxes. Her mother had shipped out a senior-year curriculum of novels, history books, and mathematics. She had even included essay topics and assignments for Becca to complete. At the top of one box, Becca found a letter, and just seeing the familiar handwriting started her lower lip trembling.

My dear Becca,

I love you, darling. I don't know if I even had time to tell you at the train station, but I do love you, and the thought of you being away for so long saddens me deeply. I predict your time in Kansas City will be very difficult, and I want you to try to keep your mind off your circumstances. To that end, I have enclosed plenty of schoolwork— you might as well come home well read—and do try to keep up with the piano. I have arranged for a tutor for you through Mrs. Lawton so that we can be sure you are making academic progress. Your father is still in New York with Edward. He should be back in Pittsburgh in a few weeks. Please write, as he asks about you often. I know it pains you to keep up the finishing-school ruse, but it will spare you a lifetime of shame.

Love, Mother

Becca read the letter several times. She shook her head. Charlotte Brontë and Charles Dickens would never take her mind off what she was going through. And why was her father taking so little interest in her education? "The finishing school your mother identified has a fine history of educating girls to become women who will take their places in society," he had said, with a satisfied nod. Had he really made no inquiries into the faculty or the curriculum, after he'd orchestrated every move her brothers had made? Her heart sank as she reread her mother's last words: "spare you a lifetime of shame." She knew there was no way she would be spared.

Every morning after breakfast, Becca took a walk in the park across the street, despite Mrs. Lawton's warnings against exerting herself too much. A recent arrival on the hall, Eleanor D., took to accompanying her. As they circled the park, Eleanor told Becca all about Houston. Her Texas drawl and descriptions of the larger-than-life characters back home made Becca laugh for the first time in months.

"There were scads of parties when all the boys came back, and lots of heavy drinking," said Eleanor.

"Sounds like the party my parents threw at Eden."

"Mama was so relieved that the war was over. The only reason I think she cared was because I was at risk of becoming an old maid!" Eleanor said.

"At twenty?"

"So she powdered my face, and did up my hair, and after a few months, I had a beau. Mama was beside herself. Well, things started moving pretty quickly. I wasn't sure what to do, but he said not to worry, that we'd be getting married."

Eleanor's story was like others Becca would hear: all about betrayals by men who said they would marry the woman they'd impregnated. "He turned out to be some donkey. Lord, it would have hurt less if he had just reached in and ripped out my heart. His mama's got a whole lineup of debutantes for him to choose from."

Becca told Eleanor about her older brothers and described Eden from top to bottom, how she had survived the Great Hurricane with her father and how her family had spent the following years rebuilding the house.

"A hurricane! That must have been terrifying," said Eleanor.

"Yes, it was, but also gave us a fresh start. Then my brothers left for the front in Europe, and when they came home, there was a magnificent party. And that's when . . ." Becca pointed at her stomach.

Eleanor took Becca's gloved hand in hers as they crunched through the dried leaves circling the park. A steady wind blew, bending tree branches and sending more leaves flying through the browning grass.

"Was he your boyfriend?" Eleanor asked, after a brief silence.

"No."

"It wasn't your first time, was it?"

Becca nodded, her tears welling.

Eleanor put an arm around Becca. "Who was he?" she asked.

"Just a soldier at our party. I had too much champagne," Becca cried. "I don't remember a thing. I feel like the world's biggest fool."

"Oh, bless your heart. *I* was the fool; you were just innocent."

Becca nodded, but when she remembered how closely Sal had held her during the slow songs, she wasn't sure. She hadn't pulled away. Had she implied something? Was it the way she had looked into his eyes? Was there a language between men and women that she didn't understand?

* * *

Her mother wrote that she had told Becca's father some story at Christmastime, about a debilitating flu that would make it impossible for Becca to travel home. Becca found it hurtful that her father had settled for that; she'd been half hoping he'd drop everything and show up in Kansas City to rescue her. Her mother later wrote that they had traveled to New York to visit Edward and Robert and Ruth. Her mother's note concluded, "We are hoping for the *big* announcement soon!"

Sitting at her desk, Becca crumpled the note and threw it into the trash. She swiped *Jane Eyre* off the surface as well, sending it under the bed. She stared at the massive icicles hanging from the eave outside her window.

Her mother sent an overwhelming deluge of presents for Christmas and for her birthday. Becca hadn't experienced such extravagance during the war, and she hesitated at the brown paper and red bows. Her mother's efforts were insulting, really. Christmas here was plain depressing. No matter how much Mr. and Mrs. Lawton tried to enliven the mood with a decorated tree and an evening singing carols around the piano, it wasn't home. The only bright spot was that her mother's package included cards from her father and brothers. Thomas and Edward sent perfunctory notes, but Robert wrote a real letter. He asked about her school and her classes and explained all about his new job at a bank. He wrote about his love for Ruth and how he was sure Becca and she would get along famously.

Eleanor sat by her side, oohing and aahing, as she unwrapped bulky sweaters and bottles of French perfume. Becca didn't pause to admire the gifts, embarrassed by it all.

"Would you like one?" she asked, holding up a pink cardigan.

"I prefer the blue." Eleanor giggled.

Becca gave the bottles of perfume to the nurses and then trudged up the stairs to her room. She lay on the bed, curled up on her side, and pulled the quilt over her legs. She looked out at the tree branches scratching her windowpanes. She'd been born at Christmastime, it had always been her special time of year. She remembered the trees she'd put up with her father. Her brothers had never had the desire to decorate them, so they'd given Becca all the say in where the ornaments went.

Her chest ached at the thought of her family carrying on without her. The tears started slowly; then she got worked up, sobbing, dwelling on the unfairness of it all, the absurdity of what had happened to her. And then she felt it—a little somersault in her abdomen. She sat up with a jolt and put her hand on her belly, hoping that if she stopped crying and got very still, she might feel it again.

* * *

A lecture was scheduled for after New Year's. Girls streamed into the living room, where a fire burned on the hearth and the smell of balsam filled the air. When Becca and Eleanor arrived, there were few seats left. Some girls sat at card tables, playing gin rummy; others were knitting. But when the speaker introduced herself, they put away their cards and sat up straight.

"Good evening, ladies. My name is Amanda Howard. I am a nurse at the Fairmount Maternity Hospital, and I am here to speak to you about birth control."

Some girls snickered.

However, once Nurse Howard began her presentation, the chatter stopped. She was another tall nurse, but with dishwater hair and a plain face. Her demeanor was serious, and she spoke with confidence. She taped large diagrams up on the wall and spoke about body parts that Becca didn't even know she had—a uterus and ovaries? Becca twisted uncomfortably in her chair during certain parts of the presentation, imagining the places on her that Sal might have touched. Heat rose up the back of her neck as she tried to conjure up any memory of what it had felt like.

"You girls should demand birth control options from your doctors if you want them. If yours won't prescribe birth control devices, find a new, modern-thinking doctor. From here on, you should have a say in when you become pregnant and how many children you have."

She took a moment to let the message sink in. "Are there any questions?"

Becca looked around. She wanted to ask if every sex act between a man and a woman resulted in pregnancy if birth control was not used, but she wasn't going to be the only one to raise a hand. Nobody spoke, so Nurse Howard folded up the charts and her easel and put on her coat.

Mrs. Lawton returned to the parlor and said, "Girls, let's thank Nurse Howard with a round of applause." There was a scattered clapping of hands, and then Mrs. Lawton escorted Nurse Howard to her car.

Becca was dumfounded. Why had her mother never taken the time to explain the link between her monthly bleedings, her eggs dropping, and how the eggs become fertilized? She remembered rushing into her sitting room when she was about thirteen, scared by the discovery of blood. Her mother had reached to the uppermost shelf in her closet for a pink box labeled MENSES STARTER KIT and handed it to Becca. It contained a garter belt–like elastic band and an absorbent pad.

"I expected you would need this soon. Now, here is another box of pads; be careful not to soil your clothes or the bed linens. You will have this bleeding monthly, and it will last three to five days. If you have any pain, I can give you one of my pills." With that, her mother went back to the news of the war on the radio.

Becca read in the daily bulletin that Nurse Howard would be returning in March. She looked forward to hearing this intelligent, bold woman speak again. Maybe if there was a private moment, Becca could ask her questions. However, when she discovered the topic of Nurse Howard's talk would be "the fortieth week," she wrestled with wanting to be informed versus dreading the specifics of her fate.

The living room was cool, as the fire was not yet lit, and Becca and Eleanor, now both visibly pregnant, teetered into the room together. Becca braced her arm on the sofa as she lowered herself down, and then held out a hand to help Eleanor. Becca presumed the lack of a fire explained why a larger crowd had not collected for the lecture, but Eleanor corrected her.

"People were upset by the last one," Eleanor said.

"Really?"

"I overhead Olivia at dinner. She said pushing birth control like that is akin to tampering with God's will. Then Alice said, 'I can't imagine what a husband would say if he found out his wife was using birth control.'"

Becca was shocked. Wasn't the lack of birth control what had put them all here in the first place? Using it sounded like a smart idea to her—would husbands actually object to such a thing?

Becca, Eleanor, and a girl named Diane from New York were the only three at Nurse Howard's second presentation. Again, Becca kept her questions to herself while the nurse packed up her pointer and diagrams and made her way to the door. Becca wished she had helped Nurse Howard with all she had to carry, but she was sure the clique by the front door would have had something to say about it.

"Our youth is over," said Diane, lingering on the couch. "Just being here, and knowing what I now know, I can never go back, can't even pretend to go back." Becca was growing weary of this same conversation night after night.

Eleanor said that her mother had sent news of her ex-boyfriend's recent wedding announcement. "I'll never trust a man again."

"It's the water breaking and the contractions that scare me," Becca said. But how could she tell them what really bothered her was her indifferent father, her brothers going on with their lives, and her mother's assuredness that this had been the right thing to do? Sometimes she dreamed of running away, taking that twenty-hour train ride toward Long Harbor with a little bundle in her arms.

The three girls snuck into the dining room later that night and stole a box of graham crackers. Eleanor put the box under her sweater, and the three of them giggled on the way back to Becca's room. Halfway through the box, Diane started to cry.

"Let's promise to stay in touch," said Eleanor.

"We'll stick together. Everyone else is a damn liar but we'll be true." Diane said.

They made a pact, but Becca knew remaining friends was unlikely. She'd seen how the Willows didn't accommodate goodbyes. A girl whose "time had come" would just disappear, not show up at breakfast one morning. Becca knew it was only a matter of time before she'd be the one to vanish, eliciting whispers and speculation for a day or two about where she'd gone to start over. She recalled her first dinner with Mabel and her friends and finally understood what they'd been trying to say.

Chapter 35

LONG HARBOR, RHODE ISLAND
Saturday, July 4, 2000

Rachel's mouth watered at the scent of meat on the grill as she entered the fireworks party. She paused momentarily, admiring the colorful crowd flocking to the grassy area between the terrace and the eighteenth green. Children were hurrying to join the line of others waiting to get their sunburned faces painted, and adults huddled in small groups of conversation, their festive attire set off crisply against the green grass.

Despite the irritation she harbored toward her daughter, Rachel stuck close to Sarah's side. They approached one of the long bars at the perimeter of the crowd. It took them ten minutes to reach the front of the line, where Rachel ordered a white wine for herself and a Diet Coke for Sarah, signing the chit with her mother's membership number. They emerged from the cluster of the bar, drinks perspiring in star-spangled cocktail napkins in one hand, pretzels in the other.

Rachel and Sarah remained on the fringe of the party, nibbling their snacks. They watched Becca take Ruth by the hand and present her to all their old friends. "It's Ruth! You remember— Bobby's wife." Rachel's mother suddenly seemed so nostalgic for the old days. Was it her way of avoiding what was going on now?

"I think Gran enjoyed the cocktail party," Sarah said, filling in the silence.

"I suppose," Rachel said, scanning the passersby from behind her sunglasses.

Suddenly, a throng of blond-highlighted young women in Lilly Pulitzer dresses scurried toward them. "Sarah!" the tallest one shrieked. Rachel recognized them as Sarah's childhood friends from her tennis clinics. Unlike Sarah, Rachel's closest summertime friends had worked at the ice cream parlor, town kids who never frequented the club.

"Sarah! When did you get here?"

"I've been here most of June, just lying low," said Sarah.

"We have so much to talk about!"

"We do, we do."

Sarah had been unique among them, remaining single and driven toward academic pursuits. Two of them had been married several years and had their own children in tow. One had a baby resting on her hip as she leaned in to give Sarah a kiss.

"I guess I do have some news . . . ," Sarah said, brushing her hand against the baby's cheek. Rachel listened as Sarah divulged her pregnancy. More shrieks. God, how things had changed—her daughter enjoyed so much freedom.

Rachel went to the bar to get another drink, and by the time she returned, the young women had moved on. She returned to her daughter's side.

"So, Mom, are you nervous to meet Lee tomorrow?" Sarah asked.

"Who?"

"You know, your *sister*? Gosh, that sounds so odd."

Rachel shook her head. "No, that's not it," she said. What made her shudder wasn't just Lee's existence, or the knowledge that her mother had had sex with Mr. Fabbrizzio, or what Camilla had said to her on the beach; it was that Sarah was now talking about her pregnancy in public. "Everything is converging at once," Rachel said, inhaling deeply. She had a pit in her stomach and feared any more introspection might lead to tears. Thank God for her sunglasses—she would not be seen crying at the fireworks party.

Another prolonged silence passed between them before Rachel asked, "Would you like another soda?" Rachel hadn't finished her second drink yet, but she planned on draining it while standing in the line for the next one.

"Okay," Sarah said.

The line for the bar was a safe place to be. There was nobody Rachel wanted to make small talk with at this party. She averted her gaze from a group of women passing by. She'd once been on the periphery of their crowd, when Sarah was little; they were the mothers of her childhood playmates. They'd gathered in the sand most afternoons while the kids made mud pies and splashed in the water. That mutual experience had somehow bonded those women for life. Except for Rachel, who felt nothing in common with them anymore.

Inching closer to the bartender, Rachel caught sight of Celia Baker, new to Long Harbor and described as having "married well but divorced better." Celia and her new husband were not members and must have been attending as guests of their neighbors. Celia was in her fifties and looked as if she had put some lucky plastic surgeon's children through college. She was tipsy, walking away from the buffet line in high-heeled pumps, and when she caught a bit of turf, she let out an awful yell and the food tray she was carrying went flying through the air.

Rachel gasped, reaching for the edge of the bar. "Oh my, I guess that's it for her," she snickered.

Refill in hand, Rachel gestured toward the popcorn machine. "I can't resist any longer; let's go get some," she said to Sarah, leading her along the edge of the lawn toward the terrace. She was now concentrating hard on the turf in front of her but still overheard tidbits of the conversations they passed.

"Is that Rachel Fitzpatrick behind those sunglasses?" She looked up, startled, catching herself from spilling her drink. It was Mrs. Notman, one of her mother's oldest friends. But unlike her mother, Mrs. Notman had put on weight in her old age and was using a cane.

"Yes, Mrs. Notman, it's Rachel."

"Oh, dear, you can call me Martha. Now, listen, where is that mother of yours? I haven't seen her all summer!" Rachel made an overture to greet her with a kiss on the cheek, but Mrs. Notman kept a polite distance, so as not to spoil her makeup.

"Well, she's here somewhere with my aunt Ruth. And Andrew and his family are here from London."

"Oh, so you've got a houseful?"

"Just about."

"Oh, and Sarah! Hello, dear. My, just look at you." Before the conversation could proceed into dangerous territory, Rachel finished her wine, then pointed to her empty glass.

"You'll have to excuse us, Martha. We were just going to freshen our drinks."

Rachel was imagining her family's turmoil becoming the centerpiece of all these clusters of gossip. She tried to steady herself as she did an about-face toward the bar. She momentarily lost track of Sarah but had to keep moving, her ears ringing with the medley of voices swirling through the air.

"Mom!" Sarah said, finally catching up with her. "I don't want another soda, and you don't need another drink." Heat rose up Rachel's back at the sound of her daughter's outburst. She sensed heads turning their way. She just kept walking without acknowledging Sarah.

"Can you hear me?" Sarah asked again.

"Yes, I heard you," Rachel said in a ferocious whisper, not wanting to draw any further attention. "Why don't you go back to the terrace and get me a basket of popcorn?" Sarah looked astonished by the demand but retreated nonetheless toward the terrace.

Rachel didn't know how she'd find the rest of her family. Where were her mother and Ruth? Where was Andrew's clan? She felt safest waiting at the bar, but a tinge of impatience flared up in her because the line was so long, now three deep. It hadn't been like this in prior years. It was all the "new people" in town.

New people. She was starting to think like her father. He had been the most outspoken about the "new money" outsiders permeating Long Harbor. He defended the spirit of Yankee frugality that had led to a gradual shabbiness of the town, driveways of crumbled seashells bleeding into patchy green lawns and sporadically trimmed hedges. It was a lot more run-down than the Founders would have cared for, primarily because the second and third generations were no longer flush with cash.

When a forty-year-old investment banker and his family moved in two houses down the beach from Eden, their multimillion-dollar renovation, not to mention their perfectly sodded lawn and instant landscaping, really raised Rachel's father's ire. He complained about the way people were subdividing their lots, creating houses that were no longer hidden at the end of long driveways. He grumbled about their suburban play structures and the fencing around their swimming pools.

When the wife of the investment banker inquired about joining the Long Harbor Garden Club, she was not-so-subtly informed that there was a great difference between being a gardener and having a garden installed. Alas, the old guard were the gatekeepers, their most auspicious bastion of power being the Paupanaug Club's admission committee. They weren't just about fending off people like Celia Baker; they were guardians of Long Harbor's values.

They had, however, gone out on a limb in the '70s, when Larry Gold, a Jew, was allowed to join. Folks in Long Harbor were aghast at first but made an exception because he didn't seem *too* Jewish. Regardless, Rachel's father had made a stink. "Jews ruined Yale, and now this." Rachel would never forget the dinner at which her father made that slur. She'd assumed it was just the pitcher of martinis talking, and that he hadn't actually forgotten that Bunny Meister, his own father-in-law, was also born a Jew.

Rachel signed her mother's name on yet another drink chit. She looked up into the glare of the setting sun and felt dizzy for a moment. She put her wine back down on the bar and caught her breath. In that instant, she spotted her mother, Ruth, and Andrew's family heading to the buffet line. She clutched her glass, which sloshed a bit as she hurried to join them. She picked up a brownie à la mode from the dessert table, before catching up with everybody.

"Enough room for me?" Rachel asked, a few steps behind them.

"Oh, Rachel, there you are. Of course, of course," her mother said.

Sarah plopped down in the seat next to her, placing an overflowing basket of popcorn on the table. "Nutritious dinner, Mother," she said, eyeing the brownie and ice cream. *How dare she take that judgmental tone with me!* Rachel thought.

Everyone shifted their white plastic chairs around to make room for Sally and Walter, who were approaching with full trays of food. "What an extravaganza," Camilla said, scanning the crowd.

"Yes, they really do a great job," said Becca, who had wrapped her shawl around her shoulders in the night air.

"I ran into Mrs. Notman," Rachel said. "She was looking for you, Mother."

"That's nice, but no more mingling for me. I'm staying put," her mother said with a smile, resting her hand on Ruth's forearm.

"When do the fireworks start?" asked Walter.

"About nine," said Andrew. "Once it's really dark."

Rachel put a kernel of popcorn in her mouth, felt its saltiness dissolving between her tongue and the roof of her mouth. Next, she took a bite of the brownie and ice cream, its sweetness an exquisite counterpoint to the popcorn. She took a deep breath and noticed a tremor in her hands. It became more prevalent as she lifted her drink to her lips. She took another deep breath, taking an inventory of the faces around the table. This was her family, but she couldn't think of a word she wanted to say to any one of them. She had never missed her father more.

"I think I'll head home," Rachel announced. "I've got a monster headache and I've already had enough fireworks for one weekend." Her mother let out a sigh, although no one else protested. She passed the bar, the crowd now dispersed among

the dinner tables, and asked for a vodka tonic. Then she proceeded down the hill along the eighteenth fairway, taking her
shoes off as she crossed the dunes and eelgrass, turning slowly
down the beach in the direction of Eden.

Chapter 36

KANSAS CITY, MISSOURI
1945

L ying under her crisp white coverlet, searching for the moon and stars through her window, Becca felt the poking and kicking turn into a maelstrom. At her last exam, she had mentioned the increased movement to the nurse, who had assured her it was the sign of a healthy baby. "It's when the movement stops for five or six hours that you have to worry." Becca sang a Brahms lullaby her nana had taught her as she caressed her tummy. *"Guten Abend, gute Nacht, mit rosen bedackt . . .* I know you are scared, little babe. So am I, but it is time for us to go to sleep."

Becca yawned at the breakfast table. She and Eleanor lingered over eggs and a crossword puzzle. "Did you hear about the new girl from Boston?" Eleanor asked.

"No," said Becca.

"She ran away last night."

"My word!" Becca shivered. Being early on and relatively thin was the only way the girl could have managed it.

"Ronald was dispatched to the train station to be on the lookout, but he still hasn't returned," Eleanor said, arching her eyebrows.

That afternoon, Becca went to her interview with Mrs. Winter, the social worker, tapping lightly on the open door to announce her presence.

"And you must be Becca M.," Mrs. Winter said, reading the tab of a manila folder that sat on top of the large wooden desk in front of her. This office had been Mr. Lawton's and hung on to its masculine air with forest-green walls and heavy draperies. Mrs. Winter reviewed the first few lines of the sheet of paper in the folder, then sat back in her chair. "Please, sit down. I'll need to ask you some questions about yourself and the baby's father in order to complete the adoption file."

"Oh," said Becca, taking the hard wooden chair on the other side of the desk. Her face flushed, and she glanced down her wrist-watch, waiting for Mrs. Winter's first question.

"Do you have someplace to be?" Mrs. Winter asked.

"Oh, no. I'm sorry, ma'am. I'm just afraid it's been a while since I felt my baby move, and I'm starting to worry. I think I might go see the nurse after we're through."

Mrs. Winter removed her reading glasses, letting them dangle around her neck. "What are you worried about, exactly?"

"About my baby," she said quietly.

Mrs. Winter took a deep breath and looked straight into Becca's eyes. "While your conscientiousness is admirable, dear," she said, "let me remind you this will all be much more difficult if you continue to think of the baby as *your* baby. It is *the* baby, and you should consider yourself the vessel sustaining it before I find suitable parents."

Becca's body heated with shame, and her eyes filled with tears. "I know, but . . ."

Mrs. Winter double-checked the name on the front of the folder, "Becca," she said sternly, "you are a mere girl and not a suitable mother. A child needs two parents, and if you were to return home with an infant as an unwed mother, there is not a chance anyone would marry you, and you would bring incredible disgrace upon your family. You must understand the only option is for you to give this baby up."

"No, Mrs. Winter, that's not it," Becca stammered. "I know I can't take her home. I couldn't do that to my family. It's just that

I've been feeling her grow and I think she's trying to get my attention. She's part of me, and I want her to remember me."

Mrs. Winter shook her head, put her glasses back on, and began to read off questions.

"Father?"

"Bernard Meister," Becca answered.

"Not *your* father, Becca, the *baby's* father."

"Oh, he's a boy—I mean, a man—named Sal Fabbrizzio."

"Was this man your boyfriend?"

"No."

"Is he aware of the pregnancy?"

"No," said Becca.

Mrs. Winter checked off two boxes on a page inside her file. "I see," she said, and Becca was sure she heard Mrs. Winter cluck her tongue against the roof of her mouth.

* * *

For the next several months, Mrs. Winter's tongue clucking featured prominently in Becca's nightmares. But when she woke early one morning in late April, it was not because of the disturbing snickers of that dreadful woman but because of a sharp pain that wrapped around her abdomen. She sat up in bed and soon felt another one. She put her coat on over her nightgown and retrieved the bag she had packed with her toiletries, a fresh nightgown, and a dress to wear home from the hospital. With one arm braced against the corridor wall as she walked, she stifled a scream through the next contractions. She stopped briefly on her way to the medical wing to slip a note underneath Eleanor's door and listen to the early-morning stillness, punctuated by the songs of a few birds fluttering outside the window.

After her labor progressed, Ronald drove her to the city hospital, where she breathed through the contractions until the anesthesia took hold. There was the shift of nurses changing in the hallway, people greeting each other, doctors doing their rounds.

Funny how an entire community lived and worked in Kansas City, when all she had known for the past seven months was the bubble of the Willows and the park across the street. As she slipped into unconsciousness, she overheard two nurses talking about all the maternity hospitals in town. "Seems like there's more and more of these girls every year," one of them said.

"The city council asked that the pregnant unweds stay inside. It'd be an affront to the fine folks of Kansas City to have them walking our streets," said the other.

Becca was shocked awake by an electric pain and a nurse and a doctor urging her to push. She was groggy and nauseated but gripped the sheet beneath her and pushed with all her might. "One more," a nurse urged, giving her a boost from behind. Their combined effort elevated Becca's torso off the bed. She let out a long, guttural groan as something emerged from between her legs. She caught sight of a shocking mound of wet, dark hair on a doll-size head. Where there had once been enormous pressure, she was now empty.

"A girl," the doctor said to the nurse, who took the child from his arms and bathed and swaddled her. Becca put her hand on her abdomen, fell back onto the gurney, and began sobbing.

She was sent to recuperate in the maternity ward with all the other mothers, to a room without flowers or visitors, a draped partition between her and a roommate. She was sore and bruised from the tearing between her legs, and she had been bound tightly with bandages around her chest to keep her milk from coming in. A new nurse was on duty that evening and seemed flustered by the crush of families in the hall during visiting hours, all requesting their baby at the same time. She must have been unfamiliar with the protocol that patients from the Willows were under no circumstances permitted contact with their newborns, and mistakenly delivered Becca's daughter, along with the rest.

Becca concealed her surprise, taking the baby into her arms without hesitation. She held her tightly, their noses touching. Even the harried nurse paused, smiling at the beauty of it, the primal connection between mother and child. Becca caressed the top of her baby's scalp with her cheek, saying a prayer of thanks for her good fortune. She kissed the baby's head, the fine, silky hair.

The nurse double-checked the card taped to the front of the bassinet. "You haven't decided on a name yet, ma'am?"

"Oh, yes, I—I mean we—have. Her name is Leah." She would keep the charade going as long as she needed to if it meant she could spend time with her daughter.

"Very nice. I'll update her records."

"Thank you."

The nurse handed Becca a warm bottle, then hastily left the room to finish delivering bassinets down the hall. Becca held the bottle up to the light, considering its rubber nipple. Her breasts ached, and with her free hand, Becca pulled the binding down around her abdomen. The infant's small mouth searched for her nipple like a baby bird with its beak wide open. Her tiny lips finally latched on. The ecstatic release of warmth from her breast sent a surge of sensation down her legs. She dropped her head back on the pillow, murmuring, "Drink, little Leah, drink."

She nursed her baby for a full thirty minutes, knowing intuitively just what to do. In those beautiful moments, Becca metamorphosed. Even after the supervising nurse came to snatch Leah away and stormed back to the nursery, Becca knew she would never be the same. The transformation was more than just lost innocence. It was more than maturity as well. It was a knowing, a knowing of true love, combined with an incredibly weighty sadness, a knowing of what loss meant.

She was transferred back to one of the Willows' post-delivery rooms to wait for her mother's arrival. Becca was in no hurry to go, wanting to wallow in this place for a while. She sensed Leah's presence in the nursery down the hall and wanted to stay close. She thought she might try to walk the length of the corridor, maybe catch a glimpse of her angel. But the nurses had seen it all before and kept the door to the nursery locked.

The afternoon Ronald drove her mother to the Willows, Becca was fully dressed and sitting upright on a bench in the foyer.

She noticed her mother first, watching her put her hands on the countertop of the nurses' station and look up at the ceiling, breathing in deeply and letting out a sigh.

"Mother," Becca said.

Her mother spun around on the linoleum floor to face her.

Their eyes met. "Your granddaughter is in the nursery down the hall, but they won't let us say goodbye," Becca said.

Her mother smiled, acting as if she'd not heard her words.

Becca remained sitting, making their embrace uncomfortable. Her mother stood back and searched her face.

"I'm ready to leave," said Becca, pointing to her suitcase.

"Is this all you have?" her mother asked, looking at the small valise on the floor.

"I gave the rest away," Becca said, standing up, shaking out her freshly bobbed hair with her fingers.

As they exited the Willows, her mother stopped to thank Mrs. Lawton for taking good care of her daughter, nudging Becca to do the same. She squeezed out a smile and politely extended her hand, now fully understanding how Mrs. Lawton was able to be so warm and loving: her counterpart Mrs. Winter did all the dirty work.

Sadie checked them into a hotel near the train station. They would stay overnight, then board a train headed northeast. "I can't wait to get to Eden," her mother said over dinner. "There's a wedding being planned!"

Her mother's enthusiasm enraged Becca. "Mother, I know you said you never wanted to speak of 'it' again, but there is something I want to tell you," she said over dinner.

"All right," her mother said, clearly taken aback.

"The nurse on the ward didn't know the rules and brought my baby to me, and I held her. I held her for a long time. And now I can't help it—I miss her, I do, and I can't believe I'm leaving her."

That statement hung in the air for several minutes as her mother took a spoonful of soup, then picked her napkin off her lap to dab the corners of her mouth, before she said, "Oh, darling, I'm so sorry about that nurse. How awful for you to have to hold the baby."

"But, Mother, it wasn't awful; it was wonderful. I loved holding her. I loved it. I love her."

Her mother reached calmly across the table and caressed Becca's clenched fist. "Becca, you no doubt felt something for that baby—miraculous wonder, perhaps? But it's not birthing a baby that creates love. It's what comes afterward, the day-to-day caring and living. It's the relationship. That baby will have a new mother to bond with. She'll be fine without you. You'll get through this. Now, let's think happy thoughts. Think about a bridal shower for Ruth."

A waiter delivered their entrées to the table, but Becca waved hers away and went to bed. During the moonlit nights in her room at the Willows, she had imagined a modest and simple homecoming. She looked forward to seeing her father and her brothers, to one of Mr. P.'s clambakes, or simply a swim with Robert. She imagined napping on the back porch, curled up under an afghan. She looked forward to some long walks on the beach, where she might cry into the wind. She even hoped Ruth would be around, but not with the commotion of a wedding.

Their travel east seemed endless. She was not an enthusiastic shopper during their stop in New York City; she let her mother and a saleswoman select a wardrobe for her new figure, dwelling on what might work best for the wedding. Her mother complained that she took the fun out of their shopping trip, but Becca just wanted to board the next train and complete the final leg of the journey.

When they finally arrived at the station in Kingston, Becca was the first to spot her father, waiting on the platform as the train slowed to a stop. "Oh, Daddy," she sighed. It had been so long, but now there he stood, as tall and solid as ever. His slicked-back hair was almost completely gray. His trench coat was draped over his forearm in the warm May sun. He shaded his brow with his free hand, searching the windows. Becca and her mother smoothed out their crumpled skirts and brushed their hair back in place. Her mother applied fresh lipstick, then offered it to her daughter.

Becca batted her hand at it before rushing ahead, homing her vision onto the sight of her father, filling her lungs with the salty air. She bounded down the stairs, leaving her mother behind. "Daddy!" she yelled.

He turned at the sound of her voice, bending at the knees, like he might have greeted a girl of twelve, not eighteen. He stretched out his arms and swept her up off her feet. "Princess," he said, as he held her tightly. They remained that way for several minutes, until her mother came up behind them.

"I told you I would bring her back safe and sound," her mother said.

"Seems as though my princess just doesn't want to let go."

Becca finally stepped out of her father's arms, exposing a red, tear-stained, face. She knew no matter what he called her, she'd never be his princess again.

Chapter 37

LONG HARBOR, RHODE ISLAND

Sunday, July 5, 2000

Becca and Lilly were up early, moving between the kitchen and the porch in an old, familiar way, Becca carrying the linens to the table, Lilly mixing the batter for her muffins. They worked well in concert, as they had in the days when entertaining was Becca's mainstay.

"Give me a hand?" Becca asked. She took one end of the long white tablecloth and Lilly took the other, ballooning it out it over a long table for ten. Becca folded the napkins, laid out the silverware, and carefully placed Sadie's china at each setting. She retrieved blue-and-white-striped cushions from the closet and clapped them together on the lawn, dust particles rising in the sunlight. She placed the cushions on the chairs, then stepped back to admire the scene.

The white table set off the gray-painted floor, sunlight reflecting off the glassware. A picture of serenity. It could have been a magazine cover; still, her stomach churned. Something was missing. She placed her index finger on her chin. Flowers. She would arrange a centerpiece from the garden. Was this pure craziness, introducing Lee to the family? Well, it was too late to turn back now.

Gardening shears in one hand and an armful of snapdragons in the crook of her elbow, she pried open the screen door. "Gran!" It was Sarah calling to her, coming over the dunes with Hennessy on his leash. Becca waited, holding the door open with her knee.

"Good morning," Sarah said cheerfully. "What an exciting day!"

"What about your bed rest?"

"I'm feeling fine, Gran. Just really restless." Sarah leaned in to give her a kiss.

Becca headed to the pantry sink and stuck the flowers in a pitcher of water. She began stripping the lower foliage, following the activity in the kitchen out of the corner of her eye. Lilly was baking coffee cake. Fresh eggs were piled high in a basket on the counter, waiting to be cracked open. As she snipped flower stems, Becca listened to the whir of the juicer, the sizzle of bacon on the griddle, and the occasional squeak of the oven door opening and closing.

"It smells delicious in here," said Ruth, coming down the back stairs.

"No peeking," Lilly said, catching Sarah opening the oven door and giving her backside an affectionate swat with a dish towel.

Ruth went to the pantry sink and stood behind Becca as she trimmed the stem of a snapdragon. "How are you doing today?" she asked, rubbing Becca's shoulders.

"Feeling some butterflies," Becca whispered.

"Has anyone seen my mom?" Sarah asked.

"You know your mother never rises before ten," Lilly said.

"I know. It's just that I haven't seen her since she left the party last night, and I'm wondering if she's calmed down."

"Did you all enjoy the fireworks?" asked Lilly.

"I'd forgotten what a show it was," said Ruth.

The Paupanaug Club had gone all out, as usual. The fireworks were set off on a strip of beach at the bottom of a steep hill. Each shot erupted over the heads of the assembled crowd on the eighteenth green. The spectacle lasted three-quarters of an hour, and a brass band played a spirited rendition of the 1812 Overture during the grand finale.

* * *

Lee's car crunched up the gravel drive at eleven o'clock sharp, not a minute late. Becca untied her apron and searched for her lipstick, taking two steps toward the screen door. Sarah scurried past her to the bay window, the choice vantage point for spying on people in the driveway. Becca saw her mouth drop wide open. "Oh my God, she looks just like Mom," Sarah said. Ruth rushed to Sarah's side, peering out the window as well. Becca's stomach tumbled again.

Lee was taking some time collecting her things from the car. Finally, she stood straight and shook out her long, dark curls, somewhat dulled by intermittent streaks of gray. She swung a purse over her shoulder and carried a small box in her hands. She wore tortoiseshell sunglasses, a bright white T-shirt, and a gauzy light blue scarf draped around her neck. Her long, flowered skirt swirled around her ankles, exposing Birkenstock sandals.

She pushed her sunglasses on top of her head and shaded her eyes, squinting toward the screen. "Hellooo," she called through the mesh.

"Oh, Lee, do come in." Becca said, walking briskly from the place where they had all been watching from the window. She pushed the door open and embraced Lee once she crossed the threshold.

"I didn't know what to bring, so I figured chocolate always works," Lee said, handing the wrapped box to Becca.

"How nice. Thank you, dear," Becca said, radiating the kindest smile she knew how. Lee looked like she needed reassurance. "Let me introduce you to everyone," Becca said, holding her hand.

"Lilly, I've met before," said Lee, turning toward the stove, "but I don't think you understood my relationship to Becca."

"Oh, I had my suspicions. There's quite a family resemblance, you know," said Lilly. "It's good to meet you again." She took off a quilted oven mitt and clasped Lee's hand in hers.

"Hi!" Sarah said, rushing forward with excitement in her voice. "It's great to meet you."

"You must be Sarah, I've heard so much about you. A baby on the way!"

"Gran told you?" Sarah said, putting her hands on her hips and turning toward Becca.

"Your grandmother and I speak on the phone quite frequently," Lee said, eliciting surprise on Sarah's face.

"I'm proud to have a great-grandbaby on the way, Sarah!" she said, biting down on her smile. "Of course I shared the news with Lee." She hoped this wasn't jealousy on the rise; Sarah would always assume a central place in Becca's heart. Thankfully, Ruth stood close by to divert the attention. Becca turned to bring her into the circle. "And this is Ruth, my dear sister-in-law from Washington, DC."

Ruth shifted her weight from foot to foot, uncharacteristically antsy. "Hi!" she said, extending her hand and giving Lee a kiss on the cheek. "Welcome to the family!"

"Goodness, I don't know what to say," said Lee, fanning herself with a flattened palm. They surrounded her in a semicircle of wide grins. Becca felt everyone's anxiety begin to dissipate, but then she noticed tears welling in Lee's eyes.

Becca wished they could linger there indefinitely. The women in the kitchen cast her family in such a loving light. She dreaded the formality that awaited them out at the table, with the whole clan. She had forgotten to ask Thomas and Andrew not to wear jackets and ties.

"The food is warm," Lilly said eventually.

"Then we'd better sit down," said Becca, taking Lee's hand again, leading the way. They entered the living room to find Andrew, Camilla, Walter, and Sally standing, huddled together in quiet conversation. "Andrew," Becca called, the four of them dispersing at the sound of her voice. "I'd like for you to meet Lee," she said.

"Well, hello," said Andrew, taking a large stride in her direction and towering over them. He shook Lee's hand as if they were about to conduct business. Lee stared up into his eyes for what Becca perceived as a bit too long, and sensed Andrew's discomfort mounting.

"Andrew," Lee finally said. "Seeing all of you, people I have a blood relationship with, well, it's more powerful than I imagined."

Becca could see the wheels turning in Andrew's head, but

he was unusually slow with a response. Camilla saved him from having to find the right words, by inserting herself at that moment. "And I'm Camilla, Andrew's wife, and these are our children."

Becca cleared her throat, then asked Andrew to man the bar. "I'm sure people might like some champagne, or a mimosa, or perhaps a Bloody Mary?"

"Certainly, Mother. Lee, what can I get for you?"

"Wow. Oh, gosh. Well, I guess this is sort of a celebration. How about champagne?"

Andrew chuckled, nodding in agreement. "That's right. This *is* a celebration," he said. "I believe this morning calls for champagne all around." Andrew had taken to making pronouncements on behalf of the whole family, just like Dan used to.

They went out onto the porch, where Becca introduced Lee to Thomas and Carol. "Thomas is the spitting image of my father," she said.

"The infamous Bunny Meister," said Lee.

"That's right," said Thomas, raising an eyebrow.

It wasn't until the champagne was poured and people started arranging themselves around the dining table that Becca realized Rachel hadn't appeared.

"Where's Rachel?"

"I'll go get her," said Lilly, placing a basket of muffins on the sideboard, where the rest of the elegant buffet was.

"She's never been a morning person," Becca said, checking her watch. "Please serve yourselves while the food is hot."

"I'd like to propose a toast." Andrew raised a glass. "To family," he said, winking at Lee.

"Andrew, you should wait for Rachel!" said Becca, but she could see everyone was anxious to get the meal started. The familiar rituals of proposing a toast and serving a meal were distractions they desperately needed.

Becca took her own plate to the buffet line and stood behind Sarah and Lee. They were spooning scrambled eggs and bacon onto their plates. "You're really a midwife?" Sarah asked Lee.

"Yes, I'm a partner in a practice over in Mystic. Know anyone in need of my services?"

"How about an appointment next week?" Sarah asked with a smile.

"Nothing would please me more," said Lee.

People sat around the table, turning their attention to Lee, dwelling on what she had to say. Ruth asked questions about where she had grown up and how she had found Becca. Lee told them about her childhood in Cincinnati and how it had been easy to find Becca once she had gotten the records from the Willows. Becca was proud of Lee's composure and noticed Sarah leaning in extra close to hear every word. Andrew sat kitty-corner from Lee and asked his own set of questions, clearly aimed at understanding her financial situation.

Becca had a single bite of coffee cake. From the head of the table, she gazed across her family's faces, her throat tightening at the sight of Rachel's empty place. She heard Walter and Sally make bets on whether Aunt Rachel would come down at all, and then Camilla scolding them for being rude.

Thomas and Carol were deliberating which train to take in the morning. "The pace of this town is exhausting," Carol said.

"It's the height of the season," said Thomas, taking a long gulp from his Bloody Mary.

"When we used to come for Labor Day weekend, it was more peaceful."

"There, there, Carol—we can rest when we get home," said Thomas, trying for the type of soothing voice Becca had never heard from her brother before.

She heard footsteps crossing the living room floor, then turned her attention from Thomas to see Sarah's worried expression. Lilly was returning to the porch alone and bent down to whisper in Becca's ear, "She's not there. Doesn't look like she slept in the bed."

"Oh dear," Becca said, flicking the cinnamon crumble topping off her coffee cake with a fork.

"What is it, Mother?" Andrew asked.

"Rachel's not in her room."

The conversations around the table stopped. "Would you like me to make some calls?" Andrew asked.

"No, don't bother the neighbors on a Sunday. She's a grown woman. She'll make it home eventually," said Becca, twisting her wedding ring. Where could she be? Walter and Sally suppressed laughter. "Go ahead, the two of you," Becca said, glaring at her grandchildren. "You're excused. Please leave the table."

Becca sensed Camilla's displeasure at her children being reprimanded. She stood up in allegiance with them. "Why don't we go refill the fruit bowl?"

Becca put her hand against her collarbone. She caught Lee's attention and mouthed, "I'm so sorry." Lee stretched her arms behind her back, seeming to shrug off the disappointment of Rachel's disappearance.

Walter and Sally began to make a ruckus, scraping their chairs against the floor and clattering silverware on the china plates, so that Becca heard the commotion in the living room only once it was right upon them.

It was Rachel's voice, louder than necessary. "Come on! Mom would love for you to join us! You're practically family!"

Becca turned stiffly in her seat to see Rachel, still in her clothes from the night before, tugging on the arm of an overweight, balding man, dragging him onto the porch.

"Oh dear! Looks like we're tardy and they started without us." Rachel's speech was slurred.

"I'm so sorry to interrupt, ma'am," the man said to Becca. "Please excuse me. I just wanted to bring Rachel home." He attempted to backpedal toward the door, but Rachel held him tight. "I found her down by the ice cream shop, on a bench by the seawall this morning. Rose brewed her some coffee."

Becca felt heat rise from her toes to the crown of her head. It was Sal Fabbrizio, dressed in an old T-shirt and sweatpants. He'd probably found Rachel while he was out sweeping in front of his shop. Oh, what had Rachel done?

"And you must be Lee!" boomed Rachel, dragging Sal toward the table with her.

Lee stood up. "Rachel?"

"Yes, I'm Rachel! I'm your sister!"

Lee smiled warily, extending a hand across the table. Andrew pushed his seat back and quickly took Rachel by the shoulders. She flinched at his touch. "Leave me alone!" she said, glaring at him. "Lee, look who I brought with me!"

"Rachel!" Ruth cried out. Her abrupt interference caught Rachel off guard. She turned in Ruth's direction. "You must be hungry," Ruth said, using a calmer tone. She spooned some eggs onto a plate. "Sit down and have something to eat."

"Oh, muffins!" Rachel said, spotting the basket on the sideboard. She let go of Sal's arm. "I love Lilly's muffins. Lee, Lilly is a wonderful cook—you know, she practically raised me." Rachel sat down at the table. "Sal, come sit next to me," she said, pulling out a chair. "Have one of these muffins. Pass the jam, Sarah, would you?"

Becca was perspiring. She pulled her arms from her cardigan sweater, letting it fall around her waist. She stretched protective fingers over Lee's hand and studied Rachel's red face as she devoured a muffin. Maybe a little food would help, soak up the alcohol in her blood, which, in combination with the heat of the day, she feared, was threatening explosion.

"What are you pouring this morning, Andrew? Champagne?" asked Rachel, looking around the table. "Where are your manners? Sal and I would like some, too."

Becca shot her son a look of warning.

But he just shrugged. "What the hell?" he said, pouring out what was left in the bottle into Rachel's glass.

Chapter 38

LONG HARBOR, RHODE ISLAND
1946

B unny held the black telephone receiver to his ear. Even the long-distance crackling couldn't obscure Thomas's displeasure. "I had to go to Washington, DC, in June for their wedding," he said, "and now Mother's ruining my August holiday with another three-ring circus at Eden."

"What can I tell you, Thomas? Playing the hostess seems to make your mother happy, and she wanted to do something for Robert and Ruth on our own turf." Bunny tried to console his son. Over their thirty-year marriage, keeping Sadie's mood elevated had become his highest priority.

"Last summer it was the welcome-home party for the soldiers, and now one for Robert and Ruth in the middle of my two weeks," Thomas continued. Bunny allowed him the last word.

Instead of hiring a car, Bunny made the trip to the train station himself. He'd always enjoyed the thirty-minute drive back to Eden, and the private time it allowed him with his children.

"So, are Robert and Ruth here yet?" Thomas asked, laying his sport coat across the backseat of Bunny's shiny new Packard Clipper.

"Yes, they're knocking around the house, trying to be helpful, but they seem anxious for the party to be over, too. That Ruth— what a girl. Why, she's got the patience of a saint."

"Do you mean to put up with Mom or because she's marrying your 'simple son'?"

Bunny shook his head—better to let him get it out now. "Thomas, your mother is wound up. Take my advice and do what she says."

"Great," said Thomas, shaking his head as he took in the scenery.

"Also, you might invite Becca to go fishing or something. I don't know what the hell they did to her at that finishing school, but it's like the life's been sucked out of her."

Thomas smirked. "Maybe our little princess had to study for once."

"No, it's more than that. Something about her is different. You'll see."

"She's growing up, Dad. Heck, she'll probably be the next one married."

Bunny reached across to the passenger seat and swatted the air playfully with the back of his hand.

"Surely it's only a matter of time. Mom had a taste of Robert's wedding; now I bet she's dying to be the mother of the bride."

"Thomas, please. I said she's wound up, but that doesn't mean we're ready to marry Becca off."

Bunny honked the Packard's horn as they pulled into the driveway, rousing Robert, Ruth, and Becca from the kitchen. Becca wore a full skirt and blouse, while Robert and Ruth were in their tennis whites and holding rackets under their arms. Thomas ducked his head getting out of the car and went directly to his small greeting party. He shook hands with Robert and gave Becca and Ruth kisses on the cheek.

"Where's your mother?" Bunny asked.

"At the club, choosing table linens," said Robert.

Mr. P. emerged from the kitchen with three glasses of Bunny's favorite scotch on a silver tray, complete with linen napkins and a dish of cashews. "Cocktails on the porch, sir?"

"Mr. P., you're a man among men. Thomas, Robert, care to join me?"

"Of course," said Robert, handing Ruth the rackets.

"Brilliant," Thomas said, taking up his drink right away and digging his other hand into the nuts.

On the porch, Bunny sat in his usual lounge chair with a satisfied sigh. The wicker chair beside him strained under Thomas's large frame. His eldest son's stomach hung over his belt, and a soft double chin had ballooned under his jaw. He was working awfully hard; it was nice to see the sun shine on his white complexion. Robert trailed behind, picked up his scotch, and leaned his elbows back against the porch railing.

"Round of golf in the morning, Father?" Thomas asked.

"Absolutely."

"Robert?"

"Depends on whether we can get out of here before Mother gets hold of me."

"Getting used to answering to women?" Thomas winked.

Ruth came out on the porch with a plate of cheese and crackers, followed by Becca, carrying a crystal bowl with eight jumbo shrimp on ice and red cocktail sauce. They set their hors d'oeuvres down on the glass tabletop in front of Bunny.

"Thank you, dears," he said, dipping a shrimp into the cocktail sauce.

"So, how's married life?" Thomas asked, raising his glass in the newlyweds' direction.

"Just great, thanks, Thomas," Robert said.

A long silence followed. The men sipped their drinks, Thomas leaned forward to cut off a piece of cheese, and Robert turned toward the ocean, the breeze blowing around the curly locks of hair above his ears.

It pained Bunny that Robert couldn't be at ease with his brother. He'd seen it unfold over the years, how Thomas had become a mystery to Robert and Edward. It had started with the seizures and his restriction from sports, but the gap had widened when Thomas had stayed home during the war. It didn't help that Thomas flaunted his wealth. An only child, Bunny wanted nothing more than for his sons' brotherhood to fortify them. That Thomas was on the outside of Robert and Edward's friendship was one of his greatest disappointments.

"And when will Edward make his appearance?" asked Thomas.

"He's still the junior man at the firm, can't leave until the weekend," Bunny explained. "He promised he'd be up from the city Saturday afternoon, in time for the party."

"He'll coast in just as the champagne is poured, avoiding all of Mother's orders," Thomas said, swallowing the last of his scotch.

"I heard that!" It was Sadie's shrill voice in the doorway. Bunny and Thomas rose to their feet. "Who's giving orders?" she asked in a mocking tone. Thomas bent down to give her a kiss. "Mother, you look ravishing," he said, before sinking back into his chair.

She did look beautiful. She sparkled when the children came home, gathered around like this. Seeing her effusive and gay, Bunny could overlook her obsession with choosing linens and centerpieces.

Sadie waved a small envelope in Bunny's direction. "Just got a late response from the Millers. They're bringing their two sons and a nephew, Dan Fitzpatrick, who I believe is a medical student at Yale." She tilted her head toward Becca, who was lingering on the fringe of the conversation, picking at her cuticles. Thomas gave his father a playful punch on the shoulder, and when Bunny looked at him, Thomas mouthed the words "next summer."

Bunny shook his head. What a ridiculous thought. Becca was just eighteen, and there hadn't yet been even one young man to call on her. It would suit Bunny fine if she went on living under his roof for many years.

"So, little brother, tell me, how's your new job going? How do you plan to provide for this lovely lady? Or will she go back to work to support you?"

Bunny winced at the jabbing. Robert stammered, describing his loan officer position at the bank. "It carries the title of junior vice president," he said, "but after a few years, I'll be a full vice president."

Ruth smiled encouragement in Robert's direction, rubbing

the small of his back. Bunny had pulled some strings. "Stash your pride, son," he had insisted. "With all these boys coming home and looking for work, let me make it easier." The only reason his son had agreed was that he had been desperate to marry Ruth.

"Well, Bobby," Thomas said, "the P and E can throw some business your way. Help the cause."

Robert turned to Ruth. "Excuse us. I promised Ruth a tennis game." He took her hand in his, and they jogged down the steps to the lawn and disappeared around the side of the house.

* * *

Four nights later, Bunny stood under the awning on the golf club's terrace, holding court near the dance floor. Standing a foot above the crowd, he kept an eye on Sadie, who was enthusiastically introducing their guests to Ruth. He watched Becca shadow Robert, then disappear into the dining room much earlier than was necessary. A brass quartet played on a small stage by the eighteenth green, the Atlantic Ocean as their backdrop.

The band members were clad in white dinner jackets and provided a jazzy soundtrack to the cocktail hour. Bunny swayed back and forth to the music, smiling and enjoying playing the host. After the sun set and the bell rang for dinner, Edward took the microphone from the band leader and raised his glass with a warmhearted smile. He recounted his little brother's undying loyalty yet dupable nature. "Ruth, he's like a well-trained golden retriever!" The crowd broke into laughter and clinked their glasses. "Hear, hear!" said Bunny, beaming with pride, having always considered a man's ability to give a good toast paramount to his success.

Sadie whispered in Bunny's ear throughout the meal. She had seated Becca in between the Millers' sons and their nephew, Dan Fitzpatrick. "I think they're really hitting it off!"

Bunny turned to study his daughter's delicate profile a few tables away. She was stunning, her thick hair up in a twist, its dark red color set off perfectly by the lime-green chiffon of her dress.

She could no doubt carry on polite conversation with the young men, but he didn't like the way her shoulders hunched. Where was her confidence? She hadn't called on one friend since she had arrived in Long Harbor, and she was spending an extraordinary amount of time alone.

* * *

Several weeks later, Becca knocked on the master-bedroom door just as Bunny and Sadie were turning out the lights. She told them that she planned to go to New York City at the end of the summer, instead of returning to Pittsburgh. Bunny sat on the edge of the bed in his robe and listened. "Ruth and Robert said they would be happy to have me stay in their extra room," said Becca. She said she needed a change of atmosphere and would take some classes there, possibly think about enrolling in college.

Sadie pulled a brush through her hair with ferocity. "Absolutely not. You're too young. It wouldn't be proper for you to live apart from us."

Bunny looked back and forth between his wife and his daughter. They couldn't even face each other. Something was definitely off. "We'll sleep on it, Princess," he said, "and discuss it in the morning." Bunny kissed Becca on the top of the head before shutting the door behind her. When he turned around, Sadie was already under the covers, a frown pasted on her face. "You mustn't even consider it. I've already gone to such lengths planning her debutante season." He turned the switch on his bedside lamp and lay quietly in the darkness.

At the breakfast table, Bunny watched Sadie's determined effort to put an end to Becca's ideas. "Robert and Ruth won't have room for you, dear," she said, stirring her coffee. "I think they want to get started right away."

"Get started?" asked Becca.

"You know, start their family."

"Oh." Becca's voice trailed off as she turned toward the window.

His daughter's visible sadness pained Bunny. He would do anything to get her to smile again. He looked at his wife's pinched mouth and his daughter's distant stare and took a big gulp of his coffee. He wiped his lips with his napkin, then put his fist down, causing both Sadie and Becca to turn toward him. "Sadie, why don't we let Becca go to New York? At least until Christmastime? She'll come back to Pittsburgh in December for the cotillion."

"Oh, Daddy, thank you." Becca jumped up, never giving her mother a chance to respond. She ran around to Bunny's chair and hugged him around the neck. Sensing Sadie's fuming, he carefully avoided her steely stare.

"Princess, I just can't believe you'd want to leave me again!" said Bunny, turning around to face his daughter.

"Daddy, I'm too old to be your princess."

"Never, Becca. Don't say such a thing."

* * *

Bunny picked ripe tomatoes and zucchini off the plants in his garden in the warm September sunshine. He turned them in his hand, checking for worms, putting the good ones in a bushel basket. He bent at the knees, pulling up weeds and refastening any fallen vines to their stakes. The kids were gone, and it was just Sadie and him left at Eden. How quickly that had happened. She held out her hand, finding him with his knees in the dirt and examining his tomatoes.

"Let's have a couple of those for lunch," she said, picking up his basket.

Bunny stood up, slowly straightening his tall frame.

"Robert sent a note," Sadie said. "Dan Fitzpatrick's been down to the city to call on Becca *three times* now."

The way she said it got to him, implying that no decent father would have let a daughter out from under his watch when there was a serious suitor in the wings. He threw his gardening gloves into his wheelbarrow and wiped his forehead with a handkerchief. Sadie sighed as she opened the kitchen door. "But what can we do about it from here?" She savored every opportunity to lord this judgment lapse over him. Bunny went to the sink to wash his hands.

Slicing into the tomatoes and sprinkling them with salt, Sadie took an unexpected tack. "On the other hand, he wouldn't be the type to take her far away. Dan would obviously prefer Long Harbor to anything *his* family could offer."

"Sadie, isn't that kind of speculation a little premature?" Bunny asked, taking his seat at the kitchen table.

"A doctor, went to Yale, and has a low golf handicap, too! Why, he could win the club championship someday."

Bunny sat at the kitchen table, chewing on his tomatoes, sweet with ripeness. They would have been better without so much salt. The young man hadn't been on the football team like his own sons, but he had captained the squash team when he was an undergraduate, a pretty precious crowd. He'd even insinuated he was Skull and Bones.

Bunny decided they would stay at Eden through Thanksgiving, in order to host the children there for the long weekend. When the time came, Sadie suggested they invite Dan to spend a day as well. Bunny organized a football game out on the lawn. Thomas sat on the porch with Becca and Ruth, sipping spiked mulled cider.

Bunny watched Dan closely, the way he sidled up to Edward and Robert, joining in their banter, inserting himself as the third man in their gang. After Dan dove for a spectacular touchdown pass, Bunny noticed Edward giving his little sister the thumbs-up sign. Sadie glanced over at Bunny with a subtle nod of satisfaction.

* * *

Later that spring, Dan called Bunny's office. When Bunny told Sadie that Dan had asked for a lunch date in New York City, presumably to ask for Becca's hand, she clasped her hands as if her prayers had been answered.

"What's the rush? Why would Becca marry the first boyfriend?" Bunny asked. She was a beauty, and *his* daughter, too, for

God's sake. That combination alone was enough to attract plenty of young men.

"Oh, Bunny, don't be silly! You have to give Dan your blessing!"

"I'm just asking if we're positive he's the right man. And what about Becca? Have we asked her opinion?"

"Of course I have. As recently as Easter Sunday. She told me she's grown fond of him. Why, Ruth and Robert think he's absolutely wonderful."

"I just can't help but feel like the timing is off." Bunny paced the floor.

"Bunny, he's a catch! We should be very happy this is finally settled." Sadie approached him tenderly, putting her hands against his chest.

"I'd just like to talk to Becca before this goes any further."

"What? And ruin the surprise?"

Bunny shook his head at his wife's stubborn insistence, as he had many times throughout their marriage. She kissed him and hugged him the way she had when they'd learned the boys had survived the war. Her excitement overwhelmed his reasoning and, hating the prospect of an argument, he went along with it.

He'd walk his daughter down the aisle at the Long Harbor chapel the following September. After he took his place in the pew with the rest of the family, he'd feel Thomas's hot breath on his neck. "Hate to say I told you so, old man," Thomas would whisper, "but your number-one son called this one."

Chapter 39

NEW YORK CITY
July 5, 2000

J oseph hung up the phone. It was his mother, and she was at
Eden, of all places. He hadn't been back there in ages, but it
had been one of the hottest Junes on record in the city and her
spontaneous invitation was alluring. Constance had just been complaining about the muggy weather, although he hardly noticed,
working as he did in an air-conditioned tower. His mother said she
had called Benjamin as well, but the trip from San Francisco would
be impossible for him on such short notice.

"Your aunt Becca invited me to Eden for the Fourth of July,
and being here is, well, powerful. *So* many memories. Becca would
love to see you and Constance and your girls."

"She would?"

"Yes, Joseph, she would. And it would be good for you. It's
less than three hours from the city. I'd love to spend a few extra
days with the four of you."

Joseph flipped his phone shut, walked into the bathroom, and
peeled his undershirt from around his belly. Constance was applying moisturizer to her forehead.

"Hey," he said, thinking of his mother back at Eden, sleeping
in the bedroom she'd shared with his father.

She looked at his reflection in the mirror with questioning eyes.

"That was Mom. She's staying at my dad's family's place in
Long Harbor for the Fourth. Wanted to know if we could come up
and join her."

Constance started brushing her teeth, shifting her glance to the water in the basin.

"Should we go?" he asked.

She shrugged.

"'Cause I was thinking," he said, "it might be fun for us and the girls to get out of the city, swim in the ocean." Joseph massaged the supple, olive skin on her shoulders, then leaned in and kissed her long neck.

She looked in the mirror again, this time with doubtful smirk. "You'll just abandon us with your relatives and go off to do conference calls, like you always do."

"No, I promise I won't." He held two fingers up in the Boy Scout pledge and slipped his other hand up under her nightshirt. She puckered her lips in contemplation and began the ritual of brushing out her silky black hair. "Hmm," she said.

Joseph caressed the smooth skin on her stomach. "Hmm?"

"I don't know, Joe. You couldn't spare the time for our anniversary, and I had to cancel all the bookings I made in Santa Barbara. Now your mother calls and you can clear your calendar?"

"It's not Mother; it's just that I've got a break in the action because everyone's on holiday, so why not take advantage of it?"

Constance turned in his arms and looked up into his eyes. "I've always wanted to see that place. Do you think it still has the sleeping porch?" she asked.

Ah, the sleeping porch. He had never slept better in his life than he had those childhood nights at Eden. He nodded yes. "I'll put in a special request, if you'd like." He leaned in to nibble her earlobe.

"Will you take the girls crabbing?"

"You remember," he said, smiling. He loved that about Constance: she listened and she remembered. When they had first met and she had asked about his father, he had given the same convenient answer he always had: "not around." But by their third date he had shared memories of his dad at the beach in Long Harbor, at this mammoth house called Eden, the sailboat he had with his uncle, the sand castles, fishing, cookouts. He had also spoken fondly of his grandfather, who had pulled him and Benjamin up onto his lap and comforted them after their father died.

"Sounds like the perfect place for a child, like a dream," Constance said.

"Sometimes I think it was."

That night Joseph dreamed he was collecting shells on the beach. His father carried a small bucket by the handle and walked with him and Benjamin down a long stretch of soft sand. He and his brother would run ahead, and whenever either of them found a promising shell, they'd go back to their father and show him before depositing it in the bucket. In the dream, Joseph took his father's free hand and walked by his side. He woke up amazed. He couldn't remember the last time he'd dreamed of his father, or even remembered a dream, for that matter.

The next morning, Constance pulled their things together: bathing suits, matching pink dresses for the girls, their white sandals, a pair of running shorts, and a few T-shirts. Joseph stared out their window, on hold with the car service, mesmerized by the ferries on the Hudson River.

Their daughters, Jessica and Monica, raced around the large loft apartment, screeching, "The beach, the beach! We're going to the beach!"

Joseph put his palm over the receiver. "Shh! We're not going if I can't get a car."

An hour later, a shiny black Suburban pulled up in front of their building and the doorman delivered Constance's luggage to the driver. Joseph helped their girls step up onto the running boards, then buckled their seat belts in the way back, the pungent scent of too much air freshener filling his nose. He took a seat in the middle row next to Constance and held her hand.

"Daddy, are the waves big in Long Harbor?" The girls began lobbing questions over the headrests from the back.

"Big, but not too big."

"Did you swim in them when you were our age?"

"Yes, but with my daddy holding on to me."

"Will you hold on to us?"

"Of course."

Constance flipped up her big black sunglasses, exposing her dark eyes. She broke into a perfect white smile and craned her head toward the backseat. "You hear that?" she said. "Daddy's going to swim with you!"

The car's fan was on full blast and cold air blew her glossy hair across her forehead. God, his wife was beautiful; he was grateful his girls favored her.

"Is that the house where your daddy saved your aunt during the big hurricane?"

Joseph chuckled. "Yes, it is." It didn't seem like they were listening, playing with their Barbies at bedtime, but his girls remembered every detail of every bedtime story he told them.

"Is it a really big house?"

"I remember it as being huge, but I haven't been back in a long time, almost thirty years, since my cousin Rachel's wedding."

Joseph's phone vibrated, and he put on his earpiece. Constance crossed her arms across her chest. Joseph put up his index finger to indicate "one"—just this one call, and then he would be all hers. He listened to his associate recount the ups and downs of his meeting with a client in Tokyo.

He watched Jessica and Monica's silliness while he was debriefed. The girls couldn't keep their hands to themselves amid the excitement of a family outing. He hadn't seen them this talkative in months, but hadn't seen them awake, either. He hadn't made it home at a decent hour since the Exron case began, and Constance believed in a regular bedtime.

Joseph looked out the window at the dense holiday traffic inching down the highway in the opposite direction. People were heading back to the city, done with their celebrating. But Joseph preferred their timing.

He was used to swimming upstream, never doing things as expected. He credited his business success to that philosophy and had even married Constance after everyone had given up on his finding someone—so much so that his mother had never even mentioned anything about Constance's being Asian. He loved her for that, for having not batted an eye the first time she and Constance had met, and for the way she embraced his wife and their love.

When they had married, he had been well into his forties and she thirty, and they had continued their fast-paced careers, living in Hong Kong, Los Angeles, and, most recently, New York. They had surprised everyone seven years ago, when Constance had gotten pregnant with Jessica. Now here he was, learning how to be a daddy at age fifty-two. He kept telling himself it wasn't that old, but he had put in decades on the road and adapting to family dinners and bedtimes was hard.

"Welcome to Rhode Island," Constance said, reading the big blue sign on the edge of the highway.

"Yay!" sang the girls.

Joseph cracked the tinted window and breathed in the fresh air. The tension in his shoulders was already easing as they left the city behind, and the drive wasn't as bad as he had assumed. His partners all had weekend places, mostly in the Hamptons, skipping out on Fridays to beat the traffic, but Joseph had bought into the old adage "you snooze, you lose." Besides, Constance had been raised on the heat and bustle of Singapore. She had such simple requests: an uncluttered apartment, the occasional meal out. It wasn't until she stopped working to raise their daughters that summers in the city felt oppressive.

Joseph leaned over the driver's seat as the car wound its way into Long Harbor. "It's that driveway over there." He pointed toward the windshield.

"It's time to turn your phone off," Constance said.

"Ha, look. Okay, now, toot the horn as we get close to the house. It's an old tradition, to announce ourselves."

* * *

"Who are you talking to?" asked Constance, hands on her hips, emerging from the water and rejoining him in a neighboring beach chair. "I leave for five minutes and you make a call."

"It's Ben!" said Joseph. "Calling my twin brother doesn't count!"

The girls were filling pails with wet sand a few feet in front of where he and Constance sat in hats and sunglasses, a picnic cooler and a canvas bag filled with reading material at their side.

"So," Joseph continued into his cell phone, "like I was saying, the place is exactly the same—down to the bathroom fixtures and the kitchen shelves. It's like time has stopped. You wouldn't believe it."

"What about the people? Have they changed?"

"Lilly is still here, for God's sake! Do you remember Lilly? She was the nanny when we were kids. . . . She's, like, seventy now, and still cooking and cleaning."

"You've got to be kidding."

"Aunt Becca's here, still the queen bee, but most of the family has left. It's just me, Constance, and the girls, Mom, Aunt Becca, Rachel, Sarah . . . Oh, and Sarah's pregnant."

Constance gave him a reproachful stare and placed her index finger on her lips. He was talking too loudly.

"Really?" Benjamin seemed to be getting a real kick out of the update.

"Yes." Joseph looked over both shoulders and spoke in a softer voice. "And get this one: turns out old Aunt Becca had an illegitimate daughter she gave up fifty years ago. Uncle Dan never knew. The whole tribe met her this weekend. We arrived to witness the fallout. A shit storm."

There was a silent moment of disbelief on the line, then, "What? Priceless, Joseph—priceless. Aunt Becca, the old bat. I wish I were there; you're having all the fun."

"Well, it's still damn gorgeous. I actually forgot how nice it is. The water is crystal clear. You've got to get back here with Melanie. And it's got to be this summer; Mom says they might have to sell the place. Hey, I even found our old fishing rods in the garage!"

"Really? And how *is* Mom?"

"She's great, joining us here at the beach in a few for a picnic. Loves telling the girls stories about when you and I were little, spending our summers here. And stories about Dad. I forgot how many pictures there are of him hanging on the back stairs. It's actually pretty cool."

"Don't forget to take the girls to the carousel, like he used to do with us."

"Check—that and an ice cream cone are on the docket for tonight."

* * *

Lilly brought them extra blankets. "You probably won't need them, but just in case it gets breezy," she said. "Isn't this fun?" She bent over to tickle the girls, who were already tucked in. "Spending the night on the porch with your mom and dad? It's like a slumber party."

The girls laughed with delight.

"I used to sleep out here with Uncle Benjamin every night," Joseph said. "Loved it."

"What's that sound?" asked Monica.

"Crickets!" said Constance.

After Lilly left, Constance spun around, her gauzy linen robe twirling at the bottom. "This place is amazing. I had no idea," she said. "We've stayed at the poshest five-star resorts, Joe, but there's something so authentic about this place."

"I know," Joseph said.

"It feels like one of those old family homes—so much history." She walked toward the screen.

"That's because it *is* one of those old family homes."

"I'm just surprised you've never brought us here before. I really love it. I know some people are looking at me and the girls sideways, wondering how we fit into the family, but I don't even care."

"You never stop surprising me," he said.

"And seeing those pictures of your dad and his brother in their military garb, home from World War II!"

Her interest made his heart swell. He looked at the painted floorboards, still worn in the spot where he and Benjamin had played cards by flashlight, and remembered his own father coming in to kiss him good night.

"What?" she asked, bringing him back.

"You're amazing," he said, wanting to bottle this feeling and take it home with him. He squeezed her long, thin fingers in his and spun her around like he used to on the dance floor. "You're gorgeous, too."

Chapter 40

NEW YORK CITY
1948

Ruth sat in the hard wooden pew of the Long Harbor chapel, next to Sadie. Robert, Thomas, and Edward were standing at the altar as Dan's groomsmen, and so it was Ruth's hand that Sadie clutched when they stood to watch Bunny walk Becca down the long aisle. Becca clung to her father's arm, a spray of white roses tied up with a pale pink satin bow in her other hand. Ruth could see Bunny's effort to shorten his stride to stay in step with his daughter. When they reached the minister and the over-size arrangements of white dahlias and calla lilies that Sadie had insisted on, Bunny bent down to kiss Becca's cheek. It looked as if he whispered something in her ear as well.

Ruth felt Sadie slip her hand away, reaching for Bunny as he joined them in the front pew. Ruth kept her eyes on Becca and Dan, the bride and groom, standing in front of the minister, happy for them. It had been Ruth and Robert who had urged Becca in this direction, confident the path they had taken would be Becca's fulfillment as well. But Becca had confided in Ruth that she was uncertain of Dan's love. "Sometimes I think it's Long Harbor he's after. If it weren't for Eden and the country club, he wouldn't be interested."

"What nonsense!" Ruth had said. "You're a beauty, you're smart, and, well, I don't know . . . There's a certain mystery about you."

"It's just . . ." Becca could never really explain.

"Listen," Ruth cut in with authority, "finding a guy who loves you and your family and won't take you away from Long Harbor . . . You are a lucky girl!"

* * *

A photographer snapped pictures of Becca and Dan leaving the chapel. Ruth heard Sadie remark, "I hope one comes out well so I can hang it with the others. It's our first Long Harbor wedding." She was a proud mother of the bride, gloating to her friends about Dan's Yale education and medical career. When they arrived at the reception at the golf club, Ruth stood in the receiving line next to Robert. "Just look at Becca," he said. "She's never had the lime-light of the family before." They all clinked glasses, then danced in a circle around Becca and Dan. Robert got Ruth laughing, puffing out his chest in an imitation of Thomas.

After a brief honeymoon in New York City, Becca and Dan returned to Eden. "So, how was it?" Ruth asked Becca, the two of them alone in the kitchen, doing the dishes. Sadie had gone to bed, and all the men had started up a poker game.

"I don't know. I was pretty nervous. I sort of thought we'd be under the covers," Becca said, scouring a pot under scalding water.

It was clear that Becca had misunderstood her question. "Oh, no, sweetheart, that's not what I was asking about. But don't worry too much about *that*—lots of young wives get the jitters," Ruth said, slowly wiping a pan dry.

Becca turned and stared into Ruth's eyes, welling up as if she might cry. "I shut myself in the bathroom for a long time. I had to drink most of a bottle of champagne."

"Oh, you poor thing—it will get better."

"I felt edgy. What if I become pregnant right away?" Becca sniffed into her forearm. "Ruth, do you use contraceptives?" she whispered.

"My goodness, no," Ruth said. They both stood silent at the

sink for a moment; then Ruth put down the dish towel and hugged Becca around the shoulders. "No, Robert and I have been trying for a baby, and you will be too, soon enough!"

Pregnant right away? Ruth would have given anything, as she and Robert had been trying for almost a year. She carried such high hopes, but every month when she spotted blood, her heart sank with disappointment. She suddenly suppressed a small panic that Becca might become pregnant before her. But by the end of the summer, thank God, she and Robert were able to make their triumphant announcement to the family around the dinner table at Eden. "Ruth's expecting!" Robert burst with pride.

Sadie leaped to her feet. "Oh, God bless!" she said, heading for Ruth's chair.

"And there's more!" Ruth said.

"What else could there be?" asked Sadie, stopping short.

"Twins!"

Bunny jumped up as well and wrapped her in a hug. "Dear Lord! How exciting. Now, don't fret about a thing. We'll be here to support you, and we'll hire some help." Bunny smiled at her in a way he never had before. Of course he saw her differently, now that she would be continuing his line.

Ruth surprised herself, becoming overwhelmed with tears. Something about telling the family made it more real than when it had just been she and Bobby who'd known. Whether they were tears of happiness or relief, or due to her now being eternally connected to the Meister clan, she wasn't sure. But once her vision became clear, she noticed Becca looking away and Dan fidgeting with his napkin.

The following year, Becca announced her own pregnancy on Labor Day weekend. Dan beamed as Becca shared the news rather matter-of-factly. Sadie shook with happiness, taking both of Becca's hands in hers and smiling. Becca closed her eyes and leaned in against her mother's chest, seeming to bask in the love. When she finally pulled away, Bunny gave her a little twirl in the air. "My princess is going to be a mother," he said.

* * *

Ruth and Robert rushed to the hospital to visit as soon as Becca's baby was born. "We're naming her Rachel," Becca said, while the nurse rolled the bassinet to Dan's side.

"Rachel? Where'd that come from?" asked Robert. Ruth had named their twins Joseph and Benjamin, for her father and grandfather.

"I think it's a nice name," said Becca. "I first heard it in finishing school, in Kansas City." Dan leaned over the bassinet to pick up their daughter. It was the first time Ruth had witnessed his ease around babies; she'd almost forgotten he was a doctor and all.

"I like it, too," said Ruth. "I hope Becca and Baby Rachel can get to Eden soon. I'll be there with the twins, and the girl your mother hired is a godsend."

"You girls should stay all summer and relax. Dan and I'll come up on the weekends," Robert said.

Ruth described the new nanny. Her name was Lilly. She was only sixteen but very capable. She'd traveled down from rural Maine, looking for work. Ruth liked her practical nature. Sadie had said a girl that age would be very "trainable." She had plenty of energy for the twin boys, who were already walking, and would continue to sleep in the nursery to take care of Rachel.

* * *

The five summers that followed were ideal ones for Eden. Like the moon's pull on the tide and the rise and fall of the sun, the household's days and weeks ebbed and flowed with the children's daily needs and the coming and going of Dan and Robert on the weekends. The weekday pattern at Eden assumed a maternal rhythm, even with Bunny there, splitting his days between the golf club and reading newspapers in his study.

Ruth and Becca walked slowly up the path through the hot dunes with the beach bags, pails, and shovels, and the children in tow. Becca helped them shed their sandy bathing suits in the driveway while Ruth rinsed their four little bottoms with the garden hose. The children danced around, glistening in the warm sun, a touch of sunburn on their cheeks. Andrew was a squirming toddler, and Rachel screamed and ran from the chilly spray. Joseph and Benjamin darted in between, daring the women to catch them. Ruth finally corralled them all with fluffy towels and sent them to Lilly at the kitchen door.

Ruth always noticed when Rachel needed something. "Maybe a bit of a sandwich for Rachel, Lilly. Her lunch got covered with sand." She could tell more easily than Becca why Rachel was out of sorts. Becca busied herself with Andrew and seemed happy to let others attend to her fussy daughter.

When Lilly herded the children up the back stairs for their naps, Ruth checked the clock on the kitchen wall and quickly poured two glasses of iced tea. Becca grabbed a stack of magazines and rushed to the back porch. Ruth would join her, sunglasses on and a law journal under her arm. They'd recline, side by side, on chaise lounges. Ruth knew that for Becca, besides cocktail hour, when she mixed her habitual pitcher of martinis, the children's naptime was her most treasured time of day.

Becca turned a few pages of her magazine and then yawned. "Andrew is still waking up so early," she said.

"Joseph and Benjamin scramble into bed with me as soon as the sun comes up. At least Andrew is still in the nursery and doesn't sword-fight across your stomach."

"Oh, but he calls for me and just won't stop."

"You should ignore his hollering."

"I bring him into bed with me, but Rachel gets awfully jealous when she finds him there."

"Rachel just seems . . . well, like she wants more from you."

"You see it, too?"

"Yes. You know how people are always saying girls are more difficult than boys."

"I didn't think that started until they were older," said Becca.

"The *teenage years*," said Ruth. "But you're the princess of the family, Becca. I'm sure you never caused Sadie any problems."

"Oh, you'd be surprised," Becca said, flipping through the glossy fashion pages.

It was times like these when Ruth felt a closeness to Becca that she'd never had with anyone, like they were sisters. Still, Becca seemed to hold back—as if she might be on the verge of sharing something important but then decided against it.

So they talked primarily about the children. Sometimes they talked about their husbands, but it was tricky because Robert was Becca's favorite brother and characterizing him as anything less than perfect was fraught with danger. Ruth couldn't exactly question the way Robert shrank in the presence of his father, or the annoying way he dropped everything when his mother made a demand. Even though Robert had not yet shed his childhood role, she believed the love in their marriage was deeper than what Becca shared with Dan. She knew Becca had once toyed with the idea of living on her own, instead of getting married. She had even picked up an application to the Katharine Gibbs secretarial school. When Robert had learned of her plan, he'd scoffed, "A secretary? God, Becca, don't ever let Mother catch wind of that idea."

Ruth liked Dan. He was kind and considerate. They shared a special kinship as both in-laws at Eden and outsiders in Long Harbor. Yes, sometimes he could get caught up in the prestige that came with being a doctor, and he cared a little too much about playing the social game, but he was a good father and had become a very good friend to Robert.

"What do you think the boys would like to do this weekend?" Ruth asked, it being a Wednesday and time to sort things out.

"Is Robert taking the train up on Friday?" Becca asked.

"Yes, he said he might catch an early one. Can Dan get out early?"

"Unlikely."

"I hope he gets here in time for the Tylers' party, but if he's late, there are three more on Saturday night," Ruth said, counting off the invitations on her fingers. The parties in the beginning of the season were always exciting, but by this point in the summer, Ruth was just as happy staying home and playing cards.

During the week, Mr. P. served dinner in two shifts, first something bland and unobjectionable in the kitchen for the children, then, after they had been tucked in, a proper dinner for the adults around the dining room table. Sitting down and putting their napkins in their laps, Ruth and Becca shared a collective sigh. They'd crossed a finish line, one marked not by a ribbon and flashbulbs but by the magical hour of a seven o'clock bedtime. Her father filled the crystal wineglasses at their places, and they toasted each other in celebration of yet another day.

"Mother, will Edward be coming up this weekend?" Becca asked.

"Not sure," her mother said, vigorously cutting her meat. Edward had a new girlfriend, whose family summered in the Hamptons.

"I believe he was a bit repelled by the fact that his bedroom was turned into the nursery," her father added, spooning more potatoes onto his plate. Ruth had heard his complaining, too, about the nappies in the sink, the high chairs clogging the kitchen, and the crying and fussing that seemed more than "the new girl" could handle. But it wasn't just the children, Ruth surmised; it also had something to do with Robert's partnering with Dan in the club's annual golf tournament.

At about six o'clock the following evening, Ruth and Becca went down to the weekly cookout at the beach club with the four kids. Thursday evening was the last night of the week without husbands, and so the club set up long charcoal grills for the mothers to barbecue hamburgers and hot dogs and roast marshmallows for dessert.

Lilly wore a cardigan and a white apron while grilling their hot dogs. The sun started setting; the blue sky took on a pink hue and the ocean a steely gray. The twins had already gotten into the marshmallows, and their fingers were a sticky mess. While deep in conversation with Mary Bell, out of the corner of her eye, Ruth watched Rachel finish her hot dog. They were debating whether families should have televisions in Long Harbor.

"Why shouldn't they?" asked Ruth. "Why does everyone want to be cut off from civilization up here?"

"It's just how it's always been."

"But don't you think retreating from the real world is dangerous? For example, watching the evening news . . ."

Ruth stopped speaking when she spotted Bunny walking onto the deck. He wore a grim expression as he approached their table. "Girls, gather the children and get in the car. We need to go." He turned toward the ocean in order to avoid their questioning faces. Ruth thought she detected a redness around his eyes. Her heart raced, and she felt a pit in her stomach as she helped gather the children and pulled Lilly away from the grill. Becca stuffed the food back into Sadie's monogrammed picnic basket, and then they all headed toward the waiting car.

Bunny's silence and firm grip on the steering wheel suggested something terrible. When they arrived at the kitchen door, Lilly took the children directly upstairs. Ruth assumed it was Sadie, but Bunny put his arm around her shoulder and guided her toward his study. "What is it? Is it my parents? What happened?" Ruth asked, but the unmistakable sound of Sadie crying in the study told Ruth who it was.

A Rhode Island state trooper in all his regalia fidgeted with his hat by Bunny's desk. Sadie rose to her feet to embrace her. "Oh, Ruthie," she wailed, "it's Bobby. He was coming up tonight to surprise you."

"Mrs. Meister," the state trooper said, addressing Ruth, "Ma'am, I'm terribly sorry to be the one to deliver this sad news, but there was a collision at the intersection of Routes 1 and 138. A tourist from Massachusetts didn't see the stop sign and broadsided your husband's car. He passed away in the ambulance."

"No, that's impossible." Ruth felt for her wedding ring, then collapsed onto the couch by Sadie's side.

Chapter 41

LONG HARBOR, RHODE ISLAND
July 6, 2000

B ecca looked at the portrait of her mother that hung in the dining room and sighed. "Well, I went against your advice, Mother," she said to Sadie's regal smile, "and now I've made some history of my own." The Sunday brunch on July 5, 2000, would go down in family folklore, referred to simply as "the Brunch." It was not because Rachel misbehaved or Camilla sneered, or because Andrew oozed his charm in order to win Lee's allegiance. It was because that brunch, the whole weekend, in fact, was a catalyst that set so much in motion. From that day forward, nothing was ever the same. Nothing could ever be the same. It was as if some cool sea breeze had blown through the French doors into the house and cleared away a hundred years of cobwebs. Indeed, after that sunny, clear morning, Becca's honesty set a new tone.

It was time to explain everything to Sal Fabbrizzio. She called him one afternoon when Lee was at the house. When he arrived at the kitchen door, Becca introduced them again. "You remember Lee from our brunch the other day. Lee, Sal is the one who escorted Rachel home." Then she herded them out of the kitchen, toward the path to the beach. She wanted to be outside, where they would not be interrupted. She also thought Sal might get upset or emotional, and she didn't want him to feel confined by Eden. Hell, he should be able to scream, or cry into the wind if he needed to.

This poor man, Becca thought. *He and his wife live a good, simple life, and they never had any children of their own. He will absolutely hate me for this.*

Sal eyed Becca with a confused expression as she slipped off her shoes at the end of the path and climbed up and over the dunes. Lee and Sal followed her, and the three of them sat on the downward slope of the sand, facing the waves for several minutes, before Becca spoke. "Sal, I never told you, but the night of the party, the night we met, I became pregnant." Becca put her face in her hands.

"What?" Sal said. "Becca, I've always carried around a great deal of guilt about my behavior that night, taking advantage of you, but I never dreamed . . . Oh, Becca, I'm so sorry. What you've had to live with."

There was complete silence, except for the waves crashing and the seagulls screeching. "Are you trying to tell me that Sal is my father?" Lee finally asked.

Becca nodded yes, lifting her face from her hands.

Sal looked back and forth between the two of them with calm wonder. "You are my daughter?" His voice squeaked, and he reached over and took Lee's hand.

Becca told him the whole story about her mother sending her off to the Willows and giving the baby up for adoption in Kansas City.

"My God," said Sal.

"I'm sorry I never told you," said Becca.

"Now I understand why you avoided me all these years."

"I didn't think you wanted anything to do with me, either."

Sal held Lee's hand and looked into her eyes. "I've had a daughter all this time. Isn't that something."

Lee shrugged and smiled. "To have found my mother and now my father, too. Thank you, Becca."

"You look so much like Rachel," Sal said.

"Sal and Rachel were very close," Becca explained to Lee.

"She was rebellious and smart, a real pistol," said Sal. "I know she was a sloppy drunk the other day, but she was a great kid. Don't write her off just yet."

Becca nodded. "Wouldn't it be nice . . . ," she said, then paused.

"What?" asked Lee.

"If you and Rachel became friends."

* * *

It wouldn't be easy, however. Rachel had retreated to her room after leaving the brunch in dramatic fashion. It all began when she found Lee and Sarah sitting next to each other at the table, deep in conversation. Becca noticed the irritated tilt of Rachel's head, straining to be included in the conversation.

"I was just saying that I might stay at Eden in the fall and have the baby here," said Sarah.

"What?" Thomas said, from across the table.

"You mean have the baby here, as in Westfield Hospital?" Rachel tried to clarify.

"No, *here* here. As in Eden," Sarah said.

"Really?" Carol asked, her eyes wide with surprise.

Rachel dropped her fork and almost fell out of her seat.

Becca marveled at Lee's calm; her methods had obviously been met with resistance in the past. She simply waited a moment for quiet to return to the table and then said softly, "I've delivered hundreds of babies in the home. It's a wonderful experience. For everyone."

All the color left Rachel's face. "Mother"—she turned to face Becca—"can you really sit here and allow this long-lost daughter of yours to reach into my daughter's womb and grab my grandchild? And what if something goes wrong? Can you picture it? Sarah, losing blood, attended to only by this midwife, up in the guest room?" Rachel stood and stumbled from the table, covering her mouth with one hand and gripping her stomach with the other.

* * *

Later that day, after the table had been cleared, Thomas found Becca on the back porch, collecting napkins. He and Carol were to leave shortly for the train station. "I thought I had it hard, being the oldest and all. My seizures, the doctors, and Mother's . . . I don't know, Mother was either hovering all around me or completely missing, painting school and such. This is the first time I've realized it wasn't a picnic for you, either. I remember kidding with Dad before your wedding—Mother was in a strange rush to marry you off. I just wanted to say . . . well, I admire your courage. And I was glad to be with you this weekend."

"Thank you, Thomas." Becca stood with her brother at the porch railing, looking out at the sea. She felt his strong hold around her shoulders. His understanding meant a great deal, but his train left in a few hours and she hoped he had found her in order to discuss the purchase.

"And how are you feeling about what we talked about?" Becca peered in the windows to see if anybody was nearby. "Will you buy out my share of Eden?"

"Becca, you're the baby of the family. You know, Carol and I, we're damn old. We look around this place, and it just seems like too big an undertaking at our age."

Her heart sank. If Thomas didn't buy her out, how could she come up with the funds to pay the bank?

"We just aren't up to all this," he said. "I think your son will agree, and Edward is on board: it's time to sell Eden."

* * *

Lilly came to find Becca next. She was concerned about Rachel. She said she'd been up to check on her and that Rachel was sitting in her room, staring out the window at Sarah's vegetable garden, sort of trembling.

"The other day when I cleaned her room, I found her bottles. I gathered them all up in a garbage bag and set them out for the trash collector. I don't think she's got anything more to drink up there. I told her it would be nice if she came downstairs at some point to talk it through, but she just started whispering.

"'Was Daddy watching over them?' she said. 'He wouldn't believe it. Mother and Mr. Fabbrizzio, who was like a father to me, had a daughter of their own. And her name is Lee. *My* older sister. And she was conceived somewhere out there!' Then she pointed past the vegetable garden to the dunes."

"Oh, Lilly," Becca said, "you're right to be concerned, but Rachel has to process this on her own. I don't know that there's anything we can do to help."

The next morning during breakfast, a taxi pulled up in the driveway, arousing Becca's curiosity as she sat at the kitchen table, drinking coffee with Sarah.

"Where are you going?" Becca asked, as Rachel struggled through the kitchen with her suitcase.

"To the train station. I'm going to a thirty-day program in Connecticut," Rachel said, heading directly for the screen door.

"Oh, Rachel, darling, wait. Rachel, I love you, dear," Becca said, rushing out behind her daughter. Rachel wouldn't turn around, however; she began lifting her suitcase into the open trunk of the taxi.

"Okay, wow. Mom?" Sarah said, rushing behind them. "Mom, bye. I love you." But Rachel had already fastened her seat belt and was staring straight ahead. As the yellow-and-black car steered down the driveway toward the opening in the privet hedge, Becca found herself standing next to Sarah and Lilly, waving goodbye in the same manner in which the Meisters had always bidden farewell to houseguests.

Chapter 42

LONG HARBOR, RHODE ISLAND
1954

The morning after the accident, Ruth, Bunny, and Sadie sat at the kitchen table with untouched plates of eggs in front of them. Bunny stirred his coffee slowly. "I need to call Edward and Thomas; then there's Kitty . . ." Ruth's hand trembled as Bunny rattled off names.

There was a faint knock at the kitchen door, and it swung open before any of them could get up. Emily Notman peered around the door frame. Their neighbor went directly to the space between Ruth and Sadie's chairs, tenderly caressing both women's shoulders. "I wanted to give you all some time, but I couldn't stay away any longer. I'm so sorry." Ruth looked up appreciatively. "I went through these details last summer when Uncle Mark passed. Let me manage the service and the reception. You should focus on your family."

Ruth loved this about Long Harbor and the Meisters' roots here. Sadie's lifelong friends from the bridge table and the tennis courts descended with food and kind words and offered to manage the logistics.

The hardest part for Ruth would be telling Joseph and Benjamin. Becca and Dan had been helpful the day right after the accident, keeping the twins occupied and away from the house, but when Ruth saw their questioning eyes at the side of her bed Saturday morning, it broke her heart. Joseph was surveying Robert's side while Benjamin jostled her shoulder, waking her from a sleep made possible only by the pills Mrs. Notman's doctor had prescribed.

Ruth summoned the strength to put her feet on the floor and put on a simple dress. She clasped each of their little hands, leading them down the stairs, out the door to the back porch, across the lawn, and up onto the dunes, where they sat facing the ocean. The sun was rising and reflected off the drops of dew on the eelgrass. She pointed to the last vestiges of the moon in the sky and said, "Daddy's up in heaven."

The boys huddled next to her, staring upward, one small body on either side, clinging to her arms. "When will he come back?" asked Joseph.

"Oh, sweetheart, he won't be back. That is, we won't be able to see his body anymore"—she tried to subdue the quiver in her voice—"but he'll always be with us." She squinted her eyes, tears streaming from the corners.

Joseph scrunched up his face, looking out toward the horizon. She kissed the crown of his head and then Benjamin's. They stretched out in the sand, using her lap as a pillow. She rubbed both their backs. They lay there quietly, the crash of the waves almost hypnotic. She closed her eyes and prayed, hoping for Robert's guidance. After some time, the screech of a seagull shocked her awake, and she lifted the boys to their feet and coaxed them back toward the house for breakfast.

Edward arrived later that day for the funeral, smelling as if he'd been drinking since he'd gotten the news. He poured himself another straight scotch as soon as he arrived, then went to Ruth's side. She smelled stale smoke and perspiration on his collar. He slurred in her ear, "If anyone had to die, it should have been me." Ruth understood that for Edward, losing Robert was like losing a part of himself. Just two years apart, and with Thomas always being carted off to doctor's appointments, they had been raised together, as one and the same—football, basketball, baseball, St. Paul's, and Yale.

"It's all my fault," said Edward, sniffling into the arm of his sport coat.

"Don't be silly."

"But it is. You see, Bobby had been trying to convince me to come up for the weekend. He was miffed I was spending so much time with Beth's folks in the Hamptons. He ribbed me all the time. Said he'd wait for me and leave on Friday." He really was the opposite of Robert—so brash, and repelled by the next generation of domesticity at Eden.

"And you told him no."

"If he'd waited for me . . ." Edward took a sip of his scotch and rubbed his eye with the heel of his hand. He leaned into her with his shoulder and choked, "Our last conversation was an argument." She had never seen a Meister lose control of his emotions. "I told him he was no fun anymore," Edward whispered now, "spending all his time with that stiff." He pointed his elbow at Dan and Becca, on the couch.

"Aw," Ruth said, rubbing Edward's shoulder, "don't blame yourself. Robert knew how much you loved him."

"But I do, you see. I feel . . ." Edward sobbed, sucking in his breath, speaking to the wall as much as to her. "I feel like I killed him myself."

Whereas Edward teetered on the verge of collapse, Thomas arrived in Long Harbor more composed in his grief. He held the car door open when it was time to drive to the chapel. Tall and substantial, he stood dutifully by Bunny's side, ready to step in at the first falter.

Despite the heat, the small chapel filled. Ruth had always loved its picturesque white clapboard construction, sitting out on a rocky crag at the end of the peninsula, with the lighthouse next door. She had secretly wished her wedding there, and the irony of walking down its aisle now, but for Robert's funeral, stung.

Inside, shards of colored light from the stained-glass windows shone on the minister's face. The congregants sang "The King of Love My Shepherd Is," and Ruth imagined their booming voices carrying out through the wide-open front doors to the harbor, wafting over the water, and being consumed by the sky.

* * *

Watching Sadie fall apart compounded Ruth's pain. Her mother-in-law rocked on the back porch, muttering, "Bobby was my baby, my sweet little baby." And Bunny was little comfort to her, retreating to his study, cringing at the disorder of Rachel and Andrew's constant bickering. Ruth wasn't sure if Becca noticed what was happening, that her mother spent days repeating the same phrase over and over, her consciousness gradually receding to some distant shore. "Becca," Ruth said in a hushed voice, "I think your father has started sleeping in the guest room."

The days that followed Robert's death lacked structure. Ruth and Sadie were awake at all hours, crossing paths in the hallway. Becca and Lilly struggled to keep the four children occupied, giving up on outings to the beach, letting them hang around the house in their pajamas instead. The family mourned within Eden's walls, the drapes drawn against the sunshine.

Becca and her children went back to Connecticut after Labor Day, but Ruth and her boys stayed on until Thanksgiving. Ruth knew she was just delaying the inevitable, not wanting to return to life in New York without Robert. She felt cared for at Eden and appreciated Bunny's interest in Joseph and Benjamin. But by the end of November, her return was past due and she needed to enroll the boys in kindergarten. After the holiday, they all packed up and went to the station in Kingston together. Bunny and Sadie would travel to Pittsburgh, after Ruth and the twins disembarked in New York. Ruth sniffed back tears when it was time to say goodbye.

"Now, you boys take care of your mother," Bunny said, patting their shoulders.

Ruth resolved to be strong, but she worried what would happen to her in-laws, especially Sadie, over the winter.

* * *

Ruth returned early the following May in order to open up Eden and then meet her in-laws' train from Pittsburgh. Life without Robert continued to be extremely difficult, but her arrival at Eden and the prospect of another season in Long Harbor filled her with promise. But her heart sank as she watched a porter unload Bunny in a wheelchair and then help Sadie down, placing a cane into her hand. Thomas telephoned days later. "I should have warned you. It's been a tough winter for both of them. I think losing Robert has set a lot of things in motion." So that summer saw Lilly trying to keep the four cousins quiet and out of the way of their grandparents, who were usually napping on the porch.

While Ruth catered to her in-laws' needs, Becca and Dan immersed themselves in Long Harbor's social life. Her changed status had driven a wedge between her and Becca. They had bonded over being young wives and mothers, but now it was as if Becca didn't know what to say. Ruth was the only one in their crowd not part of a couple, and the men, once they had a few drinks in them, made not-so-subtle propositions. Becca hadn't believed her when she'd described the way Howard Loring had offered to keep her from going frigid, passing by too closely, rubbing against her breasts.

Ruth also shook her head at the obligations Becca took on. One of the Notman sisters nominated Becca to be vice president of the Long Harbor Ladies Auxiliary, and it was as if she had found her calling. Ruth kept her calendar clear, choosing to spend time with Joseph and Benjamin. They had two jigsaw puzzles going at once in the bright sunroom adjacent to the living room.

Sometimes Ruth would find the twins propped up in Bunny's lap, atop his wheelchair. He'd tell them stories of his youth, or of Eden, or even of Robert. Sometimes Bunny would nod off midsentence and the boys would climb down gently, careful not to wake him. The sight of the three of them huddled under a blanket on his lap touched a tender place deep within her.

She was the one who noticed when Bunny stopped reading the *Wall Street Journal* at breakfast and no longer perused his gardens. Then one weekend, while Becca and Dan were playing in the two-day mixed member-guest golf tournament at the Paupanaug Club, Bunny's wheezing and coughing turned from bad to worse overnight, so much so that Sadie went to him in the guest room and Ruth shuttled up and down from the kitchen with lemon tea and hot compresses. The last time she knocked, all was silent. She pushed the door open to find Sadie clutching his hand, her ear on his chest.

"Oh, Ruthie," Sadie said, almost too quietly to hear, "I believe he's gone."

Ruth put an arm across her back.

"He went so peacefully. It makes me want to join him," Sadie said, looking intently into Ruth's eyes. Ruth left Sadie alone by her husband's side for a few hours more, while she went off to call the doctor and then try to track down Becca.

When the news spread that Bernhard "Bunny" Meister, the mastermind of the P&E and a man who had shepherded his family through the better part of the twentieth century, had passed away, the earth stopped spinning underneath Eden. Ruth understood something about Sadie's grief and her silent mourning, but she felt especially heartbroken for Becca, who had been preoccupied all weekend and hadn't had a chance to say goodbye to her father. She found Becca in Bunny's study on Monday morning, sitting, with the drapes drawn, in Bunny's desk chair, her forearms crossed over his leather blotter, her forehead collapsed onto them. Her back heaved violently as she cried. Ruth went to her, rubbing her shoulders, trying to console her.

"Oh, Ruth, please, please, just leave me alone," Becca sobbed.

* * *

Thomas boomed from the altar, representing the family in delivering the eulogy, "Our father was intelligent, an unyielding negotiator, quick to laugh and play, and set extremely high standards for his children." Ruth remembered how intimidated by Robert's eldest brother she had once been, but she certainly appreciated his steadiness at funerals now.

Later that evening, from her place at the dining room table, Sadie made an uncharacteristic toast: "No matter where your father and I are, the love we feel for you will continue on in this home. Eden was your father's dream for you." She held her wineglass high, a grand oil portrait of her hanging on the wall at her back. "To Bunny," she said.

"To Bunny," they all repeated back in unison.

Ruth gazed at her mother-in-law admiringly. Somehow, she had pulled herself together for this occasion. The aura of Sadie's fashionable youth still permeated the air like a fine perfume.

When Ruth announced she would be accompanying Sadie back to Pittsburgh at the summer's end, Becca reacted with alarm. "I feel guilty you're the one helping my mother and Aunt Kitty close down Lancaster Fells. I'm the daughter—it should be me," she said.

"Don't be silly. I'm happy to do it. Dan needs you in New Haven."

Becca nodded, acquiescing quietly.

At Sadie's direction, Ruth donated furniture to the church in Pittsburgh and gave away most of the clothing. Ruth polished china and silver and boxed it up, mostly for Becca. It was as if Sadie needed to redistribute her family's heirlooms in preparation for her own death, and Ruth was honoring this ritual alongside her.

"Now, Ruth," Sadie said, "when I'm gone, you children don't need to hang on to all of this stuff. Encourage Becca to let go of some of it, will you?"

But when Becca finally bustled in four weeks later, she looked around with an eye toward what had been set aside for her.

"I've always admired that side table, Mother. Whom did you give that to?" she asked.

Ruth's fondness for Becca soured as she witnessed the importance she was putting into Sadie's possessions. It was the last thing poor Sadie needed. She sidestepped Becca's spats with her mother, escaping to her suite of rooms, where she read to Joseph and Benjamin and supervised them as they practiced their letters in wide-lined composition books.

Ruth encouraged Becca to come to Eden early that spring. "You should be the one by your mother's side, calling your brothers, assembling the family."

"You act as if she's got one foot in the grave," Becca said.

"Oh, Becca, I don't know what a doctor would say, but she's frail. Mentally, she's elsewhere. I think she's getting ready." Ruth was reminded of her childhood cat, who stoically disappeared into the woods when it was his time to go.

* * *

After the last of the neighbors left Sadie's funeral reception at Eden, Ruth slumped on the living room couch with Becca, Dan, Edward, Beth, and Thomas. They nibbled on the last of the ham and drained the wine from all the opened bottles. Ruth scanned their faces, all young and vital. "I, for one, am ready to retire this black ensemble!" she said.

"Hear, hear!" said Edward.

The cousins dashed through the living room. "Lilly, can you feed them and get them to bed?" Becca hollered in the direction of the kitchen.

"There must have been five hundred people packed into that chapel," said Dan.

"Mother would have been pleased," said Edward.

"Sorry to change the subject," said Thomas, "but would it be all right if we go over the will? As executor, I have some concerns."

Ruth cringed at his timing.

"Specifically, I want to discuss the future ownership of Eden."

Edward's wife, Beth, chimed in: "I was sort of wondering the same thing."

"Stop it! Both of you!" Becca exploded. "We just buried Mother. Have some civility. We will not discuss this now."

"I just thought since everyone was here . . . ," Thomas said, holding his hands up in defense.

* * *

Ruth was the first one to witness Becca's maneuvering, how she shuffled up and down the hallways, carrying basketloads of clothing, as soon as her brothers departed. Becca and Dan moved into Eden's master bedroom, moved Rachel into their old room, and shifted Andrew into what had been Robert's boyhood room. Ruth was nervous about what Thomas's and Edward's reactions would be when they returned later in the summer.

She overheard their arguments. The first occurred upon Thomas's arrival. He was standing in the upstairs hallway, suitcases still in hand.

"That is not the case at all!" Becca yelled. "You could have spent more time here if you'd wanted to. Nothing would have made Mother and Daddy happier than for you to show up a little more often! Dan and I have been doing all the work around here ourselves for the past three summers. Dan spent two weekends last summer scraping and painting the balustrade on the porch! There is no reason that huge bedroom should sit empty while you're in Pittsburgh!"

Ruth chafed at Becca's claim to have done "all the work." It was as if, overnight, Becca had assumed the title of lady of the house. In addition to claiming better bedrooms, she made decisions on whom and when to entertain and on what food would be served. Ruth spent lazy days on the beach with her boys while Becca's realm turned into one of tomato sandwiches, writing prompt thank-you notes, and making lists of chores for Lilly. Ruth even caught her keeping a hostess book, making sure the same guests never sat next to each other and were not served the same meal twice.

Ruth decided to return to her childhood home, Washington, DC, in September and look for a job as a legal secretary. Joseph and Benjamin would go away to summer camp when school got out. Ruth had her opinions about the cousins hanging out at the Paupanaug Club with their upturned collars. The part of her that had wanted her sons to claim their place in Long Harbor had withered away.

Thomas and Edward didn't conceal their irritation as gracefully. They ranted to Ruth about a letter the three of them had received from Dan, requesting their share of the property taxes and annual maintenance.

"Damn doctor—doesn't even understand how Father's trusts are set up," Thomas fumed, stamping out his cigar in an ashtray.

"They must be living off Becca's inheritance," Edward concluded.

"I fear you're right," Ruth said, having watched Dan, no longer with a father-in-law to impress, lose the discipline to get back to work after the weekend. His golf game and the cocktail-party circuit had become his highest priorities.

Chapter 43

COPPER HILL, CONNECTICUT

August 2000

At the Copper Hill Hospital in Connecticut, Rachel took part in group therapy and art classes. In her hours of solitude, she continued to write in her journal. Her hand was jittery from detoxing, her disenchantment with Eden immense. She questioned everything. She fumed at her mother's hypocrisy and was miffed at Bunny and Sadie, now just distant stars who had passed on some myth about her heritage. Eden's traditions had betrayed her. It was just a veil of family togetherness behind which so much was hidden. She recalled the way her mother had ticked off names to Lee in the photo gallery and remembered how she had once stood on the back stairs as a child and wished there were more pictures of her. She had always assumed the photos stopped because they had run out of wall space, but now it dawned on her that her mother never dared mess with Sadie's arrangement. "Yes," Rachel scribbled furiously in her journal, "everything sacrosanct at Eden is from a bygone era, and all these years, Mother has been putting up a front. I have an honest-to-God sister."

She had a sister who went to college and graduate school and delivered babies for a living. And here she was, a college dropout. She'd never forget how disappointed her father had been when she'd come home after her first year at Cornell wearing a loose-fitting peasant dress, her long, frizzy hair barely contained by the braid down her back. "Mr. Fabbrizzio won't even recognize you," her father said.

"I'm done scooping ice cream. There's no way I'm wearing those stupid red shirts anymore."

"You're really marching to your own drummer these days," her mother said, eyebrow raised. "Academic probation, and now you want to quit your job?"

"I want to go to California with some friends."

"You do, do you?" asked her father. "And how might you be planning to get there?"

"We're gonna hitch," Rachel said. Andrew burst out laughing at the kitchen table.

"Silence!" her father shouted, pounding his fist on the counter. "No daughter of mine is hitchhiking! Listen, Rachel, we need to get several things straight." He laid down firm rules about smoking, drinking, and drug use. "I won't throw another year's tuition down the drain. If we don't see a turnaround in your attitude this summer, you might not go back to Cornell at all."

"Do you two even get what is happening in this country?" Rachel shouted.

"What's happening is that you are going to weed the flowerbed! There is plenty of work to do around here!" said her father.

Rachel made a point of horrifying him. She went braless in an old T-shirt and put on a baggy pair of dark green army-issued pants, the only clothes left in her closet that fit her buxom figure. She made an ordeal of lowering to her knees, sensing her father's gaze upon her. After twenty minutes of yanking and driving dirt up under her fingernails, she stood, covered in sweat. She clapped the dirt from her hands and knees and headed for the kitchen door.

"Where do you think you're going?" her father hollered from where he stood trimming the hedges.

"Dad, I have my *period*!" Rachel screamed. "My *cramps* are killing me!" Her father turned his back on her. She knew the mention of her menstrual cycle, let alone the sight of her nipples through her soaked T-shirt, repelled him.

She continued to needle her parents with defiance all summer long, even refusing to call them Mom and Dad and addressing them as Rebecca and Dan. But toward the middle of August, they counterattacked. They cornered her on the back porch, and she listened with drooping shoulders as her father laid down the terms upon which he would pay her tuition.

"A 3.5 GPA after midterms, or you're coming home."

Rachel nodded. She could do that.

"I still don't think we should let her go," her mother said. "College campuses are so dangerous now."

"Becca, it's normal—well, normal for the times we're living in. Kids are wrestling with authority, demonstrating, smoking marijuana. But if Rachel promises she'll keep her grades up, well, we should believe in her."

Her mother leaned against the railing, her arms crossed in front of her chest, her lips squeezed into a thin line. "Oh, Dan," her mother said, "I can't help feeling this is a big mistake."

* * *

Rachel spent Good Friday suffering the stale air of a five-hour bus ride to New Haven. She fought back the bile that rose in her throat and validated her mother's premonition. When they reached her stop, she took hesitant steps down to the wet pavement, her eyes squinting in search of her parents' wood-paneled station wagon. When she opened the passenger door, her mother leaned toward her, lips puckered. After a peck on the cheek, she said, "Welcome home, Rachel." Her mother inhaled deeply. "Is that smoke I smell in your hair? I'd wash that out before you greet your father."

Rachel began to cry.

"I was just suggesting you wash your hair. No need to overreact," her mother said.

"They tested my urine, Mom. I'm pregnant."

Her mother drew back toward the steering wheel, her mouth dropping open. "Are you sure?" she whispered, barely audible over the thrum of the idling engine.

"Yes," she cried, bracing for an onslaught.

"How do you feel?" her mother asked with a tender tilt of her head.

Rachel blinked, unprepared for such compassion. "Um, scared and, well, stupid. Other than that, I feel fine." More tears streamed down Rachel's cheeks.

Her mother pulled her torso closer, and they sat that way for a surprisingly long time. Her mother patted her back and whispered, "Shh, shh, shh, shh" into her ear. For the first time since she'd told Peter her period was late, Rachel's stomach stopped churning. "I expected you to kill me," she said.

"Oh, Rachel," her mother said with tears of her own welling in her eyes, "I'm afraid I left you alone a good deal when you were small."

Rachel was not sure where that apology came from.

"And the father, is he . . .?" her mother asked, reaching for tissues in the glove compartment.

"He's a guy I've been seeing for a few months. His name is Peter Stern. He's a senior," Rachel said. Her mother listened intently, then nodded some more.

"Rachel, you aren't alone," her mother said. "We'll work this out together. It's best you tell Dad this afternoon, before Andrew gets home."

Rachel's voice cracked. "Mom, I'm sorry."

"I know you are," her mother said, smoothing Rachel's hair. "But get hold of yourself. It will not be an easy conversation with your father."

Her mother slid back over to the driver's side and, with trembling hands, shifted the station wagon into drive and proceeded carefully into the rush hour traffic.

* * *

Rachel planned to tell her father as soon as he got home from work, but when he arrived, she could hear his irate voice downstairs in the living room from her bedroom. She stepped out onto the landing to hear what was going on. "What the hell kind of bull-shit is this!" he screamed, followed by the sound of ripping paper. "This family *is* Yale, for Christ's sake!"

"Calm down, Dan, please. Here—drink your martini, have a Triscuit," her mother said.

"A Triscuit? Are you kidding me, Becca? This is a disaster! I was Skull and Bones! How could Yale not accept Andrew?" A brief silence followed, during which he must have stopped to gulp his drink. "I'd heard rumblings about the new admissions policies, but I never dreamed it would affect us, with all the money your father gave! Not to mention Thomas and Edward."

"It must be true about them cutting back on legacies in order to increase the number of boys from public schools," her mother said. Rachel could hear the clink of ice cubes, her mother refreshing their drinks.

"And women! Becca, I read they're going to admit women."

"Dan, darling, I'm sure we can smooth this over. I'll try Thomas. I'm sure Yale will have Andrew."

"Oh, and I almost forgot—I got a call today from the dean's office at Cornell, on top of everything else."

Rachel chose this moment to descend the stairs. She held on to the polished mahogany banister, her legs trembling, her bare feet perspiring on the carpet's plush pile. She stood in the entry to the living room, facing her parents in their customary pose, side by side on the couch, cocktails in hand. Her father stood.

"Well, here she is. Come sit down. We need to talk," he said, patting the chair next to him.

"Hi, Daddy," she said, hiding her face behind her long hair.

"It's nice to see you, Rachel, but I can't tell you how angry I am," her father said.

Rachel looked to her mother for support, but she wouldn't meet Rachel's eyes. She stared down at her hands, folded in her lap.

"Rachel, don't look so astonished. The dean's office phoned. He said how pleased he's been with your improvement this year; he just couldn't believe you would jeopardize all that hard work.

Not showing up for your exams? You are risking expulsion. Do you hear me? Expulsion."

Rachel said nothing.

Her father leaned forward, placing his glass down on the coffee table.

Rachel looked at the carpet in silence.

"And do you know what his assistant found when she went to your dorm?" His face was now just inches from her ear.

Rachel cringed, knowing what would come next. All she could do was study the way her feet left indents on the thick carpet. She twisted the bracelet on her left ankle with the big toe of her right.

"He found out you weren't living there, that you hadn't been living there all year!" Rachel maintained her downward gaze, evoking an even louder voice from her father: "I want an explanation, and I want it now!"

Rachel's mother patted his knee. "Dan, please calm down. I know how disappointing this is, but there's no need to raise your voice."

Rachel let her father stew while she searched for the right words. "I know, Dad. I'm sorry. But, well, I was working really hard and going to all my classes, and then . . . well, and I know I should have told you guys I moved out of the dorm, but I thought you would get mad, and I figured as long as I kept my grades up, it would be okay . . . but . . . I moved into a house. I was invited by a friend. It's off campus, like a co-op, and, well, there was this guy there who I really liked. We started dating."

Her father's jaw dropped. "Do you mean to tell me you've been living with a man for six months?"

"And ten other people, too."

"In some sort of hippie commune?"

"It's not what you think. Everyone was in school. It just had a lot more freedom than a dorm. We shopped and cooked our own meals, and it was really comfortable." Rachel stood up and walked around the coffee table, facing the fireplace.

"Don't tell me about freedom," her father said. "Not when we're paying your tuition. College is not about being comfortable. Do you know when I was——?"

"Dan, please, just listen to Rachel," her mother interrupted, fiddling with her wedding band.

Rachel took a deep breath. "So this guy and I were——are—— kind of serious, I guess. And, well, we——or I——wasn't careful, and last week I . . . It's the reason I couldn't show for the exams. I was sick, and scared, because I found out that I'm pregnant."

Her father's eyes popped. "What!" He stood up, shook his head, clasped his hands behind his skull, then ran his fingers through his thinning hair. He slapped his palm down on the mantelpiece. He opened his mouth to speak, but at first nothing came out. "Rachel, I never thought you . . ." Rachel watched the color leave his face.

"Dad, I'm not . . . it's not . . . Peter and I . . . I love him." She wished she could tell her parents that Peter loved her, too. But the resentment on his face at the bus station was still seared into her memory. "Graduation from Cornell was a light at the end of the tunnel for me," he had said. "I pictured I'd finally be following my dreams. Then I met you, and I think you're fun and everything . . . It's just that I never imagined that at this point I'd have my hands tied."

Her father looked over at her mother, who sat still, her lips moving silently, as if in prayer. "You knew about this, Becca?" he shouted.

Her mother looked up, startled. "Rachel told me this afternoon. I didn't know about the house or the exams, obviously. But let's just learn more about this Peter. Rachel says she loves him, and he'll be graduating this spring."

Rachel told her parents what bits she knew about his family in California, and the ranch where they grew citrus, and his dreams of being an agricultural engineer near San Francisco. When she finished, her mother said, "Well, maybe he'd like banking. I'm sure your uncle Edward could get him a job in New York."

Rachel said, "There is another option. I know it isn't legal, but . . ."

Her father made the sign of the cross. "No, Rachel, don't even say it. If you don't want to marry this fellow, we can investigate adoption; you could go somewhere where they will find a loving family to raise your baby."

This time, her mother raised her voice. "No, Dan. Rachel will not give our grandchild up for adoption. She will call this Peter and ask that he meet us. Rachel is not far along; there could be a wedding in May after graduation. Then we'll set them up in New York City. It wouldn't appear out of the ordinary. Nobody would think twice. Rachel will keep her baby, I won't hear of anything else." Her mother closed her eyes as she finished and held up her hand like a policeman signaling "stop."

Bile rose in Rachel's throat. *Nobody would think twice?* Was her mother's only concern shocking the neighbors?

"But what about school, Mom? I really want to finish . . ." Rachel's chin quivered.

"Please, Rachel, you didn't exactly take advantage of school. College will just have to wait." A blue vein pulsed in her mother's neck as she spat out her words. "Your father and I will drive you back to Ithaca at the end of the break, and we will not leave until we sit down with this young man and work the whole thing out."

* * *

Monday morning of her second week at Copper Hill, Rachel shuffled down the hall, wearing slippers and her hospital-issued pajamas. They were light blue, loose fitting, with drawstrings, and quite comfortable. Over the pajamas, she wore the silk bathrobe Peter had given her. Jamming her hands into the pockets, she made her way to her first group therapy session of the day.

She stared around the circle at the mostly indifferent faces and continued the story she had stammered through the week before. "You see, Eden always represented a place of permanence for me. But permanence is such a dangerous ideal." She paused to glare at a young woman about Sarah's age who was mindlessly yawning and tracing the lines of her tattoos with a fingernail. Rachel continued, "Places like Eden attempt to be permanent. Maybe that's what we need to believe when we're children. But any adult should understand it's susceptible to the next natural disaster." Rachel took a deep breath. "Clinging to that place was killing me."

"You said you got a family there?" the tattooed girl asked.

"Yeah," Rachel answered.

"Your mother and who else?"

"Right now, there's my mother, my daughter, a half sister—if you can count her. Ha. And, um, I have a grandchild on the way."

"Hmm," the girl said, nodding her head as Rachel's answer lingered in the air among the other patients in the circle. The rest of the heads bobbed silently up and down. An older man with disheveled gray hair had his legs crossed and was biting his fingernails. Someone's metal chair screeched against the floor. Rachel tugged her robe tightly around her as if an unwelcome draft had entered the room. The silence continued another moment or two, before the group leader thanked Rachel for sharing.

Chapter 44

LONG HARBOR, RHODE ISLAND
August 2000

Mornings were quiet again. Becca walked into the village as the rising sun glimmered on the harbor to get the paper and the mail. Hennessy was on the leash, and they were both now accustomed to the roadside and sidewalks, instead of the beach. She dialed the combination on the post office box and thought about all the years they'd used this address, her mother fingering the same dial before her. She opened the small brass door and found a catalog for lawn furniture and a creamy envelope. The return address in the corner read "New York City"—likely a thank-you note from Joseph and Constance. So prompt. What a nice couple they were.

She bought a newspaper and folded the note inside it, tucking them both under her arm for the walk back to Eden. When she got home, the kitchen was eerily quiet. The house's emptiness felt as heavy as her heart. Sarah was still on bed rest upstairs, but Rachel was gone. She wondered if Rachel's room at Copper Hill was anything like her own room at the Willows. She hoped she had a window to look out of and a comfortable place to write, at least.

Becca passed her reflection in the window, amused by her unkempt appearance. She wore a faded green tracksuit and had stuck on a baseball cap over her mussed hair. There had been a day when she would not have been caught dead outside the house like that. She unleashed the dog and sat down at the kitchen table.

It was time to deal with her situation. Thomas, Edward, and her prying son all wanted to sell Eden. Now that Sarah was pregnant, it would take her and Lilly the rest of the summer to get the house fit for sale. She picked up the notepad by the kitchen telephone and began to make a list. Lilly and Jimmy would have their own ideas, but she was the only one who could do certain things. Like wrapping up all the pictures on the back stairs.

There was a certain burden that came with these objects. They held so much meaning, as did the gesture of bequeathing them. When her mother had passed away, Becca had wanted to hold on to all of it. But Rachel and Sarah had never been interested. The china and crystal were too old-fashioned. This was no longer a world in which things like that held value.

The icemaker in the kitchen made a loud, grinding sound. Andrew went through a lot of ice while he was here, and that old machine had a hard time keeping up. Becca put it on the list of things that needed to be addressed. She couldn't have potential buyers hearing that ghastly noise.

Lilly came down the stairs in her robe. "Are you feeling all right?" Becca asked.

"Oh, Becca, I'm exhausted from the weekend. I started stripping the beds and doing the sheets and towels yesterday. Even cleaned up Rachel's room. Up and down to the basement a million times," Lilly said, a milky cloud over her blue eyes. "I don't think I can do it anymore."

"Lilly?"

"Ma'am?"

"What are you saying?"

"Oh dear. I wanted to be here for the holiday. I wanted to help you through this week. I thought I could make it through the whole summer."

"We're both getting old."

"I should have shown you this sooner," Lilly said, handing over a tattered piece of paper.

Becca put on her reading glasses, unfolded the letter, and

scanned the first few lines. "Well, they've obviously been thinking about this for a while. It seems to be our only choice."

"No!"

"Lilly, with Dan gone and our estate the way it is, I can't afford this anymore. I asked Thomas to buy my share, but after all the excitement of the weekend, he and Carol decided to pass. They all want to sell."

"Oh no." Lilly bent over to hug Becca, her robe falling open, exposing an old cotton nightgown. Becca caught a whiff of Lilly's powdery soap. "I'm so sorry."

Lilly faltered as she stood up, her elbow brushing the folded newspaper and knocking it onto the kitchen floor. The creamy envelope she had retrieved from their post office box slid under the table. Becca bent down and picked it up while Lilly retrieved the newspaper.

"Lilly," said Becca, "you sit down. I'll make our breakfast this morning." With that, Becca started the coffeemaker, poured juice, made toast, and fried two eggs. While she padded across the floor between the refrigerator and the stove, Lilly asked questions.

"When will it go on the market?"

"We need to patch up some leaks and touch up the paint, clean out some closets and get the clutter off the shelves."

Lilly nodded.

"We'll aim for the middle of August, before the season is over."

"Think there are still folks who need a house this big?" Lilly asked.

"Somebody will probably buy her for the view, tear her down and start all over," Becca said, rubbing her eye.

"That would be a crime!" said Lilly.

"Let's not get ahead of ourselves. We'll just focus on spiffing her up for her showing," Becca said, sitting down at the table with two warm plates in her hands. "Hand me that envelope, would you, Lilly?"

Becca held it between her fingers, opened it with her knife, pulled the folded note from the envelope, and read for several minutes. When Becca finally looked up, Lilly was mopping up the last drips of yolk with her toast, while her own plate had gotten cold.

Lilly looked at her. "What is it?"

"I don't believe it. Listen to this!"

Dear Aunt Becca,

Thank you so much for your generous hospitality. Constance, the girls, and I had a wonderful time being in Long Harbor with you. It was magical walking back in time through my childhood. I don't know why it took me so long to make my way back to Eden. Maybe the memories it evoked of my father were too difficult when I was young. But now, as a father myself, I felt as if he was alongside me as I swam with my girls and played with them in the sand. I actually dreamed of him while sleeping out on the porch and even heard his voice.

Constance was enamored by the tradition and the Meister legacy you have so tastefully preserved. It is something she has never experienced. Again, thank you so much for having us up to spend time with Mother in the middle of this awful heat wave. The invitation was a godsend.

I want to broach a sensitive topic. Mother mentioned that you, Uncle Thomas, and Uncle Edward may be considering putting Eden on the market. If that is the case, I would very much like to speak to you about buying it. I think it would be the perfect escape from the city for us. It would also be nice if Eden stayed in the family. I hope you will be in touch.

With love,
Joseph

Chapter 45

LONG HARBOR, RHODE ISLAND
August 2000

Constance and the girls returned to Eden for the month of August. They moved in gradually, quietly, conscientious of all the transitions taking place. But Becca didn't want them to feel as if they needed to wait in the wings. "Constance, you should have your pick of the bedrooms," she said. "I'll move my things out of the master."

"Becca, there's no sense in disrupting this summer. Joseph and I will be happy in a guest room, and the girls wouldn't dream of leaving the sleeping porch," Constance said. "We'll be doing some renovations over the winter, so we can pack up personal items then."

Becca walked the beach every morning and spent as many afternoons as possible lying on a chaise on the back porch, listening to the crashing of the waves. She stopped going to bridge luncheons and meetings at the club, choosing to listen to the girls play with their dolls on the sleeping porch instead. It had been their grandfather, after all, who had rebuilt the porch after the hurricane. It was their turn to grow up at Eden.

Throughout the remainder of the summer, Becca invited Lee often to Eden, where they sat with Sarah in the shade, drinking iced tea. Constance sometimes joined their conversations, curious to learn all she could about Joseph's and Eden's history. Lee asked about her grandparents and aunts and uncles, keeping a notebook in order to get it all straight. Sarah asked about her days at the Willows and how it had felt to keep such a secret from Becca's father and brothers. "Sarah," said Becca, "I had no choice. But a part of me died in that place."

Joseph took the train up every weekend from the city and met with plumbers, roofers, even a landscape architect, who suggested they put in a pool in the middle of their great expanse of lawn. Sarah raised an eyebrow in Becca's direction when that idea came up.

"But we'll keep the gardens as they are," Constance assured them, probably feeling chastised by Sarah's expression.

When she got Sarah in private, Becca said, "Don't you dare say a thing about the swimming pool. We're lucky enough that they're letting us stay on. I'm so grateful your baby will be born here."

"Of course I wouldn't, Gran," Sarah said, laughing. "I'm the one who loves swimming pools. It was you and Poppy who despised them, remember?"

* * *

Their afternoon gatherings on the back porch became a daily ritual. Lee came by in the late afternoon, work permitting. Constance and the girls joined them, freshly showered after the beach. Sarah and her big belly were at the center of it all. Lilly prepared pitchers of lemonade and snacks. "Consider it afternoon tea," she chuckled. Lee had shown the girls where the mint grew in the garden, and they'd return to garnish all the glasses.

"Has Alistair responded to your letter?" Becca asked Sarah one afternoon as they all sat around, soaking up the vanishing rays of sunlight. It was late August, approaching Labor Day, and the sun was sinking earlier and earlier.

"He actually called the other day."

"He did?" Becca asked, surprised Sarah hadn't already mentioned it.

"No change. He said he *does* miss me and cares for me a great deal, *but* he's been married before and already has two grown children, and a life with me and a child isn't what he wants."

"Oh," said Becca, her shoulders drooping.

"Are you okay with that?" Lee asked.

"Yeah, it was good to have a civil conversation and apologize for all the mean things we said. He didn't make any promises, but he said he'd like to see the baby."

"Aha!" Becca said. "He'll come around."

"Oh, Gran, don't get your hopes up," Sarah said.

Lilly massaged Sarah's shoulders. "I think your grandmother is right."

* * *

Becca folded old linens into boxes. She would be taking another load to the shelter in town. Sarah was officially released from bed rest just as it became time to prepare the gardens for the dormant season. Becca watched from the window as her granddaughter pulled dead foliage, fertilized the earth, and then covered it with a blanket of seaweed that she dragged up from the beach. Lee worked with her amid the earthy colors of autumn: yellow and red chrysanthemums, rust-colored dahlias, beach roses turned to berries, and now-purple bay bushes.

Becca watched the bond between Lee and Sarah tighten as they rooted around in the earth. Becca imagined their conversation.

"Did you feel loved?" Sarah would ask.

"I did, very much. My parents loved me. . . ."

"But?"

"Ha, yes, there is a 'but,'" Lee would say. "I guess it's the fact that where I ended up was random, unintended, that it never had to be me they adopted; it could have been any child. And then I always wondered about who left me and why they would do such a thing. So the answer is I felt loved, but with an asterisk."

"And in my case, my parents were the ones who created me," Sarah would say. "I was their flesh and blood. They said they loved me, but there was so much resentment, it permeated everything. They hadn't wanted me, they hadn't planned on me, and because of me, their lives were indelibly changed. So I guess I felt loved, but with an asterisk, too."

We reap what we sow, Becca thought, as she watched the two women working side by side.

* * *

It was an extremely active hurricane season. Joseph's contractor came over in October to board up the big windows in the living room. They were pelted with rain and whistling wind from one week to the next. Joseph and Constance and the girls had been back in the city since the start of the school year and planned for the renovations to begin the first of the year.

Sarah was due in November. She walked the beach with her grandmother when the weather allowed, but otherwise back and forth down the long upstairs corridor of Eden. Lee told her walking was important. When her labor finally started, Becca moved her from her tiny bedroom into the large guest room, where the plywood had been removed from the window so she could have a view of the ocean. Lee arrived with her assistant from Mystic and took charge.

Another storm with high winds was passing through. The lights flickered on and off. Becca stayed out of the way, planting herself in a lounge chair against the wall. The wind seemed to call to them, howling off the ocean. Sarah's head was perched up on several pillows, and Becca watched her contractions come like long waves, crashing, then receding back, pulled by a strong undertow. Lee coached her through the breathing, massaging her back between sets. As the sun faded, Lee lit candles and incense and played classical music on a CD player. The bare branches outside scraped against each other and against the side of the house in the wind.

As she waited for her great-grandchild to be born, Becca thought about the abundance in her life: having Lee back; a great-grandchild on the way. She thanked God for keeping Eden— the paradise her father had built, with the sky and the sea at its doorstep—in the family. She planned to return to New Haven for the winter, to live in a small condominium she had purchased with her share of Eden's sale proceeds. Joseph and Constance had been most generous, inviting her to return during the summer for as long as she liked. "You and my mom can pal around like sisters again," said Joseph.

There was an ebb and flow to their lives. Everything that had happened before would happen again; all the stories, the drama, the goodness, the struggles, would be re-created over and over. She sat by the window, watching the full harvest moon rise and the dark storm clouds blow out to sea. Becca had finally found her peace, while Sarah was in the thick of her labor.

Becca had received a letter from Rachel the day before. Phone calls had been difficult, so they'd turned to written communication, with much better luck. Over the course of several letters, Becca had learned that Rachel's rehabilitation stay had been worthwhile; she was sober and less angry. It had been an opportunity to do some writing; in fact, she had finally completed the first draft of a novel. She was back in New York City now, teaching. Reading those words made Becca proud. She scanned her daughter's familiar cursive for a hint of an invitation, but there was none. She yearned to see her, but Rachel would come home when she was ready. Becca folded the letter in thirds and tucked it into her book, before closing her eyes and laying her head back against the chair.

She woke in the early-morning hours to the sound of the baby's cries rising above the wind. Lilly brushed past her in the candlelight, delivering more hot water and towels to the bedside. Lee took the little girl in her expert hands, washed her, and folded her tightly in a blanket. She turned and handed the baby to Becca, who kissed the crown of her head before laying her across Sarah's breast. Becca could see the relief in Sarah's face, then watched her granddaughter's eyes shine as she became a mother, prepared to let go of everything for the sake of this new life.

"I'd like to name her Rae, for my mother," Sarah said.

"That will make her very happy," Lilly said.

Lee wiped Sarah's forehead with a damp cloth. They had been huddled around the bed for several moments, admiring the baby, when Becca cleared her throat. "There's something I'd like to read," she said, pulling a piece of paper from her pocket. "It's a baby blessing I found among my father's things."

She placed a hand on the crown of Rae's head and read:

In every birth, blessed is the wonder.
In every creation, blessed is the new beginning.
In every child, blessed is life.
In every hope, blessed is the potential.
In every transition, blessed is the beginning.
In every existence, blessed are the possibilities.
In every love, blessed are the tears.
In every life, blessed is the love.
There are three names by which a person is called:
One which her father and mother call her,
And one which people call her,
And one which she earns for herself.
The best one of these is the one that she earns for herself.

ACKNOWLEDGMENTS

I would never have finished this book without the support of my amazing husband. John, as the song goes, you are my first, my last, my everything. Thank you to my children, who, when filling out school forms that asked for their mother's occupation, wrote "author." Team Zebra lovingly held my feet to the fire.

Dad, thank you for, at every opportunity, praising my writing. That has meant more to me than you will ever know.

Thanks to my Cambridge writing group—Bette, Deb, Louise, Beth, and Lallie—who suffered through early pages of this work. Thanks to Maria Canale and Beth Madison, enthusiastic readers of early drafts. Thanks to Sophie Powell and my classmates at Grub Street who critiqued and encouraged me. I can't say enough about the community at Grub Street. You gave me the courage to go the extra mile. And Carol Michael, thank you for doing one last read. Your blessing meant so much!

Thank you to Jessica Keener and Mary Carroll Moore, editors, coaches, and "book doctors" extraordinaire. Thank you to April Eberhardt for helping this novel find a home.

Annie Tucker, you are a superb editor. Your caring, insight, and humor made the eighth revision of this book a pure joy! Thank you to Brooke Warner, Cait Levin, and everyone else at She Writes Press and BookSparks for your innovative vision and for setting the bar high.

ABOUT THE AUTHOR

J eanne Blasberg is a voracious observer of human nature and has kept a journal since childhood. After graduating from Smith College, she surprised everyone who knew her by embarking on a career in finance, making stops on Wall Street, Macy's and Harvard Business School, where she wrote case studies and business articles. A firm believer that you are never too old to change course, Jeanne enrolled at Grub Street, one of the country's pre-eminent creative writing centers, where she turned her attention to memoir and later fiction. *Eden* is her debut novel. Jeanne and her husband split their time between Boston and Westerly, RI. When not writing, she can be found playing squash, skiing, or taking in the sunset over Little Narragansett Bay.

For book group questions and to learn more, please visit www.jeanneblasberg.com

Author photo © Sharona Jacobs Photography

9/6

SELECTED TITLES FROM SHE WRITES PRESS

She Writes Press is an independent publishing company founded to serve women writers everywhere. Visit us at www.shewritespress.com.

Bittersweet Manor by Tory McCagg. $16.95, 978-1-938314-56-8. A chronicle of three generations of love, manipulation, entitlement, and disappointed expectations in an upper-middle-class New England family.

Things Unsaid by Diana Y. Paul. $16.95, 978-1-63152-812-5. A family saga of three generations fighting over money and obligation—and a tale of survival, resilience, and recovery.

Stella Rose by Tammy Flanders Hetrick. $16.95, 978-1-63152-921-4. When her dying best friend asks her to take care of her sixteen-year-old daughter, Abby says yes—but as she grapples with raising a grieving teenager, she realizes she didn't know her best friend as well as she thought she did.

The Rooms Are Filled by Jessica Null Vealitzek. $16.95, 978-1-938314-58-2. The coming-of-age story of two outcasts—a nine-year-old boy who just lost his father, and a closeted young woman—brought together by circumstance.

Shelter Us by Laura Diamond. $16.95, 978-1-63152-970-2. Lawyer-turned-stay-at-home-mom Sarah Shaw is still struggling to find a steady happiness after the death of her infant daughter when she meets a young homeless mother and toddler she can't get out of her mind—and becomes determined to rescue them.

The Geometry of Love by Jessica Levine. $16.95, 978-1-938314-62-9. Torn between her need for stability and her desire for independence, an aspiring poet grapples with questions of artistic inspiration, erotic love, and infidelity.